heavy PETTING

ERIN NICHOLAS

NEW YORK TIMES BESTSELLING AUTHOR

The Series

Boys of the Bayou-Gone Wild
Things are going to get wild when the next batch of bayou boys falls in love!

Otterly Irresistible
Heavy Petting
Flipping Love You
Sealed With A Kiss
Head Over Hooves
Say It Like You Mane It
Kiss My Giraffe
Better Safe Than Safari

available in digital, paperback, audio, and special edition paperbacks!

About the book

He's her best friend.

A reformed bad boy turned hot teacher.

And after one spur-of-the-moment Vegas wedding... her husband.

Jordan Benoit and Fletcher Landry have been best friends since they were six. He's always been The Guy. When she needed picked up, cheered up, or lifted up--like literally, to see the stage at a concert--Fletcher was the guy.

So when her boyfriend dumps her--on national TV--Fletcher immediately gets on a plane and comes to her rescue.

And when she ends up in a Vegas wedding chapel and needs someone to say, "I do"...yep, Fletcher's the guy. Of course.

But being The Guy 24/7 is a lot. He just wants everyone to give him a freaking minute to get this marriage thing right. Including his sexy, sweet new wife who he's wanted for three years. Who is exasperatingly, temptingly all-in from minute one.

Jordan knows what she wants. A life in her hometown. A job with alpacas. And Fletcher. Not necessarily in that order.

They've said the vows. They'd told the world. They've told their *grandmas*. Forget taking things slow. Forget just heavy petting. Forget any chance of backing out when things get tough. They're going to have to go all the way, in every way.

After all, friends becoming lovers should be the easiest thing in the world. Right?

Prologue

"STAY WITH ME."

Jordan spun to face him.

"What?"

Fletcher sucked in a breath. He was putting it all on the line.

Jordan Benoit was his best friend. She had been since they were six.

But she was more than that now.

He couldn't lose her.

Again.

Two years ago, she'd moved to Nashville with her boyfriend Jason. Fletcher had wanted to ask her to stay then, but he hadn't. She and Jason had been together for nine years at that point. He was going to Nashville to pursue a music career and Jordan was his cheerleader and his biggest fan. Of course she was going along.

Besides, Jordan knew that Fletcher wanted more. If she'd wanted Fletcher, she knew she could have him.

A year before that, in Galveston, things had changed between them. Fletcher had kissed her.

He shouldn't have, of course, but being stuck together, just the two of them, in a roadside motel in the middle of a tropical storm, he hadn't been able to hold back.

And she'd kissed him back. At first anyway.

But eventually, she pushed him away and told him that she couldn't do it, because of Jason.

So when she told him she was moving to Nashville with Jason six months later, Fletcher bit his tongue.

Not this time.

"Don't go with Jason. Stay here. With me."

She stared at him. They were standing outside behind his grandmother's bar. Inside was the wedding reception for three of his cousins who had just gotten married to the loves of their lives.

He didn't know if it was the general love-is-in-the-air feel surrounding the weddings or the fact that this girl—who, at one time, he'd truly believed he could never lose—had actually, essentially, left him twice already, but hearing her say that she was joining Jason on his debut world tour as an opening act for country music star Brett Eldredge had made Fletcher's gut tighten and he knew he had no hope of keeping the request inside.

"I can't stay here. What are you talking about? I have to go with him."

"No, you don't. You know you have a choice. This tour isn't about you. You're really willing to quit your job, quit teaching— the thing you love more than anything—to follow him around? You're the girl who would rather curl up in her pajamas at eight o'clock on a Saturday night and watch movies with sub sand- wiches than go out even to a local bar where you know every- one. What are you going to do on red carpets and at after-parties and hanging out backstage at country music concerts? That isn't who you are."

"But if it's Jason, then it has to be me."

Fletcher stepped forward. He'd known this girl her entire life.

He knew things about her that she probably didn't even know. She was fierce, brave, funny, loyal, and loving.

It was that those last couple things that were screwing him here.

She'd been with Jason for so long, she felt obligated.

Even though Jason's life was going in a totally different direction than she'd planned, even though there was nothing about what Jason wanted that matched up with her dreams, she felt that she had to go now.

She was a small-town girl from Louisiana. Her family meant the world to her. She was passionate about teaching.

None of that matched up with what Jason was asking.

"If he cared about you, he wouldn't ask you to do this," Fletcher said.

She pressed her lips together and her frown looked a lot more scared than angry. "You're wrong. He shouldn't have to give up his dreams just because I don't want to live in a big city."

"Isn't a relationship supposed to be about *both* people?" Fletcher pressed. "What about you? Why do you have to give your dreams up for his?"

"I love him."

You just don't know any different. But Fletcher kept those words inside.

Jordan and Jason had met when they were fifteen. Jason had been her first... everything. He'd asked her to the Valentine's Day dance when they were freshmen in high school. And here they were eleven years later, and she was still with him. No one else had even had a chance.

Fletcher hadn't had a chance.

Hell, it had taken eight years for him to realize he even wanted a chance.

Well, maybe she needed to be reminded that she had options. Really fucking good options.

Fletcher reached for her, wrapping one arm around her waist, and the other hand cupping the back of her head. He tipped her head back and leaned in to kiss her.

But this time she didn't melt into him the way she had in Galveston.

Maybe she hadn't had enough tequila.

Maybe she'd been expecting it this time.

Maybe she really had chalked that all up to one crazy, stormy night, far from home.

Her hands came up to his chest and she pushed.

He stopped, just inches from her lips.

"Knock it off." Her voice sounded choked.

He straightened immediately, letting go of her but not stepping back.

"Jordan—" he started. But his breath lodged in his throat. She was crying.

Fuck.

He'd seen Jordan cry before, but he'd never been the cause of it.

He shoved a hand through his hair, then tucked his hands into his back pockets. "I'm sorry."

"Are you? For which part? For telling me that I shouldn't go with Jason? For being angry with me for quitting teaching? Or for kissing me when I'm with someone else? Again?"

Fletcher swallowed. He should say that he was sorry for all of that. The truth was, he wasn't sorry for any of it.

"For making you cry."

She reached up and brushed the tears away. She sniffed, then blew out a breath.

"Tell your grandma I will send her that signed poster from Jason when I get back to Nashville."

Fletcher sighed. It was bad enough that he was losing this woman to another man. But of course, it had to be a famous other man. And, of course, his grandmother had to be the president of the Autre branch of the Jason Young Fan Club. Literally. They met at her bar once a month and watched any interviews or acoustic performances he'd done in the past month on her laptop while eating loaded chili fries—Jason's favorite thing at the bar and something Fletcher's grandmother told *everyone* and even printed on her menu.

"I'll tell her," Fletcher finally said to Jordan.

"I'll…call you."

That long pause was telling. He and Jordan talked and texted all the time.

But would he be able to handle hearing about her life on the road with Jason?

If she was happy, and he was a good friend, he'd be happy for her. But he was starting to think that maybe he wasn't as good a friend as he'd thought.

Because the idea of her being deliriously happy with Jason Young while giving up all of the things she'd ever wanted made Fletcher want to punch something. And if he heard about how miserable she was on the road with Jason, that would also make him want to punch something.

But finally, he nodded. "You better," he said.

Because, at the end of the day, no matter how painful it was, *not* hearing from Jordan Benoit would be much worse.

He was just gonna have to find something to punch.

One of his brothers would surely piss him off soon enough.

She took two steps towards her truck, but then turned back. "You know I love you, right?"

He nodded. He did know that. It just wasn't the love he'd started feeling for her three years ago.

"I do. And you know I love you, right?"

He wasn't sure if she knew that he was *in love* with her, but they'd always loved each other.

She nodded. "I do."

Then she turned and walked away.

And Fletcher let her go.

CHAPTER

One

FLETCHER LANDRY'S life was about to change. Forever. Irrevocably. He was never going to be the same.

This was going to be the worst day of his life.

And his grandmother was throwing a party for the occasion.

Not only that, but she had threatened to cut him off from her gumbo for two weeks if he didn't show up.

So now he was sitting at a huge table at the back of her bar with the rest of his family, bracing for the moment when everything went to hell.

At least there was lots of food. There was always lots of food when his grandmother was in charge. There wasn't much that her jambalaya couldn't make better.

It was a small comfort.

"Shut up! It's starting," his grandmother told the group.

Ellie Landry, the matriarch of the family, pointed the remote at each of the televisions in the bar, turning the volume up to he-couldn't-ignore-this-if-he-tried level.

Fletcher groaned. Not only was this whole event going to suck, but he was going to watch it on television, with his whole family gathered round, with the volume set to blaring.

And he was going to have to listen to Jason Young sing as a warm-up.

Jason Young was the hottest rising country music star in Nashville. But he wasn't from Nashville. He was from Bad, Louisiana, the town just up the bayou from Fletcher's hometown of Autre. Fletcher had known him since they'd played football against one another as pee-wees. Jason was good-looking (according to others), talented (also according to others), and charming (to people who didn't know him very well). And did things like giving to charity and visiting sick kids in the hospital.

Fletcher hated the guy.

Because Jason had also been dating Fletcher's best friend, Jordan, since they'd been fifteen. Which meant that Fletcher had hated Jason since they'd been about fifteen and a half, and Fletcher had realized Jordan was going to keep dating him.

At first it had been fine. Fletcher had liked seeing Jordan happy and it seemed that Jason treated her well. Of course, Fletcher threatening to end his life if he didn't might've had something to do with that. It hadn't hurt, either, that he'd been backed up by his cousins Mitch, Josh, and Owen. All of whom also had no trouble getting a little bloody for the right cause.

They all would have considered Jordan the right cause.

But then Jordan had actually fallen in love with Jason and told Fletcher all about it with a sweet smile on her lips and a dreamy look in her eyes.

He'd started to hate Jason then.

He hadn't stopped since.

Jason did three numbers and the family all ate in relative silence. There was never *total* silence when it came to the Landry family, but when there was food involved it was a little better. And the way Ellie had the TVs turned up, it was difficult to make conversation. Thank God. It was maybe the first time he'd been grateful that his grandmother was a huge fan of Jason's.

Because he was sure that his family, specifically his twin brothers, Zeke and Zander, would be monitoring his reactions to Jason and whatever he had up his sleeve tonight. Not having to talk while he struggled to hide his reactions would be great.

The thing that made the whole situation even worse, was that Jason was actually pretty good. Fletcher would never buy an album and he would continue to turn the radio away from any of Jason's songs, but it wasn't like his ears were bleeding or anything.

"Vegas, wow, that's fun," Tori, the wife of one of Fletcher's cousins, said. "I'll bet Jordan's having a good time."

Jason was performing at the MGM Grand in Las Vegas.

Yeah, he was doing very well in his career.

The fucker.

"Shhh!" Ellie told her. Everyone's eyes widened. Tori *never* got snapped at. She was sweet and kind and patient. And pregnant with Ellie's first great-grandchild. She'd basically been treated like a princess since she'd moved here and like a queen since she'd shared the baby news.

But Ellie really was a big Jason fan. And the rumor was that he had something big planned for his live show tonight.

The further rumor was that he planned to propose to Jordan. On stage.

Fletcher pushed his plate away. Not even jambalaya could make *that* feel good.

Jason moved to the microphone, grinning into the camera. He had a room full of fans at that casino as well.

"Hey, everybody, thanks for coming out tonight!"

The crowd roared.

His grin widened.

Fletcher sighed.

"This past year and a half or so has been pretty crazy for me. All my dreams seem to be coming true and there are some really important people who have been a part of that."

He thanked his manager, his parents, and a couple of people Fletcher didn't know. Then he said, "But there is one very special person who's been here with me from the beginning and who I have a very special question for tonight."

The crowd went crazy. Ellie gasped and grabbed her husband Leo's arm. The women at the table sat a little straighter.

Fletcher rolled his eyes.

This was where things were *really* going to start to suck.

The noise in the casino was incredible and Leo reached for one of the remotes to turn the volume down. Ellie slapped his hand, but thankfully he managed to reduce it by a few notches.

"Yeah," Jason said grinning. "I hope she feels the same way about it. Now I just need her to come out here with me."

The camera swiveled and focused on a beautiful blonde who had just stepped out from backstage.

It was Jordan. Kind of.

Fletcher's chest tightened and his heart thumped hard against his breastbone. He'd know that face anywhere, of course, but a lot of people who knew Jordan would be shocked to see her tonight.

Jordan was a tomboy. A natural beauty. A girl who wore lip gloss on Saturday nights. Maybe. If she remembered. The first time she'd ever tried to use mascara, she'd ended up with an eye infection. The most she'd ever done with her hair was having her girlfriends curl it for prom and she'd bitched all night long about her head aching from the bobby pins.

She was most at home in denim and bare feet and she had a perpetually sun-kissed glow to her skin and a smattering of freckles across her nose from being outside all the time.

The woman who was walking across the Las Vegas stage in three-inch heels looked nothing like his best friend. She wore a form-fitting sparkly black dress and had her hair swept up in a fancy twist. She had heavy eye makeup on and lipstick.

The only thing that looked slightly familiar was the denim jacket she wore over her dress. But even that was studded with rhinestones that caught the spotlight and sparkled.

"Daaay-um," Zeke said appreciatively. "Jordan's got great legs. And other stuff."

Fletcher ignored him. Zeke said shit like that to him about Jordan all the time. But he'd seen her legs a million times. Bare. Long. Tanned. The girl was from Louisiana. She didn't wear a lot of clothes a lot of the year.

Yeah, okay, he'd seen a lot of her "other stuff" too. Not bare, but…

He stopped those thoughts right there.

He was good at that. He'd been doing it for the past four or five years on a regular basis.

And of course, she had great legs. She had always been athletic. She loved sand volleyball, and to swim, and could kick his ass at a game of one-on-one basketball up until he'd really had his growth spurt. They'd continued to play though. She was fast and had a really great three-point shot.

He guessed she was working out in hotel gyms now, though.

He rolled his eyes about that too.

But now, of course, he couldn't stop looking at her legs and thinking that, yeah, *daaay-um* worked.

It was the dress.

The fucking dress.

Jordan wasn't a dress girl so when she did wear them, they always kind of knocked him on his ass. Because they did make him think of her as a *girl*.

That had been happening a lot more since about the time they'd turned eighteen.

Then when she turned twenty-one, it got worse. She'd started going out to clubs and bars with her girlfriends and she'd started dressing up more. Lipstick. Curls. And dresses.

And she'd often asked him to join them. Or to pick them up after.

But beyond the dress, the lipstick, the heels, Fletcher homed in on something more important tonight.

Jordan looked terrified.

Some of it was probably having to walk across a stage in front of thousands of people in high heels.

But he also knew that she wasn't a huge lover of the spotlight or big public displays.

And she had to know what was about to happen. Everyone knew what was about to happen.

And a knot formed in Fletcher's gut as he watched her. He breathed a small sigh of relief when Jason met her partway and took her hand. At least she wouldn't end up on her ass on national television.

"Oh my gosh," Maddie said. "This is pretty exciting."

"I would die," Paige added. "I hate public proposals."

The group, sans Fletcher, laughed. Paige had been proposed to five times before she had come to Autre and fallen for Mitch. And at least a couple of those had been public, from the sound of it. She was somewhat of an expert.

But it was the word *proposals* that made the knot in Fletcher's gut tighten and, for possibly the first time in his life, made him regret even the few bites of jambalaya.

"You already promised me that you would ask Mitch to marry you here at the bar in front of all of us," Ellie told Paige.

"I guess I don't consider you all public," Paige said with a smile. "You're family."

"Awww," Juliet and Tori said together.

"Shhh!" Ellie said, sharply waving her hand to shut them up as Jason pulled Jordan to the microphone at the front of the stage.

The girls exchanged wide-eyed looks but grinned.

Ellie often had Jason's music playing in the bar. She also had a signed poster of him hanging behind the bar near the cash register and watched him on TV every chance she got.

Some of it was because he was a local boy, but a lot of it was because he was connected to Jordan. Jordan had been like another granddaughter to Ellie growing up, constantly in and out of the bar and on and off the boat docks where Boys of the

Bayou, the family business, operated their swamp boat and fishing tours. She'd swiped cookies, boudin balls, and fried pickles right alongside the other grandkids.

Ellie adored her. But Fletcher had a sneaking suspicion that as Ellie had listened to Jason's music she'd actually decided it was good.

The casino crowd had been cheering this whole time, but as Jason swung his guitar to his back and went down on one knee, they quieted.

Ellie's bar—and, miraculously, the Landry family—also fell silent.

"We've known each other forever," Jason said, with Jordan's hand in his.

Fletcher felt his heart squeeze and the jambalaya in his gut roil.

He wasn't sure he could watch this.

Yes, Jordan was his best friend and this was a huge moment in her life. That was how Ellie had gotten him to come to the bar and sit down in the first place. Well, that and the threat of cutting him off from gumbo for two weeks. But he'd been dreading this moment for at least two years.

Jordan and Jason had been together for a decade. Of course at some point he was going to propose. Jordan was amazing and Jason was a lot of things, but an idiot wasn't one of them. Of course he'd want to get a diamond ring on her finger. And of course she'd say yes. Fletcher had given her a chance to break up with Jason in the past. Two chances actually. To choose him instead. And she'd turned him down flat.

So yeah, Fletcher had been expecting Jordan and Jason to get married.

Though he'd figured he'd get this news by phone call. A phone call where he could fake a happy tone of voice and say all the right things even as he was cussing internally and planning to break things as soon as they hung up.

Witnessing it in person, and with an audience who would be very interested in his reaction, was pretty much hell.

Especially because the look on Jordan's face was even more terrified now than before.

Fletcher frowned. Surely she'd been expecting this. The entire country had been expecting this. There was no way she'd gotten all dressed up like that just to stand backstage all night.

Then again, he didn't really know how any of this worked for her now. Maybe she did get dressed up like this every night. It was true that every time he caught a glimpse of her on television on the entertainment news—always at Ellie's because he didn't watch that shit—she looked fixed up.

He supposed that when you were a big star touring the country with other big stars, there were people like hair and makeup artists to help out. Maybe that extended to the significant others of the big stars.

They wouldn't want to risk having Jordan make Jason look bad, after all.

Fletcher realized his hand had curled into a fist and he consciously made it relax.

He and Jordan were friends. The best of friends. They'd known each other since first grade. He'd known her longer than Jason had and she'd told him, more than once, that no matter what happened they would always be friends.

But, over the past couple of years they'd drifted apart. Especially since she'd moved to Nashville with Jason and started only substitute teaching so that she could travel with him more.

And especially since April, when she'd been home for the family weddings and told him that Jason had gotten a spot on this big tour and she was quitting her job entirely to go with him.

Fletcher had told her exactly what he thought of that.

Jordan was a teacher. A gifted teacher who loved her chosen career. Fletcher had bitten his tongue a lot over the years when it came to Jason, but that time he hadn't been able to.

He'd also given her the chance to stay in Autre. With him. As a lot more than his best friend.

She'd turned him down.

And she'd cried.

And they'd not spoken for over a week. For the first time in their lives.

He wasn't doing that again. Jordan knew that if she ever wanted to leave Jason, Fletcher would be there for her. Hell, she knew that he would be there for her no matter what. She knew he thought she should be teaching and that she deserved to have dreams too. He'd had his say, she knew where he stood, and it had made her cry. So he was done with that.

When Jordan became Jordan Young, Fletcher would be happy for her. At least as far as she would know.

"We've been through a lot together," Jason went on. "It just seems right, at this point in my journey, that I ask this question."

Loud whistles and a smattering of applause came from the audience, but for the most part everyone watching stayed quiet.

"I love you, Viv. Will you marry me?"

Fletcher frowned at the television. What the fuck?

Surely he'd heard that wrong.

Had Jason just said *Viv*?

"Wait. Who the hell is Viv?" Zeke asked.

Okay, so no, he hadn't heard it wrong. Jason had just fucking said the wrong woman's name. And yeah, who the hell was Viv?

Ellie swung to look at him. "Does he call Jordan Viv?"

"What? Is that like her middle name?" Zeke asked.

No, it wasn't her middle name. No, Jason didn't call her Viv. Jason called her Jordan. Fletcher couldn't even remember hearing Jason call her sweetheart or honey, for that matter.

But he didn't bother answering his family. His eyes were glued to the television and, more specifically, Jordan's face.

The camera had zoomed in on both Jason and Jordan.

They both looked like they were about to puke.

Jason quickly got to his feet, grabbing both of Jordan's hands as she started to pull away. "Oh fuck," he said, directly into the microphone.

Well, they bleeped the word for television but it was clear what he'd said.

Zeke snorted.

Fletcher realized his hand was curled into a fist again.

That "oh fuck" was all he needed to hear. Jason had said the wrong name. Accidentally, obviously. But there *was* a Viv.

He wanted to smash Jason Young's face in.

It wasn't the first time he'd had that urge, but this was the strongest it had ever been and if the guy had been in front of Fletcher in the flesh at that moment, he wouldn't have been breathing normally out of his nose ever again.

"No, I'm sorry, Jordan. Jordan. Of course. I want *you*."

Suddenly there was a crash and the camera panned to the drum set that was now lying on its side, as the drummer bolted off her seat and ran for the side of stage.

"Oh, that's Viv," Zander said.

"*What?*" Ellie demanded.

Zander nodded. "Vivian Holbrook. Jason's drummer."

Ellie turned to face Zander, her hands on her hips. "What are you saying?"

"I'm saying that Jason Young basically just proposed to Vivian."

"Why would he do that?" Ellie asked.

"Maybe because he's actually in love with her but his management team told him that breaking up with a sweetheart like Jordan would look bad for him right now," Zander said.

"How do you know this?" Ellie demanded.

"I might have…read it…somewhere," Zander said.

Ellie narrowed her eyes at him. "Do you follow country music celebrity gossip?"

"Maybe," Zander said slowly.

Ellie nearly gasped. "I can't believe you've been holding out on me! We could have been talking about Kelly and Brandon and Brett?"

Zander rolled his eyes. "Well, apparently, you wouldn't have been that great to gossip with. People have been talking about Jason and Viv for a while and you seem shocked."

"Don't you tell me Jason Young has been cheating on Jordan," Ellie said.

"Okay, I won't tell you. But *he*"—Zander pointed at the television—"basically just told you."

"Maybe he was just nervous in front of all those people," Ellie said, obviously not wanting to believe it. "This is kind of a big deal. Maybe he just said the wrong name. Obviously he knows Vivian really well too."

Zander snorted. "Asking a woman to marry you *is* kind of a big deal. But not exactly something where you get the wrong name. Especially when you've been with the woman you're asking for ten years."

"But—" Ellie started.

Suddenly Fletcher shifted back from the table and stood. He threw his wadded napkin onto his plate and headed for the back door.

"Where are you going?" Ellie called after him.

He yanked the door open and turned back. His eyes flickered to the television screen again.

Tears were streaming down Jordan's face and she'd turned to run off stage. Jason had started after her, but a bodyguard stopped him. His manager was now in his face and they were having a heated discussion.

Fletcher looked at his grandmother. "Vegas."

CHAPTER
Two

"ARE THOSE *SCISSORS*?"

"Jordan, *no*. Put the scissors down."

Jordan sighed. "A haircut would help."

"It really wouldn't," Charlie Landry, one of the women on the Zoom call with Jordan, and one of her best friends, said.

"Not a haircut you give yourself anyway," Naomi LeClaire, Jordan's best friend from high school, agreed.

Jordan let the scissors she'd borrowed from the gift shop employee clatter to the marble countertop. She sighed and leaned in, bracing her hands on either side of the computer. "I went out to get coffee and a bunch of people recognized me," she told the girls. "They were all in line to order. They saw me right away and started asking questions about me and Jason. I didn't even get coffee!"

"Oh my God, honey. I'm sorry," Naomi said sympathetically. "That's so hard."

Naomi herself had been a celebrity, dealing with way larger crowds who wanted photos, autographs, and gossip. As a child TV star it had definitely shaped who she was today. Namely a woman who barely left her tiny Louisiana hometown.

Jordan's shoulders slumped. "I'm sorry, Naomi. This is

nothing compared to what you've been through. It just surprised me. It's stupid. I just panicked."

"You're fine," Naomi assured her. "Panic is normal when something like that happens. But now just enjoy your coffee from room service and wait it out."

"Wait it out?" Charlie asked. "For how long? She can't just stay in Vegas in that hotel room indefinitely."

"These people are all in town for Jason's concert last night," Naomi said rationally. Naomi was almost always rational. It was one of the things Jordan liked best about her. Because rational was something that had been somewhat lacking in her friends growing up. And that included Charlie. Jordan had a very *irrational* tattoo of Oscar the Grouch on her left hip thanks to Charlie Landry, as a matter of fact.

"It's Sunday," Naomi went on. "Most of them will probably be going home today so they can get back to work tomorrow."

Charlie nodded. "Okay, good point. Just hold tight," she told Jordan. "Don't do anything crazy."

"Well, um…"

Both Naomi and Charlie looked at their computer screens with eyebrows up.

"What did you do?" Naomi asked.

Jordan turned her head to the right. Both women gasped.

"Jordan!" Naomi scolded. "You know you're supposed to call us before you do anything like that."

"That is…totally salvageable," Charlie said diplomatically.

Jordan sighed. "It's a purple stripe in my hair."

"It is," Charlie nodded. "And in your blond hair it looks very—"

"Obvious," Jordan filled in.

"Well, yes," Charlie agreed with a shrug.

"How did that happen exactly?" It was clear Naomi was trying not to smile.

"I ducked into the gift shop because there was a crowd in front of the elevators to come back up to the room. I was going to wait and catch the next one, hoping there would be fewer—or no —people on it."

She'd seen the peanut butter cups first, but the hair dye had been on the shelf straight across from the candy and an idea had been hatched. What could she say?

Okay, she'd been actively searching for the peanut butter cups. Still the dye was right there and had seemed like a good idea at the time. When she'd been sleep deprived, insufficiently caffeinated, and hiding her face from people behind a king-size candy bar.

Of course she'd gotten the king-size. She was *hiding*.

"And it's temporary hair dye," she added quickly. "It's supposed to wash out in three shampoos."

"But it's bright purple," Charlie said. "You couldn't have gone with a dark brown or even a black?"

"I was just thinking about disguising myself," Jordan said.

Her friends laughed out loud at that.

"I hadn't. Had. Coffee. Yet," Jordan reminded them. "And I've never been recognized in public without Jason. I honestly wasn't expecting it. It freaked me out."

Naomi nodded. "A little freaked out is understandable. We are going to fix this."

"For the record, in retrospect, I realize that purple is going to call *more* attention to me than if I had dyed my hair brown or black," Jordan said.

"Well, it's just one stripe. You could go back downstairs and get black and cover up the purple," Naomi suggested.

"And buy some big sunglasses. Oh, see if they have any with plastic noses and mustaches underneath them," Charlie added with a laugh.

Jordan blew out a breath. "I'm not going back downstairs for more hair dye." That much she knew for certain. More peanut butter cups were not off the table entirely though. "That gift shop is right in the main lobby. I'm seriously trying to figure out how to sneak out a back door of this place as it is."

"Okay, so we need to figure out what to do about your hair," Naomi said. "It could be worse."

"Yes, it could. And *no* to sneaking out. You need to lean into this," Charlie said. As a marketing guru, Charlie didn't believe in bad publicity. Actually, she didn't believe in publicity she couldn't turn into something good.

"Lean into it?" Naomi asked. "No. She needs to just get through this as best she can. Lay low. Let it blow over."

"But she needs to control the narrative," Charlie insisted. "She should dye her hair in purple stripes, put on something sexy, do her makeup big and dramatic, and walk through that casino like she's never had a better day."

Charlie pointed at Jordan. "You need to get down there before anyone talks to Jason. Answer their questions. Tell them you stayed because you knew Jason needed you—which is true —but you're happy that you can both walk away as friends and move on with your lives."

Charlie started typing on her keyboard as she talked.

"I'll send you these talking points in an email. You're going to act like the most mature, most well-adjusted, best ex-girlfriend anyone has ever had. Everyone will talk about your class and grace. There's not going to be any craziness, you're not going to have any big meltdown. This was a single chapter in your…no, wait…" She kept typing. "It's a single *verse* in your whole song and you're ready for the second stanza."

Charlie looked up. "Is stanza the right word? Is there something better?"

Jordan and Naomi exchanged wide-eyed looks. Charlie was something when she got going.

"I think stanza works," Jordan finally said.

Charlie nodded. "Okay. You say that you have big plans that have been on hold and you're ready to get going on them." Charlie was still typing. "I just reserved JordanBenoit.com." Charlie looked up. "Tell people to watch that site for future announcements about your plans."

Jordan was staring at Charlie. This was Charlie 2.0 in action. Jordan had heard about it from Fletcher when he'd told her about how Charlie was growing the Boys of the Bayou petting zoo. And Jordan had definitely witnessed Charlie talking people into and out of things—herself included—for years. Charlie didn't understand the word 'no' and she rarely met someone she couldn't get her way with.

But this Charlie was older and had even more experience getting her way and talking other people into all of her crazy schemes. Plus she was even more confident now that she'd convinced Griffin Foster, the grumpy, stubborn wildlife vet that worked at the petting zoo, to not only let her have her way with the programs at the zoo, but to fall in love with her too.

If she could win Griffin over, Jordan didn't stand a chance. She already loved Charlie.

"But I don't have any big plans. At least not big plans that are worth having a website for," Jordan said.

"Worry about that later," Charlie said with a wave of her hand. As if the actual *plan* was just a tiny detail. "You just need to exude confidence and happiness. Walk through that lobby like you're Audrey fucking Hepburn."

"Audrey Hepburn, huh?" Naomi asked.

"Oh, I totally see Audrey in Jordan," Charlie said.

Naomi seemed to be thinking that over. She nodded. "Yeah, I would've said Marilyn Monroe maybe, but Audrey has a cooler façade. Sweet but elegant."

"Definitely," Charlie agreed. "Marilyn comes off more warm and bubbly."

"I'm not warm and bubbly?" Jordan asked dryly. She definitely wasn't feeling bubbly. That was for sure. But she didn't care about this. She was pretty sure she couldn't pull off Marilyn *or* Audrey.

"You're very warm," Charlie said. "But you need to be more cool and unruffled now."

"Marilyn is more the purple hair type though," Naomi said.

Charlie nodded as if this was actually a serious consideration.

Jordan sighed. "I have *one* stripe. That's why I called you guys. I did one and then had second thoughts." She ignored her friends' grins. Yeah, yeah, thinking it through *before* putting the color applicator to her hair would've been good. "The question now is, do I do it all purple or do I keep doing stripes?" That was seriously the most profound decision she could handle at this moment.

"Stripes," Charlie decided.

"Okay, faster and easier, and less to wash out," Jordan agreed. "But I can't see the back to do stripes evenly."

Suddenly there was a loud banging on the hotel room door. Jordan scowled.

"So since I'm on my own here, I just have to go all purple, right?" she asked.

"You're not going to answer the door?" Charlie asked.

"No."

"What if it's Jason?" Naomi asked.

Jason Young had known Jordan for eleven years. There was no way he was at her door knocking right now. He knew better.

They'd talk again eventually probably, but he'd know not to come after her right now.

"Room service has been here with coffee. There's no one else I want to see."

"You sure?" Naomi asked.

Something in her friend's tone made Jordan perk up. It would be just like Naomi and Charlie to have gotten online while they talked and sent her a giant cookie bouquet. Or liquor.

Jordan picked up the computer and started for the door.

Oh, or a woman to do an in-suite spa treatment. Sure, she might be here for a massage or pedicure, but Jordan could pay extra for help with the back of her hair.

"You guys are the best," she said as she carried Charlie and

Naomi with her from the bathroom, through the bedroom, and into the living room of the suite.

"Us? You don't even —"

"Jordan!" A male voice yelled through the door. He pounded again. "Jordan! It's me, let me in."

Jordan froze with shock.

That was Fletcher's voice.

Immediately her eyes filled with tears.

She hurried to the table by the window and set the computer down. "Be right back," she told the girls.

"Jordan! Dammit! Let me in!"

She ran to the door, twisting the deadbolt, fumbling with the chain, and finally yanking it open.

Fletcher Landry was on the other side, his fist raised, ready to knock again.

He froze.

They stared at each other for a long moment.

Then she launched herself at him.

He caught her easily, his big arms wrapping around her. He stepped through the doorway with her, her feet dangling three inches off the floor. He kicked the door shut behind them and then just squeezed her.

There was nothing better in her life than Fletcher hugs. That had been true since she'd been six years old and had fallen on the playground at recess, scraping her knee, and he'd come over to check on her and hugged her. That was it. Fletcher Landry had been hugging her and making things better for the past twenty years and this moment was no different.

But, as she buried her face in his neck, she realized this was totally different.

He hadn't had to come.

Things had been awkward between them for months. She'd cried the last time they'd been together. He'd asked her to choose between him and Jason.

And clearly, she'd made the wrong choice.

But still, he'd come. Now her best friend in the entire world and the person who could always make everything okay was here. As if by magic.

Of course, it wasn't magic. Fletcher had, clearly, gotten on a plane immediately after finding out what happened and had flown to her.

He let go of her with one arm and reached behind him to re-lock the door and replace the chain. Then he walked to the sofa in the living room of the suite.

He sank down onto one of the cushions, taking her with him. He pulled her into his lap and continued to hug her tightly. Jordan curled into him, her arms around his neck. He was warm and solid and familiar.

So familiar.

They sat together on the couch, hugging, for several minutes.

Eventually, she lifted her head from his shoulder and looked up at him.

He met her gaze, but didn't say anything.

He didn't really need to say anything.

"Thank you," she told him. She didn't need to say anything either, she knew, but she wanted to.

He just gave her a single nod.

She pulled back slightly, studying him. His jaw was tight and though he was holding her and hugging her, his eyes were stormy.

"Are you okay?" she asked.

He gave a soft snort. "I think that's my line."

She shook her head. "Well, obviously *I'm* not okay. I've never been more humiliated in my life. But you look…" She narrowed her eyes. "Really pissed."

"Accurate."

Yeah, that made sense. Fletcher wasn't a huge fan of Jason's. In spite of her best efforts and desires over the years, Jason and Fletcher had never been friends. They tolerated one another.

Mostly because she insisted on it. But there was a tension between the two and always had been.

Jason had, at times, been jealous of Fletcher. At least in the beginning. When they were fifteen and had first started dating, everything about relationships had been new to both of them. Her being close to Fletcher had made Jason suspicious. But after some time, he'd realized that she and Fletcher truly were just best buddies.

It probably helped that Fletcher had been a playboy from a young age. He was a Landry and the Landry males were well known for being too charming for their own good. They all had more than their share of female attention and they all wallowed in it. Fletcher had been no exception. He'd dated extensively through high school and had been very familiar with backseats and lost panties long before Jason even got lucky with his long-time girlfriend.

For some reason, thinking about that now, she became acutely aware of the fact that she was in Fletcher's lap.

She'd sat in Fletcher's lap lots of times. Usually when there had been too many people packed into someone's pickup heading down to the bayou for a bonfire.

Was that the safest situation? Of course not. Would they have been pulled over and ticketed by the cop if he'd seen them? Probably. But if they were ever short on seats, whether in the pickup or on someone's couch for movie nights, she'd always plopped down on Fletcher. Sometimes not even just because they were short of seats. She'd sat on his lap and shared blankets around bonfires and ballgames a number of times.

But it had been a while.

And for some reason, at this moment, she was aware that he was bigger and harder than she remembered from past lap-sitting situations.

Of course he was. He was twenty-six now. This was defi-nitely not the same body she'd cuddled up with in high school on the pontoon boat when the sun dropped and things got chilly on the bayou.

This was, however, the body she'd pressed up against in that motel in Galveston…

She'd been thinking about Galveston on and off ever since it had happened. Suddenly kissing her best friend had been pretty unforgettable. But she'd especially been thinking about it since the night of the weddings in Autre when Fletcher had asked her to stay. With him. He'd specifically said "with me". She hadn't been able to forget that.

And now, in his arms again, all of that, and everything from Galveston, came flooding back. It wasn't just him in general that was big and hard. There was a specific part of him pressing into her right butt cheek at the moment that definitely could be described as big and hard.

She wiggled.

His hand clamped down to keep her from moving. And that was when she became aware that one of his big, hot hands was resting on her hip.

Her mostly bare hip.

Because she was wearing the t-shirt she slept in and panties. And nothing else.

She'd changed back into the shirt to dye her hair, not wanting to risk staining anything else in the limited wardrobe she had with her.

And she hadn't covered up to answer the door.

So now she was sitting on Fletcher's lap, barely dressed, in a hotel suite, and he seemed very happy to see her.

"Fletch—"

"Ignore it."

Yeah, he knew what she'd noticed. As always, they were on the same page without exchanging many words.

She shifted again, his grip tightened on her hip, and she was shocked to feel tingles dance across her skin.

"I don't know if I can."

"I'm ignoring the fact that you're half-naked. You can ignore my reaction to it."

It was completely stupid, and probably inappropriate, but Jordan snorted.

"Your 'reaction' would indicate that you're not actually ignoring me being half-naked."

Fletcher gave the soft chuckle and squeezed her hip again. Then he nudged her off his lap.

Jordan stood and gave him a smile. "You've seen me in less."

They'd swum together many, many times. She'd worn bathing suits, bikinis, and they'd even skinny dipped a couple of times. Never just the two of them and, as far as she knew, he'd never gotten a good look. But he'd probably seen a flash of her ass at least. And she'd gotten one really good full frontal view the summer after they'd graduated. It had been quick, right before he dove into the water, and she'd, of course, been completely caught up in Jason, but she'd understood what the girls of Autre and the surrounding area had been gushing about.

Fletcher stretched up from the couch and Jordan had to take a step back to give him space.

"Who's saying that I didn't have this 'reaction' then too?" he asked.

Jordan grinned. This relationship was so easy. They could talk about almost anything and there was very little filtering of language or topics. At least it had always been that way. She was incredibly relieved to think that was still true. They hadn't really been "them" for a while, but now standing here, looking up at him, after two years of being physically apart and three and a half months of things being awkward and tense in phone calls and texts, she desperately needed them to be them again.

"Thanks for saying that," she told him.

"Thanks for shaving your legs," he returned. His eyes dropped to her bare legs.

Again, he'd seen them many times in shorts, skirts, and bathing suits. But he'd also known her through many awkward growing-up stages. Like before she'd started shaving her legs. And after she started shaving her legs and hated it. She'd sometimes go a few days even in the summer when she was wearing shorts and he always gave her shit about it. To which she would always reply, "I'm only hanging out with you, it doesn't matter."

Right now, though, she was really glad she'd shaved her legs too.

"Did you see that damned dress I was wearing last night? *On stage*? How could I *not* shave?" she asked.

"I did see that damned dress. And that damned stage."

His joking tone was gone.

She sighed. "Yeah. So that sucked."

He didn't respond directly to that. Instead, he said, "Get your stuff."

"What?"

"I'm taking you home. Get your stuff."

"Home?"

Fletcher blew out a breath. "Well, what else are you going to do?"

He had a point. But if she went home, she couldn't *not* have the conversation with her mother that she didn't want to have.

She would have told her mom and dad that she and Jason had actually broken up two weeks ago, but Jason's manager, Ethan, had somehow talked her into keeping that a secret for four more months. And faking an engagement.

How had he talked her into that again?

Oh, yeah, she was really nice and genuinely cared about Jason and his career—even if she no longer wanted to be his girlfriend.

The fifty thousand dollars Ethan had offered hadn't hurt either.

But now that Jason had ruined the entire thing—and seriously, he couldn't remember her *name* for his fake proposal after dating her for eleven years?—she was definitely in a weird predicament.

She was suddenly single. And homeless, since the apartment in Nashville was Jason's. And even if she was going to get her own, she didn't have a job—also thanks to Jason and her quitting her job to travel with him four months before he told her he was in love with someone else.

But she didn't want it to be in Nashville anyway.

She'd worked for a very short time in New Orleans, but even then she'd shared the apartment with Jason. It was now August, and schools would have, obviously, hired all the teachers they needed for the year. She could substitute, she was sure. But that was much less steady work, it didn't come with benefits, and, frankly, she didn't want to live alone in New Orleans. She loved the city, but didn't know it well enough to feel safe and secure there by herself. She'd been living in Nashville and traveling the country with Jason, but she was still a small-town girl at heart.

She'd clearly taken too long to respond, because Fletcher said, "You need to come home."

"Sure, why not? Everyone already saw the most humiliating moment of my life, I might as well slink back home with my tail between my legs, jobless, boyfriend-less, pathetic, and miserable."

It took Fletcher about three seconds to answer. "Yeah, you might as well."

That was not going to make it into the pep talk Hall of Fame, but Jordan felt her mouth curving into a grin. "At least there'll be moonshine and good coffee." It seemed no one outside of Louisiana believed in chicory coffee, which was a true travesty.

"Have you had anything for breakfast besides peanut butter cups?" he asked, his tone gentler now.

She shook her head. She'd only been able to focus on coffee. But her stomach growled at the mention of breakfast. Then she frowned. "How did you know I'd had peanut butter cups?"

He gave her a *really?* look. "Good guess."

Yeah, okay, he knew her well. They all did. "Yes, I could probably use some real food."

"I'll order room service. Go get ready."

She opened her mouth to respond, but realized she didn't have a response. That all sounded like a really good idea.

It was her experience that most of Fletcher Landry's ideas were good. Actually, if she was being totally honest, that wasn't true. Just his ideas when it came to *her*.

Fletcher had gotten into plenty of trouble and made plenty of stupid decisions growing up, like all kids did. Like all boys did. Like all Landry boys did. But when it came to her, he seemed to have an innate ability to know exactly what to say and do. He always made her feel better. He always knew the right things to say. He always fixed things for her.

And four months ago when he'd told her to stay with him in Autre…she should have listened. Look at her now. She was on her way back there anyway. With him.

And she wasn't upset about it.

"I'm really glad you're here," she said.

His eyes flickered with emotion but he just gave her a little nod. "Of course I'm here."

Of course he was here. She probably should've been expecting it.

"I just really —"

"Jordan," Fletcher interrupted.

"Yeah?"

"You need to put some clothes on."

She looked down at herself. Her shirt was a pale peach color and hit about three inches below the lower curve of her ass.

"But I shaved."

Fletcher tucked his hands into the front pockets of his jeans and braced his feet apart. He nodded. "Yep. And I'm wondering just how much shaving you do."

Her eyes widened and her mouth dropped open. She stared at him. There was very little off limits between her and Fletcher, but there were just some things they naturally steered away from. How much shaving she did was one of those things.

"I can't believe you just said that to me."

He shrugged. "It's the truth. Also that shirt is a little see-through when you're standing in front of the window."

She glanced behind her. The sun was coming in through the huge window. She looked back at him. "I—"

"And I can see your nipples."

Again she felt her mouth drop open. She was very rarely speechless around Fletcher. Then again, Fletcher very rarely talked about her nipples. In fact he had *never* talked about her nipples.

She crossed her arms over her chest instinctively. It seemed that her nipples liked being talked about because they were a little perkier than they had been a moment ago. "Wow," was her only response. Very eloquent.

Again, he just shrugged. "Thought we could always say anything to one another."

"We…can…I just never…had you comment…my nipples before." She couldn't believe she was stumbling over her words with Fletcher.

"You sure?"

"Very."

"Huh." Fletcher seemed to be thinking about that. "Well, I'm sure I've noticed them before, so I must've been trying to be a gentleman by not commenting."

"And you're not feeling gentlemanly today?"

"Not especially."

"And why is that?"

"It just you and me, Jordan. And you're now single. Do I need to be a gentleman?"

She took a deep breath, studying him. Fletcher seemed a little wound up. Not his usual laid-back, easy-going self. She realized he was worried about her. And upset about what happened to her. And honestly, that was really nice. So no, he did not need to be a gentleman.

"Nope," she said.

"Good. Now go get dressed."

Or else what? She thought. But she didn't say it out loud. She wasn't going to taunt Fletcher about her near naked state and her nipples. That was ridiculous. And inappropriate. Probably. For some reason.

Why didn't that feel inappropriate and ridiculous?

That was probably something she should think about later. But she was acutely aware now of her near-naked state and her nipples and getting that all covered up seemed like a good idea.

"Be back in a bit," she said, pivoting on her heel and heading for the bedroom. She closed the door behind her and took a deep breath.

CHAPTER

Three

WOW, what was going on? For some reason, she felt even more discombobulated right now than she had when she'd been recognized in the hotel lobby by Jason's fans.

Jordan pressed a hand to her chest.

Okay, Charlie had said she needed to face all of this with confidence. Naomi said she needed to lay low and let it blow over. Fletcher was now saying she needed to go with him, get on an airplane, and head back to Autre.

Oh crap.

All of a sudden she remembered Naomi and Charlie and her computer. They were still out in the living room. Unless they'd hung up. Surely they'd hung up.

She pulled the door open and peeked out. She didn't see Fletcher right away so she stepped into the living room.

He was across the room by the phone. He had the room service menu in hand. He glanced over with a questioning look.

She pointed at the computer as she crossed to it.

Fletcher glanced over. "Oh, hey, ladies."

"Hi, Fletcher," Charlie greeted cheerily.

Clearly, neither of her friends had thought to disconnect once

Fletcher showed up. Which meant they'd witnessed all of the weirdness.

Jordan picked up the computer, lifting it right in front of her face. "You guys knew he was coming?" She started for the bedroom again.

Naomi nodded. "But we didn't want to say anything because we didn't know when he'd get there, for sure. And we thought we should focus on the hair emergency."

"And you might've gotten dressed if you'd known he was coming and that would've been a whole lot less entertaining." Charlie gave her a smirk.

Jordan shut the bedroom door behind her. "Stop."

"No, seriously, I didn't know you and Fletcher talk like that to each other," Naomi said.

"Yeah, I didn't realize you and Fletcher had so much chemistry. I clearly haven't been around you guys together in a while," Charlie said.

Jordan set the computer on the bed. "Fletcher and I talk about almost everything."

"Nipples and erections?" Charlie asked.

Jordan's cheeks flushed. "Well, no." She went to the closet and started sliding hangers from one side to the other, rifling through her outfits.

"Well, you've talked about nipples and erections now," Charlie pointed out.

Jordan really wanted to *stop* talking about nipples and erections. At least, *her* nipples and *Fletcher's* erections.

She sighed, turning back to her friends. "I don't know what's going on. I feel like I'm going to wake up and all of this was a weird dream."

"It's definitely not a dream," Naomi told her.

"Dammit."

"But Fletcher is there now. It's all going to be okay," Charlie said.

Naomi nodded. "Right. No worries now."

"So I need to get on the plane and come home," Jordan said. "I guess that makes sense."

"Well, there's no way he's leaving you there," Naomi said. "And he can't stay. He's got work tomorrow. And I can't imagine him thinking you should go back to Nashville."

"So I should just do whatever Fletcher tells me to do?" Jordan asked dryly.

There was a two-second pause and then both of her friends said, "Yes," simultaneously.

Jordan laughed.

"I'm serious," Charlie said. "You're having a hell of a morning. I think, in light of everything, you should just let Fletcher take over the decision making for the next…twenty-four hours. At least."

Jordan frowned. "That seems extreme."

It also sounded amazing. The only decision she'd been sure of so far today was that she wanted *caffeinated* coffee. She was even second-guessing the king-size peanut butter cup purchase. She probably should have just gotten a regular.

"Nah. Let's say…until your hair is back to its normal color," Naomi said with a grin. "Let the sweet guy who knows you best and adores you and would protect you no matter what take care of you for a bit."

Jordan felt a long breath leave her lungs. It felt like…relief. "That's okay then?" she asked, finally giving in. "I mean, I *really* want to do that. I want to just say I'm done for the day. But it's not even noon and I'm a grown woman."

"Oh hell, take advantage," Charlie said. "It's not every day a knight in shining armor shows up. Fletcher's got you."

Yeah, he did. He always had. And now he was *here*, in the flesh, looking protective and determined. It would be *so* easy to just turn it all over to him. If he thought she should go home, then she could just nod and say, "Okay." No thinking, no weighing pros and cons, no worries. Just "okay."

"You cannot be trusted to make decisions today," Naomi agreed.

Jordan frowned. "Hey."

Naomi pointed to her own head.

Jordan's hand flew up to touch her hair where it was now streaked purple. Dammit. She tipped her head back, took a long deep breath, then focused on her friends again. "Okay. Fletcher's in charge."

"And have Fletcher help with the hair," Charlie said, matter-of-factly.

"I could try washing it out."

"It won't all come out," Charlie said. "It will fade and look weird. Just go for it. Dark purple stripes. And wear the silky red dress I saw in the closet."

"No way," Jordan said quickly. "If I'm getting on a plane later and coming home to Louisiana…" The reality of that hit her.

She couldn't stay in Vegas. She couldn't even stay in this suite for another night. This was Jason's suite. He had let her stay, not even calling her or coming up last night—again, knowing better. But eventually he would want access to his room. And she sure wasn't going to *share* it with him.

"She needs to look casual," Naomi said. "Just relaxed and comfortable and happy. Like she barely gave any thought to how she looked. Because it didn't even occur to her to care."

Jordan liked the sound of that. It seemed less likely to involve high heels, for one thing. For another, no hairspray. She was so sick of hairspray. Her naturally straight hair refused to hold curl without a gallon of the stuff and Marci, Jason's hair and makeup girl, had been insistent that Jordan's hair be curled. For some reason.

"Yes. Casual," she agreed. "I want that."

Charlie rolled her eyes. Charlie knew Jordan would always choose casual. For a girl who liked heels as much as Charlie did, Jordan could be very frustrating. Of course, Charlie's blond hair was perfectly wavy and always gorgeous, even without hairspray, so she didn't really understand Jordan's aversion to spending time in front of the vanity mirror.

Naomi, on the other hand, got it. Growing up on television, from age eight to fourteen, she'd had her hair messed with on a daily basis. She often talked about the time spent by hairstylists on straightening her naturally coiled hair into sleek black strands. The process had done a lot of damage. Now Naomi preferred her hair untouched and wore her hair in braids a lot of the time.

Of course, Jordan's aversion to all the fussing was just general laziness and not wanting to mess with it at all. Naomi had much better reasons.

"Fine." Charlie sounded put out. At least Naomi did like lipstick and doing her nails and other things Charlie liked. "Go get Fletcher. Get your hair fixed."

She didn't have a better idea, so Jordan set the computer on the bathroom counter and went to the bedroom door. She pulled it open.

"Hey, Fletcher?"

"Yeah?"

"Could you come in here for a minute?"

He crossed the room. "What's going on? You're not dressed."

She turned her head and pointed to the purple stripe in her hair. "I could use some help."

He lifted a brow. "Yeah, I noticed that. What happened?"

"Momentary freak out while downstairs in the gift shop."

Half his mouth curled up into a grin. "So what do you need help with?"

"I need you to help me finish my hair in the back where I can't see it."

He looked puzzled. "Help you do what to your hair?"

"More purple stripes."

"I don't know how to do that."

She stepped back and swung the door to the bedroom open

wider. "Lucky for you, Charlie and Naomi are still on my computer."

"And they agree this is a good idea?"

"They agree that there isn't a better option." Jordan said.

He sighed and stepped into the bedroom. "Okay, show me what to do."

Jordan turned and led him into the bathroom. This was one thing she definitely appreciated about Fletcher Landry—he was easy-going and particularly with her. If she said she needed something, he didn't ask a lot of questions. He just stepped up and did what needed to be done.

In the bathroom, she showed him the box of dye and both Charlie and Naomi weighed in with tips.

"You have to be dressed like this while we do this?" Fletcher asked from behind her.

They were both facing the mirror, with her in front of him. His hands were in her hair, combing his fingers through it and for a moment she couldn't focus on what he'd asked her. Damn that felt good.

She was trying to remember if Fletcher had ever run his fingers through her hair before. And if so, why she didn't remember it. He had really big hands. She was sure this wasn't the first time she'd ever noticed that but suddenly she couldn't stop thinking about it. Big hands, and long thick fingers.

"Jordan?"

Her eyes went from her hair gliding between his fingers to his eyes in the mirror. "Yeah?"

"I asked if you need to wear this while we do this. Can you put something else on?"

"No, I don't want to get dye on anything else. You need to focus."

Which was completely hypocritical of her to say, considering all she could think about was how intimate this suddenly seemed. Even with her two best girlfriends on the computer essentially watching. She was barely dressed, they were standing in a hotel bathroom, his hands were in her hair—his big, hot hands—and he was about to…do something. She couldn't quite remember the details. Hair dye. Right, he was going to help her dye her hair. But honestly, she would've had to think for a few seconds to come up with what color.

That was super weird.

She was distracted by Fletcher.

She knew all of Fletcher's tricks and quirks and could easily ignore them or look past them. But now he had his hands on her and she couldn't think straight?

This had to be a product of being dumped on national television, sleeping like crap, and the craziness of being recognized as a public figure downstairs in the hotel lobby.

Or something.

She became aware that Naomi and Charlie had apparently given Fletcher his next instructions as he leaned past her to reach for the applicator. His chest pressed against her upper back and his arm brushed the side of her breast.

Tingles raced through her body.

Yeah. Super weird.

Over the next few minutes, Fletcher applied the hair dye in four long strokes down the back of her head. When he got to the right side, he met her eyes in the mirror. "Want me to keep going or do you want to do it?"

She simply shook her head. "You."

She was suddenly too flustered to put hair dye on her own head.

He stroked the applicator in more stripes then leaned to put it away. Finally. Each time he leaned forward to get more dye, his body had pressed and brushed against hers.

This was not new. Why was she acting like this was new? She and Fletcher had been comfortable around each other physically since they were six.

She studied him in the mirror as he chatted with Naomi and Charlie and examined his work on her hair.

He looked really good. He had a couple days' growth of scruff on his jaw. He'd worn his hair long for several years now. Not as long as his twin brothers Zeke and Zander, who pulled their hair back into "man buns", but Fletcher's hair was long enough to hang past his shirt collar, and when he reached up and ran his hand through it, he definitely made waves in it. It would blow in his face at times when he was outside working so he would pull it back into a ponytail. It looked good on him. It was a little wild, a little nontraditional for an elementary school teacher, and gave him just a hint of the bad boy he'd been in high school.

But that bad boy was mostly gone. He'd grown up and took being an elementary educator very seriously. He knew he was a role model and knew that a lot of the parents of the kids he taught were aware of his reputation. Heck, some of those parents had been at the same parties, fights, and drag races that had resulted in that reputation. And most of the moms had found that edge, that reputation, attractive. At least at one point.

A lot of the parents who had kids in Fletcher's class were a bit older than Fletcher and Jordan, but Autre was a small town and everyone was aware of everyone else. Some of the parents had run around with Fletcher's older cousins—Sawyer, Owen, and Josh—and Fletcher had tagged along at a much younger age than most kids.

"Okay, so can we eat breakfast while your hair turns purple?"

Jordan became aware that there was a knocking on the suite door again.

"You already called room service?"

He nodded. "I've been sitting in airports all night. I'm starving."

"You have?"

"I headed straight to New Orleans after I saw what happened. But there were no last minute flights and nothing direct. I camped out there and got on standby on the first flight out, but had a long layover." He spread his arms wide. "But I'm here now."

He'd sat in airports and been on planes all night. For her.

"Yes. Of course. Let's eat."

Fletcher's eyes dropped to the front of her shirt. Then traveled down past the lower hem to her bare legs. "Can you put more clothes on *now*?"

Actually, having more clothes on suddenly seemed like a great idea.

"Yeah, I'll put on a robe or something," she said. "I have to wash my hair after the time is up for the color though."

He nodded. "Okay. I'll meet you out in the living room." He turned to look at the computer screen. "Thanks, ladies. See you soon."

Naomi and Charlie were both watching intently. They nodded and said goodbye.

As soon as he left the room though, Charlie said, "Oh my God."

"Seriously," Naomi added.

Jordan frowned at them. "What?"

"That was so sexy," Charlie said.

Jordan shook her head. "What was so sexy?" It had definitely been sexy.

"Watching you and Fletcher just now," Naomi said. "Talk about foreplay."

"Foreplay? Stop it. I was just dumped *last night*. He's helping with my hair because I'm an idiot and started dying my hair purple without thinking it through. That's all that was."

Except that four months ago he'd essentially told her he wanted her and had asked her to choose between him and Jason. And then there was Galveston…

Charlie and Naomi didn't know about either of those things though.

"Whatever you say," Naomi said.

"Sure, okay," Charlie said.

Jordan leaned in closer to the computer screen. "I just got out of an *eleven-year* relationship less than twenty-four hours ago."

Charlie snorted. "Stop it. You already told us everything."

Jordan sighed. When Charlie and Naomi had called that morning, concerned about her, she'd told them about the fake proposal and that she and Jason had planned to pretend to be engaged for the next four months while he was on this tour to preserve his image.

It sounded way stupider when she'd explained it out loud than it had in her head though. Or than it had when Jason's manager had explained it to *her*.

The whole a-breakup-at-this-point-in-his-career-will-ruin-everything had seemed dramatic to Jordan, but then she'd been recognized in the lobby of the hotel that morning and now she realized Ethan had reason to be concerned. The fans in line at the coffee shop had called out things like, "Team Jordan!" and, "he's a scumbag!" and, "I've already deleted his album!"

So, she was glad she'd said yes to going along with the whole idea.

And then Jason had botched it anyway.

Jordan could only imagine what Ethan had said to *Jason* about that last night.

"Okay, well, I better get going," she told Charlie and Naomi. "But I guess I'll see you guys in a few hours."

Her friends smiled brightly at that.

"I can't wait to have you here with us," Charlie said. "Oh my gosh! You can come work at Boys of the Bayou Gone Wild with me!"

"At the petting zoo?" Jordan perked up at that. They had alpacas. She loved alpacas. And they now had lemurs and a sloth. How cool was that?

"Of course. You can take over what Fletcher did all summer with the educational talks and stuff," Charlie said enthusiastically. "With school back in session, he can't do them anymore. We've talked about alternatives." Then she gasped as a thought clearly occurred to her. "We can *expand* our educational offerings! You're a teacher! We could put together some really amazing programs. Maybe some online stuff. We could—"

"Oh my God, Charlie!" Jordan broke in, laughing. "Okay. We'll definitely talk. Let me get there first."

"And she's not supposed to make any decisions for the rest of the day," Naomi reminded them both. "Fletcher's in charge."

Jordan pulled in a deep breath. Yes, that really did sound nice. "Exactly. I'll see you when I get to Louisiana."

"Okay. But I'm typing up notes as we speak," Charlie said.

And she literally was. The creative part of Charlie's brain worked constantly. Jordan knew that in the hours it would take for her to get to Louisiana, even with a layover somewhere between Vegas and New Orleans, Charlie would have some amazing plan worked out.

"I love you both. Thank you for being here for me this morning," Jordan said, carrying the computer back into the bedroom.

"Of course," Naomi said sweetly.

"I would have been pissed if you hadn't picked up," Charlie told her.

Laughing, Jordan disconnected the call.

She pulled on one of the plush robes provided by the hotel. She supposed if she got purple dye on the robe it was Jason's problem, since this was his room.

He could fork over the money for a new robe at least after messing everything up last night and leaving her scrambling for a plan this morning.

She hadn't wanted to say yes to the proposal. She hadn't wanted to be proposed to, period. But she'd been willing to go along with it for *his* image.

Hell, she was living out of a suitcase, sleeping in a new city and having her hair curled and sprayed and having to be sure her legs were shaved *every night* because of him. When she could have just stayed in Autre with Fletcher four months ago and could now be living the life she'd always dreamed of…

She stopped that train of thought.

There was no use going there.

She'd made her choice. It had been the wrong one, obviously, but there was no use doing the whole what-if thing.

She took a deep breath and stepped out into the living room.

Fletcher looked up. "Thank God." He used his foot to push the chair on the other side of the table by the window out for her.

"Thank God?" The aroma of coffee and *bacon* hit her. Yes, the day was definitely looking up. "You didn't have to wait for me to start eating."

"I didn't."

She looked at his plate as she took her seat and tucked her foot under her. It was empty except for one piece of bacon and a few crumbles of what looked like scrambled eggs.

"Then what are you so thankful for?"

"You're covered up."

She rolled her eyes. "Come on. It wasn't *that* bad looking at me."

He shook his head slowly. "Nope. It wasn't bad."

"So what's your deal?"

"Single looks really good on you."

Her eyes locked on his. There was something in his tone that made her heart hammer. She took a breath. "Thanks."

What else was she supposed to say? That she was getting a little hot with this robe on and she thought she should take it off?

"Here. Eat." Fletcher leaned over and lifted the silver dome that was covering the plate in front of her.

The cheesecake was the first thing she saw.

Her eyes flew to his. He was watching her, smiling.

"Cheesecake is basically just a softer and more triangular bagel with cream cheese," he told her.

It was an exact quote of what she'd said to him every time

she had cheesecake for breakfast. Which wasn't often, but it had definitely happened in the past. More than once.

She found herself actually a little choked up over the piece of cheesecake with the chocolate drizzle and strawberries on the side.

"I love you," she told Fletcher sincerely. "This is perfect."

A strange flash of emotion went across his face, but he gave her a half smile and said, "I've always got you."

He really did. What would she do without him?

She took a breath, realizing that she was feeling *very* emotional over a triangle of cream cheese and sugar.

But… cream cheese and sugar. On what was one of the most confusing mornings of her life. Except that Fletcher had fixed it. From her hair to her breakfast to giving her a plan and a place to go.

She pulled the plate toward her, cradling it like a newborn baby.

Fletcher reached to pour the coffee.

She watched him as she took the first bite of cheesecake.

Yeah, this all felt pretty much perfect.

Of course Fletcher Landry was the one delivering exactly what she needed.

Just like a good best friend.

CHAPTER
Four

FLETCHER WATCHED as Jordan took the last bite of cheesecake. She gave a soft moan as her eyes slid shut, and he had to shift on his chair trying to get more comfortable behind his fly. That was nothing new. Jordan had been making him hard with random, seemingly silly things for the past three years.

He'd known her, and been hanging out with her, for twenty years. He'd seen her in less than the t-shirt she'd been wearing this morning. He'd slept next to her multiple times. He'd even kissed her on at least three New Year's Eves that he could think of.

He always thought she was attractive, in that objective every-guy-would-think-she-was-pretty way. He was aware of her long, silky, dark blond hair. He knew every shade of blue that her eyes would turn, depending on her mood. The freckles that were scattered across her cheeks and nose were as familiar to him as the freckles on his own mother's face. He not only would have been able to tell where all of Jordan's scars were, but he'd be able to tell the stories of how she'd gotten them.

He also remembered when her curves had first developed. He also remembered threatening bodily harm to the other guys who also noticed and commented on it. Hell, he'd been with her the first time she'd bought tampons on her own.

But one dark and stormy night in Galveston, Texas, she'd suddenly become a *woman* to him.

Since then, he'd noticed things like the way her eyelashes curled, how pale the skin under the strap of her sundress was compared to the rest of the smooth skin on her shoulder, how her ass looked in blue jeans, and, most definitely, any time her nipples got hard.

Oh, and the moaning. He definitely noticed the times she moaned.

"My God that was good," Jordan said, opening her eyes and giving him a smile as she set her plate and fork on the table between them.

Fletcher felt stupidly smug about getting her that cheesecake. He was also glad that room service had offered it and was willing to put chocolate sauce on it instead of the strawberry drizzle they offered. He probably wouldn't have gone so far as to find the nearest restaurant that served cheesecake, take a taxi there, and get her a piece. Probably. But there was very little he would not do for Jordan Benoit.

"So, other than having purple-striped hair now, you seem good," he said.

She really did. She didn't seem angry or hurt. He had to assume the purple hair thing was a reaction to everything that had happened. But she wasn't a blubbering mess or wanting to set shit on fire, so really, she was doing better than he'd expected.

She picked up her coffee cup and settled back in her chair, tucking her foot under her butt again. She cradled the cup in both hands and gave a nod. She sipped the coffee, then sighed. "Well, the hair was because I got recognized in the lobby this morning by some of Jason's fans. That freaked me out and I panicked."

"You thought this would be some kind of disguise?"

She grinned. "Exactly."

"I don't think it's going to work."

She laughed. "Me either. So the plan now is to walk out of here as if I'm totally fine and am the best ex-girlfriend ever."

God, he *really* liked that she was Jason's *ex*-girlfriend. "How not fine are you?" he asked. He needed to be prepared for a breakdown later on if one was imminent, he figured. He'd grab a box of tissues, some more chocolate, and make a beeline for the bar at the airport.

She studied him for about ten seconds before answering. "I'm actually totally fine."

He lifted a brow.

"Seriously. Everything is…good. I mean now that I have a place to go since I've just about overstayed my welcome here in Jason's penthouse suite."

"That was your only concern this morning?" Fletcher asked. He wasn't buying it.

"I was also not sure how the plane ticket back to Nashville on the record label's dime was going to work now that we're not together anymore," she said. "I figured they'd probably let me fly back to Nashville. I mean, it's *his* fault that everything went to hell last night. But the flight isn't for two more days and I didn't know if they'd pay to move the date. I don't want to stay *here*. And I don't want to sit next to Jason on the plane even if they did let me keep the ticket. That would have been confusing. So…I was just mixed up about what to do."

Fletcher stared at her. "Seriously? Those were the things you were worried about?"

Jordan lifted a shoulder. "Yep."

He studied her. She meant it. What the hell?

He sat forward in his chair, resting his forearms on his thighs. "Okay, *why* are you good?"

She sighed. "Because you were right. I should have listened to you."

"You should have." He paused. "About which thing?"

She gave a soft laugh. "You were right that I shouldn't have moved to Nashville with him. And I definitely shouldn't have gone on this tour with him."

Fletcher froze.

That night in Autre, when he'd asked her to stay, had replayed in his mind about four thousand times over the past four months. Fletcher shifted on his seat again, but this time not due to any increased firmness behind his zipper. He didn't regret what he'd said that night, but he wasn't sure he wanted to rehash it either. "What do you mean?" he finally asked.

"I think I knew, even when we first moved from Louisiana, that we were going to break up."

"Really? Things were bad?" Fletcher worked on keeping his tone and posture casual.

He and Jason Young had had words about Jordan over the years. Jason had generally been a good boyfriend, which had been the reason Fletcher generally stayed supportive of their relationship. However, over eleven years' time, there had been a few arguments and a few tears on Jordan's part. Fletcher had always warned Jason that if he hurt Jordan, Fletcher would hurt him. And Jason knew the Landry boys' reputation well enough to know that it wouldn't be *emotional* pain.

It wasn't particularly mature, at this point in their lives anyway, but Jason and Jordan had started dating when they were kids. From about fifteen to eighteen, Fletcher had cared a lot more about Jason treating Jordan right than he had about being diplomatic or mature.

"I wouldn't say *bad*," Jordan said. "We just started drifting apart. We'd been together for eight years when we moved to Nashville. I had figured by then we would be buying a house and planning for at least our first baby. Once we got to Nashville, it became clear pretty quickly that his plans had changed in those regards."

"But he went to Nashville to pursue his music," Fletcher pointed out. "You didn't talk about the change in plans then?"

Jordan winced. "So I'm going to confess a really bad girl-friend thing right now."

Fletcher didn't say anything. They had so many secrets from so many years together that there was nothing she couldn't tell him.

"When he said he wanted to go to Nashville to try to get a recording contract, I figured, I had to let him try. But…" She bit her bottom lip, clearly not proud of what she was about to say. "I didn't think it would happen." She winced again.

"You didn't think he'd get a contract?"

She shook her head. "I really didn't. And I know that sounds terrible. He's talented. I've always thought so. I just never dreamed that he had what it would take to become an *actual* country music star. So I thought we'd move to Nashville and give it a try for a couple of years, then we could always move back home. But while we were there, we could get married and work on starting a family. Then when we moved back to Louisiana, we'd be ready to settle down."

Fletcher couldn't help the small smile that started to crawl across his lips.

"Don't laugh," Jordan said. "That's terrible of me. I just assumed he was going to fail."

"So why did you decide to go on this tour with him?" Fletcher asked. "That was a pretty good sign that things were taking off for him."

She blew out a breath. "Yeah. Obviously. But then I was telling myself that lots of country music stars have families and houses and real lives."

"Not a life like you want to have."

She nodded. "I've been miserable on this tour." She met his gaze. "As you knew I would be."

Fletcher shook his head. "We don't have to go there." He'd been right, but it wasn't giving him a lot of satisfaction at the moment. He really just wanted her to be happy.

She sighed. "Okay. But, I was unhappy even before the tour

started. I thought maybe the tour would bring us closer together. I mean, we haven't had sex in six months."

Fletcher coughed slightly at that and shifted on his chair again. He hadn't been expecting that. He was thrilled to hear it, if he was being honest with himself. But she'd just been dumped last night. This was not the time to be thinking about what this could mean for them. Even if that meant fighting the urge to entertain *all* of those thoughts every other minute.

"But he was *proposing* last night," Fletcher pointed out. "And you knew it, right?"

She pulled her bottom lip between her teeth and nodded.

"So, what was that? Had he told you about Vivian or something and you were trying to work it out? Was that some kind of—"

"Publicity stunt."

Fletcher stopped and blinked at her. "What?"

She nodded and chewed the inside of her cheek.

"What the hell do you mean it was a publicity stunt?" Fletcher couldn't explain the tightness in his chest suddenly.

Jordan blew out a breath, then pushed up from the chair. She set her cup down and paced to the window.

"It was all fake," she said, looking out the window and hugging her arms around her middle. "We were going to pretend to be engaged for the next four months of the tour, then figure out a way to end it. After ticket sales didn't matter anymore."

Fletcher processed that. He ran the words through his mind three times. Then he shot up from his chair. "*What?*"

Jordan turned. She didn't seem intimidated, or even startled, by his roar.

"You're not going to like this," she warned.

"Tell me," he demanded.

"Fine. Jason is up-and-coming. He's doing well, but he's just getting started and he needs to maintain the image that's attracting fans. Thanks to Suzanne, one of his publicists, I'm all over his social media accounts and the fans love me." She gave him an adorable modest smile.

He didn't return it and she rolled her eyes.

"They love that we were high school sweethearts," she continued. "They love that Jason's first number one hit was written for me, they love that I've been there for him through it all, from the first time he took the stage at a talent show in high school to moving to Nashville with him and supporting him while he pursued his dream. Everyone has fallen in love with our love story."

"Jesus, enough," Fletcher muttered, shoving a hand through his hair.

"*Anyway*, the fans would have been devastated by a breakup, and that could have negatively impacted tour ticket sales, so somehow Ethan, Jason's manager, convinced me to go along with a fake engagement for a few more months. Then I'd break up with him and he'd still get to be the good guy, probably write some sappy broken-hearted song that would go to the top of the charts, Vivian would be there to comfort him, and it would all end happily ever after."

"For him," Fletcher said flatly. It was so like her to be willing to be the bad guy to make Jason look good.

Jordan shrugged. "I kind of think Ethan believed we'd patch things up and stay together. But I agreed to it because I do care about Jason and his career. And it's not like I have a life of my own to get back to that couldn't wait four more months."

Those words landed like she'd just punched him in the gut.

"But you *could have*," he said, his voice low and tight.

Jordan's eyes flew to his. Her mouth opened into a little O.

He wasn't sure if it was because she'd realized what she'd actually said. Or if it was because he looked as pissed as he felt.

"Anyway, it was *not* a perfect solution," Jordan went on, clearly unsure what else to say. "Jason and Vivian had to hide their feelings and not be together, at least publicly, for four more months. And *she* would have had to watch us pretending to still be together and in love. That would have been so hard for her." She blew out a breath. "In some ways, this worked out well."

Yeah, it sure fucking had. *He* was taking her back to Autre *tonight*. For good. Away from Jason. To give her the life she wanted and deserved.

He just watched her, a bit amazed and a bit frustrated. She definitely wasn't heartbroken. Which was awesome. He didn't want his best friend hurting, first of all. He also didn't want the woman that he was half in love with pining for another man.

But *God*, did she have to be feeling bad for Jason and Vivian, for fuck's sake? How could she be *that* good of a person?

Of course, this was all an adjustment for him mentally. He'd spent three years telling himself that he had no business thinking of Jordan that way and that she and Jason were going to be together forever and he just had to accept that.

She'd been single for about twelve hours now. And damn, it really did look good on her.

"Jason should have broken if off if he wanted to be with someone else. Hell, Vivian should be mad at him for that too," Fletcher pointed out.

"He did," she said.

"What?"

"He told me two weeks ago that he was in love with Vivian. That's when we decided to break up. And when Ethan freaked out and came up with this plan."

"How long has he been cheating on you?" Fletcher asked. It was kind of a dick question, he knew, but he didn't care at the moment.

"He says he hasn't," Jordan answered. "He said that he'd been fighting it. But they fell in love anyway."

Fletcher wasn't sure he bought that, but he *was* sure he didn't care. Jordan was done with Jason. And she was fine. That's what mattered.

"Wow…" Jordan went on, musing out loud. "They've known each other for almost two years. They met shortly after we got to Nashville. They met at a writers' gig and started writing together every week." She smiled, almost to herself. "They definitely have so much more in common than we do now. Viv understands all the music stuff, everything with the business, shares that passion." Suddenly Jordan's eyes went wide. "Oh my God!"

"What?"

"He wrote that song about *her*. He wrote it *with* her."

"What song?"

"'Sweet Southern'. That number one song. His big breakout hit." She started chewing on her bottom lip. "Wow, and everyone thinks it's about me. He said that in all the interviews and everything. That poor girl."

Fletcher blew out a breath. "Okay, so you're good? Really, actually, honestly, for sure good?"

It was no secret, to him or anyone in his life—including Jordan—that Jordan being good was one of his primary goals. All the time. No matter what.

But she shook her head. "I am exactly the opposite of where I wanted to be at age twenty-six. I'm single. Homeless. Jobless." She sighed. "I don't even have a dog."

And she was also just a touch dramatic. "You can have all of those things by dinner time tomorrow," he told her.

"Yeah, I'll crash with you for a while." She looked up. "Okay? As far as the world knows, I was dumped. Moving back in with my parents would be just a bit *too* pathetic."

"Of course you can crash with me." He'd figure out how not to push her up against any doors in his house to kiss her. Probably. For a while anyway.

"And getting a dog is easy," she said. "And Charlie's already talking about a job with the petting zoo. Or I can substitute teach or something." She sighed heavily. "But I'm single. I do not want to be single, Fletcher."

Fletcher felt his gut tighten, not only because he always

wanted Jordan to have what she wanted to be happy, but because he was actually quite happy she was single. Not that he would tell her that. This wasn't the time.

"You'll only be single as long as you want to be," Fletcher said. "You can snap your fingers and be in a serious relationship tomorrow."

She narrowed her eyes slightly. "With who?"

Me.

"With whoever you want. The guys in Autre are a lot of things, but they're not stupid. Most of them anyway."

She shook her head. "I don't want to date. God, that sounds terrible."

He chuckled. "Dating is okay."

She rolled her eyes. "What you do is not dating, Fletcher. What you do is flirting, and partying, and sex."

"I buy dinner. Sometimes."

"That's your definition of dating?"

"What's *your* definition of dating?"

"Getting to know one another. Figuring out your likes and dislikes. Figuring out if you're compatible. Figuring out if this is a person that you actually want to spend every day of the rest of your life with."

"Jesus," Fletcher said. "No pressure."

"What's the point of dating if you're not trying to figure out if the person is *your* person?"

"Having fun?"

"But you can have fun with friends. And with family. Dating should be about more than that. Figuring out if you and this person fit together in a way that you don't fit with anyone else. And if you want to fit that way forever."

"No offense," Fletcher said, "but you might not be an expert on this."

She lifted a shoulder. "You've got a point. I've dated one guy. And I started going out with him when we were fifteen. We figured everything out together. He was my first boyfriend. My first date. My first kiss. The first guy who bought me a birthday present. The first guy who took me home to meet his family. The first guy I went on vacation with. The first guy I lived with. The first guy I broke up with." She sighed. "And the *only* guy I've done those things with."

"Not true."

She frowned. "What do you mean?"

"I got you birthday presents nine times before Jason bought you one. I took you home to meet my family when you were six. We've gone on at least three vacations that I can think of. And I've kissed you. In fact, I was your first."

She was looking at him with a mixture of emotions. The predominant one however, was clearly affection.

She nodded. "I stand corrected."

"You do remember that then?"

"We were eleven, we were playing truth or dare at Mitch's birthday party, and Zander dared me to kiss you."

"And because it was Zander, and you could never let Zander get the better of you, you agreed and laid a major one on me, as I recall."

She grinned. "My grandma loved romantic movies."

He laughed. "It showed. I remember that fondly."

"I remember so many things fondly with you, Fletcher. You're the best."

Her expression and tone of voice were both full of genuine fondness and Fletcher felt his chest warm. No matter what else he felt for this woman, the predominant emotion would always be love. A soft love that came from a long history and many, many wonderful memories. He would do anything for her.

"You were my first too," he said.

She nodded. "I figured."

He lifted a brow. "Oh yeah?"

"I don't think you'd watched too many kissing movies when

you were eleven," she told him. "I remember girls talking about kissing you in junior high, and I was floored that they were so impressed."

"You're a brat," he told her, tossing his napkin at her.

She laughed as she caught it.

That sound—her laughter—after worrying about her all of last night while camped out in the New Orleans airport (he really should have looked up flight times *before* he drove all the way there), made him take a deep, contented breath. That was what he wanted. Jordan Benoit happy.

"So what do you need?" he asked her. "How can I make all of this better?"

"Take me home," she said.

His chest squeezed. He loved the fact that Autre was still home to her and that was where she wanted to go when things were falling apart.

Not that they would be falling apart for long. He would make sure of that.

"You are staying with me," he said. "Seriously."

She nodded. "I'm going to take you up on that. Living with you could make me pretend that things are on the right track."

"What do you mean?" His heart thumped without even knowing the answer to that question.

"I'm twenty-six. I have spent eleven years in a serious relationship I thought was going to end with marriage and babies. I know it doesn't sound very liberated, or adventurous, or even unique, but what I want is a house with a front *and* a back porch, two dogs, a yard, French toast on Saturday mornings, being able to drop in and see my mom and my grandma for lunch, big family dinners, having everyone together for birthday celebrations, and silly little things like…crawfish boils." She lifted a shoulder and let it drop. "I honestly sat in Nashville thinking more than once that I wasn't going to be able to have a crawfish boil whenever I wanted one. How do you have crawfish boils when you're living on a tour bus?"

Fletcher couldn't answer her for a moment. His chest was tight and his mouth was dry.

He had a big house on the edge of town that had a front and back porch.

He'd be happy to get a dog. Or three. Her mom lived eight blocks away from him. Her grandmother lived ten. And he made kickass French toast. Which she knew. He couldn't help but wonder if she'd mentioned French toast on purpose.

He wondered how many kids she wanted to have. At one time she'd wanted six. That was when they'd still been kids though. Maybe things like that changed. But he could see Jordan with six kids.

She'd be an amazing mom. She was funny and creative, just organized enough to keep a rowdy bunch together, but not so much that they wouldn't have a ton of fun. She was a fantastic baker. She was a great crafter. She was patient and sweet, while also being clear about her limits for bullshit. She was an incredible teacher because of all of those things, and he was certain they would spill over into motherhood.

Damn, Jason Young was a dumb ass for letting this woman go.

And he *was* letting this woman go.

Fletcher and Jason had exchanged texts over the past few hours. Jason knew Fletcher was on his way to Vegas and he knew Jordan and Fletcher's relationship well enough to know that Fletcher was not leaving here without her.

Jason knew that Fletcher would take care of her.

In the past that had been a bone of contention actually. Jason had been jealous of Fletcher and Jordan's relationship at various times over the years. But now, he seemed relieved that Fletcher was on his way.

Which made sense if Jason was in love with another woman.

What a dumbass.

"You can have my porch, my French toast, and my crawfish pot for as long as you want them," Fletcher told her.

She gave him a soft smile. "That sounds wonderful."

"Then let's get the hell out of here."

"Yes, please." She pushed to her feet. "Just let me go shower, wash my hair, and change."

"Great." He sat back. He was anxious to get her home. "Hurry up."

CHAPTER
Five

THIRTY MINUTES LATER, Jordan stepped out of the bathroom with dry, purple-striped hair and light make-up on. She wasn't going to do Charlie's dramatic make-up-sexy-dress thing, but she *might* be able to pull off some Audrey Hepburn attitude if she had Fletcher walking through the lobby with her.

At the dresser, she pulled on a white thong and matching bra. Then she paused. She glanced toward the closet where her suitcase was. She needed to pack.

With a sigh, she hauled her roller bag out of the closet, tossed it onto the duvet, and opened it. She tossed the dresses from the closet into the bag. On top of those, she threw the few clothes she had in the dresser—two pairs of capri pants and a couple of t-shirts. She didn't have a lot of casual clothes along. Very little in Jason's life had been casual lately.

See, Vivian dealt with all of the pomp and circumstance with the band and the tour and the parties so much better than Jordan did. Jason and Vivian would be really good together.

"Hey, hurry up." Fletcher nudged the door open. "We need to—" He stopped one step inside the room. And stared.

Jordan gave a little squeak. "Fletcher!" She reached for a shirt. "It's called knocking."

"I've heard of it."

She jerked the t-shirt down over her head. "Want to try it?"

"Not really. This worked out pretty well for me."

He didn't even attempt to turn away. Or avert his eyes. Or apologize. In fact, he watched her jab her arms through the sleeves with a grin.

He seemed completely comfortable watching her dress.

Jordan was completely…not uncomfortable. Which was very weird.

But not as weird as the ribbon of heat that curled through her stomach.

She and Fletcher were *incredibly* easy with one another. Fletcher had been the one to explain what people meant when they talked about "sixty-nine" and what wet dreams were. They'd belched and puked in front of one another. They'd cried on each other's shoulders. They'd covered for one another when in trouble with their parents. Fletcher had come straight to her the one—and only—time a girlfriend had told him she thought she was pregnant. She hadn't been, but Jordan was the one he'd panicked with until he knew for sure.

If anyone other than her boyfriend were to see her in her underwear, she would be most comfortable with it being Fletcher.

Theoretically.

But, while she wasn't *uncomfortable*, she wouldn't call what she was feeling *comfortable* either. She felt a little jittery. Not nervous, not worried, not awkward. But like she'd taken a shot of espresso and needed an outlet for the energy.

In other words, she was feeling turned on.

Girl, you're just horny. You should have brought your vibrator with you.

She grabbed for something to put on her bottom half. The white capris wouldn't have been her first choice for a day of travel, but she just needed to be covered up. Now.

She shimmied into the pants, grabbed a pair of white, rhinestone-studded canvas tennis shoes, and slipped them on.

Then she smoothed her hand down the front of her outfit and finally looked at Fletcher directly.

"No fucking way."

"What?" she asked.

"You're not wearing that."

His tone was bossy and firm and he was no longer grinning.

She looked down. Her t-shirt had Jason's face on the front of it.

She looked up at Fletcher. And snorted at his expression. He looked like he'd just smelled a dirty diaper.

"I've no idea what you're talking about," Jordan teased.

"Take it off," Fletcher told her.

Now, see? Having her best childhood friend tell her to take her clothes off should not be hot. Funny maybe. Weird for sure. But not hot.

It was completely hot.

"It was just the first thing I grabbed," she said. "But it will work."

Fletcher took a step forward. "Take it off. Or I'll take it off of you."

Jordan's heart thumped hard inside her chest and her stomach swooped. *What?* a little voice in the back of her mind asked.

But she knew what. And so did that little voice.

She immediately flashed back to the night she and Fletcher had spent in Galveston, stuck in a roadside motel, just the two of them, in the middle of a tropical storm.

Her nipples remembered too. They were suddenly tight and hard and she was pretty sure he noticed. Again.

She wet her lips. "It's really that big of a deal?"

He took the three remaining steps between them, stopping nearly on top of her toes. He reached for the hem of the shirt and, without a word, tugged it up. For some reason, she raised her arms over her head so that he could strip it off of her.

Yeah, her nipples *really* liked that. And the rest of her seemed to as well.

Fletcher's eyes were hot and his voice was rough when he said, "Find something else."

What were they talking about again? She couldn't really think when he was standing this close. If his hands in her hair had been distracting, *this* was forget-her-own-name stuff.

"I..." Yeah, she couldn't come up with anything.

Without breaking eye contact, Fletcher reached for her suitcase. He grabbed something from the top. "Here."

Jordan simply raised her arms again, possibly because her brain seemed to have disconnected. He drew the garment over her head and arms, sliding it down her body, and tugging it into place.

Jordan managed to pull her gaze from his to look down. She was now dressed in a pale pink tank top, white capris, and her sparkly tennis shoes.

Well, okay then. At least she was dressed. And not in a Fletcher-offending t-shirt. She could totally go to the airport like this. It was fine.

"We need to go. We have a plane to catch," Fletcher said. His voice was still rough and he hadn't stepped back yet.

Yep. An airport was a good idea. A busy place with other people. Where she would *not* be half-naked. Or fully naked. Or thinking about her best friend since first grade in very inappropriate ways.

"Great." She looked down and spread her arms. "I'm ready."

Fletcher just studied her face. Then he nodded, turned, flipped her suitcase shut, zipped it, pulled it off the bed, and left the room.

Jordan huffed out a breath. Holy. Shit. What was going on with her and Fletcher?

She followed him to the door. Fletcher pulled it open and

waited for her to step out. She looked down at the suitcase he was pulling.

"You know what? Leave that."

"Leave the suitcase?"

"Yeah. There's nothing in there I need. Most of it is dresses and heels for the events here in Vegas. I definitely don't need those in Louisiana. There are plenty of girls back home I can borrow clothes from until Jason's assistant can send me my stuff from Nashville. Heck, I probably still have clothes at my mom's house I can use."

Fletcher dropped the bag and held up a hand. "I'm fine with leaving everything about Jason behind."

Jordan grinned and started out the door. But she stopped in the doorway and looked up at Fletcher as a thought occurred to her. "Jason knows you're here, doesn't he?"

Fletcher sighed. "How did you know that?"

"He hasn't tried to call me this morning. I'm guessing he called you because he knew you would know how I was."

"I was already in the New Orleans airport when he called me last night," Fletcher said. "I told him I was on my way."

She nodded. "That's why he hasn't checked on me."

"Yes." Fletcher didn't look a bit apologetic.

It made sense. Whether he *liked* it or not, Jason knew if Fletcher was here, Jordan was fine. She nodded. "Okay, let's go."

They were in the elevator and halfway to the lobby before Jordan turned to him again. "Thanks for coming."

Fletcher was leaning against the back wall, his hands braced on the wooden railing that ran around the elevator at waist height. "If you'd thought about it for even ten seconds you wouldn't have been surprised to see me."

"You're right."

She looked forward again. They were quiet as they passed two floors.

Then she said turned again and said, "You're a good guy."

He lifted a brow. "Thanks."

She was quiet for another second. Then she asked, "Know any great guys you could set me up with?"

"No."

She'd been expecting that answer too, though she wasn't sure why. Fletcher had never introduced her to anyone, obviously. She hadn't dated any of his friends. She'd been dating someone, the same someone, from the time any of them had actually been "dating".

But she didn't want to date anyone else.

She wanted to date Fletcher.

She'd been thinking about him differently, in spite of her best efforts, ever since Galveston. She'd been thinking about him *very* differently, and not even really trying not to, ever since the weddings in Autre.

She'd been planning to go home and ask him if his offer to stay there with him still stood when her fake engagement to Jason was over.

And, well, now her fake engagement to Jason was over.

But she was supposed to let Fletcher make all the decisions today.

So Fletcher had to bring it up.

She turned, resting her left shoulder against the back wall of the elevator, facing him. "You know me best. You'd be a great matchmaker for me. And you know the guys around home. I bet you could pick the perfect guy."

"I'm not fucking doing that, Jordan."

FLETCHER REALIZED his reaction to her request seemed harsh.

But *fuck*.

She'd been single for a few *hours*.

Yes, so she'd apparently been getting over Jason for a while. And she didn't want to be single. But holy *shit*. The last time a guy had asked her out, she hadn't been single again for over a decade. She'd probably go out to one dinner with a new guy and they'd all be pushing forty before they broke up.

And yes, Fletcher wanted her single.

Because *he* wanted her.

She sighed. "You just want me to be alone? Forever?"

"Of course not." He gripped the railing under his hands tightly and pretended to study the lighted numbers on the elevator panel.

He very much wanted her to *not* be alone. But he also had very specific ideas about what *not alone* looked like for Jordan. And he needed to give the girl a chance to breathe and a chance to settle a little before he told her how he felt and what he wanted. Didn't he? There was time to talk about all of this later.

As long as she didn't even have coffee with anyone else in the meantime.

He was exaggerating. Probably. But Jason Young had asked her to the Valentine's Day dance when they'd been fifteen and Jordan had been taken ever since, for fuck's sake.

Jason had walked up to her in the parking lot after their schools' big rivalry basketball game—where she'd been standing with Fletcher, Zeke, Zander, Naomi, and Naomi's brother Michael—grinned at Fletcher, then turned to Jordan and asked her out. Right in front of everyone. Even now, Fletcher had to admit that had taken balls.

Fletcher had known Jason had done it to annoy him. *Everyone* had known that except Jordan. But dammit, she'd said yes, they'd gone to the fucking dance, and…that had been it. They'd gone and actually fallen in love and the rest was history.

So now? No, Fletcher would not be setting her up with anyone. She'd probably fall in love while they were still on the appetizers.

"Think you'll like my next boyfriend?" she asked.

"I doubt it." He was sure he *wouldn't* in fact.

"It would be good if you did," she said. "You're my best

friend. It would be really nice if you liked the man I was going to spend the rest of my life with."

"So now we're already onto the rest of your life? Thought you were talking about a *boyfriend*."

Fletcher was trying really hard not to grit his teeth. Of course, in Jordan's experience, going out for pizza with a guy was basically the same thing as saying 'til death do us part. Fletcher shoved a hand through his hair. He needed to relax. He was definitely overreacting.

But *damn*. She was just now single after *eleven fucking years*. It had been less than a day and she was already talking about her *next* boyfriend. Who she was, apparently, already planning to marry?

Maybe he wasn't overreacting. That was insane.

Why the fuck was this elevator taking so long?

"I told you, I want to settle down," Jordan said. "I'm not going to just date for fun. I won't go out with a guy I know for sure I can't be with long term."

Fletcher lost the battle to not grit his teeth.

"What if it's Zeke or Zander?" she asked a second later.

Fletcher looked at her quickly, scowling. She was poking him now, but he wasn't sure why. "It will *not* be Zeke or Zander."

"Why not? They're both great guys. They've both grown up."

"Have they?" His brothers were great guys, that was true. But grown up was a relative term.

"Zeke owns his own company," Jordan pointed out. "Zander's a *cop*."

Fletcher pushed off the back wall of the elevator and turned to face her. "No."

He didn't have much else to say about her going out with either of his brothers as anything more than friends.

"Well, what about Knox? He's still single, right?"

Knox was also a great guy. Far more mature and settled than Zeke or Zander. He was intelligent and serious and knew exactly what he wanted, and the females in Fletcher's family always commented on how hot he was.

So, not just no. *Fuck* no. Because if she went out with Knox, it was even more likely Jordan would be filling out her wedding gift registry by the time dessert came.

"You are not going out with Knox," Fletcher said. Firmly. *Really* firmly.

The elevator finally arrived at the ground floor and the door swished open. Jordan stepped out first with Fletcher right behind her.

They made it down the short hallway that led from the private elevators to the main hallway that would then give them the choice of heading to the casino, the front of the building, or to the bank of elevators that went up to the regular floors.

They started for the front doors.

But even before they made it all the way down the hallway, they heard the commotion.

They came up short as the hallway opened to the front entryway of the hotel.

Jason Young was there.

Right in the middle of the lobby. Surrounded by people. A few looked like reporters, but most were clearly just fans. His bodyguards were keeping people several feet back, but nearly everyone was holding up a phone or a camera, recording what he was saying.

He was holding an impromptu press conference.

"Oh my God," Jordan said. She reached out and grabbed Fletcher's forearm. "Shit."

Yeah, shit about summed it up.

Fletcher looked around quickly. Was there another way to duck out of here? They could turn around and head back to the casino. There were entrances on that side as well. Here in the lobby though, the check-in desks were to the left and there were a few closed doors along the right, but otherwise, it was just a huge open space with lots of marble and lots and lots of people.

He reached for Jordan's hand and started to turn, but just then he heard, "There's Jordan!"

He felt her stiffen.

Then a louder voice—Jason Young's voice, to be specific—said, "There she is! See? Doesn't she look amazing?"

Fletcher pivoted to glare at Jason. The guy was pointing Jordan out? And saying she looked amazing? What the hell?

But it only took a second to realize that this little gaggle hadn't been going well for Jason. He looked stressed. And maybe like he'd been sweating.

That was confirmed when someone said, "Jordan, are you all right?"

And another called, "Team Jordan!"

And yet another, "Be strong, girl, we've got your back!"

Had the crowd been ganging up on Jason? Were they blaming him for what happened last night? That was fair but a little surprising. Fletcher suddenly liked this a lot better.

He looked down at Jordan and squeezed her hand. "You okay?"

She looked like a deer caught in headlights, actually. But as the crowd started to press in her direction she straightened and lifted her chin. "Yeah, I'm okay."

She took a few more steps further into the lobby and gave the crowd a wobbly smile. She lifted her hand. "Hi, everyone."

Seeing that as obvious encouragement, half the crowd broke off and came to surround her. Fletcher immediately felt claustrophobic, but he kept his hold on Jordan. He was definitely bigger than most of the twenty-something women who were first to get close, and he spread his feet and angled his body slightly, making his physical space, and that around Jordan, wider.

"I'm never buying another Jason Young album again," one girl told Jordan.

Another put her hand over her heart. "I know how it feels to be cheated on. I want you to know that you have our support."

"We started an online fundraising account for you, Jordan," a young redhead told her.

Jordan stared at her. "For what?"

"For whatever you need to get back on your feet," the girl told her.

Jordan shook her head, seemingly coming out of her dazed state. "Oh my gosh, you guys," she said, taking another small step forward. "You can't do that. I appreciate it, but I don't need it. I promise I'm okay."

Another girl leaned in. "You're so strong. You're my inspiration."

Jordan's eyes were wide. "You guys don't understand. Everything's okay." Jordan looked over to where Jason was standing.

Part of the crowd had stayed near him, but everyone was watching her.

Fletcher didn't know Jason nearly as well as Jordan, of course, but he could've sworn that the man mouthed *I'm sorry* to her.

Jordan took a deep breath, squeezed Fletcher's hand, then dropped her hold on him. And headed toward Jason.

Fletcher didn't know what was going on, but he was clearly no one's concern at the moment. Everyone watched Jordan's every step and her little fan club immediately fell in behind her as she approached where Jason was standing.

Fletcher moved closer as well but stayed at the back of the crowd. He wasn't going anywhere without Jordan.

She stepped up next to Jason and turned to face the little crowd. "Hi, everybody," she started.

The crowd applauded and a few called, "Jordan!", clearly showing their support.

Jason grimaced.

Fletcher tucked his hands into his pockets and settled back on his heels to watch. Anything that made Jason Young uncomfortable was entertaining for him.

Jordan held up her hands. "I wasn't expecting to see you all today. But I guess I should take this chance to say something. I think there's been a big misunderstanding."

"Team Jordan!" someone called again.

There was more applause supporting that sentiment.

"I ripped up my Jason Young t-shirt!" another voice yelled.

"I'll never listen to 'Sweet Southern' again!"

Jason looked almost sick at this point. Jordan glanced at him, clearly concerned, then back to the crowd. She caught Fletcher's eye. He gave her a nod. He didn't know what he was nodding at exactly, but whatever she thought she needed to do, he was supportive.

Jordan held up her hands again, quieting the group. "You guys, seriously, we need to clear something up."

The crowd calmed, but nearly everyone present lifted their phones, clearly recording.

Jordan took a deep breath. "Jason and I have been together for a long time. You all know that. We are really close. I am *thrilled* at all of his success. But…this life isn't what I want. And it became clear over the past couple of years that we were moving in different directions. But…" She paused and took another deep breath. "I made a huge mistake. Instead of being honest with him and ending things, I…"

Fletcher felt his spine tighten and it seemed that the entire crowd was holding their breath together.

"…had an affair."

There was a collective gasp. Jason looked completely stunned. Fletcher felt shock and rage arch through him.

"But," Jordan said quickly. "Jason and I tried to work it out. Again, we had been together so long. We truly love each other. Still, in the end, I fell in love with someone else. I told him right before he went on stage last night. Which was totally unfair of me. So he was still shocked and hurt and felt he had to go through with the proposal. But then he realized we were over and how he really felt for Viv and…" She stopped and looked at Jason. "I'm so happy that Jason found Vivian, and now we can both move on with our lives and be happy." She reached out and took Jason's hand. "I'm so sorry and thank you for forgiving me and I'm so glad we're going to keep being friends."

The crowd was clearly shocked. No one said anything for several long beats. Which was enough time for Jordan to make it halfway to where Fletcher was standing.

But finally, someone said, "You *cheated* on Jason?"

That seemed to loosen everyone's tongues.

"Who's the guy?"

"Jason, how long have you known?"

"This is all *your* fault?"

"He *forgives* you?"

Jordan made her way to Fletcher almost robotically.

He met her partway and immediately reached for her and tucked her under his arm. He glowered at the first two people who tried to step close.

"Are you the guy?" one of them asked with a gasp.

"Who are *you*?"

"Wow, huge balls to just show up here like this!"

Okay, *now* they cared who he was.

"That's Fletcher."

The entire crowd rotated back to face forward again as Jason spoke.

Under Fletcher's arm, Jordan trembled slightly.

Fletcher glanced down at her. "What the hell?" he asked in a whisper. "You had an affair?"

She looked up at him with a frown. "Of course not."

"Then what —"

"I'm trying to make *him* look good."

Jesus. Fletcher shoved a hand through his hair. Of course she was. And of course, without having planned anything, *this* was what she'd come up with. She was willing to be the bad guy, take the blame for the breakup, let everyone go on thinking that Jason was some big hero.

Fuck.

"Fletcher and Jordan have been friends since they were in first grade," Jason said. "He came to be with her after everything happened last night. I'm really grateful for their friendship. I felt huge relief knowing he was here with her."

Fletcher met the other man's eyes. He realized Jason was trying to downplay what people thought was going on between Fletcher and Jordan. Maybe just to help them get out of the casino without a mob scene. But he was clearly lending Fletcher his support and, in essence, telling the crowd that he was not a threat or someone they should be angry with.

Well, he did not need Jason Young's help.

"Okay, so if you'll excuse us, Jordan and I have an appointment." Fletcher said, raising his voice to carry over the cluster of people.

Then he turned, with his arm still around Jordan, and started for the second door on the right.

He yanked on the gold handle and nudged Jordan through the door.

The last thing he heard before the heavy door bumped shut behind them was, "Oh my God, they're getting married!"

CHAPTER
Six

"HELLO, CAN I HELP YOU?"

Jordan looked at the woman coming across the lobby of the wedding chapel toward her and Fletcher.

The *wedding chapel.*

Well, one of them needed help.

And yeah, it might be her because her heart was pounding and her stomach felt like she'd swallowed a hundred butterflies.

She and Fletcher weren't actually getting married.

But dammit if she wasn't feeling pretty swoony about the way he'd swept her off in front of everyone that way.

She'd really been trying to help Jason. Did she want to be labeled a cheater in the press? Well, no. But it wasn't like she'd planned that out. And did it matter? It was much better for her to be the pariah than Jason, who was losing fans over the breakup.

And then Fletcher came in and swept her off to a *wedding chapel*? How could she not feel a little swoony? Maybe they thought she was a cheater, but at least she was in love and getting married to the guy.

Wait, people did think that Fletcher was the guy now, right? She hadn't *said* that. And Jason had made it seem that Fletcher was just a friend. But now they were in here and so surely people would realize Fletcher was the one.

Though, they weren't *really* getting married…

"Hi, we're interested in wedding packages," Fletcher told the woman.

Jordan felt those butterflies in her stomach start doing the Hokey Pokey.

"Oh, wonderful!" the woman said. She was dressed in a pencil skirt, heels, and a silk blouse. Her nametag read *Avery*. "Do you have something in mind?"

"Simple. And today," Fletcher said.

Avery's smile widened. "Well, great. Do you have your license?"

Jordan barely spared the woman a glance. She was too busy staring at Fletcher.

He was just making conversation. Right? Acting interesting in wedding packages made more sense than telling her they were hiding out from Jason Young fans.

So why was her heart hammering as if Fletcher was being serious?

Why was her brain saying things like *this seems right*?

It didn't seem right. It didn't make sense. Did it?

Her and Fletcher married. That should seem crazy.

It didn't.

"I knew all those movies about getting spontaneously married in Las Vegas weren't entirely accurate," Fletcher told the woman with a grin.

God, he was good-looking. All the time. But especially when he grinned.

Jordan barely heard the woman laugh and say, "Well, you do need a license, but they're not difficult to get. It can take just a few minutes if there's no line."

"Is that right?" Fletcher gave Jordan a glance and her stomach swooped.

Her stomach *swooped*? Sure, he'd made her stomach swoop

when he'd pressed her against the inside of the hotel room door and kissed her in Galveston.

But stomach swooping, when it came to Fletcher, was not a usual occurrence.

Then again, it'd been a really long time since anything had made her stomach swoop. And that was pretty sad considering she'd been practically engaged to country music's newest hot star.

"Yes," Avery said. "You just need to go downtown to the Clark County Marriage Bureau, pay the fee, fill out some paperwork, and you can have a license in under an hour. Especially at this time of day on a Sunday. Bring it back here and by the time you get back, we can have your ceremony ready to go."

"You have an opening?" Fletcher asked.

He's just making conversation. He's just trying to make her think we're not crazy.

But in spite of Jordan's self-talk, the stomach swooping continued. Maybe you couldn't just walk in off the street and have a wedding ceremony in a snap, but it sure didn't sound complicated. It definitely sounded like she and Fletcher could leave Las Vegas married if they wanted to.

Her heart also did a little swooping thing at that thought.

"If you want to do it right away today, then yes, I can fit you in," Avery assured him.

"The sooner the better," Fletcher told her. But he was looking directly at Jordan.

"Excellent," Avery said. "Do you want to look at our packages and make a selection?"

Fletcher shook his head. He was still looking at Jordan. "Just put together the best you can in the time you've got. Nothing but her saying 'I do' really matters."

The woman's face brightened, and Jordan could only assume she worked on commission. "Excellent. It can be fun to play with nontraditional plans."

"I just need the address for the clerk then I guess," Fletcher told her.

"All of the taxi drivers will easily be able to take you straight there."

Fletcher chuckled. "I guess that's a good point."

"Can I get your names?"

"Fletcher Landry and Jordan Benoit," Fletcher said.

"Wonderful, I'm Avery. Fletcher and Jordan, it's a pleasure to meet you. I look forward to seeing you back here in a little bit with your license." She handed Fletcher a card. "Please call me if you have any questions or if things take longer than an hour or so."

Fletcher tucked her card into his back jeans pocket. "There is one more thing you could help us with."

"Sure, what can I do for you?"

"Is there a way out of here where we don't have to go through the lobby? There are a couple of people we're trying to avoid at the moment."

Avery nodded. "I can take you through our outdoor entrance."

Jordan had to assume that working in a wedding chapel in Las Vegas, Avery had seen a lot of things and had probably learned not to ask a lot of questions.

They followed her across the chapel lobby and down a short hallway that opened into another smaller lobby. There were double doors leading out to the parking lot.

As Avery helped him plug the address in for a car pick-up, Jordan continued to study him. Would she marry Fletcher Landry if he asked?

Yes.

The only thing surprising about that was how quickly she was able to answer.

People talked about marrying their best friend all the time. Or how their husband or wife was their best friend. The only difference between what she and Fletcher had now and being married, was that she and Fletcher didn't have sex.

And she was not opposed to the idea of sex with Fletcher at all. Not. At. All.

Fletcher was hot. Maybe if Galveston hadn't happened, this would all seem stranger. But it had. It definitely had. And she knew for a fact that Fletcher knew what he was doing when he put his hands and mouth on a woman.

A lifetime of that plus hanging out with his family, eating his French toast, and laughing with him over old reruns of *Whose Line Is It Anyway?* sounded pretty damn good.

Their car pulled up and Fletcher stepped forward and opened the back door for Jordan. He turned back to Avery. "Thanks a lot for the information." Jordan slid into the backseat as Avery assured him it was no problem and she was excited to see them again in a little bit.

There was stomach swooping again just hearing Avery say she was expecting them back.

She was expecting them back at *a wedding chapel*. To *get married*. If that wasn't stomach swooping material, Jordan didn't know what was.

Fletcher joined her in the backseat and shut the door.

"Which airline?" the driver asked.

"Delta," Fletcher told him.

The driver pulled away from the curb and Jordan frowned. He'd answered, "Delta" instead of, "take us straight to the clerk to get a marriage license".

Oh. Okay. So he hadn't meant any of what he'd said to Avery. It really had just been a cover for why they were in the chapel and a way to get out another door.

It had been convincing, Jordan had to admit, but more than that it had served its purpose. They'd escaped the casino without any further run-ins with any of Jason's fans and were now on the way to the airport as planned.

Fletcher was good. When he set a goal, he accomplished it.

Jordan sat back in her seat working very hard not to feel disappointed. That was ridiculous. Them getting married was a ridiculous idea and being disappointed that it wasn't happening was silly.

Besides, if she wanted to marry Fletcher, she could bring it up back in Louisiana. Or on the airplane. Or…

"I've been thinking about what I need," she told him.

He'd been typing something into his phone—she assumed a text to someone back home letting them know what was going on—but he stopped and looked over at her. "I've been thinking about what you need too."

She lifted an eyebrow. "Oh yeah? Does it include eating your grandma's pecan pie until I can't move?"

He nodded. "Yes. And more."

"So, dancing with Zeke, kicking Zander's ass at darts, binge watching baking shows with my grandmother, and playing chess with your grandpa, too?"

Fletcher put his phone down and turned to face her fully. "Yes. And swimming in the bayou, hanging out with a couple of lemurs, and a hard game of one-on-one with me."

Maybe I just need to get laid.

That was her first thought. That would explain why the "a hard game of one-on-one with me" sent her mind in all kinds of dirty directions. He was talking about basketball. They'd played one-on-one since they'd been eight or nine. But this time the phrase made her think about naked body parts and getting sweaty with Fletcher in a whole new way.

And the fact that it took a good fifteen seconds for the word *lemurs* to even sink in said a lot about which naked body parts.

"Yes. To all of that."

He grinned.

It was the grin, she figured, that made her say, "But I also think that I need to—"

"Marry me."

"Date you."

They spoke at the same time.

Then stared at each other.

"What?"

"What?"

They spoke simultaneously again.

Jordan ignored the butterflies in her stomach that thought he'd said something about marrying him. She held up a hand to keep him from talking and took a deep breath.

"I was trying to get you to tell me *we* should date in the elevator earlier when I was talking about Zeke and Zander and Knox. Because Naomi and Charlie said I should do whatever you tell me to do today and not make any big decisions myself. So I figured if *you* said you thought we should date, then it would mean it was a good idea." She frowned at him. "But you didn't say that."

"I was trying to give you some fucking *space* before I said anything." He seemed very annoyed suddenly.

She leaned in, bracing her hand on the seat between them. "The last person I need space from is you, Fletcher. I mean, we've basically been dating for twenty years. If dating is about getting to know someone and figuring out how well you fit with them and figuring out if you want to spend the rest of your life with them…we've done that. I've always envisioned us growing old together, sitting together on your back porch and watching the sunset over the bayou when we're eighty."

"You were going to marry Jason. Up until, what, six months ago?"

She shrugged and nodded. "I know. But…I guess I thought we would both marry someone else, have those lives, stay friends, of course, and then after they died, we'd end up living together in Autre and sitting on the porch every night."

Jordan watched him process that. She'd never told him that before, but it was true. She didn't know when it had first occurred to her or why she'd never thought it was odd, but she'd always figured, no matter what other paths they took, she and Fletcher would end up together somehow. Even if it was just side by side in their rocking chairs.

He shook his head. "You have *got* to be one of the most exasperating people in my life."

Her eyebrows rose. "Considering your twin brothers are Zeke and Zander, being one of the most exasperating people in your life is pretty huge."

He shook his head. "Absolutely exasperating. To think I could've kissed you when we were standing next to a king-sized bed and you were only in your bra and panties and you would have been all in."

Jordan felt her cheeks flush, but she grinned widely. "God, I really am a pain in the ass."

"You really are." His gaze dropped to her mouth.

Jordan felt a zing of excitement go through her. She *really* wanted him to kiss her.

"I think you dating me is a great idea," he said after a moment."

Thank God.

"You're sure you're done dating other people? Having fun with all those girls? All the casual relationships?" she asked.

"If it means I get to be with you? Absolutely."

Her stomach swooped, harder and faster than before. "This isn't crazy?"

"It makes a hell of a lot more sense than anything else. Like you dating other men. Or either of us being with anyone else."

"We've never talked about this before."

"You've been taken for eleven years," he said simply.

Right. That was true. And Fletcher was too good of a guy to go after another man's girl.

She still felt compelled to say, "Galveston was a long time ago."

Why was she bringing that up? She was *very* attracted to Fletcher and she'd seen the heat in his eyes in the hotel suite. He commented on her nipples this morning, for God's sake. He'd been hard when she'd sat on his lap. They had chemistry. Even Naomi and Charlie had seen it. She didn't need to worry about that part.

"What are you thinking about?" Fletcher asked, reading her clearly as he so often did.

"The physical part," she said honestly. "It's been three years since anything happened."

"Again, because you've been taken." His voice dropped. "*Only* because you've been taken, Jordan."

Her heart skittered at that and she wet her lips. She thought about her next words carefully. Several seconds ticked by. Then she said simply, "Prove it."

And she realized a split second later, as Fletcher reached out, wrapped his big hand around her wrist, and tugged her close, that *this* was why she'd brought Galveston up. She wanted to kiss Fletcher. Right now. Not because she was afraid there was no spark, but because she just really, really didn't want to wait any longer.

He cupped the back of her head and brought her in until they were nose to nose. "This changes everything," he said. Almost as if it was a warning.

"I know."

"I'm the last frog you're ever going to kiss. So be sure you want it now."

Oh, damn. That was exactly what she'd wanted to hear without even realizing it.

"Oh yes," she answered softly.

He gave a quiet almost-growl then covered her mouth with his.

His fingers sank into her hair. He held the back of her head still as he tasted her.

At first the kiss was gentle. Tasting and seeking. Their lips pressed and released. He tipped his head, changing the angle slightly. Then again, deepening the kiss just slightly.

But it wasn't enough.

Jordan was sure she was the first one to give a little moan and press closer. But Fletcher answered the noise and the movement. They both opened their mouths at the same time.

His tongue stroked along her bottom lip and she felt the tingles racing from the top of her head to the hot ball of need that had already gathered in her lower belly. Heat arrowed between her legs and she had to be closer.

She fumbled with her seatbelt, unlocking it, not caring what possible consequence that might bring. She'd gladly pay a fine to get closer to Fletcher.

She climbed into his lap, straddling his thighs. His hands immediately went to her hips and she felt him press her closer. He was hard behind his fly and she instinctively ground against him. That definitely elicited groans from both of them.

She met the stroke of his tongue boldly, wrapping her arms around his neck and pressing as much of her body against his as she could. His fingers dug into her hips, and then slipped back to her ass. He felt amazing. He tasted amazing. The things his mouth and hands were doing to her body were amazing.

This was such a good idea.

They made out for a few minutes. Jordan almost regretted starting this in the car because her natural instinct was to keep going. She wanted to touch him. She wanted to feel him against her. She definitely wanted to strip out of everything she was wearing and rub herself all over him.

But eventually, the driver coughed, and Jordan pulled back. She stared at Fletcher, breathing hard. His breathing was ragged as well.

"Anything else you need to know?" he asked.

She shook her head. "I'm good."

He gave her a knowing, cocky grin and the arrow of desire that speared through her was enough to make her moan softly.

The car came to a stop and the driver turned to look at them. "We're here."

Fletcher didn't take his eyes from Jordan's. "Actually, we need you to make a different stop. Any chance you could take us down to the clerk where we can get a marriage license?"

Jordan's eyes went wide. "What? Really?"

He lifted her hand to his mouth and placed a hot kiss in the center of her palm. "Marry me, Jordan."

She sucked in a quick breath. Oh God. Married? Seriously? To Fletcher?

Married.

To *Fletcher.*

But...she felt her head nod.

The driver chuckled and pointed out the window. "That's where we are, man."

Fletcher and Jordan both glanced over at the same time. They were definitely not at the airport.

Fletcher looked at the driver. "How did you know?"

"It's not like I can't hear every word you say back there."

Jordan felt her heart hammering in her chest.

She wanted this. And Fletcher thought it was a good idea. She could always count on him to know what she needed.

She reached up and took his face in her hands. "Do you promise to make French toast at least twice a month?"

He paused, then a smile curved his lips. "I do."

Her heart gave a little flip.

"And do you promise to make me the Oreo fluff stuff you make at least once a month?" he asked.

She couldn't help the wide smile spread across her face. "I do. And do you promise to watch science documentaries with me at least once a week?"

"I do. If you watch kids' shows with me. I have to keep up on what my class is into."

She laughed. "I do. And do you promise to do at least half of the laundry? And scrub the toilets every other time?"

He nodded. "I do. Do *you* promise to help clean up the yard from our two or three dogs?"

She laughed. He was going to get her dogs. She loved him for that alone.

"I do. And do you promise to always help me cheat when I play poker against Mitch and Owen?"

"I do," he said with a chuckle. He already did that. "Do you promise to sleep in just a shirt like the one I saw you in this morning every night, forever?"

"I do. Unless, of course, you'd want me to wear nothing at all."

She felt his fingers digging into her ass. "I do."

She grinned.

The driver cleared his throat. "I'll keep the car running."

Jordan laughed. "So you think we should do this?"

"I've been married three times. If I'd said vows like any of the ones you just did, I might still be with one of them."

Jordan and Fletcher grinned at each other and got out of the car.

There was no line inside the clerk's office. They got their license and were back in the lobby of the chapel at the MGM Grand thirty minutes later.

"Do you, Fletcher Landry, take Jordan Benoit to be your lawfully wedded wife?"

"I do."

The look on Fletcher's face as he said those two words was the look that every woman wanted on the face of the man she loved.

It hit Jordan hard as the officiant asked her if she took Fletcher to be her lawfully wedded husband.

She loved him.

She sucked in a quick breath. She *loved* him. Not the way

she'd always loved him, as a friend, almost a brother, the most important person in her life. But she was *in love* with him.

Wow.

She blew the breath back out.

That shouldn't have been stunning.

And…it wasn't. As it settled in her mind, and her heart, she realized that she wasn't stunned. At all. She'd been ignoring it, fighting it, telling herself that *wasn't* what she was feeling ever since he'd asked her to stay in Autre with him in April.

But it was. When he'd asked her to choose him, she'd wanted to. The *yes* had been on the tip of her tongue. Walking away from him that night had been the hardest thing she'd ever done. She'd been convinced that was the last chance she'd have. That he would find someone else, that he would belong to someone else, that he'd never be hers and, despite the fact she'd been leaving to join her *boyfriend* on his world tour, it had killed her to think about losing Fletcher.

But now…he was hers. She could admit how she felt. Not just to herself but to *him*. To the *world*.

"I do," she said, gazing directly into his eyes.

The look on his face as she said her vows to him was hot and sweet and stomach-swooping in a way she never would've imagined.

"Then, by the power vested in me by the state of Nevada, I now pronounce you husband and wife."

Fletcher reached up and cupped her face in his hands tenderly. He looked at her for a long moment, drinking her in. She wrapped her fingers around his wrist, holding him in place.

"I love you, Jordan."

"I love you too, Fletcher."

He lowered his head and kissed her. It was the gentlest, sweetest, hottest kiss of her life.

She kissed him back. It wasn't a hot, wet, passionate kiss. This kiss was full of emotion, promise, and happiness.

Eventually they separated. They looked at each other for

another long moment. Then Fletcher grinned. "How about we head home?"

A few hours ago "home" had meant Autre. Now home was even more specific. It was Fletcher's house on the end of the road that led out of Autre and down to the bayou. She now had a house with the front *and* back porch. And she would bet really good money that she was going to wake up to French toast in the morning, even though it wasn't Saturday.

She wasn't sure she'd ever been happier.

"Yes, take me home."

Their driver had agreed to wait for them. He'd even shut the meter off. He said he was invested in this story now and wanted to see them after they got married.

He was leaning against the side of the car when they emerged from the chapel.

"I can tell by the smiles on your face you did it," he said, opening the back door for Jordan.

"Of course we did it," she told him with a grin. "This guy's a catch."

The driver chuckled.

Fletcher slid into the backseat next to her and she cuddled up against his side.

"You need to have your seatbelt on," Fletcher chided.

"Yeah, I know. I just can't quit touching you."

Fletcher cleared his throat, shifted on the seat. "It's a long trip home, Jordan. You're killing me already."

She gave him a grin. "Yeah?" She put a hand on his thigh and ran it up and down.

He immediately clapped his hand down on top of it stopping the motion. "Mrs. Landry, you need to behave."

Oh, that Mrs. Landry thing was hot. Now she was regretting that they had to get on an airplane.

"Maybe we can stay another night here. Get a hotel room?" she asked.

He groaned. "Tempting. Very tempting." His eyes were hot

on hers. "But I really want our wedding night in my house, in my bed. *Our* house."

Jordan's whole body felt like hot sparkles were dancing through it. She wanted that too. "Our house. Our bed," she agreed.

His voice low and rough, he said, "Yeah, our bed."

It was going to be a very long trip home.

FLETCHER BLEW out a breath as he pulled his truck up in front of Ellie's bar and turned off the ignition five and a half hours later.

"You ready for this?" he asked.

Jordan grinned. "Definitely."

They got out and met at the front bumper. He laced his fingers with hers.

"No nerves at all?"

"Walking into Ellie's bar where all our friends and family are? Definitely no nerves." She sighed. "This already feels so good."

Fletcher felt his chest tighten a little. Making her happy had been easy when they'd been kids. Even as teenagers. Hell, even in college. It had only been when she'd been farther away and he hadn't been able to be there physically whenever she needed something that he'd started to feel like he couldn't do as much.

And he was a *doer*. He could talk, and listen, and give advice, of course. But he was best when there was *action* too. Even with his kids at school. When he taught a new concept, he had to address all learning styles, but the one he was best at was the hands-on approach. Whether it was science or spelling, he found ways to get the kids actively engaging. *Doing* things.

He'd always been that way with Jordan too. When she was sad, he took her on a walk or for a drive. When she was angry, he put her in front of his punching bag. When she was sick, he brought her soup and balloons. A simple phone call or sitting quietly and talking had never been his thing. And he'd always been able to make things better for her.

So her being away in Nashville, far from her friends and family and home, alone—okay, other than Jason—without even the familiar paths to walk if she was sad, had made it a lot harder to feel like he was impacting her life and actually fixing anything.

That was over now.

She was not only home. She was *his*. They were married. They were going to be sitting on his porch together when they were eighty.

Their porch.

They could walk the trails until their knees gave out. He could get her gallons of soup. He could dance her around the living room. Make her his homemade spaghetti sauce. Kiss her to make it better.

His body heated at that thought. He could kiss her now. Any time he wanted. Every time the urge hit him.

He tugged on her hand to swing her around to face him, cupped the back of her head, and covered her mouth.

She melted into him immediately, and it made him hot and *warm* at the same time. This felt right. This was good. This was what they both needed.

The front door to Ellie's was ten feet in front of them. It suddenly banged open and he heard his cousin Owen's voice boom, "There you are!" Then a chuckle and, "I see the trip went well."

Fletcher lifted his head and looked down at Jordan with a smile. "Very well."

He didn't believe for one second that Owen didn't know exactly how the trip had gone. Zeke and Zander knew. Which meant everyone knew. His brothers were a lot of things, but discreet was not one of them.

"Hey, Owen," Jordan greeted, finally looking over at the man who was technically Fletcher's first cousin but, like all of the Landry grandchildren, felt more like a brother.

"Hey, Jordi, great to see you," Owen said with a huge grin.

Fletcher knew he meant it too. Everyone loved Jordan. She'd already been a part of the family. This "transition" from friend to wife—dammit, he *loved* referring to her that way—was going to be easy for their relatives.

Fletcher let go of her as she lifted a hand to her purple striped hair with a laugh. "I've had…an interesting last twenty-four hours or so, but thanks."

Owen shook his head. "I saw you in that dress last night and you looked hot as hell, but honestly? You look even better now."

Jordan tipped her head and narrowed her eyes. Owen was a natural-born bullshitter. And charmer. Which translated to being an unapologetic fabricator—a nicer word, and more accurate, than liar—with a killer grin. Which Jordan knew very well. The suspicious look she was giving Owen was well earned.

"Yeah?" she asked.

"You'll always look better standing on Louisiana bayou dirt," Owen said with a nod.

Fletcher couldn't agree more. He looked at Jordan. And was startled to see her eyes were watery.

He stepped close, looping an arm around her waist. "What's wrong?"

She sniffed and lifted her face to give him a sweet smile. "Nothing. Absolutely nothing. Everything is wonderful."

He wanted to kiss her again. He started to lean in, but Owen interrupted. Probably on purpose.

"Get your asses in here," Owen said, pushing the door open wide. "Everyone's waiting."

Fletcher was sure they were.

Jordan looked up at him and gave him a little grin. She stretched up and gave him a quick kiss on the lips. "Hold that thought," she told him.

He wondered if she had even the slightest idea about all the thoughts he was having and would have to hold onto.

Actually, some time here would probably be good. He needed to rein it in a little. He couldn't just take her home, throw her on the bed, and go for it. This would be their wedding night, for fuck's sake. He could do better than that.

Couldn't he?

He could be romantic. And sweet. And make this memorable. And everything she ever wanted. He could be the best she ever had. He could…

"Are you all right?" she asked, squinting up at him.

Fletcher cleared his throat. Fuck. No pressure. He managed to nod. "Sure. Yeah. Of course."

"Because you're squeezing my hand so tight it hurts and you look like you're going to puke."

Well, *that* would make their wedding night memorable.

He forced himself to relax his hold on her hand, take a deep breath, and smile. Performance anxiety? Really? *Him?* He knew that would sound horrible out loud, but seriously? He loved women. Especially naked women. And he was definitely not a monk. He wasn't Zeke. Or even Zander, for that matter. But he knew what he was doing in the bedroom. And this was *Jordan.*

"Good, then let's go in. I'm starving and I can't wait to see everyone!" Jordan started toward the door, tugging him along with her.

Exactly. This is Jordan.

Fletcher scrubbed his free hand over his face. Fuck. This was Jordan. Everything mattered more with Jordan.

The moment they stepped across the threshold, the room went wild.

Yes, it was a bar, but Ellie's was really just one big rectangular building with one big rectangular room filled with mismatched tables and chairs and a long, scarred wooden bar that ran the length of the east wall. The kitchen was through the swinging doors behind the bar, the restrooms were at the back, and…that was pretty much it.

The décor was "whatever Ellie and Cora wanted to put up". There were posters, sports team banners, and photographs. So, so many photographs. From Christmases to football championships to fishing expeditions to just sitting-around-a-crawfishboil, events from all of their lives were depicted on those walls.

But he immediately noticed that the fucking signed poster of Jason Young that had hung behind the bar in a place of honor for the past four months was gone.

Fletcher didn't know if it had just been rolled up and stored somewhere or if it had been ripped up or burned. He didn't care. It wasn't hanging up where he had to see it every day anymore.

Thank God.

Ellie often said that she needed the bar because her house wasn't big enough to feed everyone at once. It seemed a house wouldn't have been big enough for her to display all of her mementos either.

Ellie, Fletcher's grandmother on his dad's side, owned the bar with her best friend, Cora—the two women had also lived next door to one another for more than fifty years now—and while Ellie dealt with the regulars and tourists up front and made the gumbo, Cora made pretty much everything else. Where Ellie was blunt and rough-around-the-edges, Cora was sweet and warm.

Ellie would greet them all after school with a chore list and Cora would greet them with cookies.

Ellie would give them advice like, "pull your head out of your ass" while Cora would say things like, "don't fear your mistakes, you can learn as much from them as the things you get right."

Ellie would discipline them by cutting them off from their

favorite foods, making the chores list longer, or, when they got older, making them sit behind the bar reading Shakespeare to her while she worked. All of her grandchildren knew all of William's works and each had a favorite. Fletcher was partial to *Much Ado About Nothing*.

Cora, on the other hand, disciplined them by scolding. And then giving them cookies.

Most of the Landry kids had been at least ten before they realized, or understood, that Cora wasn't actually their biological grandmother. And it had never mattered even after they'd figured that out. Cora was family and blood was only a tiny part of that in the Landry clan.

"Finally!" was how Ellie greeted Fletcher and Jordan.

She was, of course, the first to cross the room and grab them both in a hug.

Fletcher squeezed her back, but then disentangled himself so she could dote on Jordan properly. He'd just left Autre last night. Ellie hadn't seen Jordan in months. And he knew his grandmother was outraged over what Jason had done and had been worrying.

Jordan, like Cora, had just always been a part of the Landry family. She'd been there every day after school with him for cookies, she'd swum from his family's docks, she'd run around all of their backyards, and been a regular at every Friday night crawfish boil.

Ellie released Jordan from the hug after a long moment and a hard squeeze. "What do you need?" Ellie asked, Jordan's face in her hands. "Gumbo? Pot pie? Pecan pie?"

Jordan grinned. "Yes."

Ellie laughed. "That's my girl. And sweet tea. There's no way they had good sweet tea in Vegas."

"You are absolutely right about that," Jordan agreed.

"Move over. You can't hog her all night." Cora pushed in next to Ellie. "Darling," she said to Jordan with a sweet smile before pulling her into a hug.

"Hi, Cora." Jordan hugged her back.

Fletcher saw the way Jordan's eyes slid shut and the little smile on her face made his heart kick.

Yes.

The sense of satisfaction that washed through him was strong and welcome.

He'd done exactly what he'd set out to do when he'd left this building last night. He'd gotten her away from Las Vegas and the bright lights and the crazy Jason fans and the humiliation and confusion and brought her home. She might have purple hair, but that would wash out. She might be exhausted and hungry, but dammit, those were very fixable problems.

She was safe. She was with family and friends who loved her.

And she was his.

That's all he needed to know.

Leo, Fletcher's grandfather, pushed in next, gathering Jordan up and squeezing her tight. "About time you came home to us, girl."

Jordan sniffed as she hugged Leo back. "So happy to be home."

Leo let her go and turned her to the next person in line.

"Mom!" Jordan exclaimed.

Molly Benoit's cheeks were wet but her smile was bright as she pulled her daughter into her arms.

Fletcher looked at Ellie with wide eyes. He hadn't known Molly and Eli Benoit were going to be there. His grandmother gave him a smile and a wink. She'd invited them. She'd known he'd be bringing Jordan home and that her family should be here.

"I'm so happy to see you," Molly told Jordan, still holding her tightly. Then Molly looked up at him over Jordan's shoulder. "Thank you."

Fletcher was surprised. "For?"

"For always taking care of her."

That hit him directly in the chest. *Fuck yes.* Everyone knew that Jordan belonged with him. Even her mother. Even just a few hours after the breakup of her eleven-year relationship.

"I always will," he promised.

"I know." Molly's expression was one of pure affection for him.

Fletcher felt that to his toes.

He'd always been close to the Benoits, just as Jordan had been to the Landrys. He knew they liked him. He was completely comfortable in their home. He knew they trusted him implicitly.

The way Molly was looking at him now was how every man could only *dream* his mother-in-law would look at him. Love, trust, respect, happiness that he was a part of the family.

A niggle of guilt tickled the back of his conscience. Molly should have been there to hear him promise to love Jordan and take care of her always during their *wedding ceremony.*

Shit.

All of these people who loved them and always had their backs should have been a part of that.

No, it hadn't been something he'd planned. Yes, it had been impulsive. No, he didn't regret it. Yes, it still felt strange that none of these people had been a part of their wedding.

Now that he was standing in the bar, surrounded by his family, Fletcher realized that he never would have been able to imagine getting married without them.

Especially to Jordan.

Shit. He stepped closer to Jordan. He needed to whisper in her ear that they needed to keep their marriage a secret. For tonight at least. Until they could figure out a way to tell them all. Maybe he could propose to her. Again. In front of everyone. Maybe they could do another ceremony here and let everyone think this was the first. That would work. They could—

"Here."

His grandmother stepped in front of his hand as he reached for Jordan.

"What?"

She held out her hand. In her palm lay a ring.

Fletcher's eyes flew to hers. "What's this?"

"This was my mother's ring," she said. "We have all kinds of family jewelry, you know. Between me and Leo and Cora we have all kinds of special things. Not all the kids wanted or needed family rings, but I figured you hadn't gotten one for Jordan and since she has always been a part of the family, it would be appropriate for her to wear an heirloom."

Fletcher stared at his grandmother, feeling his throat tighten.

So many thoughts spun through his head. The first was *this feels perfect*. But the first he voiced was, "How did you know?"

"That you married her?" Ellie asked.

Fletcher's eyes darted around the crowd. "Um…"

Ellie laughed. She was speaking quietly enough, and there was ample commotion around Jordan, that no one would overhear her.

"You were in Vegas with Jordan and she was single for the first time since you've been old enough to appreciate more than the way she can bait a hook. If you *hadn't* married her, I would have slapped you upside the head and asked what the hell was wrong with you."

Fletcher shook his head. "Wow."

Ellie reached out and took his hand, pressing the ring into his palm and curling his fingers around it. "And *I'm* not an idiot, Fletcher. Put that ring on that girl's finger and never let her take it off."

He swallowed hard. "You're not mad we did this without you all?"

She chuckled. "You only did one tiny part without us."

"Kind of the biggest part, don't you think?"

"Not even close," she said simply. "The ceremony is twenty minutes in a whole lifetime. Now it's twenty-four-seven, every day, forever. We're all going to be a part of all of that."

Fletcher took a deep breath. He loved his grandmother's

practicality. He nodded. "And you're not upset you didn't get to see us say our vows?"

Ellie lifted a hand and patted his cheek. "You and Jordan have been saying vows to one another for years and we've all witnessed it. Every time one of you needed something and the other was there, we saw it. Every time you two huddled together and told secrets and laughed like there was no one else in the world, we saw it. Every time something hurt or upset one of you and the other got just as angry and hurt and was ready to go to battle, we saw it. And we saw it the day she left Autre for Nashville. And when she was home for the weddings in April and told you about the tour. And last night. We all saw all of that. Those were all vows to be there and love one another and respect and take care of each other."

Fletcher actually felt his eyes stinging. He'd like to chalk it up to lack of sleep. He'd *really* like for his brothers not to notice. But yeah, he was choked up.

"So I did the right thing."

"Marrying her? Sure," Ellie said.

"It's all good now. We're where we need to be?" he pressed. He needed reassurance, he realized, and if anyone could give that to him, it was his grandmother.

"Oh, I didn't say that," she told him, dropping her hand.

"Wait. What?"

"This is a *very* good start," Ellie said.

"Start?" Fletcher repeated. "*Start*? We've known each other forever. How is this a *start*?"

For some reason that made his heart kick. Hard.

He was the king of the grand gesture. He was the one who swept in at the last minute and saved the day. He was great at big *endings*.

Proposing to Jordan and sweeping her off her feet in front of a crowd—including her ex—was definitely his M.O.

Ellie looked puzzled. "Well, you're *married* now."

"Right. Happily ever after. The End are the words that come after that."

She laughed. *Laughed*. "Yes, that's the problem with fairy tales and romance novels and romantic movies. They end after the couple gets together and you don't get to see the rest."

"Because the hard part is over. The part where you figure out you belong together."

She shook her head, still smiling. "Falling in love and into bed is the easy part."

Then, with that, with no further insight or advice, she turned and ducked into the crowd.

That was a really cruel, not-grandmotherly-at-all thing to do. *Fuck*.

The falling in love and into bed was the *easy* part?

He'd been waiting three years for the first part. And they hadn't even done the into-bed part yet.

"Jordan!"

Finally Jordan's girlfriends had made it through the crowd of family. Fletcher watched as Naomi and Charlie and Kennedy all hugged Jordan at once. Of course, some of those girlfriends were now family too.

He felt that annoying tightness in his throat again.

"Jesus, you've got it bad."

He turned to Zander. He swallowed quickly and shook off the urge to sweep Jordan up in his arms and head out the door to start the falling-into-bed part of this whole thing.

She was just so fucking gorgeous when she was happy.

But he was going to get to see that every day for the rest of his life. They were together. Here. At home. And making her happy was what he did best.

"Are you going to cry?" Zander asked him, peering into his face. "Feeling bad for poor Jason Young, left all alone in Las Vegas with only his seventeen thousand adoring fans?"

No, he was getting all sappy again about spending his life with his best friend and the most gorgeous woman he knew.

And that was ridiculous. He should be crowing about this. Feeling damn proud and smug, as a matter of fact. He'd gotten the girl. What knight in shining armor didn't feel pretty fucking cocky at the end of a good quest?

"I'm just tired as hell," he told his brothers.

"Well, you've got a lot of night and partying ahead of you," Zeke told him, putting his arm around Fletcher's shoulders and steering him further into the bar.

"Nah, we're having dinner and heading home."

"I don't think so," Zander said, from his other side.

"What do you me—"

But the answer was as clear as if someone had hung a huge sign with gold glittery letters explaining it to him.

Because they had.

Congratulations, Fletcher and Jordan! We love you! shimmered from the cream-colored banner that hung over the enormous table full of food at the back of the bar.

And if the sign had been even the least bit unclear, the gigantic wedding cake in the middle of the table was an unmistakable indication that Ellie wasn't the only one who knew about their wedding.

Clearly what happened in Vegas didn't stay in Vegas.

Not with the Landrys.

Because of course it didn't.

"Fletcher!"

Fletcher focused on the woman standing just to one side of the table.

Elizabeth Landry was beaming at him.

"Hi, Mom."

Elizabeth came forward with her arms spread wide. Fletcher let her hug him, even as he silently groaned. Things had definitely just gotten real.

"I'm so happy for you and Jordan," Elizabeth said.

"You're not shocked?" Fletcher asked.

Elizabeth laughed. "I would've been shocked if you *hadn't*

married her while you were in Vegas together."

Fletcher shook his head. He supposed his shock over their reactions was really the unexpected emotion here. Maybe this all made sense. Maybe he and Jordan being together was exactly how this was supposed to go. He did believe that, but he'd honestly thought he might need to do a little more convincing of the people around him.

What he should do was appreciate the fact that no one seemed upset.

And hey, there was cake.

"Son." Ray, Fletcher's father, approached. He was also smiling widely. He first took Fletcher's hand, then pulled him in for a hug. "Way to go. Congratulations."

"Thanks, Dad."

"It's about time you and Jordan figured this all out," Ray said.

Fletcher nodded. "I guess we were the last to know how this should go."

"Well, maybe besides Jason," Ray added with a chuckle.

But hell, Jason hadn't even texted since Jordan had made him look like the good guy and she and Fletcher had ducked into a wedding chapel.

"No, I really think it's me and Jordan who are going to have to work on getting used to this," Fletcher said.

"Nah," Ray told him. "You and Jordan know each other better than I knew your mother when we got married." He looped an arm around Elizabeth's waist. "And we're at twenty-eight years."

Fletcher nodded. "True. So no fatherly advice on being a good husband?"

"You know better than anyone what Jordan needs," Ray said. "Just…give that to her. Keep bein' her best friend. Keep havin' fun and makin' each other laugh."

He could do that. His dad made it sound so easy.

"I'd tell you to be sure you didn't forget her birthday or

anniversaries or things like that," Elizabeth said. "But you've always been good about that. I remember her first birthday after you became friends. You insisted on calling her first thing that morning. It was seven a.m. and I was sure Molly would be put out by having her phone ring that early. But she'd been delighted. And you called her right after you woke up every single year after that." Elizabeth tipped her head. "I assume you still do that."

Fletcher just tucked his hands into his pockets and nodded.

He'd always wanted to be the first person to tell Jordan he was glad she'd been born and that had never changed. Cheesy? Maybe. But it had been true. So he called her and told her that.

It was really that simple.

Or it *had* been.

The thing about knowing someone at the age of six—you didn't have filters. You didn't worry about cheesy. You didn't think about that being misconstrued as anything other than "I'm glad you were born". Because the other six-year-old took it at face value too.

You also didn't think about how people might say things like, "ooh, Fletcher, do you wanna *kiss* Jordan?" when they hung out at recess together at age eight. Of course, Jacob Bernard had been the last kid to say something like that. Jordan had punched him in the nose for it.

You didn't think about how it might be strange for your friend to give you a big hug when she saw you at the bonfire party. Even if she was wearing only a bikini and you were in swim trunks.

You didn't think about what people might think when she sat on your lap in the back of a pickup at a barbecue because she was cold and wanted you to warm her up. Literally. Not in any kind of sexual way.

Because you'd known her since you were *six*.

And then you went to Galveston with her because you didn't want her on the road alone for five hours one way and when there was only one bed in one hotel room, you didn't think anything of it…until you did.

Until suddenly she was sexy and sweet and felt so fucking good and smelled so fucking good and you tasted her for the first time and your world tipped on its head. And never righted itself.

So, then you married her the second you were given the opportunity because you wanted to be the first person to tell her you were glad she'd been born on every birthday for the rest of your life and it would be a lot easier if she was just lying next to you in bed.

Fletcher turned and looked across the room to where Jordan was still standing with Naomi and Charlie and the other girls.

She lifted her gaze just then and their eyes met.

Across the fucking room. Like one of those romance movies that his grandma had pointed out ended when the couple got together.

Jordan gave him a small smile. A smile that said wow-these-people-are-a-lot-and-I-love-them-so-much.

God, he was so glad she'd been born.

"You're going to be great," Elizabeth told him, squeezing his arm and pulling Fletcher's attention back to his parents. "You and Jordan just fit."

Fletcher took a deep breath. "Yeah. We do."

"Why are we standing around talking when there's *cake* to eat?" Zeke called over the general din in the room.

"That's a damned good question," Zander told him. "Cora! Is this cake just for looking at?"

"Oh hush!" Cora told him, heading around behind the table with a huge knife. "Y'all act like we haven't fed you for days. You just ate dinner two hours ago and I've seen you stealing hors d'oeuvres from this table all night."

Zander laughed. "Hors d'oeuvres? What the hell is that? These are cheese and crackers and alligator balls."

Cora shook the knife at him, frowning even though Fletcher

could see the corners of her mouth twitching. "When it's a wedding reception, we call them hors d'oeuvres. Like *classy* people."

Zander and Zeke both laughed loudly at that.

"Chips and dips are chips and dips, Cora," Zeke told her, grabbing a tortilla chip from the bowl and dunking into a pinkish-red dip before popping it in his mouth. "No matter what fancy names you call them." He crunched for a moment. "Though we can call this really-fucking-good dip if you want."

Cora sighed. "I don't think I'm going to take 'classy' notes from a grown man who talks with his mouth full."

"You're gonna have to look *far* and *wide* from this place if you need notes on being classy," Zeke said.

Zeke gave her a wink and Cora shook her head, finally losing the battle with her smile.

"Why would you worry about classy now?" Leo asked, joining them. "We've all been doin' just fine for seventy-some years without any class."

He chuckled as Cora rolled her eyes, while not even bothering to try to hide her smile now.

Fletcher felt someone press against his side and an arm wrap around his waist. He knew it was Jordan even before he looked down.

She'd been hugging him, putting her arm around him, leaning against him for years. Her body against his was as familiar as the pillow he put his head on at night.

And yet…

He ran his hand down her back and cupped her ass, bringing her closer.

She gave a surprised little squeak and looked up with wide eyes.

"I can do that now. Finally," he told her.

Her smile was quick, and a little mischievous. "Finally, huh?"

"I've been trying not to look at your ass for years."

"How many?"

He thought about it. "Senior year of high school."

She lifted a brow. "Huh, I've been admiring your ass and abs and arms since at least sophomore year."

He gave a surprised laugh. "What?"

"I could hardly help it. All of the girls I hung out with—well, not Charlie and Kennedy of course," she said, naming his cousins. "But everyone else would never shut up about how hot you were. Especially when you had your shirt off working outside, or swimming, or on the boats."

"Huh." He flexed and she laughed.

"But the guys didn't comment on me, huh?" She seemed to ponder that. "I guess I was such a tomboy they didn't think about me that way. I didn't really fill out until junior year."

"I'm pretty sure they noticed you," Fletcher said dryly. "But they also knew I'd kill them if they said anything. At least to me. Made it easier to not look and pretend you hadn't suddenly gotten hips and breasts."

She pressed one of those breasts against one of his biceps she said she liked so much. "Well, you don't have to look away and pretend anymore."

His body heated several degrees instantly.

That was definitely going to be a change.

But a welcome one.

He gave her butt a squeeze—also something he was sure he was going to get used to quickly. "You have to behave. We have to cut the cake and probably do some toasts, dance a bit. You know they're not letting us out of here without a proper reception."

Her smile was full of happiness and contentment and Fletcher felt like a king.

"Yeah. I know. But I don't have to *totally* behave. You're my *husband* now. And they all know it."

Before Fletcher knew what was happening, she turned, put her hand on the back of his neck, pulled him down, and kissed him.

In the midst of all their family and friends.

A cheer went up around them and Fletcher felt her smile against his mouth.

Fueled with a sense of *fuck yes*, he cupped the back of her head with one hand, splayed one on her lower back, dipped her back slightly, and deepened the kiss.

If it was weird for any of them to see him kissing her, they were going to have to get over it. Right now.

He righted her after several long, wonderful moments.

She looked slightly dazed but happy. He looked around to find dozens of stupid, happy, goofy grins. His mother and Molly were both wiping their eyes. Leo had Owen and another cousin, Sawyer, popping the corks on several bottles of champagne. And Ellie was helping Cora shoo Zeke and Zander away from the food table.

It was all absolutely perfect.

"Okay already, cut the freaking cake!" Zeke called.

Jordan laughed but started for the table.

Fletcher was right behind her.

And he definitely took the opportunity to look at her ass.

CHAPTER

Eight

TWO HOURS LATER, the cake was mostly gone, the food looked like a swarm of locusts had descended, they were down to the last bottle of champagne and Fletcher and Jordan had barely sat down because of all the people who wanted to hug them and dance with them.

He hadn't been within ten feet of his new wife for almost an hour. They'd had their first dance—Zeke had started a Jason Young song for it, then had needed to hold up his hands to keep from getting hit in the face with boudin balls, baby carrots, and wadded up napkins as he laughingly insisted he'd been kidding. They'd danced to Ed Sheeran's "Perfect" instead and shared another long kiss at the end while everyone whistled, whooped, and clapped.

Fletcher was now at a back table with his brothers and cousin, Mitch. The table they had occupied for family dinners for years.

The Landrys all gathered for dinner at Ellie's most nights. Not everyone made it every night, of course, but there was always a group of some size. Mostly it was the grandkids, many of whom were bachelors who simply didn't want to cook for themselves. But as those grandkids had fallen in love, the group around the big back tables had grown. And at least once a week, you could find Ellie and Leo's own children in the building for a meal. Ellie and Cora loved it. It was their way of keeping up with everyone and taking care of them.

None of the family ever paid for any food inside Ellie's. Instead, they paid in repairs, errands, and other tasks that helped keep Ellie's running. Alternately, Ellie and Cora had never paid a bill for plumbing or electric work, to put in a new appliance, to replace a roof, or anything else related to the general upkeep of the restaurant and bar.

"So, big night ahead," Zeke said, sitting back in his chair, cradling his beer bottle on his flat stomach.

Fletcher had his chair tipped back on two legs, leaning against the wall behind him. It was the perfect position to watch Jordan. She was seated at the end of the bar with his cousin Kennedy and Tori, Maddie, and Juliet, the women who had somehow been talked into marrying his cousins Josh, Owen, and Sawyer.

"What are you talkin' about?" Zander asked his twin. "What's goin' on?" He was the town cop and always wanted to know what kind of "big night" might be happening in or around Autre. He glanced at the clock over the bar. "It's past eleven. What's *ahead*?"

"I mean for Fletcher," Zeke said.

Fletcher rolled his head to look at his youngest—by two minutes—brother. "What?"

"Your first night with Jordan. Ever. And it's your *wedding night*. I mean…no pressure." Zeke chuckled.

"Good thing Fletcher is so hot and so sweet and so charming and so funny," Zander said, his voice changing to a falsetto as he repeated what they'd heard so many women say over the years.

Mitch just chuckled and lifted his beer bottle, clearly choosing not to comment.

Zeke laughed outright. "Sure, except this is *Jordan*. She knows him well enough to know what's bullshit and what's not."

His younger brother studied him. "I wonder what it's like to seduce your best friend," Zeke said, obviously choosing to wonder out loud. "I mean, you always want it to be good, but with her you'll want it to be *really* good."

Fletcher felt his gut tighten. Of course he wanted it to be good. Why wouldn't it be good?

"But he knows her really well," Mitch said. "That's an advantage. He'll be able to read her. Tell what she likes, what she doesn't, what she's into. Being really in tune with someone makes the intimacy so much better."

Spoken like a man in love, Fletcher thought. God, he was happy for his cousin. Paige was amazing and they were fantastic together.

"Well, sure," Zeke went on.

Zander scoffed. "You know so much about intimacy?"

"Maybe not," Zeke admitted. "But I do know that with a lifetime of knowin' each other, he'd better be careful not do or say something that might remind her of the time he couldn't camp out with us because of the Stephen King book he'd read that freaked him out. How he headed back to town and then asked Jordan if he could sleep on her bedroom floor so he didn't have to admit to Mom and Dad he got scared."

"And so he wasn't sleeping alone," Zander said with a nod.

"Jesus," Fletcher said, scrubbing a hand over his face. "I was *nine*."

"Sure. Just sayin' that if something reminds her of that, she might be reminded of other not-sexy-at-all shit. And Jordan knows *a lot* of that about you," Zeke said.

"Like the time you puked on her," Zander said.

"Which time?" Zeke asked. "There are two I can think of."

There were three actually. And now that they were talking about it, it was a damned miracle Jordan was even still his friend.

"The time they ate blue cotton candy, blue snow cones, and

blue..." Zander turned to Fletcher. "What was the other blue stuff you guys ate?"

There was absolutely no point in pretending he didn't know what they were talking about. "Blue gummy bears and blue cupcakes. But we also had blueberries."

Jordan had seen the blue cupcakes at the fair stand that was promoting some business whose tagline was *It blew me away*. She'd decided it would be fun to eat only blue food the rest of the day. God knows why. Or why he went along with it.

Actually, it was easy to figure out why he'd gone along with it—because it had made Jordan smile. Still, it had been a *bad* idea.

Zander nodded. "Right. Then they went on the Octopus ride three times in a row. Jordan's yellow t-shirt turned a gross green color with the blue puke all down the front of it."

Fletcher sighed. "We were *eleven*."

"Right. But in the middle of getting naked with her, all it takes is the thought of something blue to remind her of the puke and to ruin a mood," Zeke told him. "Doesn't matter *when* it happened. And she knows tons of un-sexy stuff about you."

"This is really helpful, guys, thanks," Fletcher said dryly. "Just what I need to hear."

And *fuck*, they kind of had a point.

"And not just un-sexy stuff," Zander said, as if Fletcher was *actually* thanking them. "She also knows things like how you always wore that one cologne when you were going to try to kiss a girl for the first time."

Fletcher groaned. His brothers knew stuff too. The assholes.

"Because Jordan told you to wear it because it was *delicious*," Zander added with a grin.

"What's the good of having a girl for a best friend if she can't give you girl advice?" Mitch, easily the *nicest* of the Landry grandsons—hell, maybe of *all* the grandkids—asked.

"Exactly. Thank you," Fletcher told him.

"Oh, sure, it was helpful, no doubt," Zander said. "We're just pointing out that one sniff and Jordan will know what you're thinking."

"You don't think she'll assume her new *husband* wants to kiss her on their *wedding night*?" Mitch asked.

Good point. But Zeke and Zander had made their point too. Very well.

And then Zeke went in for the kill.

"Oh, she'll probably assume he wants to kiss her," Zeke agreed. "She'll probably also assume that he remembers her telling him that she hates giving blowjobs."

Mitch and Zander had both just made the mistake of taking a drink from their bottles.

Mitch sucked beer into his lungs and started hacking and coughing. Zander actually spit his out.

Fletcher, on the other hand, knew better than to take a drink when Zeke was on a roll like this. Instead he leaned in, one forearm on the table, scowling at his brother. "*What* did you say?"

Zeke lifted a shoulder. He knew that if Fletcher hauled him out of his chair and hit him, it would be a pretty even match. He couldn't be sure which side Zander and Mitch would take, of course, but Mitch at least was out of commission for the moment, trying to clear beer from his breathing passages.

"Jordan doesn't like giving blowjobs. She told you that once. Those are the kinds of things you should really keep in mind."

"How the *fuck* do you know she told me that once?" Fletcher asked.

Had she? Yes. Did he remember it? Absolutely.

He and Jordan had been the kinds of friends who talked about *everything* and nothing had been awkward about even sex talk until they'd kissed in Galveston. After that, he had *not* wanted to know what she liked and didn't like about sex, because she was having that sex with someone else and he wanted her to be having it with him.

Until then, though, it had seemed natural to talk about it. In fact, it had been an awesome part about having a best friend of the opposite sex. Seeing inside the female mind had been fascinating. And helpful. And he didn't just get Jordan's insights, but he got to hear about how her girlfriends thought about and talked about guys and dating and sex and everything too.

But they'd kept each other's secrets.

Or so he'd thought.

"We heard her tell you," Zeke said simply.

"You heard her…" Fletcher flashed back to the conversation. They'd been in the family room at his house. It had been after midnight. They'd been eighteen. Jordan had asked him if blowjobs were really *that* good. He'd assured her that yes, they absolutely were. She'd been disappointed to hear that because she didn't like giving them. "You were fucking listening?" Fletcher asked his brother.

"We always eavesdropped on you and Jordan," Zeke said.

"We were always hoping we'd catch you two kissing. Or more," Zander added. "But we got some awesome insights into girls by listening to Jordan."

Fletcher sighed. How could he fault them, really? Maybe Jordan had made them better guys when it came to women with her advice, unknowing as it may have been. He'd say better boyfriends, but neither Zeke or Zander had ever really been a *boyfriend* to anyone. They'd certainly made sure to spread their… charm…around though.

"So, sorry about your luck with the blowjobs," Zeke said. "But there's plenty of other fun stuff to do, right?"

Mitch and Zander both chuckled. Because the answer to that question was *of course.*

"Then again," Zander said. "There's a chance she could learn to like them."

"You think?" Zeke asked.

"Well, I mean she's only been with one guy. Her blowjob experience is very limited. And if she started giving them when they were teenagers, it's very possible the experience was less than ideal," Zander said.

"Hey, yeah, she's kind of a blowjobs virgin," Zeke said, almost perking up as if this directly affected him. "I mean, if she didn't like it and they stopped doing it, then maybe it's been a while." He looked at Fletcher. "You could introduce her to the glory of blowjobs. She doesn't know what she's missing."

Fletcher felt his gut tighten. It was, of course, in part because his brothers were discussing his sex life. Or more specifically, Jordan's sex life. Which always annoyed him. Having them speculate about what Jordan had or had not done in the past with Jason and what she would or would not be willing to do with him, was not helpful in the least.

But, even more than that—they were making sense.

Jordan had only been with one other man and she and Jason had gotten together when they were very young. In spite of the eleven years together, that did mean she had relatively limited experience.

Damn.

Then Zeke made it all worse by putting Fletcher's exact thoughts to words.

"She's maybe kind of a virgin in a lot of ways."

Zander frowned. "What you mean? She and Jason were together a long time."

"Sure," Zeke agreed, "but they were kids when they got together. They maybe don't even know all the things they could have been doing. Could be all kinds of things Jordan hasn't even tried." He grinned at Fletcher. "This could be fun. I've been with a couple of virgins and I'm telling you, when they're enthusiastic about learning, it can be a really good time." He paused. "Of course..."

Fletcher did *not* want to encourage this conversation. He already had a knot in his gut. He and Jordan were going to have to talk about this, weren't they? He'd need to know how experienced—or not—she was. Which meant hearing about what she'd done with Jason.

He did *not* want to know that.

"Of course what?" Zander asked.

Zeke lifted a big shoulder. "Just…it's some pressure too, you know? I mean, you wanna make it good for them. First time and all. And Fletcher always has to be *The Guy* with Jordan."

"The Guy?" Mitch repeated.

But it was Zander who nodded. "Oh yeah. For sure. Fletcher has to be the guy who comes through—no pun intended—for Jordan no matter what."

"Well at least he was smart and got her hitched the second he could," Zeke said. He reached over and clapped Fletcher on the shoulder. "Now all you have to do is be the best she's ever had. Erase all those memories with that other guy. What's his name again? Big hot super star—"

"*Okay.*" Fletcher cut his brother off with a sharp tone.

His heart was pounding and not in the good, hot, I-get-to-have-sex-with-Jordan-tonight way.

Fuck. Zeke was right. And while that happened more often than most of them would admit, it was significantly unpleasant in this case.

Sleeping with Jordan was a much bigger deal than with anyone else. He'd known that would be the case. He was in love with the girl, after all. Her being his wife should make this easier though, shouldn't it? But damn…their first time together would also be the beginning of the only sex either of them would ever have again.

And she was kind of like a virgin. Not technically, of course, but he would only be the second man ever in her bed. And the first had gotten her naked for the first time when she was sixteen.

Yes, he knew that too. She called him right after Jason had dropped her off.

In fact she'd talked to Fletcher about it before it happened.

She and Jason had discussed it for nearly six months before it happened and she told Fletcher all of her feelings about it. How she was nervous, how she didn't know if it was the right thing to do, how she really wanted to do it, how sweet Jason had been waiting, how she was sure she was going to marry him so surely that made it okay.

Fletcher got to hear all of that. At age sixteen it had been fine. Fletcher had never imagined sleeping with Jordan himself. His only concern had been Jason treating her right, and using a condom.

Which he had told Jason when he'd found him after football practice over in Bad the next afternoon.

He'd threatened to be sure that Jason was never able to father children if he did anything to hurt Jordan, told him that one single "no" from her meant Jason better fucking stop no matter how far along they were, and then he'd slapped three condoms into Jason's hand before turning and stomping away.

So yeah, he knew when Jordan had officially lost her virginity. He knew she didn't like giving blowjobs. He knew she was on the pill. He knew she'd sprained her ankle once trying shower sex. And he knew, that even with all of that awkward knowledge between them, he still wanted to be the last man to ever make love to her.

Yes, he wanted to erase all of the other memories and be the best she'd ever had.

Yes, he was used to being the guy who did everything right with her. And yes, he really fucking liked that.

So yes, fucking hell, he was definitely feeling the pressure.

He hadn't expected to be thinking about spending the night in her bed when he'd picked her up this morning. He definitely hadn't expected to be married to her.

This was all going too damned fast.

"You realize, I hope, that Zeke doesn't really know what he's talking about when it comes to relationships, right?" Mitch asked.

He was leaning in, giving Fletcher a very concerned look.

Fletcher swallowed hard. "Yeah, I know," he said, trying for nonchalant.

He apparently didn't pull it off.

Mitch shook his head. "I mean it, man."

"He's right," Zander added. "Zeke's idea of a serious relationship is when he lets the girl shower at his place in the morning instead of just driving her home."

Mitch looked over at Zeke. "When was the last time you let a woman shower at your place?"

Zeke had to think about it. "A year. Maybe more."

"What if she has to work in the morning?" Mitch asked, looking entertained.

"Then she better get up in time to get home and get ready," Zeke told him.

"Why don't you let women shower at your place?" Mitch asked. "Seriously? What's the big deal? If they've already slept over?"

Mitch hadn't let women spend the night at his place. He'd been basically celibate for about six months after meeting Paige and she was now living with him, but even before his trip to Iowa where he'd met the sassy blonde, he'd had a rule about no women in his personal space.

Zeke had no such rule. Except when it came to his shower, apparently.

"Long hair," Zeke said, lifting his beer and taking a long drink.

Mitch laughed. "What about it?"

"It uses more shampoo and clogs my drain."

Mitch and Zander both snorted.

"*You* have long hair," Mitch pointed out.

"So adding *more* would be a big problem," Zeke said.

"You're not having women shower at your place because they use up your shampoo and you might have to snake your drain more often?" Zander asked. "Wow."

Zeke shrugged. "Guy's gotta have rules."

"What about shower sex?" Zander asked.

Which, of course, took Fletcher's thoughts back to Jordan's sprained ankle and her declaration that she was *not* into sex in rooms other than the bedroom.

At the time he'd laughed.

He wasn't laughing now.

Shower sex. Kitchen sex. Of course living room couch sex. Even we-couldn't-make-it-upstairs-before-we-tore-each-other's-clothes-off-on-the-fifth-step sex. There were so many possibilities.

"Shower sex is harder than it sounds," Zeke informed them.

"Mitch and I have shower sex all the time," Paige said, as she joined them at the table.

Specifically, as she slid into Mitch's lap and wrapped an arm around his neck.

Zeke smirked at her. "Well, you're tiny and do yoga. You can probably assume some positions a regular girl can't."

"Nope," Mitch said, shaking his head. "You're not going to sit here and imagine Paige in the shower."

"It's *instructional*," Zeke said. "Paige is declaring that something can happen that I don't think can. She's educating me."

Mitch shook his head. "No, she isn't." He looked up at his girlfriend. "Don't encourage him."

She laughed. "He doesn't need encouraging. He's also full of it. There's no way he's not having shower sex. You told me Zander put built-in benches in all your showers when he remodeled your bathrooms."

"And you're all very welcome," Zander said, lifting his beer.

"I *really* appreciate it," Paige told him with a grin.

"I use my bench for holding up my bottles," Zeke said. "I've got plenty of other surfaces for sex."

"Bottles? How many bottles are we talkin' here?" Zander asked.

Zeke counted silently for a moment. "Six."

Fletcher had to admit his eyes widened too. "Six?"

"Shampoo, conditioner, body wash, shave cream, shampoo, and body wash," Zeke said, ticking them off on his fingers.

"You said shampoo and body wash twice," Zander pointed out.

"I have two of each."

"*Why?*"

"Sometimes I want to smell like spring rain and sometimes I want to smell like a mountain morning," Zeke said, as if that were obvious.

The guys just stared at him, but Paige leaned over and gave him a sniff. She nodded. "Very nice."

"Yeah? Which one is it?" Zander asked.

"Beer and buttercream on a mountain in the rain," she said.

Zeke gave her a wink and they all laughed.

"But seriously," Zeke said. "Shower sex is more work than bed sex. It just is. And it's not just the hair in the drain. You have to worry about slipping, you have to remember to take the condom in there, you have to hold on tighter, then when it's over everybody has to dry off. And then her hair gets my pillow all wet."

"Oh my God, it's about the hair again," Zander said. "Have you considered dating a bald girl?"

"I have actually," Zeke said. "I dated a girl with a super cute pixie cut. I let *her* shower at my place."

Mitch, Paige, and Zander laughed and even Fletcher felt himself smiling.

"I've never met a man so obsessed with women's hair," Zander told his twin.

Zeke gave him a smug grin. "Well, when you have so many to choose from, you can be a little pickier. I guess you wouldn't understand that."

Zander just flipped him off.

Fletcher even chuckled at that. He was sure Zander had to

snake his drain on a fairly regular basis too and that it wasn't all because of *his* long hair.

Fletcher glanced toward the bar where Jordan was sitting. The thing about Zeke and his aversion to long hair clogging his drain, was that he hadn't met the right girl yet. Fletcher would have no trouble dealing with Jordan's hair all over his house.

Just then she looked up and caught his eye. She gave him a little smile and he felt his heart thump against his ribs.

It was their wedding night. They were fucking sitting in Ellie's bar with all of their friends and family eating their *wedding* cake at their *wedding* reception.

How the hell had this happened?

He watched her say something to Naomi and Charlie that caused them to glance in his direction and nod. Jordan slipped off the barstool and started across the bar.

Again, his heart thumped hard. God, he loved her. And she was his now. And he was supposed to be giving her a night to remember. That was one thing Jason had never done. Given her a wedding night.

Yeah, no pressure.

Fuck.

A moment later she slid into his lap the way Paige was sitting on Mitch. Instinctively Fletcher's arm went around her, happily settling his hand on the outer curve of her ass. While she'd sat on his lap many times in the past, he'd never been able to touch her quite that way. Or move her back slightly so the curve of her butt cheek was pressing into his cock. Or lean in and put his nose against her neck and breathe deeply.

Spring mornings on mountains had nothing on how Jordan smelled.

She looped her arm around his neck and put her lips against his ear. "I don't have to ignore it anymore."

He and his cock knew exactly what she was talking about. Just like that morning, the moment her sweet ass hit his lap, his cock had said hello.

And he did not want her to ignore it.

At all.

But she didn't like giving blowjobs, she only liked sex in the bedroom, and she hated when Jason slept with one of his legs draped over her because he was hot and made her sweaty.

It was possible he and Jordan knew too much about one another.

Dammit. He needed a little more time to prepare for taking Jordan to bed. They were both a little sleep deprived—a lot sleep deprived—and they'd both been drinking. Twenty-four hours ago they hadn't even been dating. Now they were married.

Essentially, he'd married her so he could date her. Or at least so no one else would date her. They'd certainly gotten to know each other well over the past twenty years. There was no question they were compatible and could live together. But maybe they needed some romance. A chance to get to know each other physically. Some heavy making out.

Maybe they needed to work up to the sex thing. Even if it was their wedding night.

"Hey, Zander," Fletcher said. "Jordan was talking about how she hasn't beat your ass at darts in a long time."

Zander glanced at Fletcher's new wife. "Is that right?"

"Did I say that?" Jordan asked.

Well not in so many words, but she'd mentioned that playing darts with Zander was on her to-do-back-in-Autre list. Besides she and Zander had always loved their dart games.

"Yeah, remember?" He was counting on the fact that she was more sleep deprived and probably more tipsy than he was.

"It has been a long time," Jordan said.

Zander was looking at Fletcher with a knowing expression. Fletcher almost blew that off. There was no way his brother knew what he was up to.

But when Zander said, "It *has* been a long time. And, you're now officially my *sister*, which means I really don't have to take it easy on you. Rematch, right now, shots all around," Fletcher realized that Zander knew exactly what Fletcher was hoping would happen.

"Take it *easy* on me? Oh, bring it on," Jordan said, pushing off Fletcher's lap and taking Zander's challenge.

Exactly as expected.

Neither Zander or Jordan had ever walked away from a dart game. Period.

They always needed to be *carried* away.

When they played, they always drank tequila, something neither of them handled particularly well. They claimed it was because they were both so good at darts they needed some kind of handicap to make it even competitive.

The truth was, they were the best dart players in the southern half of Louisiana—for what good those bragging rights were. When they played against one another, it was a toss-up as to who would win. Their records were pretty even.

When they played as partners—as they had for a couple of years in a league that even included tournaments—they were undefeated.

They were *stupidly* proud of their three trophies—that, of course, sat on a shelf at the west wall of Ellie's.

Zeke groaned. "I call dibs on Jordan."

"No way," Fletcher told him as Jordan headed for the bar with Zander to retrieve the darts and the tequila. "She's going home with me. I've got her."

"You've *always* got her. And she's way lighter than Zander," Zeke groused.

They'd both had to do firemen carries on the dart champions in the past.

"Plus, Jordan gets sweet when she drinks tequila. Zander gets…more Zander-ish."

Fletcher chuckled. That was also true. Whiskey made Jordan sassy and got her riled up. But tequila made her sappy and sweet. All liquor just made Zander more sarcastic and stubborn.

"Guess *you* should have gone to Vegas and married her,"

Mitch said to Zeke, clapping him on the back. "Then you could have carried her home."

"Yeah, well, you just fucked up your wedding night, man," Zeke said, looking past Fletcher.

He turned to watch Jordan and Zander clearing people out of the path of the dart board and getting ready for their first throws.

He pivoted back to his beer, but not before he caught Mitch's knowing look.

Okay, so Mitch and Zander had both figured out that he was trying to get his wife so drunk she wouldn't be up for any fooling around tonight.

He just needed a little time here.

He was *married* to his *best friend*.

She'd once puked *orange* all over the floor of his car, by the way. And she'd *bled* on him. He'd also had to carry half of her left third toe on their way to the hospital. And they hadn't even been able to reattach it. Yeah, Jordan only had half of a third toe. And in sixth grade he'd read her diary about how cute Michael LeClaire was and how she wanted to kiss him "so much it hurt".

Yeah, he knew plenty of gross and embarrassing things about *her*.

But as she threw her first dart and thrust her arms into the air with a triumphant cheer and beamed at his brother, Fletcher realized that he *had* to make this work.

He always made everything work for Jordan.

Obviously their *marriage* had just moved to the top of that list.

JORDAN'S HEAD was pounding when she opened her eyes and she promptly squeezed them shut again.

It didn't help much.

Fucking tequila.

Fucking Zander Landry.

Fucking competitive streak and her inability to let anyone beat her, especially a Landry boy, without giving it her all.

Okay, she'd let Zander win at the end, the way she always did. But she'd definitely made him earn it.

She was never drinking again.

Okay, she was never drinking *tequila* again.

Jordan was aware that she'd made that very promise at least a dozen times in her life.

And that Zander Landry always made her forget tequila hated her and had been invented for the sole purpose of torturing her.

He was the devil.

She moaned and pressed a hand against the center of her forehead where her brain was threatening to pound through her skull. She felt as if someone had bashed her over the head with the tequila bottle rather than just pouring the contents of it into a glass. Repeatedly.

She was really going to have to get her shit together. If she was going to be living in Autre and seeing Zander on a regular basis they were both going to need to grow up. He couldn't be feeling any better than she was right now.

She hoped there was a major cop issue for him to deal with today. Well, not a *major* cop issue. Cop issues could get pretty bad and she didn't want any of that happening in Autre. But maybe a couple of neighbors could have a fight over one of their dogs pooping in the other one's yard or something equally annoying. And loud.

She took a deep breath, knowing that her only hope was a large bottle of Gatorade, a bunch of carbs, and caffeine. And ibuprofen. Lots and lots of ibuprofen.

Which meant she was going to have to get up to get those items.

Which meant she was going to have to move.

Which sounded like a generally terrible idea at the moment.

She took a deep breath. Then another.

Oh, that was nice. That smell. That was…Fletcher.

Her eyes flew open. Then she groaned and let them slide shut again.

But she breathed deep again. The smell was nice. Even if the bright sunlight in the room wasn't.

The room smelled like Fletcher.

Because this room was Fletcher's.

She was waking up in Fletcher's room. In Fletcher's bed.

In *their* bed.

Her heart thumped inside her chest and she took another deep breath, this time less to savor the scent and more to calm the butterflies that were suddenly having a house party in her stomach.

She slowly opened her eyes, willing herself to tolerate sunlight as she rolled her head to the left. *Ouch.* Yep, that was the window in Fletcher's bedroom. Not that she'd ever seen it from this particular angle, but she'd been in this room before. Fletcher had lived in this house for about four years now. Ever since they'd graduated from college. She'd helped him move into it. Taking another deep breath, she rolled her head to the right, more slowly this time. Yeah, that was his bedside table, his alarm clock, and his lamp.

She was definitely lying in Fletcher's bed. Which made sense, she supposed, considering she was his wife.

Holy shit. She was Fletcher's *wife*. She was waking up in his bed. The morning after their wedding. She started to sit up at that thought. Then realized that was a horrible idea and let herself back down—gently—onto the pillow.

Great. She'd gotten wasted with Zander on her wedding night.

Which meant she hadn't really had a *wedding night*.

Dammit.

That was really too bad.

She had a hot, charming, rumored-to-be-amazing-in-bed husband now. He'd literally flown to her rescue yesterday and swept her off her feet. He'd kissed her like he'd been starving for her for years. He'd promised to love her and cherish her 'til he died.

And she'd felt what he had behind his zipper against her butt. Twice.

Yeah, she'd messed up last night. Big time. Pun intended.

Okay, she had to get up.

The most difficult thing she'd do all day would be going from horizontal to vertical. She needed to get it over with.

Getting upright, getting water, even brushing her teeth would help her feel better. And surely Fletcher had ibuprofen.

With a deep breath and her eyes squeezed shut, Jordan pushed herself up to sitting, bracing against the pounding in her head. When it lessened to a dull roar, she threw the covers back and pivoted to sit on the edge of the bed. After two minutes she opened her eyes.

Okay. She was going to live. Maybe she hadn't had as much tequila as she thought. The long emotional day, the lack of sleep, and the champagne with the cake had probably all combined to make even a small amount of tequila seem more potent.

Some good food, a gallon or two of coffee, and maybe a nap later and she'd be good to go.

Jordan swallowed and ran her tongue over her teeth. Ew. And she needed her toothbrush. Like right now. She shoved herself off the edge of the bed and stood. She immediately felt the cool air on her legs and looked down.

She was wearing only her thong and the pink tank top from yesterday. Yuck. She needed a shower and new clothes too. But she didn't have any other clothes here. She was going to have to call Naomi or Charlie. But where were her pants and bra? Had Fletcher taken them off? She supposed those were automatic enough activities that she could have done them even drunk, but she didn't remember.

Her body got warmer thinking about Fletcher undressing her. Too bad she'd missed it. It'd been sexy when he'd taken her t-shirt off in Vegas. Last night in his bedroom they wouldn't have had to stop. In fact, they would've been practically required to keep going since it was their…

Ugh. She covered her face with her hands. It had been their *wedding night.*

And she'd ruined it.

Okay, she had to pull herself together. No more acting like— well, like she always acted when she visited Autre. This wasn't a quick trip home for the weekend or holiday to catch up with everyone and party and depend on Fletcher to get her home and keep her safe.

She was here to *stay* now. With him. As his *wife.* And while she'd always love having that hot, sweet Louisiana boy take care of her and he'd always love doing it, there were new ways for him to take care of her now. Fun, hot ways. That she definitely wanted to be sober for. Even if it was just him undressing her.

A hot shiver went through her and she headed for the bathroom with renewed determination to not be a hungover mess today.

The sunlight streamed in brightly here too and she had to blink against the glare off the white and light gray marble and tile.

The bathroom was just the right amount of clean and uncluttered. The counters were wiped and dry, there were no globs of toothpaste drying in either of the two sinks, towels were all hung up. But there was an uncapped bottle of cologne sitting out, a stray sock on the floor, a hooded sweatshirt hanging on the inside doorknob, and the medicine cabinet was partially open.

But there was also a new, unopened toothbrush lying on top of a clean, folded dark gray towel and she smiled. He was taking care of her even when he wasn't here.

The bathroom was the newest room in the house. Fletcher, Mitch, and Zander had all moved into Landry family houses passed down by the older generations. Zeke had chosen to build his own, but had put it with the others at the end of the dead-end road that butted up to several acres of open land that led to the bayou. Open land except for the area where they put the lemurs and sloths that were part of the Boys of the Bayou Gone Wild.

She was heading down there today in fact. Charlie was going to show her around and they were going to discuss a new job for Jordan.

She felt the flip in her belly. She was excited. Not just about a job potentially working with a sloth—though that was very cool —but just being here. She was home. She was going to get to see the people she loved most in the world on a regular basis. Hell, she was *married* to one of the people she loved most in the world. She was definitely going to see a lot of him. Hopefully a lot of him without his clothes on.

Jordan laughed. She wasn't used to thinking about Fletcher that way, but wow was it easy. Grinning, she reached first for the medicine cabinet and the bottle of ibuprofen. Shaking three into her hand she turned on the water to wash them down and glanced in the mirror. And nearly screamed.

She'd forgotten about her purple hair. It looked especially wild sticking up on the left side and paired with her bloodshot eyes with the dark circles under them and the what-the-hell-was-that stain on the front of her shirt.

"Holy. Shit. Pull yourself together. You are a mess."

She had to pray that her new husband wasn't into adoringly watching her sleep. She couldn't really imagine that, thankfully.

She remembered Fletcher telling her once that the worst part of having a woman spend the night was getting her downstairs the next morning. Once they were dressed and having coffee, even breakfast, everything then seemed okay. But in the bedroom the morning after was awkward. His theory was that meals—even a meal in his own kitchen—were a more normal part of everyday life. Lots of people had meals with lots of other people all the time.

Waking up together, on the other hand, was not a normal part of everyday life for just every group of people. It was definitely more intimate. So he made a point of getting up and out of bed before the woman woke up. He made it seem romantic by making breakfast, but truly he wanted to get out of the bedroom before she was conscious. He could then have the kitchen be the first place they faced one another the morning after.

Jordan frowned as she added toothpaste to the new brush and started scrubbing her teeth.

Fletcher had gotten out of bed before her today. Of course, she was hungover and he had to go to school today. Still...he could have kissed her good morning. Or whispered goodbye.

Though Jordan would admit she wasn't a hundred percent sure she would've heard him. Maybe he'd tried and she'd slept through it. She scrubbed her teeth a little harder. She was also maybe glad that he hadn't tried to kiss her this morning before toothpaste.

Then again, she wasn't like the other women he shared that bed with. For one thing, she'd shared a bed with him before. As kids they'd camped out in the backyard numerous times. She'd crashed in his bed after a handful of parties in high school. They'd shared a bed in a hotel room in Dallas when a bunch of them had road tripped to a concert. And then there was that time in Galveston.

Interestingly, now that she was thinking about it, he'd gone to the lobby of the hotel in Galveston to get her coffee and a muffin the morning after. Nothing had happened and yet he still felt awkward the next morning.

Jordan frowned and kept scrubbing. But she was his wife now. That made this different. Didn't it?

She finally rinsed her mouth and pulled Fletcher's brush through her hair and found a hair tie in the top drawer under the sink.

Jordan pulled her hair into a ponytail, then, feeling a lot closer to normal, stepped back into the bedroom. Now she needed clothes. She'd borrow a t-shirt and athletic shorts she could cinch with a drawstring from Fletcher for now and call one of the girls for something she could wear out of the house.

Charlie was curvier—i.e. had great boobs at least two cups sizes bigger than Jordan's. Naomi was taller than Jordan so any shorts would be long on her, but she'd be covered at least until her own clothes got here. She could also run up to New Orleans today to shop for a couple of things. Or she could maybe check out the closets of her new cousins-in-law. Josh's wife, Tori, was very pregnant now so it was likely she had some pre-pregnancy clothes not being used.

Jordan was bent over rummaging in Fletcher's dresser for shorts when she heard the bedroom door open and the surprised, "Oh."

She looked over her shoulder to find Fletcher standing in the doorway staring at her. More precisely, staring at her ass. She was still wearing her thong so her butt was almost entirely exposed. The tank top was definitely not long enough to cover her hips and butt even when she was standing straight and certainly not when she was bent over.

"Morning," she greeted. She took her time taking out a pair of shorts and then straightening and turning to face him. He was going to have to get used to having this particular woman in his bedroom in the mornings.

"Morning." His voice was a little husky.

Jordan was careful not to hold the shorts or the shirt she had chosen in front of her. She let them both hang at her sides. The tank top was silky and clingy and without a bra her nipples were prominent behind the pale pink fabric.

His eyes traveled over her. Slowly. She felt her scalp tingle, her nipples tighten, her stomach clench, and her inner muscles tighten.

"I thought you'd left for school."

"I thought you'd still be in bed."

They spoke at the same time. Jordan stopped and smiled. Her eyes went to the mug he was holding in one hand and what looked like a garment in the other.

"I brought you coffee and clothes." He held up what turned out to be a cherry red sundress with tiny white dots on the bed. He cleared his throat. "Charlie brought this over."

Now it seemed he was trying to avoid looking at her completely. She frowned. "That was nice of her."

"Yeah, so I should get going. To school. Need to get some stuff done."

"You look hot," she told him, ignoring his excuses. It was early. He didn't need to be at school quite yet.

His gaze came up to hers. "What?"

She smiled. "You know the teacher look does it for me."

She'd shared about her crush on their sociology professor

their freshman year. Definitely the distinguished-older-man-in-glasses-and-in-charge was her type.

Fletcher was dressed in khakis and a dark green button down shirt, brown dress shoes—scuffed but still dress shoes—and he was wearing his glasses.

What could she say? The dress-shirt-and-glasses-geeky-about-something guys were her real turn-ons.

He didn't wear his glasses all the time and she *loved* when he did. They got in his way when he was out on the bayou, helping Zeke with construction projects, or playing sports, but he wore them when he was at school because he needed them mostly for reading.

He cleared his throat again. "Yeah, I didn't need to know what you are willing to do for an A in sociology."

She laughed softly. "That was two a.m. and I was delirious from studying for a test I was certain I was going to fail. I didn't really mean that."

He gave her a look. "You meant it sixty percent."

She thought about that. Then grinned. "Maybe forty percent."

Their sociology professor had been in his fifties. But he had been very handsome and the gray at his temples had been sexy and he'd had a great sense of humor. She'd ended up with an A in that class without needing any "extra credit", of course. She would never have done anything immoral for a grade, but she'd enjoyed teasing Fletcher about it.

Now that she gave it more thought, Fletcher had reacted with jealousy and she'd kind of liked that. That was weird. She hadn't thought about it much then, but it was clear looking back that had been why the joke had been fun. Immature, for sure, but fun.

"Just realizing that I can play out my hot teacher fantasies all the time now," she said stepping even closer. "I have my very own hot teacher twenty-four-seven now."

Fletcher's jaw tightened. Then he cleared his throat. "I need to get going."

She was half naked, two feet from the bed, and teasing about hot teacher fantasies, and he was ready to head out?

She stepped even closer and he suddenly thrust the coffee mug out. Straight out. As in arm-fully-extended as if it would fend her off. Some of the coffee even sloshed over the rim. What the hell?

"Here."

Fletcher was uncomfortable having a woman in his bedroom in the morning. But this was *her*. This was the first morning of many to come.

She took the mug and the dress from him, but as soon as he let go, he started backing toward the door.

"So…see you la—"

"Fletcher."

He stopped. "Yeah?" But now he was looking at the window past her shoulder.

She set the mug on the bedside table and tossed the dress on the bed.

"You can't leave without kissing me goodbye."

He didn't move. In fact he went completely still. "What?"

"Shouldn't husbands kiss their wives goodbye when they leave?"

He was looking at her now. Their gazes were locked, and she could see emotions swirling in his. What was going on? He seemed to be trying to resist her. But that was ridiculous. Was he upset about last night? He would have a right to be.

"I'm sorry about last night," she told him. She stepped closer and lifted a hand to rest on his chest.

He stayed completely frozen, but she could feel his heart hammering under her palm. "For what?"

"I completely ruined our wedding night. I should never have started playing darts with Zander. We both know how that always ends."

In fact, Fletcher probably should've stopped her when she and Zander went to get the darts. But she was grown up. He didn't need to babysit her. Her head throbbed and she amended that to he *shouldn't* need to babysit her.

"You didn't ruin anything. It's fine. I'm not mad."

She believed him, actually. He didn't seem mad. And this was Fletcher. He would tell her if he was mad. But why did he seem so uncomfortable? If this really was about feeling awkward the morning after, he was going to need to get over that. Plus, it wasn't really the morning after anything, other than sleeping.

Then a terrible thought occurred to her. "Oh God, did I do something embarrassing last night? Did I talk in my sleep? Or did I karaoke? Or did I puke on the way home in the car? Or in here?" She spun, looking around the room.

Fletcher's hand landed on hers on his chest. "No. None of that. You played darts, you let Zander win, you came over, sat in my lap, and fell asleep on my shoulder. I carried you to the truck, carried you into the house and up here, and put you to bed."

She winced. "I'm sorry." Then she glanced down. "Did you undress me?"

"Well, your pants. I pulled your bra off with your shirt on, the way you showed me in college."

Jordan grinned. She'd showed him the trick women knew for getting bras off without fully undressing by unhooking and then pulling the straps off through the sleeves. "I'm impressed you remembered that."

His thumb was stroking over the back of her hand now, and Jordan moved in close again.

"I guess a *wife* can kiss her *husband* goodbye." She ran her other hand up his neck to the back of his head, slipping her fingers into his hair, and pulling his head down.

He didn't resist. He let her pull him into the kiss. She touched her lips to his, softly at first. She probably should let him go with a simple kiss.

But she couldn't.

He smelled so good. Laundry detergent, soap, coffee, and the cologne from the bathroom.

She sighed and opened her mouth slightly. She wanted more and she pressed closer, lifting on tiptoe.

It took about three seconds, but Fletcher finally gave a soft groan and cupped the back of her head as he deepened the kiss. His mouth opened and he licked along her bottom lip. Heat immediately shot through her and she met the stroke of his tongue with her own.

The ibuprofen or the endorphins or both were kicking in it seemed because she was feeling no pain. She started walking backward, pulling him with her. He nearly stepped on her foot and with a frustrated growl, scooped his hands under her ass and lifted her. His big palms on her mostly bare butt sent licks of fire along her limbs. She wrapped her legs around him and he carried her to the bed. He lowered her, following her down, settling deliciously between her thighs as he pressed her into the mattress.

Oh yes, this was good. This was very good. She needed to be *against* him. It was the craziest urge, but she wanted to feel skin and heat, the weight of him on her, and as many inches of him against as many inches of her as possible.

Jordan linked her ankles at his lower back and lifted her hips trying to get the front of her thong against the front of his nerdy-hot-teacher khakis. She ran her hands up and down his back and happily returned his hungry kisses.

After a few long moments, he shifted, one big hand running down her side to her hip. He squeezed then lifted her as he ground into her. The pressure against her clit was delicious. But she needed more.

"Fletcher," she breathed against his mouth.

His hand ran up her side, dragging the pink silk of her tank with it. His palm covered her left breast, his thumb teasing the hard tip, plucking and rolling until she whimpered.

"Fuck." He lifted his head and stared down at her, breathing hard. Then his gaze dropped to her breast and he gave another low growl, before lowering his head and taking her nipple in his mouth.

He sucked hard and she felt sparks shoot from there through her belly straight to her clit. She rubbed more insistently against him, needing more pressure and friction.

"More," she begged softly. She'd gone from warm and tingly to need-my-clothes-off-now in seconds.

His hand glided down her belly and his fingers slipped under the top edge of her thong. He didn't drag it down, but his hand ran from her hip to her mound and paused.

She arched up into his touch. "Please, Fletcher."

He lifted his head from her nipple and took her mouth in another deep kiss. He ran his thick middle finger down over her clit and she almost cried out from that simple touch alone.

The way she clutched him, her fingers digging into the hard muscles of his back, must have communicated her pleasure, because he continued the slow, sweet strokes over her clit for another few seconds, before dipping lower and pressing his finger inside to the first knuckle.

She wiggled under him trying to get her legs further apart, trying to lift closer, trying to do anything that would help relieve some of the need she was feeling. It had been forever—okay, six months and a few days—since someone else had touched her there. She did fine on her own but it was nothing like *this*.

"More. Harder."

She wanted to feel more of him too. She wanted his shirt off, she wanted to put her hand on his bare cock and squeeze. She wanted him inside her. She wanted it all at once.

Her fingers went to the buttons on the front of his shirt and she started tugging. She knew she needed to unbutton them carefully, but she was fumbling with even that simple task, hovering on the verge of an orgasm the way she was.

"What do you need, Jordan?"

His voice was rough. She moved her head back and forth on the bed.

"I don't know. I'm not sure. Something. More."

"Help me out," he said, moving his finger lazily.

She got three buttons open on his shirt, but it wasn't enough.

What she really wanted was for him to just take over. She'd only been with one other man and for all she knew, they'd been doing everything wrong.

Okay, that was probably unlikely. But there could be so much more to her sex life than she even knew. She was looking forward to Fletcher's experience actually. She wanted him to take the lead. To show her things she might not know. She definitely wasn't used to talking about what she wanted. What she wanted was an orgasm. That was simple enough, wasn't it?

"*You* help *me* out," she said, again trying to lift her hips closer to his finger. "Show me what I've been missing."

For some reason, that was the wrong thing to say. He suddenly froze. He took his hands from her body and rolled to the side. He scrubbed a hand over his face and let out a long sigh.

"Fletcher?" Jordan realized she was breathing a little harder. She rolled toward him. "What's wrong?"

"I can't do this."

Ten

"YOU CAN'T DO THIS?" Jordan knew her eyes were wide even though he wasn't looking at her. "What does that mean?" Her body was still humming, her clit tingling.

He pushed himself to sit up on the edge of the bed. "Do you remember that time when you first tried mascara and you poked yourself in the eye with the stick thing and you ended up with an eye infection and your eye got all red and goopy?"

Her I-was-this-close-to-an-orgasm brain cells were jumping and she had to tell them shut up to process his question.

She sat up, pulling her tank top down. "Um…yes."

"Yeah." He nodded. "Me too."

She stared at his back. "*What?*"

He pushed up from the bed and ran a hand through his hair. "Fletcher?"

He didn't look at her. "Yeah?"

"*That's* what you were thinking about just now?"

"Yeah."

"That's…weird."

"Yeah."

Her body was still buzzing and hot. But now her left eye stung a little at the memory of that infection.

"What the hell does that have to do with anything?" she asked, rubbing her eye.

He shrugged. "I was just thinking about that." He started for the door.

"So that's really it? Seriously?"

She scrambled off the bed but didn't go after him, just stood beside it, her hands on her hips. She had no idea what was going on.

"You know a lot of gross and embarrassing things about me," she commented.

He stopped in the doorway and turned back. "I really do."

She narrowed her eyes. It was true but it wasn't particularly gentlemanly of him to bring it up. Then again, Fletcher had never been all that worried about being a gentleman with her. Nor should he have been.

She stepped forward.

He stepped back.

She rolled her eyes. Then she focused on the front of his pants. And his still-evident erection. "Doesn't seem that my gross, infected eyeball is really that much of a turn-off."

He shifted his weight. "Maybe I should think about the time you went to pee in the bushes at the bonfire party and peed on your shoe accidentally."

"Hey! You try squatting behind a bush in the dark with your pants around your ankles, trying to avoid sticking your ass in poison oak, and *not* pee on anything you shouldn't." She shook her head. "It's amazing it only happened that one time." And she definitely hadn't told anyone else, even about *that* time. Now he was using it against her? "You swore you'd take that to your grave."

"I won't ever say anything about that to anyone else," he said. "But I know it. I can't *not* know it."

Okay, so he knew gross and embarrassing things about her and apparently that was an anti-aphrodisiac.

Great.

If that was true, they were never going to have sex. Because the list of things the two of them knew about one another that they couldn't *not* know, was extensive.

"Well, I know a lot about you too", she said. "Like your credit card number. Which is going to be handy since all my vibrators are in Nashville right now. I need to order a couple. Or head to New Orleans."

Fletcher's whole body went still.

"Not really something I can ask to borrow from a friend like clothes, you know?"

He swallowed, then sucked in a breath. "Speaking of your friends—" he said, his voice definitely rougher. "Charlie is still downstairs."

Jordan's eyes went to the bedroom door. "What?"

"She said you're going to talk about the job at the petting zoo."

Yeah, Jordan definitely remembered that. Charlie was a great saleswoman and, as expected, she'd had plans ready to pitch by the time Jordan had walked into Ellie's last night.

Jordan was willing to take the job *today*. Educational Director for a petting zoo that Charlie intended to grow into a bigger animal park? It sounded fabulous. She could develop educational programs for the park, as well as outreach programs that could keep their visitors from around the country engaged even after their visit to Autre.

But Charlie had promised to give her a full pitch, complete with park sketches, tour, and program ideas today, and she'd told Jordan she could hold Slothcrates, the sloth, while Charlie talked.

Jordan was doing *that* for sure so she was going to string Charlie along for a bit.

"Well, I guess I better get in the shower then." Jordan pulled her tank top up and off, tossing it in the general direction of Fletcher's hamper.

His eyes, predictably, immediately went to her breasts. Until she slipped out of the thong.

Then his gaze tracked over her whole body. His eyes were hot, and the path they took from her breasts to her toes and back up again, slowly, felt hot and tingly. But she stood, letting him look.

His jaw was tight as he took in the sight of her completely naked. For the first time ever.

Jordan couldn't forget that *tiny* detail.

She also definitely didn't miss the way Fletcher looking at her completely naked made *her* feel.

Annoyed.

Because he wasn't going to do anything about it.

"I guess you get the answer to your question from yesterday," she said.

"Which question?"

"How much I shave." She pivoted on her heel and sashayed toward the bathroom door, satisfied that at least she wasn't the only one who was leaving the room worked up. And she was going to have a lot easier time taking care of her problem on her own than he was at the moment.

She felt his gaze on her back and looked over her shoulder with a small smile. "You didn't know about *that*."

"Nice… magnolia," he said of the tiny flower tattoo on the lower corner of her right shoulder blade. It was the Louisiana state flower.

"That also got a little itchy," she said. "You want to come check for any other new ink or piercings?"

He knew about all the rest. She had a tiny alligator on the outside of her left ankle—Fletcher did too—and the Oscar the Grouch tattoo on her hip. She had four piercings in each ear, and Fletcher had gone with her for three of them and had helped her do the fourth at home. That had hurt like a son of a bitch. And it had gotten infected too.

"Well, I wouldn't want you to sprain your ankle. Again."

She stopped and turned back. He had *not* just mentioned how she'd sprained her fucking ankle the first time she and Jason had tried to have shower sex. Wow.

He definitely knew a lot. About a lot.

"I've gotten *a lot* steadier on my feet," she told him, haughtily.

"That right?"

"Yep. Even just standing on one foot while the other one is—"

Suddenly he was there, right in front of her. He'd crossed the room swiftly and was now taking up all of her personal space and making it hard to breathe.

She backed up and he followed. She bumped into the wall behind her.

They stared at each other for a long moment, breathing hard.

Then their mouths crashed together.

Fletcher's big hands dropped to her hips. Jordan's fingers went to the buttons on his shirt.

It was really convenient that she was already naked. His hands gripped her hips as he pressed her into the wall and kissed her hungrily.

She pushed his shirt from his broad shoulders. He flexed his arms, letting it drop to the floor. He lifted his head as his hands went to his belt buckle.

"Is this what you want, Mrs. Landry?"

She licked her lips. "God, yes. Especially the Mrs. Landry thing." That was hot as hell.

His eyes flared with heat and he reached into his back pocket. He pulled out his wallet, flipped it open, and withdrew a condom, took it between his teeth, then tossed the wallet to the carpet.

Jordan sucked in a breath. That condom wasn't in there for her. Who knew when he'd put that in his wallet? Had it been before a specific date? Or did he always have one with him? Those thoughts made her acutely aware of how many more times he'd done this, and that it had been with many more people. It made this all feel a little taboo. And it made a hot shaft of desire arc through her.

He was hers now. This sexy, charming, funny, amazing man was all hers. All of those women in the past, any woman in the future who might have hoped that condom was for her, were out of luck now.

He undid the button on his pants, lowered his zipper, and pushed his boxers out of the way.

And Jordan saw Fletcher's cock for the first time. She swallowed hard. Then reached for him.

She took his shaft in her fist and he let out a long, slow breath.

He braced a hand on the wall by her head and when she looked up, his eyes were closed and his jaw tight. The condom was now gripped in his other hand.

Oh, she liked having an effect on the big, much more experienced guy. She squeezed slightly. He groaned. She stroked. He growled. And grabbed her wrist.

"Enough."

"What? That wasn't *nearly* enough," she protested.

He ripped the condom open and moved her hand so he could roll it down his length. His impressive length. His impressively long, hard, thick…

The next thing she knew, he'd lifted her again and had her pressed against the wall.

They were eye to eye, her hot center pressed against his cock, her breasts against his chest. She gripped his shoulders as he gripped her ass.

"Love your hands, but I've felt them before," he said, his voice thick and rough. "There's something else I want to feel right now."

"You haven't felt my hands like *that*." Her voice was soft and breathless.

"True." The corner of his mouth kicked up. "We can come back to that. But need your sweet pussy now, Jordan."

Her breath rushed out of her. Whoa. Fletcher saying the word pussy to her was…something. She felt hot and melty and achy. "Yes," she replied softly. "God yes."

He didn't bother to kick his shoes off, he didn't even push his pants any further down, he just shifted her against the wall, pulled his hips back slightly, then pressed forward.

She felt him at her entrance, then the slow, delicious slide of his thickness into her. Her breath caught and she let her head fall back against the wall. It was a tight fit. It had been a while. And Fletcher was big.

She wanted every inch. She tried to shift or arch, to *move*, to bring him more fully in, deeper. But pinned to the wall like this, she was at his mercy.

And it was amazing.

She trusted him completely and the idea of turning everything over to him was still a dream come true.

"*Fletcher*," she moaned.

"God," he ground out between clenched teeth. "You feel fucking amazing."

"Ditto. More," she coaxed.

"Don't want to hurt you."

She opened her eyes—she hadn't even realized they'd slid shut—and met his stormy gaze. "Not possible."

"Jordan," he groaned. But he pulled back and thrust again, deeper.

Her toes literally curled. "*Yes*. More."

"I've wanted this for so long. I'm trying not to go too fast."

Hearing how much he wanted her, in his words but also his tone, made her inner muscles tighten and he gave a reactive groan.

"Please, Fletcher, more." The need and heat were swirling in her lower belly and pussy, coiling tighter and she needed release. She put her hand between them, circling her clit.

His eyes dropped to watch for a few seconds, his breathing ragged. Then he let out a long, low, "Fuuuuck."

He gripped her more tightly and thrust deep. Then again. And again. Hard and fast, stroking her deep, making her body tingle from where they were joined to her nipples to the top of her head. She felt her whole body tightening and straining toward an orgasm.

Her finger moved faster, pressing and circling. She was well acquainted with how to give herself pleasure but it was so much *more* with Fletcher buried deep inside her.

"Yes, yes, Fletcher."

"God, Jordan."

His hips drove into her and she felt her climax building. She circled faster, lifting her other hand to her breast, and squeezing her nipple. Fletcher's fingers gripped her ass. His breath was hot and fast against her cheek.

She felt it coming and she tightened around him. Her heels dug into his ass, her pussy clenched around his cock, holding on as she cried out his name, her orgasm rolling through her hot and fast.

"Yes!" Fletcher thrust deep, then came, his body tightening as the swells of pleasure were still coursing through her.

Jordan clamped her thighs around his hips, loving the feel of him letting go like that.

He leaned into her, pinning her even more securely, as he rested his forehead on the wall over her shoulder and sucked in long, full breaths.

She wrapped her arms around him, holding on tight.

A couple of minutes passed before he finally lifted his head and looked at her.

She smiled up at him.

He blew out a breath. Then shook his head. "That was not how I planned for this morning to go."

Then he shifted back and let her slide down the wall. Once she was on her feet, he stepped into the bathroom, she assumed to deal with the condom. She heard the water run and she looked around. But there wasn't anything for her to do. Getting dressed didn't make sense since she really was getting in the shower soon.

He came back out, zipped and buttoned up again. He bent to grab his shirt and shrugged into it. His gaze tracked over her still naked body once before coming back to her face as he fastened the buttons.

"That was…"

She lifted a brow. "If that sentence ends in anything other than 'even better than all the times I've imagined fucking you against the wall', just keep it to yourself."

He looked surprised, then turned on, then like he was fighting being turned on. He nodded. "It was definitely that."

"Good answer." She gave him a smile. "Now have a nice day, Mr. Landry. And be sure to stay away from the south side of the football field. Or at least keep your pants on this time if you do go over there."

Yeah, she might've accidentally peed on her shoe at that bonfire party, but she had *not* gotten poison oak on her ass. Unlike Fletcher, who had taken a blanket and a sophomore girl named Ashley to that field one Saturday night.

He hadn't been able to sit down comfortably for three days. He hadn't told anyone, except Jordan, about the poison oak and where he had the rash.

Of course, she'd gotten him a bottle of calamine lotion and a pair of boxers that said *Burnin' Love* across the butt, but she'd otherwise kept his secret.

He wasn't the only one who knew embarrassing things.

But they wanted each other anyway. He'd better remember that.

She blew him a kiss, then stepped into the bathroom and pulled the door shut behind her.

BY THE TIME she was showered, dried, dressed, and downstairs, Fletcher was gone.

Charlie was sitting at the kitchen table, sipping coffee and, well, working it seemed. She had her electronic tablet open along with two folders spread out in front of her and a pen in hand. Charlie was a go-getter and Jordan doubted she ever really had downtime. From what Charlie had shared with her on the phone and via email over the past few months, she was growing Boys of the Bayou Gone Wild by leaps and bounds. Which was a funny, yet appropriate phrase to use in reference to a petting zoo, Jordan supposed.

"I need to go to Ellie's," Jordan told her without preamble. "I need some grits and strong coffee right now."

Charlie lifted a brow. "Your new husband made you coffee and breakfast."

In spite of the way her stomach flipped every time she heard or thought the word *husband*, Jordan shook her head. "I had some of his coffee upstairs. It's too weak for this. Plus, there's no way he made grits."

For the same reason that no one in the Landry family ever

made gumbo or jambalaya or bread pudding—it simply would never measure up to what they could get at Ellie's.

"No, I think he made you bacon and French toast."

Oh my God. Jordan suddenly felt a little choked up. He *had* made her French toast.

Sex and French toast and bacon. She was loving married life.

Jordan moaned. "Okay, I'm taking the bacon and French toast to go. But I need stronger coffee. And… grits too. I worked up an appetite." She gave Charlie a grin.

Her friend shook her head. "I know. I was really regretting taking my earbuds out of my purse."

"Sorry." Jordan wasn't sorry. Though she *was* still a little confused by Fletcher's attempt to refrain from their morning fun.

"I just went on a little walk," Charlie said. "Hey, that dress looks great on you."

Jordan looked down at the red sundress. "Oh thanks. I appreciate this. *And* the underwear."

"There are more of both in the bag over there." Charlie gestured toward the purple roller bag that was sitting next to the kitchen's center island.

"You're a lifesaver," Jordan told her sincerely. "I'll email Jason's assistant today, but it will be a couple of days before my stuff gets here."

"You're welcome to anything in my closet or my bathroom," Charlie promised.

Jordan grabbed her purse off of the back of the chair where Fletcher must've hung it last night, put three pieces of bacon between two pieces of French toast like a sandwich and wrapped the whole thing in a paper towel. Then they headed out to Charlie's car. Jordan could already taste the grits and couldn't wait to have a cup of strong chicory coffee in hand.

Ellie greeted them with smiles and hugs and they had coffee and beignets to get them started within minutes of taking seats at the big back table where the Landry family usually gathered. At this time of day, they were all out working, but around lunchtime there would be a handful and at dinnertime even more.

The French toast sandwich and half the beignets were gone by the time the grits and Naomi showed up ten minutes later.

Naomi took in the plate of fried donuts, the huge cup of coffee, and the bowl of grits. "A pitcher of water, some eggs, and toast, please?" she asked Ellie.

"You've got it," Ellie told her.

"You haven't eaten yet?" Charlie asked her.

It was a fair question. Naomi's grandmother and mother were both amazing cooks and lived within easy walking distance of Naomi's little house. It was a rare meal that Naomi ate outside of one of their kitchens. She always said that was one of the things she had missed the most living in California. They'd had a cook who had been amazing, but it hadn't been the same as home cooking out of her grandmother's cast-iron skillet.

Naomi shook her head, looping her purse over the back of her chair. "That's all for you," she told Jordan. "The grits are going to soak up the alcohol in your stomach, but you're gonna need some protein and a ton of water to get you feeling better."

Jordan regarded her friends.

Charlie's pale skin had just a touch of a tan now that she'd spent her summer in Louisiana. Her long hair fell in waves past her shoulder blades and had streaks of lighter gold that were hard to tell if they came from the sun or a salon. Her make-up was fully done from her arched eyebrows to her pink lips. She had a quick smile, talked fast, and was a problem solver, but she was spontaneous and often leapt before she looked. Then dealt with the consequences.

In contrast, Naomi had always been cool and collected. She was the epitome of had-her-shit-together. She planned ahead, was ready for anything, and handled everything with grace and class.

Her warm, medium brown skin was smooth and flawless this morning. Because of her time spent getting her makeup and hair done while acting, she now preferred an easy, natural look. Her long black hair was in braids and the only hint of makeup was mascara on her incredibly long lashes and a hint of berry color on her lips. She wore a simple white sleeveless blouse with denim capris and sandals. She looked relaxed and casual and perfectly put-together.

And while Charlie had pulled Jordan into crazy, spontaneous plans, Naomi was the calming influence. She mothered them all, but in a low-key, non-judgmental way that they all loved. Having Naomi around meant never being without a Band-Aid, a breath mint, a tampon, or duct tape. And yes, Jordan had borrowed all of those things from Naomi at one point or another.

Naomi was also the voice of reason more often than not, giving level-headed, thoughtful advice.

Jordan needed Naomi right now for sure.

She leaned in. "So, my new *husband* didn't want to have sex with me this morning."

Naomi frowned. "What?"

"But you *did* have sex," Charlie said. "Right? I mean, that's what it sounded like."

"We did. After we made out and argued."

"You argued while you were making out?" Naomi asked.

"No, after he stopped right in the middle of making out and reminded me of my eye infection."

Naomi and Charlie looked at her in confusion. Then they looked at one another. Then back to her.

"You have an eye infection?" Charlie asked.

"I *had* an eye infection," Jordan said. "When I was *thirteen*. At least that was the one he was referring to."

Charlie wasn't from Autre. She'd spent her summers down here with her grandparents and cousins, but she'd grown up in Shreveport, so had missed a few of the childhood shenanigans.

Naomi had retired from acting when she was fourteen and had moved back to Autre. While she'd been living in California, she'd visited and spent holidays in Louisiana when she was able, but neither of these women had been around to see some of Jordan's more embarrassing moments. Unlike Fletcher.

"I mean, it was gross," Jordan admitted. "But why was he thinking of it at *that* moment? And why would he bring it up even if it did come to mind?"

"What were you doing exactly?" Charlie asked.

"I was half naked, we were on the bed, his hand was in my panties."

Just then Ellie arrived with her eggs, toast, and water.

"And he just suddenly stopped and brought up an eye infection?" Charlie asked.

"Yep."

"But then you did end up having sex?" Naomi clarified.

"Yes. But he was definitely trying to resist. We argued and I took my clothes off and he…came around." Jordan couldn't help her little grin as Naomi, Charlie, and Ellie all snorted. "But—" she said the next second with a frown. "Why did he mention my eye? Oh!" she added, remembering their bickering. "He also brought up the time I peed on my shoe at a party."

"Ew. What?" Naomi said.

"Don't 'ew' me, Naomi LeClaire. I was at a party and all we had were bushes. You're too classy for me and we both know it, but you love me anyway," Jordan said.

"Of course I do and I am not. I've peed in the bushes myself but on your shoe? That's an amateur move," Naomi told her. "You've been squatting in bushes since you were little and didn't want to take time to run inside at crawfish boils."

Jordan laughed. "*Anyway,* I didn't expect my husband to bring it up while I was all hot and bothered and begging him for more."

"Sounds like he was trying for a distraction," Ellie, Fletcher's *grandmother,* said, propping a hand on her hip. She'd been shamelessly listening to the conversation.

But Jordan didn't even blush. The Landry family had very few filters. And, after all, she and Fletcher were married.

Honestly, even to Fletcher's grandmother—even if Ellie wasn't a typical grandmother in any way—it had to be a surprise that he'd pulled back when they'd been getting hot and heavy.

"A distraction?" Charlie asked. "Why would he want to be distracted right *then*?"

"So things didn't go too fast. Lord knows he's been waiting for this girl for a long time. He was probably pretty worked up," Ellie said.

"And he didn't have time to spread out the rose petals, light candles, and tell you all of the things he loves about you from head to toe," Naomi said with a grin.

Ellie nodded. "That's a good point."

Jordan frowned. "What do you mean?"

"It may have hit him that this morning wasn't romantic enough," Naomi said. "I mean, I assume you weren't up for much last night. So this was your first time."

Jordan thought about that. Okay, the Landrys were a huge, grand-gestures, over-the-top-romance-crazy family. And yeah, it had been their first time. But…it had been hot. Why did it have to be a big, romantic production?

But that did make sense.

"Well, he should know he doesn't have to do that for *me*."

"Why would he know that?" Ellie asked.

"Because he knows me better than anyone."

"But he doesn't know what you like *in bed*," Ellie said, matter-of-factly, as if they were talking about Fletcher not knowing how she took her coffee or liked her eggs.

And hey, he'd sure known how to make her happy against the wall.

"But he has to know I'm not the rose petals and candles type," Jordan insisted.

"How?" Ellie asked again. "You've done everything together since you were tiny. Except this. This is a whole new world for you."

Jordan slumped in her chair. "I thought being such good friends for so long would make this really easy."

"Being friends is important," Ellie agreed. "But marriage is more than that. It's more than sex too. It's a blend of those things and a whole bunch of other stuff."

Jordan waited for Ellie to elaborate on the "other stuff". "Such as?"

"You'll see."

Jordan's eyes widened. "No advance preparation? No insight?"

"Well, every couple's stuff is a little different," Ellie said. "Hell, Leo and I have done it twice and each time the stuff's been different."

Jordan frowned. "So…how do I prepare for the stuff? How do I know we'll figure that out?"

"That's where the friendship and sex come in," Ellie told her.

Jordan blew out a breath. "That is very vague."

"It's actually very specific," Ellie said. "When the stuff happens, you lean on the friendship and the sex to get through. And that's why your friendship is important. And why you need to figure the sex out. Which, it seems, Fletcher realizes."

"We need to figure the sex out? We can't just keep doing it?" Jordan asked.

"Take your time," Ellie told her. "Enjoy getting to know each other this way. Just necking and heavy petting can be a damned good time."

Charlie snorted. "Necking and heavy petting? You sound like an old lady," she teased the seventy-something year old.

"And making out is such a great term? What does that even mean?" Ellie asked. "At least heavy petting sounds like what it is —running your hands all over each other and rubbing and stroking—"

"Okay." Charlie held up her hand. "Got it. You're right. Back to Jordan and Fletcher." She rolled her eyes. "So Fletcher didn't want to just jump right in this morning."

"Right. He *really* tried not to," Jordan said.

Naomi nodded. "Well, if he was going to overthink the sex thing and put a bunch of pressure on himself, it would definitely be with you, the woman he always wants everything to be perfect for. The woman he always has to fix everything for."

"I don't want him to feel weird about sex with me," Jordan said. The sex that morning had been *great*. It had been so hot. And this was her and Fletcher. *Nothing* should be weird. She'd hated the last few months of awkwardness since he'd asked her to stay in Autre and she'd said no…

Oh.

Shit.

Jordan felt her spine stiffen as the realization hit her.

He'd asked her to choose between him and Jason. And she'd chosen Jason.

She'd more or less rejected him four months ago.

She'd also chosen Jason when she and Fletcher had been in Galveston and it had been clear that he wanted more from her. She'd pushed him away. Because of Jason.

Then the moment things went bad with Jason, Fletcher was there for her, and she jumped into his arms and asked him to save her.

Oh, wow. Yeah. Maybe Fletcher had a reason to doubt this sudden change in their relationship and just how solid it was.

"People's hearts override their heads all the time," Ellie said.

Her words hit Jordan hard.

She thought maybe in this case it was Fletcher's head that was overriding his heart, though.

Someone called to Ellie from the bar and she stroked her hand over Jordan's hair in a familiar, affectionate gesture before turning and going to tend to her customer.

Jordan sat staring at her coffee mug.

All of this made sense. Fletcher did like fixing things for her. He definitely liked being the guy she could turn to no matter what. He'd been there for her yesterday in spite of everything that had come before that. And now, they were married. And he would definitely take getting that right seriously. Every part of that.

"I say enjoy it," Naomi said.

Jordan looked up at her friend. "Enjoy Fletcher being stressed out about having sex with me?"

Naomi shook her head. "Let the hot, sweet, charming, fun guy who wants to take care of you do his thing. Wallow in him wanting to make the sex the best you've ever had."

Charlie nodded. "Agreed. Fletcher has always been great at making you happy. Just sit back and let him. He was the one who always remembered and celebrated the day you *met*, for God's sake. Now you've got that stuff twenty-four-seven. Enjoy it."

Jordan rolled her eyes. But yes, Fletcher *had* always remembered the anniversary of the day they'd met in first grade. And he always gave her a card and, when they got older, took her out to celebrate the start of their friendship. Which did seem a little over-the-top, but was also perfectly Fletcher's M.O. Her girl-friends had always swooned over it.

"So, he thinks the sex has to be perfect. Romantic and sexy, and —"

"And you have to come hard multiple times, seeing stars, and praising his name," Charlie said.

"Don't all guys think that that's how it should be?" Naomi asked.

Jordan shrugged. "Actually, in the beginning they probably do. But after you're with a guy for eleven years, he relaxes a little bit."

"So, you and Jason did become like an old married couple?" Charlie asked.

"It's just that when you're with someone for so long and you're living together, you're going to have nights when you're too tired or when your head hurts. Or when you're just not in the mood," Jordan said. "And yeah, Jason and I got to that point."

Naomi sighed. "In some ways that would be really nice."

Charlie laughed. "Speak for yourself. I'm still in the newly dating phase and I am very happy with all of the sexual energy."

Naomi rolled her eyes. "Oh yes, we know. You and Griffin can hardly keep your hands off each other. But what I mean is, it would be nice to be to that comfortable place where you can just be yourself and where you know that the sex can be rocking and hot, but it can also be sweet and soft and it can also just be… nothing. You can just sit on the couch and watch TV and then go to bed and sleep together."

Yeah, that *was* nice too, Jordan agreed. She and Jason hadn't drifted apart because of any of that. If his music hadn't become the center of his life and taken him down a path she didn't want to follow, they would probably still be together.

And she would have missed out on being with Fletcher.

She was really glad Jason's career had taken off.

Jordan picked up her spoon and dug into her grits with renewed optimism.

Naomi waited until she'd taken a few bites, then pulled the bowl away and pushed the eggs in front of her. She also filled a glass of water. All without a word.

Jordan rolled her eyes, but grinned and reached for the water. "Okay, enough about me. What's been going on with you girls?"

"Well, of course, Charlie's been falling in love," Naomi said smiling at their friend.

Jordan nodded. "Of course. How's that going?"

Charlie's cheeks got a little pink, but her smile was bright and instantaneous. "It's going great. He's amazing. And I've never loved Autre more."

Jordan was grateful that she and her girlfriends had stayed in touch in spite of her moving away. They emailed regularly and texted. She also talked to both Naomi and Charlie on the phone on a fairly regular basis. She knew Charlie was head over heels in love and it was awesome to see.

"How's your grandma and everybody?" Jordan asked Naomi.

"Ornery and doesn't listen to anybody. So completely normal," Naomi said with a little laugh.

"Your grandma or everybody?" Jordan teased.

Naomi nodded. "Yes."

The LeClaires were like the Landrys in a lot of ways. They were loud, loving, opinionated, and had deep roots in Autre. Which, of course, also meant that they were as involved in the community—and the gossip in that community—as the older Landrys were. In fact, Naomi's grandfather Armand was a regular at the end of Ellie's bar. He and Leo had been telling each other stories and one upping one another for at least fifty years.

Just then male laughter boomed from that side of the room and Jordan, Naomi, and Charlie exchanged grins. Speaking of the devils. Leo and Armand were in here right now. Jordan was surprised *her* grandpa wasn't there with them. He would be by lunchtime, she knew. The whole thing made her chest feel warm. She was going to be able to see them all every day. This was definitely where she wanted to be.

"I could tell you about the new Director of Education position that's opened up at the Boys of the Bayou Gone Wild," Charlie told Jordan with a grin.

And it was not just a happy or excited grin. This was an I-have-a-huge-plan-and-I'm-so-going-to-talk-you-into-it grin. Jordan had seen that grin several times growing up. She'd ended up with a drastic haircut after seeing that grin once. She'd ended up on an airplane to Orlando—without permission at age sixteen—after seeing that grin another time.

Charlie Landry could talk anyone into anything.

Thank God, she could also talk almost all of the adults in her family *out* of being mad at her and that charm had extended to Jordan's mom and dad. She'd never seen anything like it. She'd grown up thinking Charlotte Arabella Clementine Landry was magic. She wasn't so sure she *didn't* believe that now.

Jordan held up a hand. "Do I have a sloth on my lap right now?"

Charlie sighed. "No, you do not."

"That is one of my conditions. I need to be holding a sloth when you tell me about the job. You promised."

"I'm shocked you can remember anything from last night after the dart game with Zander," Naomi said.

Jordan groaned. "Don't remind me. Zander and I are going to have to come to an understanding."

"Okay, I can wait. For *a little bit*," Charlie said. "But I feel like the subject is going to come up anyway."

Charlie was smiling at something over Jordan's shoulder. Or someone. Jordan turned to look.

Sure enough, Ellie's front door had just opened and a petite, pretty brunette Jordan didn't recognize was making a beeline for their table. She was the epitome of bouncing energy. She seemed to actually be vibrating as she came across the floor.

"Who is that?" Jordan asked, watching the woman, who had an exuberant smile and couldn't have been more than five-foot-one, come toward them.

"That's Fiona," Charlie said. "She's the one who helps us obtain our new animals. She runs an animal park in Florida and is a longtime friend of Griffin's. She's the one who brought us the lemurs and the sloth. Along with some other things."

"Oh my God, hi!" Fiona greeted them, pulling out a chair, dropped into it, and reached for Charlie's glass of tea. She took a long drink, then sat back in her chair with a big sigh. "I'm here!"

"Well, hi," Charlie said with a laugh. "Zander let you go with a slap on the wrist?"

Fiona fanned her face. "I begged him to handcuff me and he said no." She grinned. "But he did call me darlin' with that drawl, so there's that."

"Zander picked you up for something?" Naomi asked.

Jordan had to agree that sounded out of character. Zander was willing to do what it took to keep Autre safe, but he didn't get riled up about much. She couldn't imagine what Fiona could have done to get him to actually pull her over.

"Well, I rolled through the stop sign right in front of him, on purpose," Fiona said.

"And he knew she wanted him to stop her," Charlie said with an eye roll.

"Oh, got you. Zander *is* fun to flirt with," Naomi said.

Jordan could confirm that. Zander was like a little brother to her, but he was a lot of fun and definitely good looking.

"Fiona has a boyfriend back in Florida," Charlie said. "They run the animal park together."

Fiona waved her hand as if that was unimportant. "Oh, Colin and I aren't that serious. I'm mostly with him for the giraffes."

"You have giraffes?" Jordan asked, leaning in.

"Of course. What is the point of having an animal park if you can't have giraffes?" Fiona asked.

Jordan looked at Charlie. "Are giraffes on our list?"

Charlie laughed. "I just got Griffin to say yes to the porcupines. We'll have to work up to giraffes."

"Porcupines?" Jordan turned wide eyes to Fiona. "When are we getting those?"

"Today. It's why I'm here. Well, and because I've started loving these regular trips to Louisiana."

"What else did you bring?" Naomi asked.

Fiona slid Charlie a little grin. "Remember what you asked me about?"

Charlie gasped. "You got me a zebra?"

Jordan sat up a little straighter.

Fiona shook her head. "I told you, zebras can be real assholes. Especially if they get spooked or defensive. So you really have to be ready for those. You'll need to have the pen ready and everything.

"But you can get one?"

"Of course I can get one," Fiona said. "In fact, I can get you two. But I think we should talk more about the red pandas. They are way more fun for people to watch. Zebras are basically striped horses. They'll roam around and graze. Red pandas are playful and cute. And take up less space."

Charlie shrugged. "Why can't we have both?"

Fiona laughed. "That's my girl."

Charlie looked at Jordan. "Fiona, this is Jordan. She's going to be our new Director of Education. What do you think, Jordan? Would red pandas be a good addition?"

Jordan couldn't believe she was actually having this conversation. They were actually talking about getting a zebra and red pandas? And she got to have some input?

"Wait, you're Jordan?" Fiona asked.

She nodded. "Hi."

"Oh my God, you're the one who just broke up with Jason Young and married Fletcher," Fiona said.

Jordan shook her head. It was weird that all of that had happened only yesterday. She felt like it had been months ago. She supposed that meant she had definitely moved on. "Yup, that's me."

"Zander said if I saw you, I was supposed to tell you he really thinks you both need to grow up a little bit and figure out how to play darts without tequila," Fiona said. She shook her head. "The guy looks like crap. Still hot, don't get me wrong, but like crap."

Jordan nodded. "Zander is one thousand percent correct, and we will be having that conversation when I see him next."

Fiona laughed. "Okay, so what do you think about red pandas?"

"I think red pandas are amazing and I can't believe that we're actually talking about this," Jordan said. She glanced at Charlie. "But I also don't remember taking the position as educational director."

"Oh, you're going to take it," Charlie said. "If I can talk you into streaking across William DuPont's backyard during Fourth of July fireworks, I can talk you into this."

Jordan groaned at the memory. Charlie Landry was trouble. "In my defense," she said quickly for the other two women, "William was supposed to be having a party that night in his backyard, but I knew it had gotten moved to Landon Bassett's house." She had streaked across an empty, dark backyard. And she'd insisted that Charlie still pay her the twenty dollars she dared her. The dare hadn't included how many people would be in attendance at the party. "And it wasn't full on streaking, I had a bra and panties on."

Charlie laughed. "Still, you know you can't resist me."

Jordan did in fact know that. It seemed no one could.

"I can only assume that you knew the parrots you were bringing us would cuss like sailors."

All four women turned to look at the man who had just approached the table.

From where Jordan was seated, she had to tip her head way back to look up at him.

"Hey, Knox," she greeted.

Knox was tall. And big. With his wide chest and shoulders, big muscles, long hair, and scowl, he looked like a bad boy member of a rock band or motorcycle club.

Jordan knew him well. He'd moved to Autre in high school and had taken every high school defensive football award for the next three years. But underneath all of that bad boy exterior, he was an even bigger nerd than Fletcher or Zeke. He'd been their valedictorian and he was now Autre's city manager.

His eyes flickered to her and he gave her a slight nod, but he clearly hadn't come over here to talk to her. His gaze bounced right back to Fiona.

"Why do you think I brought them to you? I can't have parrots saying, 'you're a motherfucker' at my animal park," Fiona said. "We run a clean family attraction."

"And Boys of the Bayou Gone Wild is going to be what?" Knox asked. "An R-rated animal park?"

Fiona grinned. "Wow, you're hot and nerdy and a prude. I have no idea why that's attractive." She tipped her head, studying him. "Maybe it's because I like the idea of making you do naughty things."

Knox ignored that. "I've gotten phone calls. And emails. I assume the tourists complain to Sawyer and Charlie and the rest. But the locals complain to *me*."

"About the parrots?" Fiona asked. She didn't seem apologetic. "What do they expect you to do? You don't work for the petting zoo."

"No, I work for Autre. When people in Autre have problems, and they're not sure where else to go, or they're not getting satisfactory answers"—He cast a glance at Charlie—"I get to hear about it."

"Hey, we dealt with the parrots." Charlie sat up a little straighter, looking offended. "They don't swear unless they're together, so we spread them out. There are two up by the barn, one in the otter enclosure, and two over by the lemurs and the sloth. They're behaving well now."

"We have swearing parrots?" Jordan asked.

Fiona laughed. "Only two. The others just mimic them. Those two only swear at each other. And when they have an audience. They do it, get laughs, and it eggs them on. When they're separated, everything is fine."

Jordan glanced up at Knox, knowing he would not appreciate what she was about to ask, but still asked, "What all do they say to each other?"

"One of them will say, 'you're a motherfucker' and the other will respond with, 'shut the fuck up.' Then the rest will repeat it." Fiona grinned. "They obviously don't know what it means. They're just going for the attention."

"I can't believe you brought those to us," Knox said.

"They were a special request from Owen Landry." Fiona sat

back in her chair and crossed her legs. The move caused the skirt she was wearing to hike up on her thigh. Then she inched it up a bit more. "I can't say no to men begging me for things with a Louisiana drawl. I'm weak. I'll say yes to almost anything."

Jordan looked up at Knox. Fiona's body language, and tone of voice, indicated clearly she was flirting with him. He seemed unimpressed. Though he did check out her thigh.

"You're a problem for me," he informed her. "The first time I ever saw that gigantic purple truck, I knew you were going to be."

"It's funny how every time you see that big purple truck parked out front of Ellie's, you head straight in here though," Fiona said. "Seems if you wanted to avoid me, it would be quite easy. Instead, it's like a bat signal or something."

"But if I avoid you, I'm not able to inform you of the problems you're causing for me."

"And how many times has you informing me of something you don't like resulted in me stopping?" Fiona asked.

Knox sighed. "I keep hoping that the more times I express myself, the more pause it gives you when you're back in Florida thinking of ways to make this petting zoo even crazier."

Fiona gave him a sly smile. "If that's your way of trying to find out if I think about you when I'm back in Florida, the answer is absolutely. And I love knowing that you're thinking of me even when I'm not here."

"You love knowing that I'm cursing your name?"

"I don't consider *Oh God, Fiona*, exactly cursing but you can call it whatever you want."

Knox's jaw tightened. "Huge. Problem."

Fiona just batted her eyes at him. "By the way, it would make it easier for me to 'curse' *your* name, if I knew what it was." She used air quotes with her fingers around *curse*.

"Knox."

She shook her head. "Online it says your name is F. Knox. What's the F stand for?"

Jordan looked up at the big man. She didn't even know this. He'd always just gone by F. Knox. Even teachers had referred to him as Knox. When his name had been announced at football games or read off in class it had been simply, "F. Knox." She supposed at some point or another they all knew Knox was his last name, but no one had pressed for his first. He was just Knox. He also never really had been a guy you pressed for information he didn't want you to have.

"It's just Knox."

Fiona shrugged. "Okay, play hard to get. I work with wild animals all the time. It doesn't intimidate me. It just makes me more intrigued."

The way Knox sighed made Jordan think he was actually considering giving Fiona his real name just to keep her from being intrigued.

But in the end, he just shook his head. "Email me a copy of the licensing paperwork for whatever you brought to town this time," he said.

"You just like getting emails from me because of the hugs and kisses at the end right?" Fiona asked.

"Just email the paperwork." He suddenly sounded tired.

Jordan took a drink of water to hide her smile behind her glass. Watching someone not only not be intimidated by Knox, but also wear him down, was something. She wasn't exactly intimidated by the guy. She'd hung out with and partied with him in high school. He was a good guy, and even had a sense of humor under the gruff exterior. But he was definitely not the easy-going, playboy, party guy that most of the Landry boys were.

Knox turned, without a formal goodbye, and stalked out of the bar.

"Bye, Ferdinand!" Fiona called after him.

Charlie shook her head and laughed. "You really like messing with him, don't you?"

"Oh yeah, he's hot when he gets all grumpy and bossy."

"Did Owen actually ask you for cussing parrots?" Charlie asked. "How did he even know you had them?"

"Owen asked for parrots," Fiona said. "But I picked the cussing ones for Knox."

Jordan finished her eggs and her second glass of water that Naomi had kept filled and had to admit she felt much better. Plus she was ready to see this petting zoo and meet the animals she was going to be interacting with.

She pushed back from the table and stood. "Okay, sloth time."

Charlie nodded. "Finally." She looked at Fiona. "We can take the new animals over and show Jordan around."

"I want to come," Naomi said. "I have a little time before I need to get back."

Jordan took in the three women as they stood and gathered their things. She already adored and had great memories with Naomi and Charlie and was thrilled with the promise of future girls' nights. Now it seemed that Fiona fit right in and she couldn't wait to get to know her better.

She glanced around the bar. It was one of the most important places in her life. It was full, even now, of people she loved, and she knew that she could stop in here at any time on any day and find people who would support her, love her, and make her laugh.

And then there was her hot, charming, sweet, mixed-up husband.

"What's that smile about?" Naomi asked her as she pushed her chair in and pulled the strap of her purse up onto her shoulder.

Jordan sighed. "I'm just so glad that Jason dumped me."

Naomi laughed and gave her a side hug. "Me too, honey, me too."

CHAPTER
Twelve

HE COULDN'T BELIEVE he'd fucked Jordan against the wall in his bedroom.

It was the thirty-seventh time he'd thought that since leaving his house that morning.

It was still true.

Their first time, their first time as *husband and wife*, had been a quickie against the wall? Really?

His phone dinged with a text and he reached for it, hoping it wasn't Jordan.

Please don't let her be sending me some sexy text or a naked picture or…

Zander: *I hate you.*

Fletcher grinned at the message. *What's wrong, little brother?*

Zander: *I got your new wife drunk for you so you didn't have to work through your performance anxiety last night, and you didn't even stop in to buy me breakfast? Dick move.*

Fletcher frowned. But then blew out a breath. He wouldn't have called it "performance anxiety", but yeah, he'd had a little *general* anxiety about his first time with Jordan. He'd wanted it to be perfect. And yeah, Zeke had gotten into his head about all the stupid shit he and Jordan had done and been through and knew about one another and it had reminded him that he knew everything about her...except how to rock her world in the bedroom.

And he *definitely* wanted to rock her world in the bedroom. Needed to, even.

He *always* knew exactly what Jordan needed. He always made things perfect for her.

Sex could be no different.

And for that, he needed a little fucking time.

They'd gone from having a fight in April and not speaking much for *four months* to married in the span of a few hours. He'd seen her naked breasts for the first time ever the morning *after* their wedding.

They were going fast and rather than being a big-romantic-swoop-in-to-save-the-day gesture, his grandmother had pointed out that the wedding was just the *start* to everything he was going to need to give Jordan as her husband.

Then his asshole brother had gotten in his head about that night being their first together as well as their wedding night and his usual need to make everything perfect for Jordan had reared its head and...

He'd panicked.

Then that morning his sexy, sweet wife, who he'd wanted for three fucking years, had been all in. In spite of thinking about one of the gross things he knew about her to temper his desire, he hadn't been able to walk out of that bedroom after all.

So he'd fucked her against the wall.

For their first time.

No, he hadn't been able to handle stopping by his grand-mother's for breakfast and coffee. Because he'd known his brothers and cousins would be there. And they'd all be giving him knowing grins. And he would have been unable to hide the fact that he was still panicking about his ability to pull off being the perfect husband to Jordan.

Fletcher took a deep breath.

Normally the smell of markers, books, and glue filled him with contentment and made him smile.

Not today.

He was sitting in his classroom waiting for his kids to file into the room to start the day, thinking that being surrounded by colorful flags from around the world and multi-colored supply bins and the guinea pigs his class had adopted would cheer him up.

Instead, he was brooding about how the one thing Jordan needed now was an amazing husband. And how he wasn't so sure he had what it took. And how he was pretty much stuck with the gig anyway. And how there was no way in hell he would ever give the job up to anyone else anyway.

Zander: *Nothing to say for yourself? Well, you owe me.*

Fletcher: *I do. Have Ellie put your breakfast and lunch on my tab.*

That was a joke because none of them had actual tabs. Though Ellie did keep track of who owed her what and when the toilets at the bar backed up, the person who had the highest "bill" was the one she called to show up with a plunger.

Zander: *Already did.*

"Hi, Mr. Landry."

Fletcher focused on the little boy who was standing on the opposite side of Fletcher's desk. He pocketed his phone and leaned forward in his squeaky wooden swivel chair.

Okay, Landry, pull it together.

"Mornin', Samuel," he greeted. He even managed a smile. "How's it going so far?"

"What is 'disown'?"

"Use it in a sentence."

"My grandma said she'll disown me if I get married in Las Vegas the way you did."

Ah. Fletcher shouldn't have been surprised. He was sure Samuel's grandma wasn't the only one talking about it. "I see. Well, it's when you don't let somebody be in your family anymore."

Samuel frowned.

"But I wouldn't worry too much," Fletcher told him. "I've known your grandma a long time." Fletcher had played football with Samuel's youngest uncle and his grandma had been the loudest in the stands. She was all about her family and a doting grandmother. "I don't think she'll actually disown you."

Samuel shook his head. "No, my Grandma Mimi wouldn't do that."

"Then why did she say it?" Cameron, another boy in class, asked.

Fletcher looked at Samuel. "Did she say it right to you?"

"No. She was telling my Aunt Courtney that if anyone in our family did that she'd disown them."

Fletcher nodded. He'd figured it was something like that.

Samuel tipped his head. "Aunt Courtney said your wife was on TV."

Fletcher nodded again, slowly. "That's true."

"Wow, really?"

"Yep." But he swiveled his chair to address Cameron's question. "Sometimes people exaggerate," Fletcher said. "Do you know what that means?"

"It means to say things are bigger or better or badder—"

"Worse," Fletcher corrected.

Cameron nodded. "Worse than they really are."

"Right," Fletcher said. "People exaggerate to make things more interesting or shocking or scary so that other people pay more attention to what they're saying."

"Is exaggerating like lying?" a little girl named Katie asked.

"It's the truth but made bigger, to make a point," Fletcher said. "So it would be like if I gave you a piece of pizza that was hot and I didn't want you to burn your tongue. I might tell you it was *really, really* hot so you'd be extra careful. The 'really, really' part is the exaggeration."

This was one of the things he loved most about teaching this grade level. The kids were sharp and ready to learn and picked up on everything.

It was also, often, like walking through a mine field.

"Do people here exaggerate a lot?" Katie asked.

"Here in Autre?" Fletcher asked.

"Yeah."

"Well… why do you ask?"

"Because my mom says everyone here is at least a little full of bullshit. Is that the same thing?"

"She said bullshit!" Samuel exclaimed, acting horrified, but clearly delighted.

"She was quoting someone," Fletcher told him. "That's not the same thing as saying it herself." He looked at Katie. "Because I know *her* grandma would not approve of that."

Still, Katie gave Samuel a smug look.

"And yes, that's kind of the same thing," Fletcher acknowledged. "As long as the bullshit"—He held up a hand as Samuel and at least three others gasped—"and don't go tellin' your parents I was cussing in class. We're *discussing* and I needed to use the word to explain it." He gave them pointed looks. Though he was sure at recess the kids would pass the news that Mr. Landry had *cussed* out loud in class. It would be quite the scandal. "But as long as the…B.S.—that's short for bullshit and most people don't consider it cussing," he told them. There, they'd learned at least one thing today. "As long as the B.S. is at least partially true, I suppose it's like exaggerating. And yes," he added, "there's a lot of that goin' on around here."

The kids all giggled.

He turned to Cameron again. "I think Samuel's grandma's just exaggerating a bit to express that she thinks getting married in Las Vegas…is not the thing to do."

"Is getting married in Las Vegas *bad*?" Katie asked.

Fletcher shook his head. "Of course not."

"Then why did my mom say she can't believe you did that?"

Fletcher blew out a breath. Katie's mother, Tiffany, said that about a lot of the things he did. Like breaking up with her sister their junior year of high school. And then dating her again the summer after their freshman year of college. And breaking up with her again.

"Getting married in Las Vegas is more unusual for people from around here than getting married here in town is all," Fletcher said.

"My dad said at least you didn't marry a stripper," Zachary piped up from his desk three rows back.

Yeah, well, his father, Matthew, knew a thing or two about strippers. He'd been known to head over to Bad and the strip club-slash-barbecue joint, the Pork and Peach, even before he'd turned twenty-one. But, of course, Fletcher couldn't say that.

It was definitely interesting teaching the kids of people he'd grown up with. Most of these kids' parents were a few years older than Fletcher, but Autre was not a big town, and everyone knew everyone regardless of what year you graduated.

"What's a stripper?" Olivia Theroit asked.

"Girls who take off their clothes," Zachary told her.

Fletcher stood up, cutting the conversation off before they could get any further into the topic of strippers. And before he cussed again.

"Okay, so it seems you're interested in me getting married." He moved to the front of his desk and propped a hip on the edge. He pointed to Samuel's seat and the little boy headed in that direction. "Let's talk about it for a little bit. Instead of rumors, I'll tell you everything you want to know."

He paused. He should've known that his students would be interested in this news. He supposed the fact that he had still been processing it over the last not-even-twenty-four hours was partly why he hadn't given *this* much thought. But yes, eight-year-olds had very big ears when it came to adult conversations happening around them and Fletcher should have thought about the fact that their parents and grandparents would have been talking.

He looked around the room. "Who knows what a rumor is?"

A few hands went up and he called on Aubrey Harrison.

"It's when people tell a story about someone else that might not be true," the little girl said.

"So it's like bullshit," Katie said.

Kids gasped and giggled.

Fletcher sighed.

But she wasn't entirely wrong.

"And exaggerating," Cameron added.

Again, Fletcher held up a hand. "Those are all pretty close to one another, yes. But a *rumor* can be a story that is *not* exaggerated, so it's not made bigger just to make it more interesting or shocking, but it's just not true."

"So it's a lie," Samuel concluded.

"Kind of," Fletcher agreed. "But usually the people talkin' about it aren't lying on purpose. They're just tellin' a story." He looked around the room. "And the best way to not have a story be a *rumor* is to ask the person about what really happened."

He had everyone's attention, and he met the eyes of Sophia Abar. And she didn't look away. Surprise kicked him in the chest. Sophia rarely made eye contact with anyone and even though he knew she was paying attention in class in general because of the assignments she turned in, she was most often staring at the top of her desk when he looked out over the room.

Sophia not only never met his eyes or spoke in class, she never spoke, period. She didn't talk to the other kids, she didn't talk to other teachers, and even if she was sitting with classmates at lunch, she didn't say a word. She sat on the swings at recess and pushed herself back and forth throughout the period.

Fletcher hadn't tried to push her to do more. Her father had died over the summer and the school counselor hypothesized that Sophia either was afraid that people were going to ask about her father at school, where she might get emotional and be embarrassed, or she was simply talked out and didn't have anything else to say.

Fletcher had barely heard her voice since school started.

It seemed that Sophia was simply sad.

And Fletcher felt like a complete failure.

They'd done a class project, had gone on a nature walk, had done some show and tell about everyone's summer break. They were things that all the other kids enjoyed immensely. In every other instance, Fletcher felt like his reputation as a fun but effective teacher was well-earned.

Sophia was the only exception.

But she was doing well in class. It seemed she was learning the material anyway. And that was, after all, his primary goal. He was a teacher and as long as his students learned the subjects he was teaching them, he must be doing at least a decent job. Right?

But right now, talking about him and Jordan getting married in Las Vegas over the weekend had Sophia's attention.

Was he willing to share about his personal life, even knowing that these kids would go home and tell their parents everything he said, just to feel like he was entertaining Sophia even in the slightest?

Absolutely.

"Okay, who has a question?"

Hands shot up around the room and Fletcher chuckled. Yes, clearly this topic needed to be addressed.

"Okay, Kyrie, you're first."

The little girl beamed. "Did she wear a beautiful dress?"

Even not having a lot of girls in his family growing up, Fletcher knew that a beautiful dress was a big deal to eight-year-olds. Should he tell her that Jordan had been wearing white capri pants and a pink tank top?

"She looked absolutely breathtaking," he told the girl honestly. "I have never seen a more beautiful woman in my life."

Kyrie's smile was bright and Fletcher knew he'd answered correctly.

"Okay, Travis, what do you need to know?"

"Did you steal her from some other guy? 'Cuz that's what my cousin said."

Now see, that was more the type of thing Fletcher was expecting these kids to overhear.

He shook his head. "Jordan and I have been friends since we were younger than you guys. Her boyfriend didn't want to get married and she did and I love her so I decided I should be the one to marry her."

That was all completely true as well. And it sounded so simple. It should be simple. Of all the people in the world that it should be easy to make a life with, Jordan Benoit would be at the very top of the list for him. Or so it would seem. Then again, he'd always expected to be playing the sidekick. He'd never really thought he'd have the starring role.

"Emma, what's your question?" he asked before he got too wrapped up in his own thoughts.

"Did you wear a tuxedo?"

Lots of questions about their clothes. Interesting.

"No, I didn't."

"Why not?" Kyrie asked.

"We didn't have time to get fancy clothes," Fletcher said. "We decided to get married and just did it."

"You didn't *want* to wear a tuxedo?" Kyrie asked.

"You know that feeling when you want to go swimming and you're right there standing by the water but then your mom tells you that you have to wait so that she can put sunscreen on you before you jump in?" Fletcher asked.

Most of the class nodded.

"That's what this was like. I wanted to go swimming and I was standing right by the water and I didn't want to wait for sunscreen."

He knew he had to be careful what he said here because he knew it was going to get repeated at home. And the accuracy of information taken home was already somewhat lacking.

"My dad said that he wasn't surprised at all. He thought you would marry her a long time ago," Travis said.

Fletcher liked that. He'd dated Travis's aunt Shelby in high school too and had known her older brother David fairly well.

"Jordan is very special to me," Fletcher said. "I'm very lucky she agreed to marry me."

"Did you go to prom together like my mom and dad?" Kyrie asked.

"My mom and dad went to prom together too!" Katie said.

"Mine did too," Samuel said, as if it was obvious. Clearly in his mind, *all* moms and dads went to prom together.

And stupidly, that made Fletcher's chest feel tight. Because he and Jordan had not gone to prom together. They hadn't done a lot of things together.

Not that all married couples went to prom, of course. But he and Jordan hadn't even dated. Not really. She was right when she said that they'd been dating for twenty years in a way.

But he still felt like they'd missed out on so much.

"Nope," he said, curling his fingers into the edge of his desk. "We didn't go to prom together."

Aubrey's eyes went wide. "Did you go to bonfires together?"

Fletcher nodded. "We did do that." There had been lots of bonfires. "And we went to parties and barbecues and ball games. Our families are really good friends, so we did a lot together. We went swimming and boating and fishing and camping."

Aubrey nodded, as if relieved. "My mom and dad went to lots of bonfires together."

"Did you *kiss her* at the bonfires?" Samuel asked, his tone and grin teasing.

The other kids giggled. Even Sophia.

"My mom and dad kissed lots at bonfires," Aubrey told Samuel. She giggled. "They still do."

Everyone laughed.

"My mom and dad kiss *all the time,*" Travis told them with an eye roll. "In the kitchen. In the living room. On the porch. In the—"

"Okay," Fletcher interrupted.

"Mine do too," Katie agreed. "My sister tells them to get a room. But they have a whole house!"

Everyone thought *that* was hilarious.

Fletcher shook his head. He was losing control. But he loved when his kids were open and happy and talked lovingly about their families.

Then he looked over at Sophia.

Dammit. She looked sad again.

Her father had just passed away. There wasn't any spontaneous mom and dad kissing going on at her house anymore.

"Okay, okay," Fletcher said, redirecting the conversation. He really needed to remember that not all of the kids came from the same types of families. Not all had moms and dads. Some of them, like Emma, had never had a dad around.

Still, Emma was grinning about all the kissing talk.

He sighed. Being the fun teacher wasn't as easy as he'd imagined in college. Because being the fun teacher…still meant being a teacher. Interacting with, helping, supporting, and guiding kids.

"I thought we were talking about *me*," he said, giving the class a grin and grasping for his laid-back fun persona.

"Yeah, did you kiss your wife *all the time*?" Samuel asked.

"We…didn't kiss in high school at all," he told them. "We were just friends."

They gasped, clearly horrified.

"But…you kiss *now* right?" Katie asked. She seemed desperate for a yes answer.

And, thank God, he could give her one. "Of course."

But dammit, he couldn't shake the little voice at the back of his head that kept saying *you've missed so much. You put your hand in her panties for the first time just this morning and you're MARRIED. You don't know what kind of foreplay she likes, or what position is her favorite, or what kind of vibrator she uses...and you're* MARRIED.

He didn't care if they had known each other for twenty years. They were jumping way ahead on the game board here.

"Can she come visit our class?" Samuel asked, breaking into Fletcher's thoughts.

Which was great, because thinking about Jordan and her vibrator—or was it vibrators, plural?—while sitting in front of his class of eight-year-olds was *not* appropriate.

"You know what? She probably can," Fletcher said. "She's going to be working down at the petting zoo."

He was shocked to see Sophia straighten slightly in her seat. She was still watching him and now she seemed even more interested.

"Who all has been down to the petting zoo?"

All hands in the room went up, including Sophia's.

Over the summer, Fletcher had sent out an email to all of his past students as well as the ones coming into his class this fall, inviting them to a movie party that Charlie had thrown at the petting zoo. All the kids got dressed up in their pajamas and came to watch the movie with the goats. Who had also been wearing pajamas. Several of his students had attended. But not Sophia. Her father had been on hospice by then.

"That's great, I'm glad you've been down there. There are some really interesting animals to learn more about."

"I went to Dr. Foster's class," Cameron bragged. "I got my certification."

Griffin had started a handling clinic out at the veterinary hospital. The goal was to have kids learn how to interact with and handle some of the smaller animals like the rabbits and hedgehogs before moving on to learn how to properly interact with the larger animals. He offered a certificate printed on fancy paper that the kids could bring to the petting zoo for special interactive events.

It was a fantastic idea really. It gave the kids experience and respect for the animals before they got up close and personal, it placed the right amount of seriousness on proper handling, and it gave over-protective Griffin some peace of mind.

Additionally, it gave the kids of Autre and the surrounding area a little something special that the general tourists didn't get. The kids visiting from out of town could come and watch the animals and, at certain times of day, feed some of the goats and alpacas that were more used to human interaction, but only the local kids with those certificates could handle and hold the smaller animals.

A chorus of, "Me too!" rang out.

Fletcher noticed that Sophia did not chime in, however. Right, with her father in chemo and then a funeral and grief counseling since the petting zoo had officially opened, Sophia probably hadn't had a chance to play with any hedgehogs.

"Is your wife a veterinarian?" Olivia asked.

Fletcher shook his head. "Nope. She's a teacher. She teaches high school science. But she is going to be working at the petting zoo, putting together classes and projects down there now."

"We can go to classes at the petting zoo?" Katie asked.

"Kind of. You know those talks I did this summer where I would tell you more about each of the animals?" Many of his students had attended those and had thought it was so cool that their teacher was on YouTube. Heads bobbed around the room. "She's going to be doing those and then making them even bigger and better. And yeah, I think they hope to have all kinds of fun stuff going on there."

"So she was on TV and now she's going to be on the Internet?" Samuel asked.

Fletcher chuckled. He wasn't going to get into how much Jordan had already been on the Internet. He was sure many of the mothers of the kids in this room had seen her all over already. "Yeah, I guess so. Pretty neat, right?"

"No wonder you married her," Cameron said completely seriously.

Fletcher grinned at him. "Well, there's lots of reasons besides that why I wanted to marry her."

"Like what?" Kyrie asked.

So, Fletcher told them. He figured it was being a great role model to explain to the kids what made him love the woman he'd chosen to marry. And after about thirty more minutes of telling them about Jordan and answering their questions, Fletcher realized that he'd grown Jordan's fan club.

They finally moved on to social studies, math, and spelling.

Over his lunch break, Fletcher texted Jordan.

Fletcher: *My class wants to meet you.*

Jordan: *Oh really?*

Fletcher: *Their families have been talking about us in Vegas.*

Jordan: *LOL. I'm shocked.*

Fletcher: *I know. But you're kind of a superstar now. Want to come up for lunch tomorrow?*

Jordan: *I could. Or you all could come down here and have lunch in a couple of days. I could practice my presentations.*

Fletcher: *Perfect.* He thought about how much more engaged Sophia had seemed after he'd mentioned the petting zoo. *I'll have them all bring a sack lunch.*

Jordan: *Awesome. I'll tell Charlie.*

Fletcher: *See you tonight. Might be a bit late. Mitch and Zeke need some help on the enclosures for some red pandas after school…I understand you know something about that.*

Jordan sent him a wide grinning face. *Best job ever and I've been here like three hours.*

That was exactly what he needed to hear. Bringing her home to Autre had been the right move, for sure.

Jordan: *And I met Fiona this morning.*

Fletcher laughed: *Autre is never going to be the same with you and Charlie and Fiona conspiring.*

Jordan: **I'm* never going to be the same.*

Fletcher's heart kicked and he had to force air into his lungs.

Jordan: *Thank you. For always knowing what I need.*

His breath rushed out.

For twenty years he'd prided himself on that very thing. He was always the guy who came through for Jordan. No matter the circumstance.

But now this thing was twenty-four-seven.

Was he actually going to be able to pull that off?

She added a little heart emoji and Fletcher set his phone down with a smile. It was just a heart emoji. His mother often used those in her messages too. But this one was from Jordan and that made it different.

CHAPTER
Thirteen

JORDAN HAD AGREED to take the job after only ten minutes of holding Slothcrates. It was amazing that she would get to do this every single day. That was even before she met the lemurs.

She and Charlie, and the rest of the Boys of the Bayou Gone Wild, which included everyone from Griffin and Tori as the veterinarians to the owners of Boys of the Bayou—Sawyer, Josh, Owen, Maddie, and Bennett—would discuss details over the next several days, but Jordan already had some pretty great ideas about what she'd like to do with the position.

Kids and animals were a natural combination and Charlie already had the kids doing little "tours" of the petting zoo with maps and educational materials that took them through the animal kingdom from the local area in Louisiana to Peru where alpacas originated and all the way to Madagascar with the lemurs. She also had visions of having the kids connect virtually once they got home to share about the animals in their own backyards.

There was all kinds of potential—they just hadn't had time, or the staff, to implement much, and Jordan was the perfect person to do it. She not only had the background in teaching, but the background in science and biology specifically.

As she walked down the fence line of the alpaca pasture she found herself humming.

Just two days ago she'd woken up in the penthouse suite in a Vegas casino hotel, preparing to join Jason on a huge stage in front of a crowd of country music fans.

Now she was on her way to get to know the alpacas better.

She was going to be doing a presentation to a bunch of preschool kids tomorrow and she wanted to get the animals used to having her around so that she could talk to the kids with the animals nearby.

There were actually three pens. One where they kept the male alpacas and one for the females—the boys were a lot more mellow when the girls weren't distracting them—and one they used for more up close and personal interactions with humans and a couple of animals at a time.

Right now, Regan Reynolds, the physical therapist from over in Bad, was there working with a patient.

"Hey, Regan," Jordan called as she got closer.

Regan looked over and raised a hand. "Hi, Jordan." She looked down at her patient. "This is Carter."

Carter gave Jordan a big smile. "Hi."

"Hi, Carter. Can I come in for a second?"

"Sure." Carter looked up at Regan. "Okay?"

"Definitely."

Jordan opened the pen and stepped inside, closing the gate behind her. She made her way to where Carter was sitting in his wheelchair on a patch of dirt that was flatter than the rest of the pasture. She guessed they'd cleared the area specifically for wheelchairs. "What are you guys up to?"

"I'm doing my therapy with llamas!" Carter told her.

He looked like he was about six or seven.

"Actually, they're alpacas," Jordan said. "Do you know the difference?"

He shook his head.

Jordan reached her hand out to Alpacasso, the alpaca that,

according to Charlie, was the most docile with the kids during Regan's therapy sessions. Cass sniffed her fingers and let Jordan run her hand down the side of her neck.

"Well the main difference is their size," Jordan told him. "Llamas are bigger. And they have longer faces and ears." She pointed to Cass's ears. "Alpacas have cute, rounder faces and shorter ears. And alpacas have softer hair. They make *yarn* out of alpaca wool." She smiled at his wide eyes. "Also alpacas are a little sweeter than llamas. Llamas can be kind of stubborn. *But,* they can also be used as guard animals for alpacas and sheep. Isn't that cool?"

Carter nodded. "I love Cass. She's so nice." He stroked his hand over the animal's side.

"I'm glad you get to work with her," Jordan said. "Do you mind if I watch for a little bit?"

"Oh, we love that," Regan said. "Carter is doing *so* well. We love to show that off, don't we?"

"Yes!" Carter said enthusiastically. "I used to hate working on walking but with Cass it's so fun!"

Jordan lifted her eyes to Regan. "This is really wonderful. When Charlie told me about how you use the animals in therapy, I couldn't wait to see it."

Regan grinned. "It was something that just came up one day. Carter was actually the reason. He isn't kidding when he said he used to hate working on walking. He's got CP—cerebral palsy," she explained. "Tell Jordan what that means, buddy."

"My brain got hurt when I was born," Carter said. "And that makes my muscles not work right. It makes them tight."

Regan nodded. "Yep. So we work on movements to keep your muscles stretched and keep them strong and your joints from getting too tight and painful." She pointed to how he was petting the alpaca. "Even that much reaching and moving back and forth is an exercise."

Jordan noticed that Carter had something around his wrist. "Is that a weight?"

"When I pet or feed the animals, I have to have my wrist weights on," Carter told her.

Regan smiled. "That's our deal, isn't it? You get to play with Cass but get your therapy done at the same time."

"And Cass helps you stand up and walk?" Jordan asked. Charlie had told her the generalities as they'd done the tour of the petting zoo that morning, but Jordan was excited to see it in action.

"He uses this strap to help pull himself up," Regan said, indicating the nylon strap that was wrapped around the alpaca's shoulders. "And then he walks with her as she takes steps. She's really good about letting me lead her so it's nice and slow and steady."

"Charlie said you've been working with Cass in particular," Jordan said.

"She's a good size and has a great temperament for this," Regan told her. "She's gentle and patient. I came and hung out with the alpacas for a couple of weeks after work and got to know them before I decided she'd be the best."

"And you use some of the other animals for things too? With other patients?" Jordan asked.

Regan nodded. "I'm still coming up with ideas and researching. Mostly I'm using a trip over here to see the animals and have a chance to get up close to them as a reward." She glanced at Carter. "Or a bribe," she said with a laugh. "But I have an older guy who just had a stroke who's come over with me and we're using the alpaca to get him stretching and reaching with his affected arm and hand just like Carter. And I have a high school athlete who was in a car accident who's just generally really depressed. The animals aren't a direct part of his therapy but being here around them seems to help him get through the painful stuff a little easier."

Jordan shook her head. "Wow. That's really cool. I'd love to learn more."

"Sure. I can email you some resources and you're welcome to join me anytime."

"Thanks, I'm going to do that."

She stayed and chatted for a little longer, watching Carter and Regan work. Then she headed down the fence line to check on the other alpacas.

She stopped at the space in the fence where most of the guests were able to take photos of and sometimes even *with* the alpacas when they were feeling especially curious and friendly.

One of them, Alpaccino, the oldest of the alpacas and the one most used to human interaction, came strolling over.

"Hey, big guy," she said softly.

Charlie and Griffin had taken time earlier to introduce her to all of the animals. She'd taken notes about all of their names, but she was finding it already easy to tell the alpacas from one another.

For the next couple of days she was going to be getting used to being around animals and vice versa. Griffin had stressed that it was important the animals learn her scent and get used to her touching and handling them before she would be able to help guests do the same.

A lot of the animals were used to having humans around and many of them preferred to be looked at rather than touched. Griffin also preferred that when it came to the animals, but slowly he was getting used to the idea that this was a *petting* zoo and that with proper instruction and supervision, the animals were safe and the humans would be respectful.

Making sure the visitors understood how to appropriately interact with the animals and then supervising to be sure that it happened was going to be one of Jordan's main jobs. She was happy to take those tasks over. It wasn't all that different from teaching and supervising a classroom and this classroom came with alpacas, fresh air, and sunshine. She stroked her hand along Al's side.

Alpacaman noticed Al getting some attention and started over to the fence.

Jordan gave him some love as well. Most alpacas didn't love being touched on the head or face, but Manny did like to have his nose nuzzled and she gave him several little rubs before moving down the fence line.

In the next pen, one of the girls was already near the fence. Alpacapella, or Ella for short, looked up at Jordan. Jordan talked to her softly, but the alpaca didn't come any closer. However, she didn't run either. In general, alpacas were very gentle, curious creatures and they tolerated humans just fine. But they weren't necessarily as enthusiastic or cuddly as dogs. Still, they all had their own personalities and Jordan was interestingly already picking up on a few of those different traits.

Movement caught her eye and she turned to look down the fence. She was surprised to see their smallest, youngest alpaca at the very end of the pasture. His name was Chewpaca, or Chewie.

Griffin had told her that the littlest alpaca had been orphaned on a farm in Iowa, and Tori's friend Drew, who owned the alpaca farm, had asked Tori if she would take him. His mother had died and he'd been rejected by the other females in the herd. He'd needed more hands-on attention, like bottle-feeding, than the farmers could give him. Tori, of course, had jumped at the chance and she, Josh, and Mitch had gone back to Iowa to retrieve him.

They'd also come home with three other alpacas. And an in-love Mitch.

Then Paige, that Iowa girl Mitch had fallen for, had showed up on Mitch's doorstep and had been here ever since.

Unfortunately, while Chewie had done well with his human handlers, he had been standoffish from the rest of the herd and spent a lot of time alone.

It had been bothering Tori ever since he'd been introduced.

Right now, though, he was being quite friendly. With a little girl.

He was standing at the fence with his chin resting on the top railing, gazing adoringly at the little girl who was talking to him and stroking his nose.

He looked completely smitten.

Jordan started in that direction.

She approached slowly, not wanting to startle the animal or the girl.

She looked around as she drew closer.

There was a mother and two other kids with the goats. They all had light brown skin, brown hair, and were talking in a mix of English and Spanish to one another. English to the animals and Spanish to one another. Jordan caught the mother's eye and waved and smiled, then pointed at the little girl with the alpaca. She mouthed, "Is she yours?"

The mother smiled and nodded. Jordan gave her a thumbs up.

"And sometimes we would go to the zoo. And he would always want to look at the monkeys the most," the little girl was telling the alpaca as Jordan got closer.

The girl stopped and tipped her head as if listening. Then she nodded. "I think he would've liked alpacas though. Our dog liked to sit in his lap and have his nose rubbed just like this."

Jordan stepped on a stick and the snapping sound made the alpaca lift his head. They both looked over at Jordan, and Chewie gave a soft snort.

Damn, she hadn't meant to interrupt.

"Hi," Jordan said.

She wasn't dressed as one of the employees yet. She and Charlie had discussed that they needed to get some kind of uniform, or at least t-shirts with Boys of the Bayou Gone Wild on them so people would recognize who they could ask for help and who was authorized to give instructions and be in the animal care areas.

Right now she was wearing Charlie's red sundress and a pair of green rubber boots.

"I'm Jordan. I work here."

"I'm Sophia," the little girl said. "This is my friend."

Jordan nodded. "His name is Chewpaca. We call him Chewie."

The little girl wrinkled her nose and looked back at the alpaca, who, surprisingly, hadn't run off. "That's a weird name."

Jordan shrugged. "It's kind of after a character in a movie. It's called *Star Wars*. Maybe your mom and dad know it?"

The little girl's face was suddenly, devastatingly, sad. "Maybe."

Jordan didn't understand exactly what the little girl was thinking, but she decided to tread carefully. "Do you come down here a lot?"

The little girl shook her head. "No. We've been too busy. But Mom says we can come more often now."

Jordan looked toward the woman with the other two kids with the goats. "Is that your mom?"

The little girl nodded. "Yeah, and my sisters."

"Well Chewie seems to really like you. He doesn't usually come over and talk to people like this."

Sophia looked back at the alpaca. The smile she gave him was heartbreakingly beautiful. "He's a good friend. He's a good listener."

"It's really wonderful that he has a friend." Jordan didn't try to get any closer. There was no need. They were having a nice conversation, the little girl's mother was nearby, and Jordan was, after all, a stranger. She propped an elbow on the fence. "He's been pretty sad for a while. He moved here from far away. And he doesn't really have any friends."

Sophia looked worried. "Where's his mom and dad?"

Jordan wondered how much she should share. But Sophia looked to be about eight or nine. "Well, his mom died," Jordan said carefully. "That's why he moved here. They were hoping that he could find a new family here, but it's been hard."

Sophia thought about all of that for a long moment. Then she turned back to Chewie and said, "We can be friends forever. I'll come visit you all the time."

Jordan felt a little twinge near her heart. Kids were amazing. And yes, kids and animals were absolutely a natural combination.

"Sophia!" her mother called.

Sophia looked over. "Okay!"

She turned back to Chewie. "I have to go. But I'll be back. I promise." She patted the alpaca's nose and he nuzzled her hand. Then Sophia looked at Jordan. "Make sure he knows I'm coming back. I don't want him to think that I left and won't see him again."

Jordan nodded quickly. "I promise I'll tell him."

"Bye, Chewie," Sophia said softly. Then she turned and ran off to join her mother and sisters.

The mother raised her hand and Jordan gave her a little wave and a smile.

She watched the family make their way out of the goat pen and head over to look at the otters. Sophia cast a glance back at Chewie and the alpaca continued to stand at the fence watching her.

Jordan shook her head, her heart full.

This job was going to be amazing.

She was *so* glad Jason had dumped her.

"SO I WAS the good guy. I backed off. I respected that she was with Jason. But fuck…if we'd just gone for it in Galveston, this would be a lot easier now."

"Are we really good enough friends to be having this conversation?" Griffin asked Fletcher as he pulled on rubber boots outside of the otter enclosure.

Fletcher thought about that. "Probably not," he admitted after a moment.

"So you want to wait for Zeke, right?" Griffin asked, hopefully.

"I already know what Zeke will say about this." Fletcher sighed. "He'll tell me I was an idiot that night in Texas and that I'm being an even bigger idiot now."

"Are you?"

Fletcher frowned. "It's *Jordan*."

"Thought she was your best friend. Haven't you known her forever?"

"Yes. Exactly."

Griffin opened the otter enclosure door and stepped through. He held it open for Fletcher as if expecting him to follow.

"I can come in?"

Griffin was very protective of his otters and who got to interact with them. Actually, he was very protective of all of the animals. But there was something special about the otters.

"You're not done talking, are you?" Griffin asked.

"You want to keep listening?"

"My feelings about listening have never stopped anyone named Landry before."

Fletcher had to grin. Griffin wasn't a warm, fuzzy, spill-your-guts kind of guy but he'd definitely opened up since Charlie had shown up. Honestly, once Charlie had decided she was interested in Griffin, the guy hadn't stood a chance.

"I swear I just came by to talk to you and Zeke about the red pandas and to ask Zeke what he meant by his text earlier," Fletcher said.

Zeke had texted simply *ZEBRAS!* with a hammer and a saw emoji.

Were they building a zebra? A wooden cut out of a zebra would look cute at the petting zoo. Or were they building a pen for zebras? But Griffin had told Fletcher zebras could be real assholes if they got spooked or defensive. So, it probably wasn't a pen.

The most important word there being *probably*.

But then Griffin had made the mistake of asking Fletcher how married life was treating him.

Griffin himself admitted it had been a mistake to ask. And very unlike him.

"So what the hell happened in Galveston?" Griffin asked, as he was swarmed by otters. "Was it that big of a deal?"

He had to raise his voice to be heard over their squeals and chatter. There were only seven otters, but they made it sound like the place was being overrun whenever Griffin showed up. They *loved* Griffin.

Fletcher was careful where he stepped as he followed Griffin deeper into the enclosure. He watched Griffin tossing fish to the otters for a few minutes. Griffin would occasionally toss one of the fish into the man-made river that flowed through the enclosure for the juvenile otters to dive after. Their parents, Gus and Gertie, were doing a great job raising and training the pups, but not living in the wild meant that they needed as many simulated activities as possible.

"Yeah, Galveston was a big deal," Fletcher said. "We were there for this science teachers' conference. I didn't want Jordan going alone so I agreed to go along."

Griffin moved to sit on one of the boulders, allowing the otters to climb up into his lap.

Fletcher took the boulder next to his and Snickers and Hershey quickly scooted up his legs and into his lap.

Griffin chuckled and handed over a few treats. The otters knew where to look and the two in his lap had been pawing at his shirt pocket.

Fletcher held a treat out to each of the ones sitting with him. "We were supposed to drive back home that night, but a tropical storm rolled in. It was too risky to be on the open road for five hours, so we found a hotel. But there was only one room. And one bed."

"Ah," Griffin said.

Fletcher sighed. It was very cliché, yes. "We were starving so we found a Mexican restaurant within walking distance. We ate, had a few margaritas, and then started back. By the time we got back to the room, we were soaked. We walked into the room and just as we shut the door, the power went out. Jordan grabbed me and…" He shook his head. "I don't know. It was a combination of tequila and the idea that we were stuck, just the two of us, far from home in a bad storm, and it was like everything just snapped. I backed her up against the door and kissed her."

Griffin pivoted on the rock to face Fletcher. "That was the first time you'd ever kissed?"

"One game of Truth or Dare and a couple of New Year's Eve kisses, but *nothing* even close to that." Fletcher blew out a breath. "It was like in a blink everything changed. I still can't totally explain it."

Even now, three years later, thinking back, he was stunned by how quickly it had happened. She had gone from being his best friend to the woman he wanted to strip naked and fuck against the hotel room door in about three seconds.

"But then you *didn't* sleep together?"

"No. We made out for a little while, but she finally pushed me back and said she couldn't do it because of Jason. We spent the night in that bed together not even touching. But…I've wanted her ever since."

Fletcher couldn't believe he'd said even this much to Griffin, a guy who didn't know him well. Should he talk to one of his brothers instead? Or cousins? A bunch of them were in serious relationships now. Or his grandmother? Ellie always had great advice. Or maybe he didn't admit this at all. Maybe he'd figure it out on his own, eventually.

But spilling his guts to a guy like Griffin, who not only had *not* known him since he was born, but who was the opposite of a gossip, sounded like a great idea. He needed to get it out, talk it through it seemed, but doing it with a guy who wasn't much of a conversationalist unless you were an otter was perfect.

"I basically gave her a choice between me and Jason that night," Fletcher went on. "And then, I did it again four months ago at the weddings." He blew out a breath. "She said no both times."

Griffin tossed another fish into the river. "And now you married her in a whirlwind, crazy trip to Vegas after she'd been embarrassed on national television and wasn't sure what to do next."

Fletcher looked over at Griffin. The guy wasn't so bad at this heart-to-heart thing after all it seemed. "Right. So is it *really* that strange that I'm thinking we need to slow the hell down? Catch our breaths? Be sure this was all really what we want?"

"You're not sure it's what you want?"

Okay, *he* knew. "Fine. What *she* wants."

Griffin was quiet for a minute, feeding and petting otters. Fletcher had to admit that having the little animals crawling on him and running his hand over their soft fur was actually quite soothing.

"You really willing to let her go if she decides it's *not* what she wants?" Griffin finally asked.

Fletcher felt his heart squeeze hard and it took him a second to answer. He shook his head. "Not without trying *everything* to *make* it what she wants first. I'll do my damnedest to make it perfect for her."

"And that should be pretty easy, right? You know her better than anyone."

Fletcher nodded. It sure *sounded* easy. "I've never *not* gotten things right. But fuck, now it's a full-time gig. That's just..." He sighed. "A lot."

Griffin laughed, startling one of the otters who scampered off his lap and dove into the river. "Well, yeah. But at least this time she did pick you. And you don't have to worry about her pushing you away while you're making out."

Right. She definitely hadn't pushed him away this morning...

"Zebras!"

Griffin and Fletcher both looked up as Zeke joined them in the otter enclosure.

"We're not getting zebras," Griffin said.

"Have you talked to your girlfriend lately?" Zeke asked.

Zeke scooped one of the otters from the ground and cuddled her against his chest as he took a seat on the log that sat along the riverbank. He stroked the otter's fur and she chittered to him happily. "Yes, Baby Ruth, you know you're my favorite."

Fletcher was relieved to see Zeke. He'd been in his head about Jordan all day. Distraction was exactly what he needed and Zeke had perfected the art of distracting people from anything but him. He was a very typical youngest child, even if he was youngest by only two minutes.

"Charlie told you we're getting zebras?" Griffin's tone was more one of resignation than surprise.

Zeke grinned. "Fiona's in town. We've got peacocks and a porcupine now. And I think we're getting a couple of red pandas before zebras. But she said we should start working on the pen and barn."

Griffin sighed. "Zebras don't really do that much. They're kinda like horses."

"But they look cool as fuck," Zeke said. He looked at Fletcher. "Can you believe we're going to be living on a wildlife refuge?"

It was true that the guys' houses sat on the edge of the land where the new lemur and sloth enclosures had been built and where Fletcher assumed Charlie intended to expand the animal park. But he didn't think any of them had really thought a lot about what that might mean.

"Is it a refuge if the animals aren't endangered?" he asked

"Lemurs are endangered, right?" Zeke looked at Griffin. "What are some other endangered animals we could get?"

"That's not really how it works," Griffin said.

Zeke shrugged. "I'm just saying, we have all this land and these animal-crazy women. If anyone were going to run an endangered wildlife refuge it would totally be Fiona and Charlie." He grinned. "Women who are crazy about animals are pretty hot."

Fletcher lifted a brow at his brother. "You're going to ask Fiona out? I thought she had a boyfriend."

"She does have a boyfriend. For now. But I don't think she's interested in me anyway."

"A woman who is not interested in you?" Fletcher said dryly. "I didn't know those existed."

Zeke nodded, pretending to be sad. "Every once in a while. But I think Fiona is into Knox."

"I think they just annoy each other," Griffin said. "Fiona likes to push buttons."

Fiona and Griffin had spent time together in Zambia working on an actual wildlife refuge before Griffin had needed to come back to the States when his parents died. Fiona had, apparently, come back about a year later.

"Naw, it's more than that," Zeke said. "Knox is easily annoyed. By almost everyone and everything. But he doesn't really let people know. He just deals with it. But with Fiona, he can't let it go. He saw her purple truck and purposely went into Ellie's. I mean, if he wanted to avoid her, it would be really easy. It's not like the girl sneaks around."

That was true. Fiona Grady was someone who got noticed wherever she went and seemed to really like that.

"Well, Charlie's taken," Griffin said. "Guess you have to find your own animal fanatic."

Zeke nodded. "Hanging out around this place can't hurt." He slid a glance to Fletcher. "I guess Jordan's pretty into everything. They said she was the one who made the final decision to go with red pandas as our next acquisition."

Fletcher had been hearing Jordan's name for twenty years.

On a very regular basis. And yet, his heart thumped hard when Zeke said her name this time. Why was that? It was weird.

Maybe it was because of the way Zeke made it seem that Jordan's involvement with the animal park had something to do with Fletcher. Which it did, he supposed. Jordan was his wife. The animal park was going to be her new job. Not only was she going to be working with his family, but she was going to be teaching again.

It wasn't a traditional classroom, that was for sure. He could admit that he had envisioned getting her a substitute teaching job at the school and thinking that she might look at area schools in the spring to see if there would be any open positions. But ever since Charlie had arrived at his doorstep that morning telling him that she and Jordan had talked about the animal park and Jordan taking over as educational director, it seemed a great fit.

Jordan was a science teacher. Animals, plants, their habitats, the food chain, the circle of life—that was all her thing. And she was creative and passionate about teaching. It would be great, not just for her but for the animal park.

And yes, if Jordan was excited about something, so was he.

But that part wasn't new. That had always happened. It was how he'd learned to make macaroons of all things. It was how he knew that Joseph Lister was the scientist who was known for coming up with the idea of antiseptic treatments and that John Bardeen discovered superconductivity which led to the invention of the MRI and CT machines. It was why he'd read *Little Women* and *The Lion, the Witch, and the Wardrobe*.

Jordan Benoit—dammit, Landry—could get him interested in nearly anything.

Especially *her*.

"Fletcher?"

He looked over at Zeke. His brother's tone indicated that he'd said Fletcher's name more than once. "Yeah?"

"So you're in to help build something for the red pandas?"

Fletcher shook his head. "Sure. On weekends."

"Yeah, Mitch and I will get the design sketched out and the supplies and we'll get started as soon as we can, but if we could get some extra hands on the weekends that would be great."

"Count me in."

"Even with the new wife at home?" Zeke asked. "Figured you'd be a little busier than usual now."

Fletcher glanced at Griffin, but Griffin didn't say a word. And somehow Fletcher knew that he wouldn't. He'd confessed a lot to the other man and he appreciated knowing that Griffin would keep his confidence.

"It's Jordan," Fletcher said. "Hell, she'll probably be down here with a toolbelt and hardhat with us."

"True."

Griffin stretched to his feet. "Okay, I gotta get going."

Zeke set Baby Ruth down and got up as well. "Yeah, me too. I'm going to Ellie's for some dinner and then I need to go over and talk to a guy in Bad about redoing a big kitchen. You know that old strip club over there? The guy's grandson is remodeling it. Making it a community center."

"No kidding." The Pork and Peach had been controversial, and Fletcher knew a lot of people who'd been happy there'd been a fire that had closed it down permanently.

"Yep. Big job but Jase is a good guy and he's paying well."

"Late hours," Fletcher commented.

Zeke clapped him on the shoulder. "Yeah, well, we don't all spend our day fingerpainting and taking naps between eight and three."

"Fuck off. I teach third grade. We don't take naps."

"But you do fingerpaint?"

"Well…we use paintbrushes." They only painted when they were doing maps of the continents or painting balls for the solar system models and things like that. But yeah, they painted. Painting was fun, dammit.

They made their way out of the otter enclosure and it wasn't until Fletcher was sitting in his truck with the engine running, that he realized he was headed home. And that there would be someone there waiting for him.

Not just someone. Jordan.

His new wife.

The woman he wanted to get naked more than anything.

The woman he'd gotten naked—okay, she'd gotten herself naked but he'd *definitely* seen her naked—that morning and couldn't stop thinking about.

The woman he needed to keep clothed until they had an important talk.

He knew so much about Jordan. Except in this one area. Yes, he knew about the sprained ankle and the blowjobs, but beyond that, Jordan's sex life had always been, thankfully, a mystery.

And now that was coming back to bite him in the ass.

Of course, the one thing he didn't know was the thing he needed to know the most.

If there was anything in his life that he had to get *right*, it was being Jordan's husband.

JORDAN HEARD the back kitchen door open and felt her stomach flip. Fletcher was home. Then she looked around. She wasn't exactly prepared for seduction. Or even for dinner. She was sitting crisscross in the middle of Fletcher's living room floor surrounded by papers, folders, a notebook in which she had already filled six pages, and her open laptop.

Dammit, the time had gotten away from her.

She looked down. She was wearing another sundress borrowed from Charlie, so at least there was that. She'd showered when she'd gotten home from the animal park too.

She'd worn rubber boots to walk around the barnyard and otter enclosure as Charlie gave her the tour. Those were obviously not the places to be wearing sandals or even tennis shoes you wanted to keep clean. But in spite of the boots and a pair of gloves she borrowed, she'd still ended up with mud—at least it had looked like mud—on her thigh and one forearm. She'd been kissed on the cheek by two different alpacas, butted in the leg by at least three goats, and had otters climbing over nearly every inch of her. She was very glad the dress she'd been wearing was Charlie's and her friend completely understood why it smelled the way it did at the end of the day. And that it wasn't dry clean only.

She didn't have any body spray or perfume with her and she'd borrowed Fletcher's deodorant. She was also makeup-less since she'd left everything back in Vegas. Not that she was missing any of that. After this second shampoo, her purple hair had faded to a very faint lavender and she'd left it down to dry naturally. She ran a hand through it now, feeling the slight dampness that remained. So, that meant she'd been sitting here working on her plans for the animal park for a couple of hours.

Fletcher appeared in the doorway between the kitchen and living room. "Um…is there something you need to tell me?"

It was crazy the way seeing him and that low, husky greeting made her stomach swoop.

She gave him a bright smile. "I took the job."

He frowned. "Yeah. I mean, I assumed. But…Jordan…there's *a pregnancy test* on the kitchen table."

Oh, right. Jordan shoved the papers from her lap to the floor and stood swiftly. She crossed the room and stepped around him. "There's also this." She handed him the paper and photo that Tori had dropped off at the petting zoo for her.

Fletcher looked down at it. "This is…" He frowned. "What is this?"

"A dog," she said. "Tori has him at her place right now. But he needs a new home." She leaned in, looking into the big brown eyes of the border collie Tori and Josh were fostering. "I told her we were looking for one."

"We…are?"

"Aren't we?" She looked up at him. "We talked about getting two or three."

He looked…freaked out.

"We did." Finally he met her eyes. "Just *yesterday*."

Jordan turned to face him. "Right. Yesterday. When we were talking about getting married."

"And the pregnancy test?"

"I saw it when I was at the store getting dog food and grabbed it on a whim. I figured we'll need one. Maybe soon." She narrowed her eyes, studying him. "Won't we?"

He took a deep breath, his eyes going from the dog's photo to the pregnancy test box, and back. Finally he nodded. "Yeah. I guess so."

"Fletcher?" She waited until he looked at her. "What's going on?"

He didn't respond for a long moment. Then he shook his head. "You know I would do anything for you."

"Yes."

"But can we just… *slow down* a second?"

She blinked at him. "Oh."

He wanted to slow down? Fletcher? The guy who'd asked her to stay with him in Autre just four months ago? Who'd jumped on a plane and flown to Vegas the second she was single?

She had not expected that. She'd been so excited by the idea that she no longer had to have her life on hold, that she could jump in with both feet with a new job and a dog and the idea of starting a family that she hadn't thought about how fast this was all going. But yeah, okay, it *was* fast. The pregnancy test had truly been an impulse buy. She'd seen it and thought, "wow, needing one of those is actually a possibility now." She hadn't intended to use it *today*, but it had just been fun to buy it.

He shoved a hand through his hair. "I'm sorry. I know that sounds a little crazy. But we *just* got married. We actually just made up after our fight in April. Now we're kissing, and fucking, and I have to explain to my kids why we got married in Vegas and then I come home and there's a dog and you could be pregnant and—"

Jordan grabbed his arm and squeezed. "Fletcher."

He blew out a breath and looked at her. "Yeah."

"Yes. We can slow down."

"Okay. Good." He suddenly turned fully and took her face in his hands. "I'm all in. I want you to know that. I want all of this. I just need it to be…"

"Perfect."

That made him pause for a moment. But then he nodded. "Yeah."

She wrapped her fingers around his wrists. "It doesn't have to be perfect. That's a lot of pressure."

"But, I always get things right with you. I always fix things. I'm the guy who's there when all else has failed."

She swallowed and nodded. That was true. Or, at least, she'd always led him to believe that all of that was true.

Well, crap.

All of this wanting to be the perfect husband was her fault.

"Fletcher, I—"

"And you've been doing the long term relationship thing where you lived with the guy and all of that. I've never done that. Not even *close*. Now, my first long term relationship is as long term as you can get and it's with the one woman that I can't screw up with."

She frowned. "Fletcher, for God's sake, you're not going to screw anything up. But even if we do make a few mistakes here and there, it's *us*. I'm the last person you should be worrying about being perfect for. I've known you forever. I've *loved you* forever. And now I'm *in love* with you too. You do not have to freak out about this."

He stared at her for several beats, then he said, "But the thing is…you and I haven't done a lot of middles. And I pretty much suck at middles."

She frowned. "Middles? What do you mean by that?"

"Come on." He took her hand and tugged her into the living room, but he paused in the doorway, surveying the papers and folders she had scattered everywhere. "Wow."

"Yeah, Charlie and I got started on some big plans." She gestured to include all the paperwork surrounding her.

"Looks like you're diving right in."

She nodded. "I've been working for a couple of hours straight. I don't remember the last time I had a project I was excited about like this."

"I'm glad." He looked down at her. "I'm really glad."

She smiled. "I know."

She believed that no matter what else was going through his mind, Fletcher would recognize that she was happy. And that would make him happy. As always.

Just then she heard a rustling in the makeshift pen she'd built in front of the sofa with pillows, cushions, and the animal carrier. "Oh! I forgot! I brought Quilly Wonka home!"

She went over and picked the hedgehog up, scooping her hands underneath the little animal from both sides to pick him up. Griffin had explained that hedgehogs had quills on top, but they were soft on the bottom. If they sensed a threat, like a hand coming at them from the top, they would curl into a ball and extend their quills, but if scooped from underneath they felt secure and the quills could be avoided.

She turned with Quilly to smile at Fletcher.

"Griffin said I need to practice handling the animals and that they need to get used to my scent and voice and being touched and fed by me so that they're calm and cooperative when I take visitors around the zoo and do presentations."

Fletcher nodded. "Makes sense."

"So can we sit on the floor to talk? We can play with him at the same time?" she asked.

Maybe having a cute little animal to focus on would make

this conversation easier. She did not want to take things slower, but if it was important to Fletcher, she would.

"Sure. Let me go change. Be right back."

She watched him bound up the stairs, then she turned her attention to the hedgehog. "This is going to be interesting," she told him. "I really hope it's not too much for your little ears."

Fletcher returned a few minutes later, dressed in gray athletic shorts and a white t-shirt. He joined her on the floor.

"Do you want to—" she started.

"So, I'm really good at endings. But I'm not so good at middles."

Okay, they were just going to jump right in. Well, that was good.

Probably.

"There's that 'middles' thing again. What does that mean?" she asked, letting Quilly Wonka explore the area of carpet and the papers strewn between her and Fletcher.

"The middle stuff. The stuff that leads up to the big grand gesture. The...hard stuff." He shrugged. "I love the grand gestures. Not so much the other stuff."

She had to admit that grand gestures were one of Fletcher's specialties.

"For example, when Anthony Howell was the lead with you in the school play but then got mono," he went on.

"Okay."

"You needed a guy to fill in at the last minute and I agreed to do it. For you. Everyone thought it was so amazing that I'd come through like that. But I didn't do the hard middle stuff—building the set or all the rehearsals. I just got to swoop in at the end when the play was already all put together and everyone else was awesome and I just happened to know the lines from helping you learn yours."

She nodded. He was right. He'd always gotten credit for being the one to save the day. To save *her* day. "And we were good enough friends that we were able to ad lib any lines that you forgot or flubbed," she added.

"I've always been there for you, but I'm always the guy who comes in when you *most* need someone and all else has failed. Like when you were learning to drive. Your dad put the hard time in. I came in at the end, when he was fed up, and helped you get over your nerves. But he taught you the basics and dealt with the tears. And the crushed traffic cones and the bent fender."

She grimaced. Her dad had *not* enjoyed teaching her to drive.

"And when you were having trouble in geometry, I helped tutor you. But you already knew the basics and Mr. Orillon saw you after school for days before I came in to help."

Okay, also true.

"And I wasn't the boyfriend," he went on, "so I didn't have to deal with your annoying habits all the time or you getting mad at me because I was going out with my friends instead of you and then getting into an argument."

"Wait, you think I have annoying habits?"

He gave her a look. "But *I* didn't have to say that. I got to be the guy who said you were awesome and that Jason was an asshole and then I brought you ice cream or flowers and I was the big, sweet best friend."

She thought about that. Yeah, Fletcher had *always* sided with her.

"And then there was Vegas..." he said dryly. "The ultimate grand gesture."

"But...I needed you."

"I know. But dammit—" He looked and sounded frustrated. "I swooped in and 'saved' you when things got really bad and went public. But you and Jason have been drifting apart for a long time. Why didn't I ever show up in Nashville to see how you were?" He shoved a hand through his hair. "See? I don't put in the tough time in the middle. But I always get to be the big hero."

"So you think you've been getting off easy all this time. Not really working that hard but getting the credit for being the one who gets me whatever I need. But it's really just that you come through when everyone else has failed and there's no way to screw it up."

She understood what he was saying. And he wasn't wrong. But some of this was on her too, for letting him think that he was Mr. Perfect.

"I *have* been," Fletcher insisted. "I've been doing it on purpose."

"What?"

"I didn't realize it at first. Like with the school play. But I always come in when it's easy to save the day. There was literally no one else who could have filled in the day before opening night of the play. They were going to push it back. I just had to stand up there and say lines that were *close*."

"You came through for me, every single time I needed you," she insisted.

"They were all times when I couldn't do anything *wrong*." He shook his head. "But I didn't realize it until we were eighteen. When your grandpa died."

Jordan frowned and hugged her arms against her stomach. "What do you mean? You were awesome."

"I showed up at your house at the end of the day."

"Yeah, when I just needed to get out and find some peace and quiet."

Fletcher nodded. "I know."

His eyes were on her knees instead of her face. Though Jordan didn't think he was really seeing her knees.

"I stayed at the back of the church during the funeral with my brothers and mom and dad. And I didn't come over to your house until I figured you were pretty cried out."

She frowned. "What are you getting at?"

He blew out a breath and looked up at her. "I couldn't stand to see you cry. It was killing me how sad you were. And I had no idea what to say. So I waited until I didn't need to say anything. Until I knew that all you needed was a drive and to listen to some music and just forget for a while."

She didn't say anything, just watched him.

"That's when I realized how much I loved being the guy who could make things better for you. But I *hated not* being that guy. I loved it so much, and I knew you so well, I could always time it just right to make me seem like the big hero. But I waited out the tough stuff. For the stuff I didn't know how to handle to be over."

Jordan took a big breath. Oh boy. She saw what he was saying. She even believed him. He did always come in at the perfect moment.

So he did it on purpose.

Did that matter? If he showed up and did what needed to be done?

She tipped her head, studying him. No, it didn't matter.

Except to *him*.

He clearly felt that he was half-assing things or something.

This was partly on her. Some of this pressure to be the perfect friend, the hero, the guy at just the right moments, came from her. Because she always let him think that he was getting it exactly right.

And he wasn't.

But the things he did do were important. And she knew he had it in him to be there for the tough stuff.

"So how does slowing things down *now* make all of that better?"

"This is twenty-four-seven now," he said. "And yeah, that's freaking me out a little. I can't just wait until the end of the day when bad things are happening. I can't just show up at the last minute anymore."

Ah. That made sense. She nodded. "Right. Okay. So what does the slowing down look like?"

"Just keeping things simple," he said. "Or as simple as we can."

"No dog yet. No pregnancy tests."

"Right." He said it emphatically.

She smiled. She understood what he was saying. She wasn't worried that he'd bail on her when things got hard, but if he needed to prove something to himself, then she could let him.

Fletcher ran his hands down his thighs, then leaned in, resting his elbows on his knees. "Look, I want the dogs *and* the kids. I want it all, Jordan. Like I said, I'm *in* here. But I want to get it right. And I feel like we've just jumped over a bunch of steps that most couples take before they get to the marriage vows."

"Like jumping to opening night of the play without building the set," she said.

He gave her a half-smile. "Yeah. Something like that."

"Does this have something to do with why you pulled back in the bedroom this morning and tried to distract yourself with gross, embarrassing memories?"

"Yeah." He nodded. Then cleared his throat. "I didn't want our first time to be a quickie."

"It was *really* good, Fletcher."

"But I'd intended to give you more…middle stuff."

"More foreplay?"

He shrugged. "And other fun stuff. I mean, hot, fast sex against the wall before rushing off to work is very much about getting to the end, right?"

"Well, I have to say that ending was *very* happy," she said, trying to keep her tone light.

"It was," he agreed. His gaze met hers with a hot intensity. "But that's just one more thing I've—we've—jumped ahead on. Most couples work up to sex. They kiss, they touch and make out. They figure out the other person's turn-ons and the spots to kiss and touch to make them crazy. To make it a *really*…grand gesture."

A ribbon of heat curled through her.

"Lots of people have one-night stands. Hookups that go from having a drink together to hot, dirty sex in the same night." She narrowed her eyes. "I'd be willing to bet you've had some of those."

He shifted, looking a little uncomfortable. She wanted to laugh. Of course he'd had some of those. Fletcher Landry had the Landry boys' reputation. They all loved women and they loved to love women.

But this was serious for him. And she understood where he was coming from. She also understood that she was going to have to help him get over this.

"You are unlike any other woman. One-night stands and hot hookups can be forgettable," Fletcher finally said. "They can be fine. They can be a good time, but that's it. That's not what we are. It has to be amazing. I won't apologize for that. You are an exception to every rule. The sex has to be everything you want and need it to be. Period."

She *loved* the deep, firm, confident tone. The ribbon of heat turned into a slow rolling wave of lust.

"So...you want heavy petting," she said, her voice a little breathless.

"Heavy petting?"

"Your grandma's term," she said with a nod and a small grin. "Making out."

"Yes," he agreed easily. "Lots of that. I want to touch you and taste you and figure out *exactly* what you want and need."

Fourteen

DAMN, that sounded good to her. Jordan leaned in and pinned him with a similarly serious stare. "I'm not worried, Fletcher."

"I'm glad."

But she realized he was. Maybe not worried, exactly, but he had an idea of how he wanted this to go.

She let a long breath out and nodded. "Okay. We can slow it all down."

"Thank you."

She sat back. "I'm *really* excited about this new job."

It took him just a second to process that she was changing the subject.

"I'm not surprised, but I'm really glad. You want to tell me about some of your plans?"

He caught on quick. "Well, if you want to slow down, I need to *stop* talking about you touching and tasting me," she told him.

Fletcher's eyes flickered with heat, but he nodded. "Tell me about your day."

She laughed softly. But this was good. If Fletcher needed to know that sweeping her off her feet in Vegas and bringing her home *had* been a grand gesture and that he'd gotten it right, telling him about all of the plans for the petting zoo would definitely reassure him. Fletcher would want her to be happy and would be excited if *she* was excited about the things happening in Autre.

"I spent the whole day at the animal park and Charlie and I have a ton of new ideas. You probably already know everything she's been doing so far."

Fletcher nodded. "I've helped her develop some of the materials, but we haven't had time to get it all done or to expand."

"Yeah, that's one of the things I got started on," Jordan said, gesturing at papers around her. "But I was thinking about another idea after I spent some time with Regan Reynolds and one of her patients. You know Regan, right?"

"She worked with a couple of kids in my classroom last year. She saw them at school about once a month so we talked regularly."

"I think what she's doing with therapy and the animals is amazing and I was thinking about it a lot."

"It is cool. The whole town is fascinated. Even if she is a Bad girl." He grinned.

Autre and Bad, Louisiana, liked to think they were rivals but truthfully, off the high school football field, there wasn't much for the two towns to *not* like about one another. The Mayor of Bad, Holly Williams, sometimes bitched about Autre only caring about exploiting the area for tourist money, but everyone in Autre chalked it up to jealousy.

"Regan is great," Jordan agreed. "And then, on top of everything I learned about her program, I met a little girl."

"Really? Who?"

"She came down after school. Her name is Sophia."

Fletcher looked stunned. "Yes. Sophia Abar. She's actually in my class."

"I was wondering if you knew her!" She was startled to see that Fletcher looked pained. "What's wrong?"

"Nothing. She's just been having a tough year. What was she doing at the petting zoo?"

"She was talking to Chewpaca, the little alpaca from Iowa."

"She was *talking* to him?" Fletcher repeated.

"Yes. About someone who would rub their dog's nose the way she was rubbing the alpaca. And he just stood there, listening to her. Chewie isn't even friendly with the other animals, but he stood there at the fence listening to this little girl as if she was the most wonderful thing he'd ever seen. When she found out he doesn't have a mom and dad, she got incredibly sad and promised him that she would come and visit him all the time." Jordan had been thinking about Sophia all evening. "I don't know why, but that just struck me as the most amazing thing. This little girl and this alpaca were having this bonding moment right in front of me."

Fletcher was quiet for a moment. Then he said, "She lost her dad this summer." His voice was tight suddenly. "After a long battle with cancer. Everyone in school knew about it all last year. There were fundraisers and things like that. I actually had her older sister in class two years ago." He took a shaky breath. "When her mom, Ana, came to me late this summer and asked if Sophia could be in my class, I took it as a huge compliment. I thought maybe I could help her move on. You know, now that his battle is over, and they're past the funeral, and they've been in counseling…"

He shook his head sadly. "I thought maybe she was ready to get back to more normal life and back to being a kid again. Those little girls went through hell this past year and had a lot of their normal childhood really taken from them. No kid should go through that."

Jordan felt a tightness in her chest. That was a heart-breaking story no matter what, but having met Sophia and seen her interaction with Chewie, it took on a whole new meaning.

"She was probably talking to Chewie about her dad."

Fletcher swallowed hard. "Yeah. And…she literally hasn't said a word in school since classes started."

Jordan's eyes widened. "What? She was so talkative at the petting zoo. Not just to Chewie, but with me as well."

Fletcher looked down at the floor in front of him. "I was really feeling full of myself. I really thought that being in the fun teacher's classroom would make all the difference. But I haven't been able to get through to her." He looked up. "I haven't been able to do anything for her."

Jordan studied him, concerned. Fletcher loved to fix things. It was most often focused on her, but it wasn't as if he didn't have that tendency with other people as well. In the Landry family no one person had to be the one fixing everything for everyone, so Fletcher hadn't felt as much pressure with everyone else. But he certainly loved having the right answers.

As a teacher, he was very gifted. He loved his kids. He loved teaching. He was definitely known as the fun teacher and he enjoyed that reputation. He was early in his career and he probably hadn't encountered a lot of kids who'd been through tragedy like Sophia had. He was clearly learning that being fun wasn't always the answer.

"You can't beat yourself up," Jordan said gently. "You can't know what to say and what to do in every single situation for every single person, Fletcher. Every kid, every *person*, is going to go through that and react to it differently. I know you're doing your best. You've only been in school for a few weeks."

"I just—" He blew out a breath. "I have no idea *what* to do. It's one thing for me to have tried plan A and it didn't work, so we've moved on to plan B or even plan C but..." He shrugged. "I don't have a plan B. I'm not sure I really even have a plan A."

"Well, then this is especially good," Jordan said. "She's opening up and talking and having a positive experience at the petting zoo. At least there's that."

Fletcher nodded. "Of course. That's awesome."

Jordan could tell it wasn't enough though. Of course Fletcher would want to be helping this little girl.

"Talking to both Regan and Sophia today got me thinking

about the animals we have. So many of them have special needs. Vincent Van Goat is missing an ear, Hermione is scared of thunderstorms," Jordan said of the pot-bellied pig. "Chewie lost his mom, Paddington was born with a cleft palate, Reggie only has three legs." She loved the English bulldog and the dark gray cat already. Reggie got along on his three legs as well as the four-legged felines. It was amazing.

"There are so many animals with varying issues, and I think that instead of just doing presentations about what hedgehogs eat and where lemurs are from and how many pups otters have, we could sometimes go deeper and talk about our animals and their specific issues. What happened, what adjustments we make for them—like how Sylvester is Hermione's comfort cat—how their issues affect their lives…and how their issues *don't*—the ways they have adapted and healed and are just like the other animals. Kids love animals. Animals are so easy to feel sympathy and empathy for, to want to help, to love. I think it could help kids who have their own stuff—anxiety, disabilities, even grief—feel less alone. And it could help other kids accept those differences in their classmates and peers."

She realized that she was watching Quilly eat as she spoke. She looked up at Fletcher. "Does that make sense?"

He was watching her with a combination of wonder and affection.

"Of course that makes sense. If a kid learns to love and understand and accept an animal with a difference, it can make it a lot easier to talk about how humans with differences need love and acceptance too."

She nodded enthusiastically. He completely understood where she was going. "Yes, exactly. And if they understand how the animals compensate for their illnesses and injuries and how they're really the same as the other animals in spite of that, it can help the kids to connect the fact that humans are like that too."

Fletcher nodded. "I love it."

She leaned in, resting her elbows on her knees. "And I would love to work on this with an elementary school teacher. Someone with a lot more experience in how kids communicate, and think, and express themselves. If you know someone…"

He grinned. "I could probably ask someone at school."

She laughed. "I'd love to work on this with *you*."

"I wouldn't let it be anyone but me," he assured her.

She knew that. Not only because of *her*, but because anything that made kids' lives better was something Fletcher would be one hundred percent into.

"I'm sure Griffin and Tori will help develop the information about how these things happen to animals, how they recover, how they adapt—"

"You know, Griffin's brother is a wildlife rehabilitation expert," Fletcher said. "He has worked in several rehab facilities around the country. I know he specializes in big cats, but he's worked with everything from eagles to turtles to wolves. I'll bet he'd add some really great perspective."

"Oh, he and Regan could talk about the similarities between human injury and recovery and animals!" Jordan reached for a notebook and made a note. "That would be awesome."

"And Donovan could talk about all the poisonous snakes and spiders he's encountered. The guy gets excited about salamanders." Fletcher rolled his eyes, but he was grinning.

"You've met him?"

"He came through for a couple of days to see Griffin in July," Fletcher said. "He's a great guy. Very outgoing and friendly. He and Bailey Wilcox got started talking about frogs and salamanders though and the rest of us kind of tuned out."

Jordan tipped her head. "Bailey? Do I know her?"

"She works for Louisiana Wildlife and Fisheries. She's with Juliet's brother Chase."

"Oh, right." Chase was in medical school somewhere, but he came to Autre as often as possible. She'd met him at Juliet and Sawyer's wedding in April. "Is Bailey the one Chase was dancing with when she stepped on his foot and they both tripped and bumped into the cake table?"

Fletcher laughed. "Yep."

The cake had already been cut and served, but several plates had ended up on the floor.

Jordan laughed. She'd missed a lot here in the time she'd been gone. She was so glad to be back.

"Well, great, maybe Bailey can come do a talk or two also. She can talk about how important it is to be careful not to do things that might injure the wildlife."

"She'd probably love that."

"And even though you're back to teaching and can't do a lot of the presenting, I would love your input on how to put it all in terms for the kids."

"Of course. I'm in. It all sounds amazing. We already know that our animals' differences are special, but this makes them even more so. They can be important in teaching kids about understanding and accepting differences in everything and everyone around them."

She sat grinning at him. She noticed that he, and the rest of the family, referred to the animals and the petting zoo as "ours". The whole thing really was a family effort, even if they didn't all work directly in the petting zoo.

Not only had she not had a project like this that she'd been this excited about in so long, but she also hadn't shared any specific passions with someone in a very long time. She'd been supportive of Jason, of course, but the music had been all his. She had been his biggest cheerleader, but she didn't play a single instrument and she wasn't terrible at karaoke, but she always let Naomi sing lead.

She loved the feeling of doing something that was the Landry family's project. Her heart flipped as she realized that she was *officially* a Landry now.

She blinked fast to keep from tearing up. "I love the idea of our petting zoo being a sanctuary," she said. "A safe place where animals and kids can come to be fully accepted and supported and understood and loved."

Fletcher gave her a smile. "And for all of us too."

She thought about that. And nodded slowly. "Yeah. It's really giving me a place to…"

"Bloom," he supplied when she trailed off." "You've been putting Jason first for a long time. Now you have a place where you can really do something for *you*."

That made her stomach swoop. "It seems like it's doing that for Charlie too," she said. She'd known Charlotte Arabella Clementine Landry for a *very* long time. She never would have imagined Charlie working for—and in love with—a petting zoo.

"It is," Fletcher agreed. "And it's helping Griffin find his passion again too."

Jordan gave a happy sigh. "Wow."

"And you've been here for *one* day," Fletcher said, his voice a little husky. "I can't imagine what you'll have come up with in a week."

Jordan felt a mix of pride and excitement swirl through her. "This feels really good."

"Nothing could make me happier than you finding your place. Especially if that place happens to be right here with me."

"Of course, it's right here with you." She gave a soft laugh. "I'm not going anywhere, Fletcher."

He didn't smile, but he nodded. "I know. Which is why it means a lot to me that you find something that makes you incredibly happy and fulfilled."

He meant that. She knew that. He wanted her to be happy even more than he wanted it for himself. It was amazing. She hadn't had someone who cared about her happiness like this in a very long time. Or ever. No one had ever loved her the way Fletcher did. "Well, I really think that incredibly happy and fulfilled is happening."

His expression was a mix of relief and pleasure. God, he was a good guy.

It was too bad there was a hedgehog and nearly two full reams of paper between them at the moment. She'd love to crawl into his lap and kiss the hell out of him.

"Fletcher—"

He suddenly shoved to his feet. Quilly startled and dove under one of the pillows at the edge of his little corral. Fletcher went to the desk in the corner and grabbed his laptop. He already had it open by the time he sat down again and started typing.

"There's probably a lot of research that's been done on comfort animals," he said.

This was exciting and fun and she felt close to Fletcher brainstorming about this new program too. Sharing this with him mattered a lot.

"There has been," she said. "People have an increase in endorphins when they're around animals and people have shown things like decreased heart rates and breathing when they pet an animal during an anxiety attack."

"Exactly. We could use that when we write up the applications for grants."

"We're going to apply for grants?"

He looked up. "We should. This program has a ton of amazing potential."

She knew that he was thinking about it in terms of potential for *her* professionally, but also for the kids they could reach. And specifically, Sophia.

That was it. They could slow down a little, but if he was going to be so amazing and jump into this passion project with her like this, he couldn't expect to *not* get kissed for it.

She scooped Quilly up and tucked him into the pet carrier. The hedgehog immediately went to his soft sleeping bag and snuggled in. Then she pushed papers out of the way and crawled the few feet to where her husband sat.

She took the laptop out of his hands.

"What—"

She slid into his lap, straddling his thighs. She ran her hands up the back of his neck and threaded her fingers into his hair, holding his head as she looked at him. His hands settled on her hips.

"It just occurred to me that we've sat and talked and brainstormed about projects together so many times, but it's never been anything as amazing as this. I can't tell you how much your enthusiasm and support means to me." She paused. "But I can show you." She put her mouth against his and said softly, "It's a *huge* turn on."

Then she pressed her lips to his, tasting him for a long moment, before she lifted her head.

She could have just left it at that. A simple, lingering but sweet kiss to say *thanks* and *hey I love talking to you like this*. But it wasn't enough. She wanted so much more from him.

And Fletcher seemed to need *something*. Something to show him that this was all worth celebrating. Yes, they were in the middle. It wasn't perfect. But all of this was worth celebrating.

Or maybe she just wanted to distract him from feeling like he was failing Sophia.

Or hell, maybe she was just really horny.

Because now that she knew what sex with Fletcher could be like, she was definitely that.

Whatever her reasons, now that she was kissing him, she didn't want to stop. For a *very* long time.

She wiggled closer, wrapping her arms around his neck and pressing her breasts against his chest. Her skirt had already hiked up around her hips and she was able to press her aching center against his fly. He was hard and the sensation ratcheted up her need. His fingers curled into her hips. She licked her tongue along his bottom lip and then changed the angle of her head. She opened her mouth, wanting so much more. She moved against his erection, but it wasn't enough.

He still hadn't opened his mouth though he was kissing her back now. His hands stayed on her hips and she felt like she couldn't get close enough. She ran her hands down his back and then around to his sides, stroking up and down through the cotton of his shirt.

Needing more, needing *something,* she reached between them, rubbing her hand down the front of his fly.

That finally got a reaction. Fletcher swiftly grabbed her wrist, and before she could speak, he rolled them so that he was on top and she was underneath. He pinned her hands to the floor above her head and stared down at her, breathing hard.

Well, she wasn't upset about *this.* But they weren't kissing anymore. And her hand was not where she wanted it to be.

"Fletcher, I want you. Please."

She opened her mouth to continue, fully willing to beg if needed, but just then Fletcher gave a soft growl and took her mouth in a deep kiss.

This time there was no holding still, no closed lips. He opened his mouth and swept his tongue into her mouth, drinking her in. Heat shot through her body, arrowing straight to her clit. She lifted her hips, needing to be closer, needing pressure and friction and heat.

Fletcher took both of her wrists in one hand over her head, while letting the other slide down her body. He lingered at her breast, kneading, then rubbing his thumb over her nipple. She wasn't wearing a bra and the sensitive tip responded instantly, wanting more.

But his hand continued lower, to the hem of her skirt. He bunched it up to her waist, exposing her thighs and her panties. He ran his hand to her ass, squeezing gently, then to the side, slipping his fingers under the silk that crossed her hip. He brushed over her mound and then down to rub his middle finger over her clit.

She moaned and again tried to lift closer. Restlessly she parted her legs, encouraging him to keep going and to go so much farther.

But instead, his hand stopped and he lifted his head.

His breathing was ragged, his eyes hot as he looked down at her. His hand was still between her legs, his finger against her clit, but it wasn't moving.

"Fletcher?"

He didn't answer, but withdrew his hand and pushed back to kneel between her legs. His hot gaze tracked over her. He couldn't see much. She was still mostly covered, but she was sure she looked willing. Her skirt was around her waist and she had one knee drawn up and splayed open.

He put his hand on her leg, stroking gently just above her knee. Even that much sent tingles racing through her.

"I need to know what you like. What you don't like. What I can do to make this the best you've ever had."

"Okay, I like when you kiss me. I like your hands on me. I *really* liked your hand where was just a second ago. I —"

"Show me."

There was something in his tone that made her stop and swallow hard. And her belly heat. "Wha—what do you mean?"

"I can make you your favorite sandwich without asking a question. I could plan the perfect birthday party for you, and not give it a second thought. I could take you on a week-long vacation, even packing the bag for you, and not tell you where we were going and still get nearly every detail right. But we just started kissing *yesterday*. I don't just want to know how to give you an orgasm. I want to know every inch of your body. I want to know exactly how you like to be touched, what you fantasize about..." He squeezed her knee. "I *need* to know those things."

"This doesn't have to be perfect to be amazing," she assured him. "Just doing this with you is awesome. I know it will be good. I know that you will take care of me."

Unfortunately, that seemed to be the opposite of what she should have said. He withdrew his hand and sat back on his heels, tucking his hands into his pockets.

"I *will* take care of you, Jordan. Which is why I need to know exactly how to do that."

She wet her lips. "What does that mean?"

"It means, you're going to tell me, and *show* me, how to take care of you."

That was hot.

Not just the words. Though, those too. He wanted to know exactly how to do what she needed him to do and him wanting to get it all right was definitely sexy. But this was also a change in their relationship. Fletcher always knew what she needed. He prided himself on that. So much, that she often let him think he'd gotten it perfectly right when…he hadn't quite.

Him *asking* her to tell him was new. She liked it.

God, he looked so good kneeling there, between her legs, fully dressed while she was rumpled on the floor in front of him. And he was being firm. He wasn't budging on this.

She could always talk Fletcher into anything. She rarely had to ask more than once. But she could tell that this was non-negotiable.

"What you want me to do?" she finally asked. "Exactly."

"You're going to show me how you like your nipples touched. How hard I should pinch or suck."

She pulled in a quick breath as one hand moved to cover a breast without thinking.

He looked pleased by that and damn if she didn't want to keep pleasing him. That was hot too. She'd always liked making Fletcher happy. It was why she let him think she liked his coffee. But this was a whole new level. She wanted to do whatever it took to put more of that oh-yes-good-girl look on his face.

What was *that*?

She hadn't been into being bossed around ever before.

But this wasn't all that different from when the girls had advised her to just let Fletcher be in charge in Vegas. And that had turned out great. Like really great.

"What else?" she asked, giving her breasts a squeeze through the dress.

"You're going to take me on a tour of your whole body.

Places where you like to be kissed and touched. Places you don't."

He wasn't touching her now. His hands were still in his pockets. But her body felt hot like he was stroking her skin as he spoke.

She shifted one leg restlessly.

His posture was casual as he gave her the instructions, but his eyes were hot and the bulge in the front of his pants was obvious. And huge.

He wanted her. She had no doubt. But he was controlling this. He wanted a "tour." She was torn between this do-what-the-hot-teacher-wants and wanting to push past that control.

"You're just going to watch me touch myself?"

He nodded. "You're going to give yourself an orgasm. While I watch. So I know what you need for that. And what that looks and sounds like."

Jordan let out a little breath. Whoa. She and Fletcher had said a lot of things to each other over the years, but this was…yeah, whoa.

Could she do this?

"Jordan, you can do this. I need you to."

When he read her mind like that, it helped. He knew her. He was right. This was someplace they'd never gone. And she wanted everything with Fletcher. Could she do this? For him? Definitely.

"This just might be a little embarrassing. I've never done this before. With anyone."

Of course he would know she meant Jason. There wasn't anybody else it could be.

His voice was rough and firm when he said, "Good."

She squeezed her eyes shut and gave a short laugh. "I don't even know what to tell you."

"Everything."

"Okay, usually there's not a lot of watching involved. And

when I'm alone with my bright pink vibrating friend, we just kind of get right to it."

"Then maybe you're going to learn some things too."

His voice was tight and her eyes opened to watch him. He looked almost like he was in pain, but she could tell it was barely restrained desire. That shot a thrill through her and she instantly understood the temptation of watching. Would she love to watch Fletcher come undone? Lose his self-restraint? Touch himself and completely lose it? Knowing she was watching? Turned on because of her?

Abso-fucking-lutely.

Yeah, she got it.

"And this?" he asked. "There's nothing to be embarrassed about. You look hotter than my hottest fantasy lying there, willing to push your boundaries with me."

She believed him, even just based on the look on his face. She wasn't sure Jason had ever looked at her the way Fletcher was looking at her now.

That wasn't true. She did know. Jason had *never* looked at her the way Fletcher was looking at her now.

She didn't know if that was because they had started out when they were so young, because things had gotten routine, or if bottom line, Jason hadn't wanted her the way Fletcher did. Whatever the reason, it didn't matter now. She was with the man who made her feel like a goddess, even while she was lying on his floor, mostly uncertain about where to put her own hands.

"There's nothing to be embarrassed about," Fletcher said, reading her again. "I remember the night you slipped when we were running across Cliff Monroe's field and landed in a pile of cow poop."

She huffed out a short, surprised laugh. "That was mud!"

He shook his head, a tiny smile tugging the corner of his lips. "That did not smell like mud."

She remembered the incident well. "You made me sit on that

old blanket when we got to your truck and you picked me up and just threw me in the bayou when we got back to the docks."

"You were wearing shorts so it didn't just get on your clothes. You smelled terrible."

She laughed, in spite of yet another gross and embarrassing memory. "You have strange seduction techniques, Mr. Landry."

His smile faded to more of a smirk. "If I can think about that, and still want you more than I've ever wanted anyone, I'd say you shouldn't worry that you'll be embarrassed during what's about to happen."

Jordan's smile died even as heat swept through her. "I really don't even know…"

Where to start was what she had been about to say. But that wasn't entirely true. What she didn't know was how fast or slow she should go here. She typically didn't need a lot of foreplay. Or at least she and Jason hadn't taken a lot of time for foreplay. When they'd first started having sex, it'd been in the backseat of his car or quickies on the basement couch. Not only had they not known what they were doing exactly, but they hadn't had a lot of time for exploring.

And then, when they'd had time and space, they still hadn't had a lot of experience with anything other than what they'd done together. And they'd been comfortable. God, now that she thought about it, she and Jason had fallen into a sexual rut by the time they'd been nineteen.

Yes, she typically liked it fast. But there was something so tempting about teasing Fletcher and taking her time with it.

"Well, Miss Benoit, you are going to give me a verbal essay and hands-on demonstration on this matter, so you better figure out what you know."

Oh my God, he was going to be the hot teacher. *Yes.* She'd never role-played but it hit her how fun this could be. And maybe helpful. If she could sort of play a part, she wouldn't think so hard about what *she* was doing.

"Okay," she said, her voice breathless. "Whatever you want, Mr. Landry."

CHAPTER
Fifteen

IT SEEMED a bit of role-playing worked for Fletcher too. He moved his hands from his pockets to the front of his pants, hooking his thumbs in his belt loops.

He looked so sexy and in charge. Jordan shifted her legs again, wanting more movement and yes, rubbing between her thighs. It looked like she was going to have to take care of that herself though.

"I hope you'll help coach me if I get stuck on something," she said. She kneaded her breast, cupping and squeezing gently. She slid her hand down her body, from her stomach to the front of her panties. The pressure on her clit was a welcome relief and she gave a little sigh.

Fletcher watched both hands intently.

She teased her nipple lightly and pressed against her clit more firmly. Okay, this wasn't so bad. This was…

"Dress off, Jordan."

Oh, *that* voice was definitely going to help this go well. And maybe fast.

She took a deep breath to try to quell the butterflies in her stomach. They were having none of that. They were dancing and fluttering with yay-sexy-times-with-Fletcher-finally energy.

She reached for the bottom of her dress and shimmied it up her body and over her head.

"Yeah, that's it," Fletcher said as his gaze raked over her. "Now put your hands back."

Her nipples were tightly puckered and a shiver went through her body as she ran the pad of her thumb over one. Heat pooled in her belly and when she rubbed over the tip again that heat slipped between her legs.

"How hard do you like it?" Fletcher asked, his voice rough. "Do I need to suck gently or can I pinch?"

Her breath lodged in her chest. "I'm…not sure."

"Find out."

She took her nipple between her thumb and finger and squeezed. "I do like that."

He nodded. "Wet your fingers."

She opened her lips and licked her fingertips, then rolled her nipple again. "The wetness is nice," she said.

"Imagine it's my mouth. Pull on it harder."

She tugged gently and gave a little moan.

"What's that do?" he asked.

"It feels so good."

"Does it make your pussy wet?"

Her eyes flew to his face. Damn, that was so hot. She licked her lips and nodded. "Yeah. Well, *wetter*. I was already wet."

"Fuck, Jordan."

God, she loved that. He sounded incredibly turned on. And she wanted so much more. She swallowed. Jason had never said "pussy" to her. And she'd never said "clit" to him.

"I feel it in my clit."

Fletcher's jaw tightened, but he nodded. "Do it again."

She wet her fingers again and rolled her nipple, then tugged, harder than before, loving the flutter of pleasure it created.

"Do you play with your nipples when you use your vibrator?"

His husky voice rolled over her and made those pleasure pulses intensify.

She lifted her other hand so that each was working a nipple. She tugged and squeezed. Her lips fell open and she was aware she was panting.

"Need one of those hands between your legs," he said after a few moments.

Yes, she really did.

She slid one hand down her body. Her skin felt hypersensitive even over her ribs and belly. She ran her palm back and forth just above the top of her panties. She lifted her hand to her mouth and wet her first two fingertips, then drew that moisture in a trail from between her breasts to the top of her panties. The stroke made her nipples tighten even further and she loved the way his eyes followed the motion.

"This is one place I would love to feel your tongue," she told him.

Fletcher nodded. "No problem there."

She liked this. Watching his reactions to her touching herself was a definite turn on, but she also loved the sensations and the idea of him traveling the same paths with his mouth and hands.

She cupped her breast and squeezed the nipple even harder. Her clit throbbed, wanting some attention too. Jordan slipped her fingers into the front of her panties, her middle finger brushing over her clit.

Sparkles of heat danced outward down her legs and up her torso. She gave a little gasp of pleasure. She had, of course, touched the spot before, but never with her senses so heightened or with so much focus. And never with someone watching her.

Suddenly Fletcher's big hand wrapped around her wrist. Her eyes flew open. She hadn't even realized they'd closed.

Even that much of a touch from him sent tingles racing from her belly to her pussy. She gave a little gasp.

"Take the panties off. I can't see." His gaze was burning into hers.

"I don't want to move my hands. You can take them off," she suggested, lifting her hips slightly. She desperately wanted Fletcher to undress her. She also really wanted him to get more involved here. This was hot. She was more turned on than she could remember being in forever. She needed *his* hands on her.

He squeezed her wrist gently then let her go. "Take them off."

His tone was firm and she felt herself reaching for the top of her panties before she even processed the thought.

Wow, bossy Fletcher did it for her.

She pushed her panties to her knees, but he was in the way of her pushing them all the way off. Clearly, he wasn't budging though. So, she only had one option. She drew one knee up toward her chest and unhooked the panties from that foot. That served to spread her legs open in a very revealing way.

Fletcher seemed to approve. He watched intently, groaning softly. She did the same with the other leg, with the same response from Fletcher, though this time he sucked in a deep breath and blew it out as if he were struggling for control.

Inspired by that, Jordan tossed her panties to the side. She left one knee drawn up and let her leg fall to the side, opening up in the most wanton way. She lifted a hand to her nipple again, twisting and tugging even more firmly than before. She began circling her clit. It had been a while since she'd done this manually rather than with one of her two battery-operated friends, but she quickly found a perfect pressure and rhythm.

"Does your vibrator only work your clit? Or do you move it inside this pretty pussy?"

She gave a low moan at Fletcher's words. There was just something about him saying graphic words to her that she'd never heard from him before that ratcheted up her desire. "I have one of each," she confessed.

"Which do you like best?"

"The one that has the clit stimulation and goes inside," she admitted. "But the other works great too."

"You use the other during sex?"

She picked up her pace, feeling the coiling beginnings of an orgasm tightening her inner muscles. She shook her head. "No. Only when I'm alone."

Almost as if he could no longer stand not touching her at all, Fletcher reached out and circled her ankle with his big hand. He stroked up and down. She'd had no idea that her ankle was an erogenous zone but that simple touch made the desire twisting deep inside her tighten further.

"Fletcher," she said softly, his name almost a groan.

"You'll use it with me. Even when I'm balls deep and stroking this gorgeous pussy with my cock, I want that vibrator against your clit."

"Oh God," she moaned.

"I want to feel the difference when your pussy milks me using that vibrator, versus your fingers, versus my fingers. We'll see which makes you come hardest," Fletcher said, stroking his hand higher onto her calf.

"Fletcher," she gasped.

She picked up the pace of her finger, pressing harder and rubbing faster.

He watched intently. His nostrils flared as he continued to hold himself back.

She was going to come like this. That was inevitable. But she knew how to make it even harder.

"Fletcher, I need you."

"I'm not fucking you yet, Jordan. Keep going."

"Help me. I need your fingers."

The groan seemed to come from the depths of his chest. "Not yet."

"Please. I'm so close."

"Finish it."

"I'll comes so much harder with your fingers inside me."

He groaned again.

And gave in.

He came forward, bracing his hand on the floor beside her hip, that arm extended. The hand that had been stroking her calf slid up her leg and immediately cupped her pussy.

She groaned at the first contact of his hand against her hot, wet center.

"You're amazing," he said. "So fucking gorgeous. So sweet and hot at the same time. God, I can't wait to make you come over and over again."

That was all he did, and she went careening over the edge of her orgasm. He hadn't even slipped a finger inside before the waves of pleasure burst over her.

"Fletcher!" she cried out.

"Damn," he muttered.

But he wasn't done with her yet. Now he slipped one big, long finger into her. The ripples of her climax were still trembling through her pussy and her inner muscles clamped onto his finger immediately. She gasped as she seemed to bounce up toward the pinnacle again. He pumped his finger deep, then added a second, stroking rhythmically and quickly.

"Again," he said, gruffly.

She rolled her head back and forth.

"Yes," he said firmly. He curled his fingers against her G-spot and she whimpered at the delicious sensation. "Again," he repeated.

Her finger went back to her clit and she started circling again. How could she argue with the man who was making her whole body sing?

She felt the climb toward another orgasm beginning.

Unbelievable.

"Tell me what else you want," he ordered. "Anything."

"I can barely think," she told him, her words coming out in breathy pants.

"Feel," he said. "What do you feel?"

"My nipples. Suck on my nipples." The answer came quickly and easily.

He groaned and lowered his head, his mouth capturing one of the stiff points and sucking hard.

His fingers continued to thrust in and out and she circled her clit faster.

"Oh God, yes, Fletcher!"

She lifted her other hand to her opposite breast, pinching that nipple at the same time.

Sensations from all over her body, the scent of Fletcher, the rustle of the project papers she was lying on, and dozens of memories from this very room, including movie nights, game nights with their friends, and just sitting and laughing and talking, all crashed in on her at once.

She shot over the summit, her orgasm pounding through her,

She cried Fletcher's name again and heard his answering, "Fuck yes."

The second orgasm went on longer than the first and was definitely more intense.

Jordan's body seemed to melt into the floor underneath her as it slowly began to fade. She felt Fletcher shift to lie beside her. His fingers slipped from her body, but he rested his hand on her lower belly as she sucked in lungfuls of oxygen.

It was several long seconds, possibly a couple of minutes, before he said, "A+, Miss Benoit."

She chuckled, and rolled toward him. "It's Mrs. Landry to you."

His hand, now resting on her hip, gave her a squeeze. "Yes, it definitely is."

She ran her hand up his arm to his neck and pulled him close. She kissed him, taking her time to really taste him. Then she pulled back and met his eyes, "I'm more on board with this slowing down thing than I was before."

He chuckled and pinched her ass. "Let's go upstairs and I'll convince you that slowing down is your favorite thing ever."

She shivered. "I'm also suddenly glad I didn't bring a new puppy home tonight."

He lifted a brow. "See? Slowing down can be a good thing."

And it was. Twice more that night.

FOUR NIGHTS LATER, Jordan looked up from her laptop at the kitchen table as Fletcher came in through the back door. After dinner at Ellie's, he'd gone with Zeke to look at the area they were thinking would be the best for the zebra pasture— she still couldn't believe they were thinking about getting zebras—and she'd come home and immediately sat down at the kitchen table to go over more information about grant applications.

Charlie and the everyone else involved with Boys of the Bayou were in favor of the program, but they needed funding to pay a psychologist to consult, for additional training for Jordan, and to develop further materials and buy supplies.

Thankfully, there was solid research around how animals helped people with a variety of issues from mild to severe. They felt good about their chances at getting a big grant from the Wallace-Hanson Foundation. But applying for a grant was a daunting task.

Jordan looked over to see what animal Fletcher had brought home with him, knowing he wouldn't be empty handed. The idea of her and the animals getting used to one another had resulted in a new animal hanging out with them every night.

Last night, she'd found herself sitting on the lid of the toilet in their guest bathroom with her laptop balanced on her knees researching grant funding for programs like theirs while the four ducklings paddled in the bathtub.

The night after the hedgehog had come home, they'd had dinner at Ellie's with everyone and then spent the evening with Baby Ruth and Skittles, two of the juvenile otters.

They'd also talked about Jordan's conversation with a child psychologist in New Orleans who was interested in being a consultant to their program and helping them develop ways to reach out to kids with anxiety, depression, and grief issues.

Hermione the pig had spent the night with them the next night. Well, until about three a.m. when the thunder started. She'd woken them up freaking out about the storm and had needed to be taken back to her barn at the petting zoo and, more importantly, to Sylvester, her comfort cat.

Jordan had helped Fletcher with the poor thing, but she'd definitely been groggy and slept in the next morning since she'd gone to bed around one-thirty after reading through a stack of articles Fletcher had brought her about talking to kids about grief and anxiety and how different species of animals grieved.

Apparently, he was using his lunch breaks at school to research additional resources.

Jordan found that sexy as hell.

He was seducing her and making her fall deeper in love with him with research articles and pigs.

Well, and the nightly "lessons" in how she liked to be touched and kissed and talked to. Thankfully, two nights ago, he'd let her do a little learning on him as well. She'd gotten extra credit—an extra orgasm—for how well she'd retained the information last night.

Now she watched as he set the tortoise he carried down on the kitchen floor.

"This is Lentement," he said with a grin.

Jordan nodded. "Lenny and I have met." Lentement meant "slow moving" in Cajun French but everyone called him Lenny.

"And I forgot to tell you at dinner that Regan was at school today and she said to tell you she has two clients she thinks would be willing to do some public talks or even just act as consultants if we'd like them to. Matt has muscular dystrophy and Amy is a marathon runner who had her lower leg amputated after a car accident."

"Wow, really? That would be amazing."

He grinned and grabbed a beer from the fridge, then joined

her at the table. "How are things going? You were up late last night."

Their new routine was to have dinner with the family, then home for some heavy petting—they both loved the term too much not to use it—and then talking and brainstorming about the program. Sometimes they brainstormed first and got naked after. Sometimes they did it all kind of at the same time. But Fletcher, the one with a job that required him to show up at a certain time and deal with a roomful of eight-year-olds all day, had headed to bed before Jordan the past three nights. She'd developed night owl tendencies hanging out with a musician and it took her longer to wind down. And to get going in the morning.

It was good the alpacas and goats and the rest didn't wear watches. And that Griffin liked to see them all—no matter what he said—and checked on them all first thing in the morning.

She nodded. "Working on the grant. But it's coming along."

"Do you want some help?"

She smiled. "You've *been* helping, Fletcher. So much. You're spending your lunch breaks and every evening on this."

"You know I love it."

She did. "You know that you're making this even better for me, right?"

He looked surprised. "I am?"

"Of course. I love doing this together."

His eyes were soft but hot when he met her gaze. "I'm glad."

She got up from the table and went to the fridge. She grabbed some lettuce and carrots out of the drawer and tossed them on the floor for Lenny. "Come on," she told Fletcher. "I have to show you something."

He followed her into the living room. She moved one of the kitchen chairs, putting it on its side to keep Lenny on the tile floor, then crossed to the coffee table, picking her way around the stacks of papers and folders that still covered the floor. There was too much paperwork to use Fletcher's desk or the kitchen table for all of it. She didn't really have a desk or office space at the petting zoo, so this was her office for now. At least until they got the education center built at the animal park. Her heart kicked at the thought. That made it seem even more official. And it was part of what they needed the grant money for.

She picked up the page she wanted him to see and sank onto the floor to sit crisscross.

Her own clothes had finally arrived from Nashville, so the sundress she wore tonight was hers. She tucked the skirt between her legs as Fletcher dropped to the floor beside her. He braced his hands behind him, stretching his long legs out in front.

"Look what I got today." She handed the page over. It was a drawing of a smiling alpaca standing in a pasture, looking over the top of a fence. The alpaca was covered in glued-on cotton balls that had been painted brown and the sunshine and the flowers in the field were decorated with glitter. It had obviously taken more time and effort than a simple drawing.

He took it and studied it. "That's cute."

She nodded. "It's from Sophia."

He looked at her quickly. "Really?"

"Yeah. She told me that Chewie wanted me to know that he's feeling happier."

Fletcher studied the artwork again.

"I think it means that *she's* feeling happier," Jordan said softly.

He nodded. "Maybe."

"I heard her telling her mom that she wanted Ana to come read a story to Chewie. When Ana asked her why, she said that she wanted to share her mom since Chewie doesn't have one."

Fletcher sucked in a quick breath. "Jesus," he muttered. "This kid is breaking my heart."

"No," Jordan said quickly. "I think it's *good*. I've been doing all this reading and one thing that animals can do for people who are grieving is give them an outlet for the pain. A reason to keep going. A way to feel like things still matter. Sophia wants to help take care of Chewie because *he's* sad and that's giving her a purpose."

Fletcher met her eyes. "You really think that or are you just trying to make me feel better?"

She smiled and put her hand on his. "I'll admit that I would just say it to make you feel better if I knew it would. But I also really think that. Her convincing *me* that he's happier means that she understands that the people who care about *her* need to know when she's feeling better too."

Fletcher shook his head. "She hasn't done anything to make me think that."

"Well, have you…" Jordan stopped.

"Have I what?"

She should have thought this through before she spoke. She did *not* want to make him feel bad.

"Jordan, have I what?" Fletcher pressed.

"Have you told her that her being happy matters to you?" Jordan asked.

"I've…" He frowned. "You don't think she knows?"

"The school year just started. She didn't really know you before you became her teacher, right? Maybe she doesn't know that *you* specifically care." Jordan bit her bottom lip, watching Fletcher process that.

Finally he shoved a hand through his hair. "Fuck. No, I haven't. I've been trying to give her space. Not pressure her to talk or anything. She's doing well with her assignments, so I've left her alone. I guess I thought maybe kids just *know* that their teachers care."

Jordan squeezed his hand. "You should tell her."

"Yeah. I guess I should." He looked over at her. "I don't know what to say."

"You don't have to know the exact words. You'll get it right."

"Am I a bad teacher, or person, if I'm relieved to think there will be another program that can help her? So I can just be the fun teacher instead?"

He looked so sheepish that Jordan's heart flipped in her chest. Fletcher Landry had always been confident and charming and funny and willing to do anything to make things right for her. He'd gotten on a plane without a second thought to fly to Vegas to rescue her. He'd walked into that wedding chapel without blinking. He was always sure of himself.

Seeing him doubtful like this did funny things to her.

Mostly, it made her…hot.

That was weird.

But Fletcher had always been so in-charge. He was the one she could always depend on to know what to do in any situation. This more vulnerable side, because he couldn't heal a little girl's broken heart, got to Jordan.

She wasn't sure she had ever been more attracted to someone than she was to Fletcher Landry at this moment.

Jordan reached out and plucked Sophia's picture from Fletcher's hand and tossed it onto the coffee table.

"Wha —"

"Saying 'I do' to you in Vegas was the smartest thing I've ever done."

His gaze heated. "Ditto."

Then she climbed into his lap and gave him a pop-quiz about how to make her come with his mouth in under five minutes.

He passed with flying colors.

And then he *really* moved to the head of the class by helping her write their first grant proposal while they fed a giant tortoise vegetables.

THE NEXT NIGHT, Fletcher, Mitch, and Zeke got to Ellie's after nearly everyone else had already showed up.

They'd been over at the site of the future zebra pen again.

Since it was essentially a pasture with a barn structure, it didn't take as much sketching and planning or special materials as the otter enclosure had when Mitch had built it a few months ago.

Now they headed for the back table where everyone typically gathered. Fletcher noted that even Naomi was there tonight with her brother Michael and his little boy, Andre. But he didn't see his wife.

He pulled out a chair next to Charlie and dropped into it. "Where's Jordan?"

"She headed home early with a headache."

He frowned. "When I texted her at lunch she didn't say anything."

Charlie nodded. "It came on really suddenly. It's one of her migraines."

Dammit. Jordan had suffered from migraines since they'd been about seventeen. They'd started suddenly and he knew her doctors thought they were hormonally influenced. He also knew she had special medication for them and that they knocked her out of commission for most of the day when they occurred. But he didn't know…much else.

Her mother had taken care of her when she'd lived at home and when she got to college she mostly handled them on her own.

But he knew what she would need the next day. She'd text him and say that she'd had one the night before and could he bring her a cheeseburger, fries, and the biggest Coke he could find.

So tomorrow he could help her.

But he wasn't sure what to do right now.

Well, he could nix the plan for Dill Prickles, one of the new porcupines, to go home with him tonight.

He pulled out his phone and noticed the text.

Going home. Headache. Just need to sleep.

He blew out a breath. Well, fuck. The thing he hated the most was when he felt like he didn't know what to do for someone he cared about. Particularly Jordan, of course.

Thankfully, he knew better than to call her or head home, wake her up, and ask what she needed.

She would be in bed, shades drawn, lights off, door shut, just wanting to be left alone.

Yeah, he'd made the mistake in college of knocking on her dorm room door when she'd had one. It had been with good intentions. He really had been concerned and wanted to help. But she'd looked so miserable, and had begged him to leave her alone, and that had been all she needed to say.

But he'd sat outside her door, doing his homework in the hallway to keep anyone else from knocking or even shouting in the hallways or slamming their own doors.

She'd almost tripped over him the next morning when she'd come out to head to the showers.

That was when she'd asked for a cheeseburger and a Coke.

He'd had to drive several miles to find a twenty-four-hour café that would make a cheeseburger at seven thirty in the morning. But he'd done it. And nothing had made him feel better than delivering exactly what she needed after she'd been so miserable.

So, he could definitely get her a cheeseburger and fries tomorrow morning. He knew that Cora or Ellie would happily make a burger for her while they were frying eggs and hash browns for the rest of their breakfast crowd.

But right now, he had nothing.

"You feeling okay?" Charlie asked.

"Useless," Fletcher said with a shrug. "But otherwise fine."

She gave him a sympathetic smile. "It definitely sucks when the person we love is upset or hurt." She cast a glance at Griffin, who was listening to Zeke tell him about the zebra pen. "And I know it's hard for you, Fletcher. But you can't fix everything. She'll be okay."

She would. In the overall scheme of things. But knowing she

was hurting right now and there was nothing he could do, defi-nitely sucked.

He really just wanted to head home with a cheeseburger. Or balloons. Or ice cream. Or take her for a drive. Or any of the other stuff he'd done for her in the past when she hadn't felt good.

But see, the timing was off. In the past, he'd known when to show up.

At the end, of course. For the grand *finale*.

Now…he was the husband. Twenty-four-seven. All the hours were his now. And he needed to figure out what to do in them.

This was the stuff he had to learn.

This was the stuff that Jason had done.

Fuck.

"What happened?" Naomi asked, leaning in.

Fletcher realized he'd said the "fuck" out loud. He shook his head. "Just trying to figure out this marriage thing. Wish there was a handbook."

"You've got a real live handbook right here," Owen said, stretching his arms out and hugging his wife Maddie to his side. "You're surrounded by people living in wedded bliss. What do you need to know?"

Fletcher looked around. He had a point. Josh, Owen, Sawyer, and Kennedy were all married. Happily. His mom and dad and several of his aunts and uncles had also been doing the marriage thing for a long time. And then there were Ellie and Leo. His grandparents had been married for fifty some years. They'd even divorced and gotten remarried. To one another. So they defi-nitely knew something about the ups and downs.

"Okay," he said to his family at large. "What if you're already married when you figure out that you might not be good at it?"

Owen looked at Sawyer, then at Josh then back to Fletcher. He nodded. "Yup, sounds like you're about right where you should be."

Fletcher frowned.

Josh nodded his agreement. "Yeah, if you're not wondering what the hell you're doing, and feeling like you're fucking it up once in a while, you're either delusional, or you're just not paying attention."

Tori leaned in and kissed his cheek. "But it's so sexy when you work on getting it right."

"For sure," Maddie agreed. "And it's not like I'm getting it right every second either. Working at it is a way to show your love, too."

"Definitely," Sawyer agreed. "And if you never mess up, you never get to have make-up sex."

"Hell, I piss her off sometimes on purpose just for the make-up sex," Owen said.

Maddie lifted a brow. "And sometimes I pretend I'm pissed off just for the make-up sex."

Owen grinned. "Yeah? You're very convincing when you're pretending to be mad at me."

"You're very convincing when you're 'pretending' to screw up," she returned with an eye roll.

Owen just laughed.

"So you already did something to require make-up sex?" Mitch asked Fletcher. "You've been married for like a minute. And I've never seen Jordan pissed at you."

Fletcher had to admit that the few times he and Jordan had ever argued had been minor. Except about the fucking tour with Jason. And she'd gone home after he'd made her cry so none of these people had seen that.

He shook his head. "Nope. She's got a migraine. Pretty sure there's no migraine sex."

Or was there? Maybe he needed to look that up. There were endorphins and things like that, right? If only sex would fix this. They were getting really good at the making out. Getting to know Jordan's body and her turns-ons and teaching her a few things she hadn't even known she'd liked had been amazing.

There had been grand finales every fucking night this week, thank you very much.

Until tonight.

Tonight he couldn't come through with an orgasm, an amazing article to help build the new petting zoo program, or a cute animal to play with. Well, he *could*. But none of it would fix what Jordan had going on.

Tonight he couldn't do a damned thing.

"Yeah, well, there's good days and bad. That's what those vows are all about," Sawyer said.

They were. Even when you made those vows spontaneously because you were trying to be the big shot knight-in-shining-armor.

"Right," Fletcher said with a nod. "I know. Just…still adjusting."

"I'm not sure it ever stops being an adjustment." Josh placed his hand lovingly on his wife's big, pregnant belly. "There's always something new to figure out."

And that was pretty much exactly the opposite of what Fletcher needed to hear right now.

He pushed back from the table. "I need a drink."

FLETCHER HEADED FOR THE BAR. As usual, there was hardly an open stool, and any place you put your ass in Ellie's meant you were going to have a conversation. The stool you chose was determined by the kind of conversation you were in the mood for.

He could talk politics or sports, he could get a sermon, he could listen to tall tales that he'd already heard a dozen times but that each got bigger with every telling, or he could get caught up with all the town gossip. Which he had probably also already heard a few times.

But no matter which one he chose, he could get advice.

Of course, the quality of that advice also varied.

Perusing his choices, Fletcher realized that all of the people sitting at the bar had relationship experience of some kind. The youngest was twenty years older than Fletcher and was happily married. There were a couple of widowers, a couple who were on wife number two or three, a couple who were sworn bachelors, and the rest had wives, kids, and grandkids.

He wasn't sure he wanted advice.

He nudged in between his grandfather and one of Leo's best

friends, Naomi's grandpa, Armand. "Iced tea," he told his grandma.

She looked toward the back table where he had come from. "Leo," she said to her husband. "Make Fletcher feel better."

His grandfather looked at him. "You need to feel better?"

Fletcher nodded. "Yeah. But I'm not sure how to get there."

"His happily in love cousins were annoying him," Ellie said.

Fletcher wondered if he would ever stop being amazed the way Ellie seemed to know what was going on with everyone. He didn't know how she kept track of them all, but she was practically omniscient.

"Pretty hard not to be happy around that group," Leo commented.

"Yeah," Fletcher agreed. "They make it look easy."

"Don't let them fool you," Leo said. "They work at it."

Fletcher knew that. He knew Josh was a little worried about being a dad. He knew Owen and Maddie were trying to get pregnant and it wasn't as easy as they'd expected. He knew Sawyer was still working through issues after losing his best friend to a tragic bayou accident and that Juliet worried about him. Still, it was clear they were all doing something right.

"So what's up with you?" Leo asked as Ellie pushed the glass of sweet tea to Fletcher.

"Well," he said with a sigh. "I'm in the middle of a relationship that means everything to me."

Leo and Armand both nodded.

"Couldn't be happier for you," Leo told him.

"Yeah, except that I suck at middles."

Leo paused with his own glass of tea halfway to his mouth. He looked at Fletcher with a frown. "What you mean?"

"For Jordan and me it's always been about grand gestures and big, flashy, happy endings. I sweep in and save the day."

"Like flying off to Vegas when she's had a breakup? Maybe proposing to her just out of the blue?" Naomi's grandfather asked with a chuckle.

Fletcher nodded. "Ultimate grand finale."

The other man tipped his head. "Except the wedding isn't the finale."

"Bingo," Fletcher told him.

"What are you talking about, boy?" Leo asked.

"For years this is how I do things with Jordan. I come in at the last minute. I come up with some big scheme that will save the day. I'm the last-minute hero. Except now, I have to be the twenty-four-seven hero. I'm in the middle of a relationship and the only part I'm good at is the ending."

"And this relationship isn't ending," Leo pointed out.

"Exactly."

Armand chuckled. "So, as usual, you rush in to fix everything for the girl. But instead of it being a quick fix with you moving on until she needs something else, you went ahead and married her. And now…"

"I'm stuck in a middle and I don't know what to do all the time. I *always* know what to do for Jordan."

Leo shook his head. "Well, yeah, you're going to mess things up sometimes. We all do. But the middle is the best part, Fletcher."

"I don't know about that," Fletcher said. "That's where the work happens. And that's where things go wrong. That's where all the stuff happens that I have to come in and fix with the big, grand gesture."

"You're lookin' at it wrong," Leo told him. "The middle is the part that makes something what it is. You can put ham and cheese in between two pieces of bread and it's a ham and cheese sandwich. You can take those same two pieces of bread and put peanut butter and jelly between them, and it's a whole different thing. The beginning and the end just hold the good stuff together. What really makes something *something* is the middle."

Fletcher looked at his grandfather. Then he looked at Naomi's grandfather. But Armand was nodding along as if Leo had just said something very wise.

"Comparing relationships to sandwiches is kind of simplistic, isn't it?" Fletcher asked.

Leo scoffed. "Things don't have to be hard to matter. Do you know Jordan's favorite sandwich?"

Okay, they were going on with the sandwich analogy. Fletcher nodded. "Yes. Italian sub."

"What does she like on her subs?" Leo asked.

"Salami, ham, pepperoni, provolone, mayo, vinegar and oil, oregano, salt and pepper, tomatoes, olives, pickles," Fletcher rattled off.

"And if you had all of that, does it matter what bread you put it on?" Leo asked.

"She prefers whole wheat."

"Okay, but does she care more about those ingredients or the bread?"

Fletcher rolled his eyes but said, "The ingredients."

"Exactly. You get that combination right, you make it the sandwich that she loves best, and the bread doesn't really matter."

Okay, Leo was making a not-terrible point. But…

"See, the thing is, all the times her sandwich was *not* an Italian sub, and she had to eat some soggy tuna salad instead, *my* job was to bring over an amazing dessert," Fletcher said. He nodded after he said it. That was actually a very good analogy. Any time things hadn't gone exactly the way Jordan needed them to, he came through with something to make up for it, to make it better. "And showing up with a double chocolate frosted brownie always worked."

"But wouldn't you rather be the sub, the thing she *really* wants, the thing that really gives her…sustenance?"

Fletcher and Armand both snorted as Leo settled on the word "sustenance".

Leo grinned. "You know what I mean. A woman can't live on Coffee Toffee Caramel ice cream alone. Be her Italian sub, Fletcher."

Fletcher chuckled. "But see, the sub is more complicated. There's more ingredients, more layers, and it's easier to forget one of the ingredients or not quite get the right amount of mayo."

Leo waved all of that away. "You can adjust. If you don't get enough mayo one time, you get it the next time. But at least the mayo was there."

"And what about all of the stuff you don't have a recipe for?" Fletcher asked.

"Well how did you get to the point where you could rattle all those ingredients off for her sandwich just now?" Leo asked.

Fletcher thought about that. "We've eaten a lot of sandwiches together."

Leo grinned. "Exactly. And you paid attention. That's really all it takes. Time and attention."

Fletcher felt a thunk in his chest. It might have been hope knocking against his rib cage.

Time and attention. He could give those to Jordan. And yeah, after all, he'd already figured out her favorite sandwich. He could come through with that, rather than having to fall back on ice cream or brownies now that her sandwich needs were his business.

"And you're still going to forget the tomatoes or accidentally put onions on her sandwiches sometimes," Naomi's grandfather said.

"Advice about what to do when I do that?" Fletcher asked.

"That's what you keep the pint of Coffee Toffee Caramel in the freezer for," Armand chuckled.

"Metaphorically and literally," Ellie added as she pushed a to-go container across the bar to Fletcher.

He gave her a smile. "You like his analogy? Sandwiches and relationships?"

Ellie gave Leo an affectionate look. "Makes complete sense to me. And Leo knows what he's talking about. After all, he's been with me long enough to know that my favorite sandwich has changed a few times. He's had to keep up with that too."

Leo nodded. "And there have been times I've introduced her to new sandwiches she didn't even know she would like."

Fletcher looked back and forth between his grandparents. "Are we talking about actual sandwiches or metaphorical sandwiches?"

"Yes," Leo and Ellie said together.

"Got it." He wasn't sure he wanted to know about all the metaphorical sandwiches Leo and Ellie had tried together.

"We're just saying that you should definitely pay attention to what sandwich she wants, but don't worry too much about getting the mayo wrong because before you know it, she'll be onto spicy mustard or garlic aioli," Ellie said.

"Or she might decide tuna salad is damned delicious," Leo added.

"Right." Ellie nodded. "Just remember…it's not the bread that makes a sandwich. The good stuff—the spicy, sweet, creamy, crunchy, interesting stuff—is in the middle. And sometimes, you'll even find flavors that blend together in new ways you didn't even think of."

Wow. When his grandparents went after a metaphor, they really went all in.

"I could do that with desserts, you know," he felt compelled to point out. "There are a million desserts. Lots of interesting blends of flavor too."

Ellie waved that away. "Too much dessert can make you sick. Be her sandwich guy."

Her sandwich guy. With all the good stuff in the middle. Right. Fletcher sighed.

"Okay, I think that's enough wisdom from my elders for the night."

Ellie swatted him with the towel she was holding, but she grinned. "Take this. You didn't eat."

He picked up the to-go box. See? She'd even noticed he hadn't eaten. "Is it a sandwich?"

"No, smart ass, it's red beans and rice and catfish."

His stomach rumbled. "Thanks." He leaned over the bar to kiss her cheek.

She patted his. "You're going to be good at this, Fletcher. She's a lucky girl to have you full time now and not just when things go sideways."

He pulled in a breath. "Thanks."

"Yeah, you're fine," Leo agreed. "You're a Landry. We've been wading into gunk and then hosing ourselves off for generations."

Fletcher chuckled and patted his grandfather on the shoulder. "Good point." Then he turned to Armand. "Thanks for the advice." He shook the other man's hand.

"Anytime. My own grandkids aren't interested in love so I gotta give all my wisdom and insight to someone." Armand cast a look in the direction of his grandkids and sighed.

Fletcher turned to go. He was *not* getting in the midst of anyone else's love life or lack thereof. He had his own sandwiches to worry about.

FLETCHER CREPT into the house ten minutes later. There were no lights on and the place was completely quiet.

He set his food, keys, and bag on the kitchen table and kicked his shoes off. Then he headed upstairs to check on Jordan.

The bedroom door was shut and he eased it open carefully.

The room was as dark as she could get it, but he could still make out her form in the bed. She was lying facing away from the window, the blankets pulled up over her head.

He felt so fucking helpless. He knew better than to go over to her. Or to speak. If she was asleep, waking her would be cruel. Sleep was the only way for her to get away from the pain.

"Fletcher."

Her whisper came to him and he felt his heart trip.

"Hey," he whispered back. "What do you need?"

"Nothing."

That wasn't entirely true, of course. She needed the pain to go away.

But that would take time. And medication.

Shit. Did she have her medication here in Autre? She'd left Vegas with only her purse.

He opened his mouth to ask, then snapped it shut. Obviously, she would have taken the medication if she had it. If she didn't, there wasn't anything he could do about that anyway.

"I'll be downstairs," he finally said softly.

"Okay."

That was it. She didn't ask him for anything because there was nothing he could do or give her to make this better.

Fuck. He hated this.

He eased the door shut again and stood outside, staring at the wood.

How long would this last? Should he sleep in there with her? Should he stay away? Would she get up in the night? If so, was there anything he could do *then*? Anything she would need? Things she'd have in her apartment in Nashville but that he wouldn't necessarily have available?

That time in college when he'd slept outside her room, she'd been a lot better the next morning. But he hadn't known when it had started for sure or how the night on the other side of the door had gone. And he'd had to head to his psych class right after dropping her burger off. He'd, of course, taken notes and shared them with her since she hadn't gone to class that day. At least that had been some help.

What would he do tomorrow? He couldn't take the day off and go feed the alpacas for her. He had twenty-two third graders to show up for.

Or should he take the day off? How would she be tomorrow?

Fuck.

He headed back down the stairs already knowing what he needed to do.

But he *really* didn't want to do it.

Still, he wanted answers even more than he wanted to never ask Jason Young for anything ever.

He had no idea where Jason was or what he might be doing tonight. Was he still in Vegas? On to another city? Back in Nashville?

Fletcher didn't know and he didn't fucking care.

Jason actually picked up on the fourth ring. "Fletcher? Is everything okay? How's Jordan?"

Fletcher gripped his phone tighter. Jason had texted a few times over the past couple of days, checking in. Fletcher had told him that Jordan was fine and to fuck off. But now she wasn't fine and Fletcher knew that Jason was the best person to ask about how this headache would go, how Jordan would do over the next few hours, and if there really was anything he could possibly do for her.

As much as Fletcher hated it, Jason was his best resource. And he would do anything for Jordan. Even talking to her ex.

He could hear background noise, as if Jason was at a dinner party or restaurant.

"Hey. Yeah, she's okay. Mostly. She's got a migraine."

"Oh. Good." Jason cleared his throat. "I don't mean it's good she has a headache, but I'm glad she's mostly okay."

Fletcher really wanted to say, "no thanks to you" but he bit his tongue. Pissing Jason off and having him hang up wouldn't help at all.

"Actually, that's why I'm calling," Fletcher said, tipping his head back to stare at the ceiling. "Was hoping you could tell me how this is going to go. And if there's anything I can do."

"Oh, hang on."

Fletcher heard Jason say something to someone but it was muffled and he couldn't make out the words. When Jason came back on the line the background was quiet, as if he'd stepped out of the room he'd been in.

"Okay, so, what's going on right now?"

"She's in bed in the dark."

"So it just started a little while ago."

"Guess so." There was a stupid jealous part of him that hated that Jason knew so much just based on Jordan being in bed.

"Nothing much you can do right now, man. If she got to her meds in time, she might keep it from getting really bad. If not, it could be a rough night. Has she started vomiting?"

He didn't even know that. He could have checked the master bathroom, but he hadn't thought of it. "I don't know. I just got home. She didn't bring her suitcase from Vegas."

"Yeah, I noticed," Jason said dryly. "But she keeps those meds in her purse so she should have them."

Fletcher blew out a relieved breath. "Okay."

"So she'll get up in the night. She'll need Gatorade then and probably painkillers. If she's not vomiting. Otherwise, those won't make a difference obviously."

"Okay." Fletcher wondered if he should be writing this down. But he was clinging to the details. Gatorade. Pain killers. Check on vomiting. "Should I…" He cleared his throat. He did not want to ask fucking Jason Young this. "Should I sleep up there with her or leave her alone or what?"

"Sleep with her."

Jason's response was smooth and Fletcher appreciated that the other man didn't sound like he thought it was a stupid or awkward question.

"If she gets up, a wet, cold washcloth to the back of her neck and the Gatorade are good. Or water if that's what she wants. But no lights, no talking."

Fletcher nodded. "Got it."

"Then just let her sleep. When she's up tomorrow, she'll want toast first thing. Then a burger and fries and a Coke." Jason gave a laugh that actually sounded affectionate. "She will *eat* tomorrow. She'll go for junk food and eat like she's never seen a carb before."

"Yeah. I remember the burgers and stuff from college. But I'm just wondering what's going to happen between now and then."

"Oh, well… like I said—sleep, maybe up in the night but maybe not."

"And then she'll just get up tomorrow and start eating?" Fletcher frowned. What about the in between part he didn't know? Where he could maybe *do* something?

"Yeah. I mean, she might sleep late. She'll be a little groggy. Like she's hungover. But once she's up, even if she's moving slow, she'll be ready to eat."

"But…" Fletcher shook his head. Jason was such a pain.

Except, maybe Jason wasn't a pain. The chances were this was all true. He'd called Jason because the other man would know better than Fletcher how this migraine thing would go.

"That's the end then?" Fletcher asked. "She gets a headache, she goes to bed, Gatorade in the middle of the night, then a cheeseburger and it's done?"

Yeah, he definitely did not need to take notes on this. That seemed easy.

"No, the cheeseburger is kind of stage two," Jason said. "Or stage three. The migraine hits, there's the middle of the night stuff, the cheeseburger and Coke, then she'll do some yoga, then it's time for chocolate, and then a neck and shoulder massage with peppermint oil." Jason paused. "Yeah, that's about it. The stages can last different amounts of time, but when she gets to the chocolate and peppermint oil stage then you're at the end."

Fletcher frowned. The cheeseburger wasn't the end? He remembered her asking for peanut butter cups in the past too, now that Jason said that. But she ate those a lot of the time anyway. Cheeseburgers too, for that matter.

"You still there?" Jason asked.

"Yeah," Fletcher answered. "I guess I didn't realize what part of the process I'd seen in the past."

"Yeah, just kind of the middle, I guess," Jason said.

His words hit Fletcher directly in the chest.

He'd been there for the middle. Maybe it didn't totally count if he thought he was at the end and was doing some big, wonderful thing by bringing her a cheeseburger when really it was just a step toward the end. Still, it had made him feel good to be there for her. And even now, knowing that he hadn't "fixed" her headaches with those burgers, he was glad he'd been able to help.

"Hey, thanks, man," Fletcher told Jason. "It helps knowing what to expect."

"Sure. Any time. Of course Jordan takes pretty good care of herself." Jason chuckled. "Let's be honest, she was taking care of me more than I was of her. I know that she put a lot on hold and to the side for the stuff I wanted and was doing."

The guy had just helped him out and had been great about it, so Fletcher bit back his initial retort to Jason's words. But hell yeah Jordan had put a lot on hold for him.

"I owe her. And I know that with the way everything happened it doesn't seem like it, but I do want her to be happy. I care what happens to her. And I want her to have what she wants and deserves." Jason paused. "I'm glad she's with you, Landry."

This should have been a strange conversation. New husbands and longtime exes probably didn't often have friendly conversations where the ex told the new guy he was glad how things worked out.

But Fletcher could hear the sincerity in Jason's voice. And he could appreciate it. Jason and Jordan had been together for a long time, and Jordan was a very hard person not to love. If Jason hadn't cared how she was doing and didn't want her to be happy, he wouldn't have been the type of guy that Jordan would've stayed with for eleven years.

Of course, without Jason in the picture, Fletcher was going to have to step up. But the idea of Jason—or any other man—never giving Jordan a shoulder massage again, was absolutely just fine with him.

"No offense, but I'm glad she's with me too," Fletcher told Jason.

Jason chuckled. "No offense taken. I know you'll take good care of her. But if you or Jordan need anything else, you've got my number."

Fletcher didn't want to need anything else from Jason. He definitely didn't want Jordan to need anything from him ever again. But it was probably good for them to stay on friendly terms.

"Okay, I'll keep that in mind," Fletcher said.

"Good." Jason did actually sound relieved at that.

Fletcher didn't know if that just made his conscience feel more clear or what, but it was all good.

They disconnected and Fletcher blew out a breath. He looked around the dark, quiet living room. So there wasn't anything he could do right now. Maybe in the middle of the night though. And at least he could sleep up there with her. That would make him feel better anyway.

Then he went into the kitchen, grabbed his shoes and keys, and headed out to his truck. He needed to get some Gatorade.

Seventeen

SHE WOKE up at some point in the night. Jordan lay on her back, staring at the dark ceiling. She knew immediately where she was. Not only from the scent of the room but because she could feel Fletcher's hot body next to her. He wasn't touching her, he was just there. And it made her smile in spite of the pounding in her head.

This was the second time she'd woken up in this bed with a splitting headache. The first time had been her own damn fault. She probably should've expected this time too. The fatigue, stress, emotional roller coaster of the preceding couple of days had set her up perfectly for a migraine.

Thankfully, she had felt it coming on and had been able to take her medication. It could've been a lot worse.

She sat up carefully, knowing that she needed to go pee and drink some water and down some additional painkillers. Okay, that wasn't so bad.

"I'll get the Gatorade."

Fletcher's whisper came to her and he was up and out of the bed before she could respond.

She opened her mouth to call after him but knew that she would regret raising her voice. Besides, Gatorade was a great idea. She always had some in the house and took it to bed with her when she had a migraine. Last she checked, however, Fletcher hadn't had any. At least not where she checked.

She pushed herself up from the bed and padded into the bathroom. Without turning on the light, she used the toilet, then washed her hands and patted her face with a cool washcloth. She wasn't nauseous to the point of vomiting, thank God. That always made her head feel so much worse. That meant she'd gotten to her medication in time to stave off a really terrible headache.

As she came back out of the bathroom she nearly ran into Fletcher. It seemed he'd been pacing on the other side of the door.

"You okay?" he whispered. "Did you throw up?"

She almost shook her head but caught herself in time. "No. I'm not okay but I didn't throw up," she clarified.

She stepped around him and headed back to the bed.

When she sat, he handed her the Gatorade. Gratefully, she took it and swallowed three tiny sips. She waited a moment, then decided her stomach was going to continue to behave, and drank a little more.

"Oh, dammit," she said softly.

"What?" Fletcher asked immediately.

"I forgot to take ibuprofen."

Without a word he crossed swiftly into the bathroom and was back within a few seconds. "How many?"

Fletcher had never been physically *with* her during the painful I-can-hardly-function part of her migraines. Once in college he had roused her out of bed at about this stage. She'd looked so bad, he'd slept on the floor outside her dorm room that night. But he hadn't knocked again. Later she'd realized that *no one* had knocked, no one slammed the door, no one had loud music playing that entire night. It hadn't taken much to understand that Fletcher had been policing her dorm room floor for her.

It'd been one of the sweetest things he'd ever done for her. And that was saying a lot.

Knowing him as well as she did, however, she could imagine that this was stressing him out. Fletcher didn't mind stepping in when she needed him, of course. He'd seen her sick before. He'd seen her struggling in math class. He'd seen her anxious and freaking out driving on the freeway. And, as had been well established over the last few days, he'd seen her in many disgusting and embarrassing situations.

Those were all the things he could fix though. This he couldn't. And she knew that would be driving him crazy.

"Three," she said holding out her hand.

He put three tablets in her palm and then set the bottle on the side table.

She washed them down with Gatorade, then sighed.

He laid a cool wet cloth on the back of her neck. "What else?" he asked softly.

Jordan found herself trying to think of something that she could tell him he could do. She did that a lot. Gave him ways to feel hopeful and heroic, she realized.

But right now her head hurt too much. And truthfully, there wasn't anything he could do. Rubbing her shoulders and neck later would be great, but right now it would make things worse. There wasn't any more medication she could take and putting anything else in her stomach might change the no vomiting thing she had going.

Right now she just needed to lie back down and, frankly, be left alone.

"Nothing," she told him honestly.

He simply nodded. "Okay. I'll be right here."

She wasn't sure Fletcher totally understood how great that was, but it was exactly what she needed.

Tomorrow she'd tell him more about her migraines and what to expect. She would have eventually gotten around to it, but they'd only been married for a few days. She'd hoped she wouldn't have to worry about a headache for a while.

Jordan lay down and closed her eyes. She felt like her thoughts were trying to make it through mud. She'd have to think about all of this tomorrow.

She felt the mattress move as Fletcher got into the bed on his side and she rolled toward him, reaching out and finding his hand.

She laced her fingers with his, and then fell asleep.

WHEN SHE MADE it down to the kitchen the next day, it was past ten.

She'd awakened, feeling better, but groggy. But the shot of adrenaline to her system when she'd seen the time had cleared some of the fogginess. She'd immediately reached for her phone and found it turned off. No wonder she hadn't heard her alarm.

Then she'd seen the note from Fletcher.

He'd talked to Charlie and everything at the petting zoo was covered for the day. He'd turned her phone off, told everyone where and how she was, told them to leave her alone until she reached out to them—she grinned imagining the threats that had probably accompanied those instructions—and said she was supposed to take her time this morning.

More ibuprofen and Gatorade, along with a shower, had helped, but it wasn't until she stepped into the kitchen that she realized everything he had done. There was another note pointing her to the food he stored in the refrigerator for her. There was a cheeseburger—the bun separate so it didn't get soggy—French fries, and a forty-eight ounce glass of Coke. Not diet. Full sugar. She only drank the stuff the day after a migraine, but it really did help her bounce back. She didn't know if it was the sugar, the caffeine, some other artificial coloring or flavoring, or the magical combination of all of those, but she didn't care. A friend in college who also suffered from migraines had turned her on to the magic morning-after elixir, and it worked every time.

She had to reheat the cheeseburger and fries, but as she took the first bite, not only did her head seemingly feel immediately better, but her heart was full. She'd been dealing with migraines for so long, that she took for granted always having the thing she needed, and frankly, having a boyfriend who knew what to expect. But Fletcher had come through. He remembered the cheeseburger and Coke combination from college. And somehow he'd known about the Gatorade in the middle of the night. Maybe he had done an Internet search. It wasn't like she was the only migraine sufferer to depend on these particular things. Most migraine patients talked about their cravings and the things that made them feel better the day after. Whatever he'd done, however he'd found this out, Fletcher had done a great job.

As always.

An hour later after doing a little bit of yoga, she felt good enough to head to the petting zoo and see if there was anything she could do.

Charlie assured her that all of the paperwork and presentation preparation could wait, so she headed over to the alpaca pen.

Apacalypse and Ella both saw her and came strolling over.

"Hi, ladies," she greeted. She let them sniff her hands and then she stroked their necks. Ella nuzzled her hair and she laughed as the animal's soft lips tickled her neck.

As she stroked their soft coats and talked to them in a low voice, she realized how relaxing it was. They were quiet animals and out here in their pen, with the soft breeze blowing, and the warm sun shining down, she felt the tension melting out of her neck and shoulders.

Two more of the alpacas noticed her, and came over to see what they were missing. She loved their sweet curiosity and that, unlike the otters, they weren't constantly looking for treats. They seemed to actually enjoy human companionship and being stroked and petted.

She noticed Chewpaca off to one side by himself. He was grazing, seemingly unconcerned with what was going on by the fence, but she found herself wishing that he wanted more interaction as well.

He was much younger than the rest of the herd, of course, and had spent his early days on a farm interacting only with the farmers. He did seem a little intimidated by the groups of people, especially younger children, who wanted to give him attention.

Except with Sophia.

Jordan wondered if there would be any advantage to bringing the little girl over a few more times specifically to get Chewie more used to being touched and petted.

She'd have to ask Tori and Griffin. She could read a lot about alpacas in general, but she needed a little more guidance from the people who knew the personalities of these animals best.

She finished talking with the alpacas, then made her way around the animal park checking on everyone and giving them their afternoon feeding. About the time school was out, she asked Charlie if she could head home. Her head was much better but she was afraid that too much commotion could change that. She could use a nap. And some chocolate and caffeine.

She wondered if Fletcher would be up for giving her a neck and shoulder massage tonight.

She grinned. She was sure he would. He'd do anything she needed him to do. She'd have to instruct him and she knew the first time wouldn't be perfect. It had taken Jason years to figure out exactly what pressure to use and he still needed coaching at times.

Still, it would make Fletcher feel good to have something to do.

She left him a note in the kitchen, telling him that she was going to try to sleep for an hour or so, but not to hesitate to wake her up when he got home.

Which he did with a sweet kiss to her forehead and a soft, "Jordan,"

Her eyes fluttered open and she looked up at him with a smile. This was a wonderful way to wake up.

"Hi."

"Hi. How are you?"

She thought about it for a moment, then nodded. "Much better."

"I brought you peanut butter cups and coffee," he said.

The aroma of the coffee hit her and she took a deep breath. Her smile grew. "You're amazing. That's exactly what I needed."

He was clearly incredibly pleased by that.

"I figured we were staying in tonight," he said. "Wasn't sure what you would feel like eating though."

"Pizza," she said quickly. "And cheesy garlic bread. And onion chips. And maybe wings."

He chuckled. "Wow. Okay. I can do all of that."

She pushed up to sit against the headboard and he handed her the coffee. She cradled the paper cup between her two hands and took a little sip. It was doctored perfectly with cream and sugar. She normally drank it without sugar, as she did her Coke, but the day after a migraine required calories. Or the comfort of sugar. Or both. Or something. She didn't argue with the results.

"Do you think you can watch a movie tonight? Or what works best the day after one of the headaches?"

She tipped her head. "Sometimes a movie is too much. At least in a theater where its brighter and loud, but here at home it should be fine. And I'm feeling pretty good." She studied him for a moment. "We've watched movies together the day after I had a migraine."

He nodded. "Yeah, but I didn't know what stage that was."

"Stage?"

"Last night was the first time I've been there through the

whole thing. It occurred to me, as usual, I was probably coming in at the end of a migraine in the past. I didn't know how long it would take you to get to that point."

She nodded in understanding. "Oh. Yeah, I'll have to tell you more about my headaches so you know what to expect."

"Sure," he said, pushing up off the bed. "But you don't have to right now. Let me go see about getting you food."

Of course he would be more comfortable focusing on actions rather than just talking. She smiled. She could help with that. "Sounds good. Would you be willing to rub my neck and shoulders later too?"

"Absolutely. Whatever you need. I had Mitch get some peppermint oil when he was in New Orleans picking up some tourists for a swamp boat tour today."

Jordan stopped with the coffee cup part way to her mouth and stared at him. "You did?"

"We had to kind of guess what you needed. But he told the girl at the shop what we were going to use it for and that you have headaches. She recommended the oil he brought home."

Jordan lowered the cup the rest of the way to her lap. "How did you know to get peppermint oil for a massage?"

Again, it wasn't some crazy secret or something that only worked on her. Peppermint oil was widely used for pain control. But for Fletcher to know that was one thing. To go to the effort of asking Mitch to pick some up for her without knowing if it actually worked was another.

Fletcher blew out a breath. "I made a call last night when I wasn't sure what to do to help you." He tucked his hands into his pockets and looked the floor rather than directly at her. He looked almost sheepish.

Jordan felt surprise and then an incredible warmth spread through her. Tears pricked her eyes. "Did you call Jason last night?"

She'd had migraines in high school when she'd still been living at home, so her mother would've known a few tricks, but they were still learning about things and trying different remedies when Jordan went to college. Jason was the person who had seen the most of her migraines and had been the only one to rub peppermint oil on her shoulders. Until now.

Fletcher nodded. "I didn't know what to do. And I figured of all the people in the world, he would. I also knew he would pick up my call."

"How did you know he would pick up your call?"

"He's been texting since we left Vegas. Just checking to see that you're okay."

She nodded. "He texted me too."

Fletcher's head came up. He frowned. "He did? What did he say?"

She shook her head. "Just *I'm sorry*. I texted back that I'm doing great and everything worked out. And that was it. I haven't heard from him again."

Neither of them said anything for a moment. Then she said, "Thank you for calling him."

Fletcher lifted a brow. "Thank you?"

"Yes. I know that was hard for you. I know how much you love to be the one with all the answers and the one fixing things for me and asking for help is a big deal. To ask for help from Jason, of all people, is a huge deal. But having Gatorade last night and the burger today," she glanced at the peanut butter cups and then down at the coffee. "And the chocolate and caffeine at exactly the right time, and now the peppermint oil for massage later, is all perfect. And I really appreciate you being willing to do that for me."

Emotions flickered across Fletcher's face, but he took a step forward and met her gaze directly. "I will always do *anything* for you, Jordan."

She believed that to her very bones.

"Okay, I'll meet you on the couch," Jordan said. "You bring the pizza and massage oil and wings and cheesy bread and…"

She laughed. "You bring everything and I'll meet you down there."

"Perfect."

He turned away and Jordan lifted the cup to her lips. But rather than leaving the room and going to hunt and gather her pizza and cheesy bread, he began unbuttoning his shirt. He shrugged out of it and tossed it into the hamper and Jordan swallowed coffee down the wrong pipe. She started coughing, which wasn't great for the tiny lingering ache at the back of her head. But it did cause him to turn back.

Fletcher looked great from behind. He had a great ass, trim waist, and hard back and upper shoulder muscles defined by doing manual construction labor with his brother all summer long. But from the front, he was downright drool worthy. Hard six-pack abs, a light dusting of hair over his chest that narrowed to a line down the center of his flat belly. And a line between the tan skin on top and the lighter skin below his waistband that teased her as his pants lifted and lowered on his hips as he moved.

His hands were on his belt buckle as he frowned and asked, "Are you okay?"

"Didn't know I was getting a strip show," she said, coughing again and clearing her throat. "But please continue. That's definitely making me feel better."

He cocked an eyebrow and unbuckled his belt. "You're not really feeling *that* much better."

It wasn't quite a question, but she could tell he was curious.

In spite of her headache, she flushed and felt her heart start to race. "I do believe there is some research out there about endorphins and pain and orgasms," she said.

"I'm going to need citations for your work, Mrs. Landry," Fletcher said with a half-grin. He crossed to the dresser and pulled open a drawer. He grabbed a T-shirt and shorts, closed the drawer, and headed into the bathroom. The door swung shut behind him.

"Chicken," she called.

He didn't respond. But she was grinning when he came back out.

"Move your sweet ass to the couch, and I'll be back soon with supplies," Fletcher told her. "And get rid of all the dirty thoughts. I'm going to give you a massage with peppermint oil and it's only going to be for your headache."

That was truly all she wanted. It was probably all she was really up for tonight. But she loved being able to tease. This was a new layer to her relationship with Fletcher. Just like him witnessing all the stages of her migraine.

In spite of being friends for so long, it seemed they had plenty of things they still needed to learn.

She made it to the couch and finished her coffee as well as several peanut butter cups by the time Fletcher got home. He'd come with everything she'd asked for plus a giant chocolate chip cookie. They ate and watched a movie, propped up on opposite ends of the couch. It was exactly like so many other nights they'd spent, but it felt very different. It wasn't just the ring on her left hand, which she twirled as she thought about everything. It was the fact that they were getting closer, something she hadn't realized they needed to do.

As the movie credits rolled, Fletcher cleaned up all of the boxes, napkins, and paper plates. When he came back to the couch, he had a tiny brown bottle with him. He handed it over.

"Is this right?"

She looked at the label. It was massage oil with peppermint essential oil added. It would be perfect.

She nodded. "Exactly right."

"Okay, show me what to do."

"Come sit behind me." She scooted forward on the couch cushion so that he could slide in behind her.

His back was to the arm of the couch, one long leg stretched along the length of the cushions, and his other foot rested on the floor. She sat between his legs, leaning into his chest. He wrapped his arms around her, resting his hands on her belly. His chin rested on her shoulder.

"This is nice," his low voice rumbled near her ear.

A tiny shiver of pleasure danced down her arm and she nodded. "It is." She let her head tip back on his shoulder and her eyes slid shut.

"But I can't reach your shoulders like this," he said. His big hands rubbed up and down her arms.

Even that felt soothing and warm.

After a few seconds she took a deep breath and then leaned away from him. She pulled her knees up and wrapped her arms around her lower legs, causing her shoulders to curl forward. She rested her forehead on her knees.

"Now you can reach."

He ran his hands up and down her back and she sighed with pleasure. He slid one hand under the bottom of her shirt, running his palm up her bare back. Oh, that was even better.

"Hang on." She sat up and stripped her shirt off. The t-shirt she'd been wearing was loose and she did not have a bra on. The fewer things squeezing and rubbing on her skin when she didn't feel well the better.

Fletcher groaned behind her.

She looked over her shoulder. "You had to know the massage oil would go on bare skin."

"Yeah, I should have known that," he agreed.

Jordan laughed. "You really didn't?"

"I didn't really think about it." He put a hot hand on her back, just resting it there. "I was just focused on there being something I could do. I didn't think any further than getting the oil and making sure it was right."

"You said you talked to Jason last night," she said as a thought occurred to her. "Did you talk to him today too?"

"Texted him. He sent me a photo of the stuff you usually use. But Mitch knew this place where they do essential oils and stuff and he said he checked there first."

"And you were annoyed when he didn't get exactly what I usually have, right?" She knew that was the case.

Fletcher sighed. "Yeah. Then I realized he was doing me a big favor and knew I had to let it go."

She nodded and turned to rest her forehead on her knees again. "I'm glad you did. The important thing is the peppermint essential oil. The exact brand doesn't matter."

"Good. I'm glad this will work."

He removed his hand and she heard him uncap the bottle and then his hands rubbing together. She gave a little shiver, anticipating his touch.

His hands were back a moment later sliding up and down her back.

She sighed. "Yes."

He gave a half-groan, half-chuckle. "Damn, I like doing anything that makes you sound like that."

"Then just keep going."

The scent of peppermint filled the air around them as his hands, hot and competent, stroked up and down her back in a gentle, even rhythm.

After a couple minutes of that, he said, "You have to tell me if you want me to do more."

"Run your thumbs along the top of my shoulders," she instructed, feeling warm contentment seep into her muscles.

He ran his hands up to her shoulders and then slid the pads of his thumbs along the tops of her shoulder blades.

"You can go a little harder," she coached.

For the next twenty minutes or so, she guided Fletcher through massaging her neck and shoulders, pressing into the knots, soothing the tension away.

When she finally pulled in a deep breath and said, "Thank you, I feel amazing," she felt him take a similar, contented deep breath.

She moved to pull her shirt back on, but when she started to shift away, Fletcher's arms came around her and cuddled her back against his chest.

"Is this okay?" He asked against her ear.

"So okay. Are you comfortable?"

"With you against me? I don't know about comfortable," he said, his tone teasing. "But I feel really good."

She smiled and settled against him more fully, letting her head fall back against his shoulder again. His arms folded over hers and rested on her stomach.

"Yeah, I can feel you're not totally comfortable," she teased.

He was partially hard, pressing against her lower back. He gave a little growl and shifted slightly. "Ignore it."

It was reminiscent of what he'd said in Vegas.

"I don't want to ignore your reaction to me."

His thumb was stroking back and forth over the back of her hand. "You don't have to ignore it. I want you to know that you affect me. Just walking into a room, just smiling, just sending me a text affects me," he said after a moment. "Tonight's not a good night though."

Her heart flipped. God, she loved all of that. But he was right about tonight. "No, I'm not really in the mood for sex. But I really like being close to you like this too. Physically, without it being sexual." She shifted slightly to look up at him. "You were right. We did skip steps. Going straight into sex without making out first did jump ahead. Now I feel closer to you. Which is weird. I've always felt like I couldn't be closer to anyone than I already was to you."

She felt his arms tighten around her in a little hug. "I know what you mean. But we do have a huge head start."

She nodded. "Yeah, I like that."

After a few minutes, Fletcher said, "You know how I said that I'm aware of being fond of grand gestures and really good at sweeping in at the last minute? And how I figured that out after your grandpa's funeral?"

She nodded. "Yes."

"I…" He cleared his throat. "I've realized that I was hoping that Sophia was past her 'middle'. That all I had to be was the fun teacher and I'd get her back to school and back to normal and she'd be okay. But…" He took a deep breath. "I've realized since you and I talked that I'm a part of the middle with her too."

Jordan nodded. "Yeah. You are."

"And then it occurred to me last night, with you, that maybe I have done some middles after all."

She frowned slightly. "Of course you have."

"I don't know about 'of course'. I think they've been accidental. But I guess I was around for some of the middle parts of your migraines without realizing it. And, while I don't love not knowing what to do, and not being able to fix it right at that moment, I want you to know that I'm getting okay with the idea of doing middle work too."

Jordan felt her stomach swoop. That was sweet. And she was so glad that he realized that it wasn't the end of the world if he didn't have a solution at the very moment something was going wrong for her. But if he thought that he was no good at anything other than grand gestures and coming in at the end to tie things up in a pretty bow, that was definitely partly her fault.

Confession time.

"You've been doing more than just the big endings for a long time," she said. "And not just with the headaches."

"I've actually kind of tried to stay away from the middle stuff."

"Yeah." She took a deep breath. "Which is why I've let you think that you always came in and fixed everything and that was it."

He hesitated. "What do you mean?"

She tightened her hold on his arms and said quickly, "You didn't actually teach me everything about geometry."

There was a long beat. Then he said, "Go on."

"Okay, all of the stuff you helped me with was huge. You helped me get over my test anxiety. And you definitely helped me understand a few things better. I went from a C to a B- in that class thanks to you."

"You got an A- in geometry."

"Right. Someone else helped me understand the rest of the stuff I didn't quite get."

There was a much longer pause this time. She felt the tension in his body and knew that, though geometry in high school seemed like a small thing now, this was going to be a big deal.

"Was it Jason?"

She blew out a breath. Well, at least he would be happy about one thing—it had not been Jason.

"No."

"Then who?"

But he was going to hate this. "Zeke."

"Zeke? My brother?"

She winced, but nodded. "He saw me after school one day after I had just done badly on another test. He grabbed my book and read through it that night and the next day told me that he could explain it to me. And he did. I don't know why, but he was the only one who could make some of it make sense."

"So my brother, who is two years younger than us, and hadn't taken geometry at all, taught you geometry when I couldn't?"

She sighed. "He's a math geek, Fletcher. And there were just a couple of things that didn't quite make sense. Like with driving."

She felt him tense again.

"What about driving?"

She chewed on her bottom lip.

"Jordan." His tone was low and full of warning. "I thought I taught you to drive. After your dad and uncle and grandpa all tried and got frustrated and quit."

She nodded. "You did. All of that is true. And after you worked with me, I was able to do almost everything. And I was definitely more relaxed about it all and didn't freak out."

Suddenly he shifted and she felt herself being lifted. He set her on the opposite end of the couch facing him again. Then re-settled on the cushion. He stared her down.

"What could you still not do after I worked with you?"

"Just a couple of little things." She winced again. "But things that would have made me fail my driving test."

"What things?"

"Fine. Parallel parking. And passing traffic on the highway."

"And who worked with you on this?"

"Does it really matter?"

"Yes, it fucking matters. Was that Jason?"

Again, it would be good news to him that it had not been Jason. But he actually wasn't going to like this answer any more than he had knowing who her geometry tutor had been.

"No, it wasn't Jason," she said.

"Was it Zeke?"

She shook her head. "No." She paused, then sighed. "It was Zander."

Fletcher shook his head for a moment. "So again, one of my brothers, who is two years younger than us and did not have his own driver's license, was able to teach you something I couldn't?"

"In his defense, Zander had been driving since he was about twelve. Not legally, of course," she noted. "But he knew what he was doing. And he, somehow, was able to teach me how to do it."

Fletcher ran a hand over his face.

"Fletcher, the point is, everything you did completely helped me. You helped me get over my test anxiety and my anxiety driving. If you hadn't done that, nothing they tried to teach me would have sunk in."

"Why didn't you tell me that you needed more help?"

She shrugged. She knew she needed to be honest here. He was her husband now. That made things different. "Because I knew how much it meant to you to be the guy who fixed everything. I was afraid if you knew that you hadn't actually done that, you would quit trying."

He just looked at her for a long moment, not saying anything.

"I loved when you helped me. I loved every night we spent studying. I loved every time we went out driving. Because the studying wasn't just about geometry. We would talk and laugh. One time we made cookies. Another time we experimented with putting different things on our popcorn. When we went driving, we always end up parking somewhere and talking. Remember the time we ended up at the farmers' market?" she asked. "To this day, I've not had apples that good again."

Finally, he nodded. "I might have stopped doing some of that," he said, almost as if he found it all a little baffling. "I really liked being the save-the-day guy. And if I'd known that I wasn't, I might've quit trying. I mean, I still would have been there for you, but I might have handed off the driving lessons or something."

She nodded. "And that's my point. You were doing all of those middle things. Those things that you think you're not good at. All of that middle stuff not only made it possible for me to learn the stuff at the end when Zeke and Zander taught me, but it gave me some great memories with my best friend. And the best apples I've ever had." She smiled at him. "You *are* good at the middles too, Fletcher."

"Yeah, maybe I am."

"Can I say something else?"

He didn't look totally convinced that he wanted to hear it, but he nodded.

"After my grandpa's funeral, that was the middle too. It wasn't like after that I was totally over everything. It wasn't like I was never sad and never cried about it again. You taking me out that day was in the middle of a lot of things I had to get used to. But you were there. And then you took me fishing the first time I ever went with anyone other than my grandpa. You went with me to see the Christmas lights in Audubon Park the first

Christmas he was gone. I had never seen those lights without him."

"I didn't know that about the lights," Fletcher said, his voice gruff. "Your family just invited me along."

She nodded. "I know. Because I knew that you being there would make it better."

He looked like he was having trouble coming up with words. He just swallowed hard and then reached out and squeezed her foot.

She gave him a wobbly smile, feeling her eyes stinging. "You've been doing middles for a long time. And it's totally my fault that you didn't know it. I wanted to make you feel good about being the superhero, so I always let you have your big grand gestures. But I didn't tell you about the little ones that meant just as much. Or more. So it's my fault you don't think you can do the middle stuff as well." She leaned forward and squeezed his foot in return. "I'm sorry."

They just sat looking at each other for several ticks of the clock.

Finally he said, "I really love you."

She sucked in a little breath. The emotion in his voice and his expression was something she'd never seen before.

She felt her eyes fill with tears, but she gave him a big smile. "I love you so much."

He didn't say anything. He just sat looking at her. And squeezing her foot.

"Do you want to make out?" she asked.

Because she really did.

That got a smile. He shook his head. "No. You need to take it easy tonight."

She'd figured that's what he was going to say.

"But there is something I'd really like."

She lifted a brow. "Okay." Anything. This guy was…everything.

She'd thought she'd been in love for eleven years. Actually, she *had* been in love. She'd definitely loved Jason. A little bit of her still did. In a way.

But she'd never felt for Jason what she felt for Fletcher.

"I'd really like to *do* something for you tonight. Something that's *actually* helpful. Something that might get you through tonight feeling better. Something *real*. No telling me you're fine if you're not, like with the parallelograms and parallel parking."

Yeah, he was going to keep bringing that up for a while.

She rolled her eyes, but smiled. "Okay. Then I think I should go to bed. And it would be really amazing if you wanted to come up and lie in the dark with me and listen to the audio book I'm listening to."

He perked up. "I could do that."

"Well, just a warning, it's a steamy romance. There might be orgasms."

He gave her a little smirk. "Huh."

"Huh? Just huh? You can handle that?"

"Listening to a book that you really like, hearing stuff that turns you on, could be *very* interesting. And educational."

"Educational, huh?"

"I'm still very dedicated to getting all of that *right*." He narrowed his eyes. "You will *not* be going to my brothers for any additional help in that area."

She laughed. "I don't want anyone else helping me with that." She squeezed his foot again, then ran her hand up and down. "You are *very* good at *those* grand finales."

Then he winked at her.

Winked.

And she realized that he'd just forgiven her for learning to parallel park with Zander.

CHAPTER
Eighteen

THE NEXT MORNING Fletcher rolled out of bed carefully, not wanting to disturb Jordan. She'd fallen asleep after only one chapter of the book, but he'd stayed awake listening to another. Mostly because she was cuddled up against him, her back to his front, tucked against him trustingly. But the book was pretty good too.

She'd slept through the night, though she moved around a lot. During the night they'd been entangled, then rolled to their separate sides of the bed, then come back together in the middle, and so on through the night. It was very comfortable. He loved sleeping with his wife. Which was a pretty great realization after knowing her for twenty years.

He made his way into the bathroom and started getting ready for work. He brushed his teeth and turned on the shower. He slipped his boxers off and stepped into the stall. He shampooed and shaved in the little mirror he had mounted on the wall. He was trying his best to ignore the urge to take his cock in hand as he'd done the last two mornings.

But damn, he was even more madly in love with his wife this morning than he had been yesterday. Sure, in the past she'd lied to him about how good he was at geometry, teaching her to drive, and who knew what other things. But knowing that he'd been there for her in more ways than he'd realized made him feel pretty damn good.

Maybe that was stupid. He'd found out that he wasn't quite as good at fixing her problems as he thought. But even as that went through his mind, he realized it wasn't true. Actually, maybe he was even better at fixing things than he thought. Maybe he didn't have to wait until the end when everything else had failed to come in and take care of her.

He grabbed the bar of soap and rubbed it between his hands, getting a lather going. He started scrubbing his chest and shoulders, moving down his arms and abs. He soaped his back and both legs. The entire time he thought about Jordan.

He thought about the time she'd fallen asleep in the backseat of Stephanie Hatchett's car with her head on his shoulder and talked in her sleep about the date she'd been on in her dream. Apparently Barack Obama had taken her to a state dinner.

He thought about the time she and Charlie had decided to get on an airplane to Orlando without permission. The phone call from her from outside Disney World when they realized how much money tickets actually cost and that they didn't have enough to get in, still made him chuckle. As did his attempt to cover for them with their parents. It had only worked for a few hours, and then he'd ended up in as much trouble as they had. Thankfully, Charlie Landry could talk her way out of anything. Even with *his* parents.

But no matter how many silly, or even disgusting stories he came up with, nothing made him want her any less. He could still replay every single second of every night with her so far and he instantly got hard and hot. He wanted her body, her moans, her orgasms.

At the moment, though, he could feel her smooth, silky skin under his hands and the smell of peppermint in the air. Giving her that massage had not been sexual, but it had been incredibly satisfying. Being able to do something to make her feel good was a turn on. Whether it was bringing her a cheeseburger, letting her have the last piece of cheesy garlic bread—and wow, Jason hadn't been kidding about how much she could eat the day after a migraine—giving her a massage, or giving her an orgasm, or just lying with her in the dark, it all made him want her on a level he'd never experienced before.

Fletcher finally gave up and took his cock in hand. Everything about Jordan made him hard. He wanted her. On every level. And dammit, he needed a release. He fisted his cock, squeezing and stroking up and down. He pictured her naked, her nipples hard, her mouth open as her breathing grew ragged. He pictured the flush on her cheeks as she grew more aroused. He remembered the sight of her fingers between her legs, playing with her clit. He remembered how her nipple felt against his tongue, how her pussy felt around his fingers, then around his cock. He gripped himself harder and stroked himself faster.

Then he remembered how she looked hugging and laughing with their families at their wedding reception. He thought about her grin when he brought her the peanut butter cups. The sound of her laughter went through his mind and he suddenly flashed through everything from the first time they'd snuck into a movie theater to see the same movie for the third time in a row, to the first time she'd run across the football field and jumped into his arms after a big victory, to the first time she'd come to his house to take care of him when *he'd* been sick.

His grip tightened again and he leaned his forehead on the arm he had braced on the wall. He let out a soft groan.

Just then he heard the door swing open. He froze, fist still around his cock.

Breathing hard, he looked through the glass shower stall. It had steamed up slightly, but he could clearly see Jordan standing just inside the door, her hand still on the knob.

Damn his brother for insisting full glass shower stalls were the way to go. A nice curtain would be good right now. Still, he was slow to let go of his throbbing cock and straighten.

"Jordan? You okay?" What if she was sick? What if she needed him for something? And here he was jerking off in the shower in the next room. He could help her with a raging hard-on, but it wouldn't be comfortable.

She wet her lips. "Um… I'm fine." Her gaze tracked over him.

She was several feet away and the glass between them was foggy. She couldn't see him clearly. But her eyes on him, even like this, made him feel like his blood was on fire.

Fletcher made a decision. He opened the shower door and extended his hand. "Come here."

Her eyes widened, but she took a step forward, putting her hand in his. He tugged her close. Her gaze roamed over him again, now without the glass between them. His body responded, heating and hardening even further.

She swallowed. "Wow."

He grinned. "Perfect reaction."

Her eyes came up to his. Slowly. Over his abs and chest as if she was memorizing each inch. "Now what?"

"You probably need a shower this morning, right?"

She nodded. "Definitely."

He reached for the bottom of the camisole she'd worn to bed. She might as well have slept naked. The thing was tiny, barely hitting the top of her panties, and was a pale peach color that nearly matched her skin. The silky fabric clung to her and the darker color of her nipples was visible through the thin material.

He stripped it off of her, loving the way her nipples tightened even further. She hooked her thumbs in the top of her panties, pushing them to the floor without hesitation. Then she stepped into the shower stall with him.

She ran her hands over his chest, sliding through the water, her palms skimming his nipples. A shudder of lust went through him. He wasn't sure how long he could last this way. With just her hands on him he already wanted to pin her to the wall and thrust deep.

He caught her wrists, pressing her hands flat against his chest. "What do you want?"

"To touch you all over."

He swallowed hard, but nodded. "Just some playing?"

"Whatever you'll let me do." She looked up at him through her long, wet lashes.

"You don't like morning sex. Or shower sex," he reminded her.

Her eyes went wide. "What? When did I say that? We had morning sex!"

"You sprained your ankle—"

"Oh my God." She pulled her hands away from his chest. "We *really* do know too much about each other sometimes."

"You're the one who told me."

"That was *so* long ago!" She shook her head.

"You were *adamant*," he told her. But he was suddenly fighting a smile.

She rolled her eyes. "I get adamant about a lot of things. I was also adamant that I didn't like pulled pork on nachos or Bruno Mars when I first heard him, but I was wrong on both counts."

Fletcher moved in close, backing her up against the wall behind her. "And morning sex?"

"If I get to watch you doing what you were doing when I walked in here, I don't care what time of day it is," she said.

Want surged through him. "What do you think you saw?"

"You were touching yourself." She licked her lips. "And it was so hot."

"I was thinking about you." He lifted a hand, cupping her face, running a thumb over her lower lip. "Thinking about you. Playing with your nipples and your clit. Making yourself come. The way your pussy gripped my fingers."

He could tell her the sweet thoughts he'd had too, the way their history and the things they'd been through made him want her even more. But this was the time for dirty talk.

Her mouth fell open as he stroked her lip. "You were?"

"Of course. I've been getting myself off thinking of you for a long time, Jordan. Now that you're in my bed, now that you're my *wife*, it's every damned day."

She smiled slightly. A sexy, oh-I-like-that smile. "It's only been a week."

"A week of having the pussy I've wanted for three years right beside me."

Her eyes went wide. "Wow."

He grinned.

"You're the one holding back," she reminded him.

He nodded. "Yep. At least now I know exactly what you look like and sound like rather than having to imagine it."

"You've been imagining me like that? When you're masturbating?"

"Absolutely."

"Oh my God." It was almost a whisper. Her eyes dropped to his cock.

His very-happy-to-see-her cock.

She met his eyes again. "I want to watch."

"You don't want to help?" His hand went to his shaft and fisted it.

"Oh, that too. But if we're learning things, this seems like a great way to learn what you like." Her gaze was locked on his hand.

He gave himself a stroke. God, this was hot. She didn't seem a bit embarrassed or awkward. And fuck, he'd loved watching her touch herself. If she wanted this, he was happy to oblige.

He grabbed her wrist with his other hand and tugged her closer. He put her hand on his chest and slid it up and down over his right pec as he stroked his cock. "I love your hands on me," he told her.

"No fair," she said, her voice husky. "You didn't touch me while I was doing this the first night."

"Okay." He took his hand from hers and braced it on the wall beside him. His left hand kept working his cock. "You can stop."

She didn't stop. In fact, her other hand came up, running over his rib cage. His stomach tightened under her touch and he squeezed himself harder.

She watched his hand moving, matching her stroking rhythm over his stomach and chest with his. Her breathing was fast.

"Do you want me to come like this?" he asked.

He didn't really have a choice. He wasn't going to fuck her now and his orgasm was already tightening his balls. But he loved talking to her like this. Graphically, openly.

She nodded. "Oh, yes." She ran her hand from his ribs down to his hip then down the outside of his thigh, heightening his need as he picked up his pace.

She kept moving her hand up and down, then shocked him by moving her other hand to her breast. She played with her nipple, rolling and tugging on it as she watched him. Then her hand slipped down her stomach and between her legs. She began circling her clit. "I want to come with you."

"Jesus, Jordan," he groaned. "Yes."

Her finger began moving faster and Fletcher knew he was only moments away from losing it.

He reached up and cupped the back of her head, pulling her in for a kiss. He opened his mouth, nipping her bottom lip and then slipping his tongue inside to taste her. He circled and stroked her tongue as if it were her clit.

He was jerking hard and fast now, seconds away from coming. As if sensing that, Jordan suddenly pulled back.

"Yes, Fletcher. *Yes.*"

He exploded, coming over his hand and her stomach.

She pulled him in for another kiss, pressing their bodies together. He cupped her head, deepening the kiss.

But her hand had stopped moving.

He pulled back. "Your turn."

"Oh, I'm—"

Before she could even finish the sentence, he'd turned her, put her hands on the wall in front of her, and slid his hand between her legs.

"Oh, God, Fletcher."

That was exactly what he wanted to hear. What he *needed* to hear. He circled and pressed as he lifted his other hand to pluck and roll a nipple.

Her head fell back against his shoulder and she moved against his hand. "More," she begged.

He moved his hand to slip his middle finger into her, keeping his thumb on her clit.

"*Yes.*" Her fingers curled against the tile, as if she was trying to hang on.

"Foot up on the bench," Fletcher told her.

Zeke had put small benches in all of the guys' showers when he'd remodeled them. He'd promised they'd thank him. As Fletcher had never had a woman in his shower with him, he hadn't realized just *how* thankful he'd be. He'd sat on the bench when he'd had a sore hamstring after a weekend softball tournament. But otherwise he'd never used it.

At the moment, it was his favorite part of his bathroom. Maybe his whole house.

Jordan put her foot up, spreading her legs. Fletcher's finger sank deep and he added a second. She gasped and again tried to find purchase with her hands on the slippery wall. But she quickly gave up, reaching back and looping her arm around Fletcher's neck.

Her body arched and he thrust deep, circling her clit faster as she ground against his hand. He squeezed her nipple. "God you're amazing."

She gave a breathless laugh. "You're doing all the work."

"I will gladly work on you like this every fucking day." He curled his finger and felt the responding tightening of her pussy.

"Marrying you was such a great idea," she said.

He wanted her to think that every single day for the rest of her life.

She moaned as he pressed harder and he felt her muscles tighten. He groaned and kissed her neck, then sucked on the spot where her neck sloped into her shoulder as he curled his fingers into her G-spot.

He tugged on her nipple and put his mouth right against her ear. "I want to feel your pussy milking my fingers all day long."

"Oh, yes, Fletcher!"

She came, clenching hard on his fingers, her hand grasping his wrist, her body arching.

Fuck. Yes.

She slumped forward in his arms a moment later. He eased his fingers from her body and turned her into the warm spray of the shower. But she pivoted in his arms, pulling him under the water with her and bringing his head down for a long kiss. She pressed close, opening her mouth and sweeping her tongue in against his. He gripped her hips, feeling his blood and need surging again.

Finally he lifted his head, staring down at her.

She was still breathing hard, but she smiled up at him as water rained down on them. "Wow."

"Yeah?"

She laughed. "Yeah."

"Right up there with the Pythagorean Theorem with Zeke?"

She snorted. "Oh, for sure. Almost as good as learning to change my tire with Zander."

He stopped, narrowed his eyes, then sighed. "He taught you car maintenance too?"

She bit her lip. "Just basic roadside stuff."

He reached for the shampoo and poured some into his hands then lifted the suds to her hair. The purple had completely washed out by now and he drew his fingers through the familiar blond strands. "No more learning *anything* from anyone else."

He started shampooing her hair and massaging her scalp and she leaned in, put her arms around him, rested her cheek against his chest, and sighed.

"Okay."

He snorted. "Just okay? That's it?"

"When you're doing that to my head? Yeah. That's it." She tipped her head back. "I mean, later I'll probably push back on you being so bossy and say that's ridiculous, but right now? Anything you say."

He massaged down to the base of her head. "I'll keep that in mind." His cock was stirring again.

She rested her forehead on his chest with another happy sigh. "And then I'll remember that I like this bossy side of you and I'll probably let you get away with it again."

"You do, huh?"

"I do. You've always been really sweet and patient with me. But I like when you push me."

Yeah, his cock was nearly at full-mast.

She noticed. And wiggled closer.

But now he needed to get to work.

"Do you remember the time when we all went out for breakfast after a bonfire and we were sitting in the booth and all of a sudden a spider crawled out of your hair, down your arm and onto the table?" he asked.

She lifted a brow. "Seriously?"

"You don't remember that?"

"I do. We'd been down by the bayou. The damn thing probably dropped into my hair from the trees and you know it. But it was creepy and weird and embarrassing. But *really*? You're trying to distract yourself *now*?"

He tipped her head back into the water to rinse the shampoo. God she was gorgeous. "Yep."

"You're so weird." She ran her hands over her hair, which, of course drew attention to her breasts.

He took a deep breath and reached for the door to the shower stall. "Still...can't get the spider in your hair out of my mind. Gotta go."

She laughed and he knew she didn't believe him for a second.

But at least he got out of the bathroom without putting her up against the wall of the shower.

This time.

THERE HAD BEEN kids at the petting zoo every day, of course, but today Jordan had butterflies.

Some of it could have been her body still humming from the shower she and Fletcher had taken together that morning. She could instantly picture everything and her body would flush and she'd lose her train of thought. She knew because that had happened in the midst of talking to Charlie twice that morning.

She now understood why Fletcher had been so determined to find ways to distract himself when he started to feel turned on. It was really difficult to get anything else done when her mind kept wanting to wander to the memory of Fletcher standing under the shower spray, wet, slippery, stroking his big, hard cock. She'd definitely gone into the bathroom knowing she'd get a look at him naked, but she hadn't expected to walk in on him doing *that*.

If she had, she would've gotten out of bed a lot faster.

But at least some of her butterflies were because Fletcher's class was coming to the petting zoo today for a field trip and she really wanted him to see Sophia interacting with the alpacas. Hearing about it from her wasn't the same as witnessing it. She knew it would make him feel better to see the little girl smiling, chatting, and loving on the little animal.

They arrived shortly after noon. Jordan and Fletcher only had time to exchange smiles in the immediate flurry of activity but even that made her feel warm and happy.

The kids ate lunch while she talked about the alpacas, giving the kids general information about the animals but then transitioning into stories about two of them—Alpacapella, the one that loved to be sung to, and Chewpaca, the one who was missing his mom.

The kids were mostly good listeners. Everything went well. Until the kids were dismissed to look around the barnyard and to pet the goats, alpacas, and pigs.

And two of the moms sidled up to Fletcher.

Nancy Howell was one of them. They'd all gone to high school together and she'd had a crush on Fletcher.

Jordan didn't know the other one. And while Nancy was laughing as if Fletcher was the funniest person she'd ever met and putting her hand on his arm, it was the other woman who was standing *against* him. As in her right breast was pressed into his left biceps and she was looking at him as if he was a piece of double chocolate cake with fudge frosting.

A *single* piece of double chocolate cake with fudge frosting. As in a not-married piece of…

Jordan blew out a breath and headed in that direction.

Honestly, in the past, she would have tried to catch his eye and see if he gave her some kind of signal that he wanted to be saved. But that past had ended about a week ago in Las Vegas. He was now hers and she didn't need any kind of signal.

"Hi, everyone," she greeted sunnily as she approached.

Nancy had the good sense to look a little chagrined and she took a step back. "Oh, hi, Jordan. I didn't know you were working here until we showed up today."

Jordan gave her a smile that wasn't *completely* fake. Nancy was married with two kids. The one in third grade had been a surprise to her and her high school boyfriend their junior year of high school. They'd gotten married and stayed together ever since. That didn't, of course, mean she wasn't fine with the idea of a fling with the hot third-grade teacher though.

"Yep, I'm back." She looked up at Fletcher.

He was watching her with an expression that was slightly amused and slightly this-might-be-interesting.

Oh, he wanted her to stake her claim? That was *fine*. She was all in on that.

She reached out her hand toward the other woman. "Hi. I'm Jordan."

The other woman had stopped leaning on Fletcher but there wasn't enough space between them yet for Jordan's liking.

"Yes, I know from your introduction to the kids. I'm Ashley Mason." She took Jordan's hand in a weak shake.

Ashley was beautiful. Blond. Curvy. Totally Fletcher's type.

Too freaking bad.

"Well, Ashley, the part you must have missed is my last name. It's Landry. I'm Fletcher's wife."

Ashley nodded. "I know. You're the one Jason Young dumped."

Ah. Okay. Jordan nodded. "I sure am. Did you see it on TV?"

"I did, as a matter of fact." Ashley gave her a little smirk.

"Didn't my ass look awesome in that dress?" Jordan asked.

Fletcher snorted and reached out, taking her hand and pulling her close. "It definitely did." He ran his other hand around and cupped said ass, giving her a squeeze.

Jordan went up on tiptoe and pressed her lips to his in a long, tongue-free but definitely not-just-friends-anymore kiss.

When she pulled back and looked at Ashley again, Jordan gave *her* a smirk.

Ashley looked annoyed.

"So anyway, I need my *husband* so..." She didn't feel like she had to ask the other women to "excuse them" or that she should apologize for taking Fletcher away with her. Ashley and Nancy would just have to find some other guy to rub their breasts on. For good. "See ya," she finally said simply.

Jordan turned Fletcher away with her arm around his waist and started toward the alpaca pen.

His arm was around her as well and he poked her in the side. "Jealous?"

She looked up at him. "Yep."

He lifted a brow. "Really?"

"Of some other woman rubbing up against you? Um, yes. That's not okay."

"You are the only one I intend to rub. Ever again."

She nodded. "I know. But *they* need to know that."

"Ashley's been making me offers for a year. She's a single mom who moved here last summer. If I wanted to take her up on something, I would have before now."

Jordan stopped and turned to face him. "I'm not worried about you, Fletcher."

"You sure? After what happened with Jason—"

"I'm not worried," she said again, meaning it. "You're...*you*. You would never cheat on me. I know that. And while you sure could have stepped away from the perky blond breasts—"

"I was trying to lean away without being obvious."

She laughed. "I'm not worried," she said firmly. "I totally trust you."

"Okay." He blew out a breath. "Okay, good. There's a lot of... that"—He inclined his head in the general direction of Ashley and Nancy—"that goes on and I haven't really dissuaded it in the past. I mean, I don't let the married moms think there's *any* chance. I would never do that. But I don't really shut down the flirting either."

"And definitely not with the single ones." She nodded. "I know. You're the hot, popular, sweet, fun teacher that all the kids *and moms* want. I've heard all about it."

He leaned in. "And you get it. Because you have that thing about teachers."

She lifted both brows. "I *so* get it. I *really*, really get it. And," she added. "I grew up here, remember? I went to school and summer camp and was in Girl Scouts and stuff with a lot of these moms. Given half the chance, I'm *totally* going to rub it in their faces that *I'm* the one sleeping with the hot teacher they all want."

He laughed even as his eyes heated. "You were with a big, hot, country rock star."

"Oh, I might have to mention sleeping with him too. If it comes up. I'm *not* above bragging about my conquests," she said.

He rolled his eyes and she loved that they could joke about Jason and their relationship already. This was why falling in love with her best friend had been such a fantastic idea. Well, one of the reasons.

"Conquests." Fletcher scoffed. "You and Jason couldn't even pull off shower sex without one of you getting hurt. And you don't like giving blowjobs. Jason did a terrible job being any kind of a sex god."

Jordan felt how wide her eyes were. "I don't like giving blowjobs?"

Should they be talking about blowjobs in the middle of the petting zoo with kids around? But a quick glance assured her that there were no kids close enough to hear them.

"According to you."

"When did I say that?"

"You asked me if guys really like them as much as everyone says. We were at my house. It was just the two of us in the family room."

"Oh, you mean in *high school.*" She laughed. "I thought you meant recently."

Fletcher had always been great about giving her the guy's perspective on things and when she and Jason had first started getting physical, she'd asked Fletcher about a few specifics. He'd told her that she should never do anything she didn't want to do and to tell him immediately if Jason ever pressured her. He hadn't, of course, but she'd known that Fletcher—and his brothers and cousins—would have made Jason very, very sorry if he had.

"Has your opinion on them changed?" Fletcher asked. His voice was a little gruffer now.

She honestly couldn't remember the last time she'd done that with Jason. And it hadn't been often. "Well, I mean…" She looked around again. She had not expected to have this conversation, or even one like it, *here* today. "We weren't really into…" She dropped her voice. "Oral stuff. But I wouldn't say I don't like it."

His voice was definitely gruff when he said, "Oh, honey, we have *so* much to go over."

She felt the hot ribbons dance down her spine and she asked, "Really?" Her voice was definitely breathless.

"Really. We are going to—"

"Mr. Landry!"

They jerked apart abruptly. Jordan hadn't even realized she'd been leaning in. Her body was tingling from the promise in his voice even without the specifics.

"Hi, Ana," Fletcher said, recovering admirably as he turned to greet one of the mothers. "How are you?"

"I'm wonderful," the woman said, with a bright smile. "I wanted to tell you Sophia has been talking at home. She talked at the dinner table last night, and the other night at bedtime she asked me if I would come and read a story to her alpaca friend." Her eyes filled with tears.

Fletcher had to clear his throat before he said, "Jordan, this is Ana, Sophia's mother."

Jordan gave the woman a big smile. "It's so nice to meet you."

"Oh, Jordan! Sophia has talked about you too!" Ana looked back and forth between them. "Are you… is this your new wife?" she asked Fletcher.

He nodded and pulled Jordan up against his side. "Yes."

Ana's hand went to cover her mouth as she shook her head.

Then she said, "Oh my, I didn't realize the two people who were making this happen for Sophia were *together*. That's wonderful."

Jordan and Fletcher shared a smile.

"It's amazing to be able to share a passion like this," Fletcher agreed. "We both love children and teaching and being able to expand helping kids reach their full potential this way, together, means a lot to us."

Jordan squeezed him. They'd started building the program so naturally. Like everything between them, it had just been so easy to fall into it together. But yeah, it really was amazing and she loved that she was able to do something to make him happy the way he always had for her.

"Well, I can't tell you how grateful I am," Ana said. "Sophia needed this so much. I would have never thought that animals could get through when people couldn't."

"Animals are so accepting," Jordan said. "And they tend to bring out the best in us. They make us into protectors and care-givers. I've been so touched watching Sophia care for Chewie and then, because of that, work through her own grief."

Ana looked around. "I can't believe how much magic is hidden in this little petting zoo." She met Jordan's eyes. "But you're making a difference for these animals *and* for the people encountering them. Thank you."

Jordan felt her breath catch. "Thank you for saying that. It was…a happy accident but, I'm going to be sure everything is very on purpose from here on out."

Ana reached out and gave Jordan a quick hug. Then she turned to Fletcher. "Is it okay for me to hug you too?"

"I insist," he said, his voice sounding tight.

They hugged and then Ana went off to join Sophia at the alpaca pen again.

Jordan took a deep breath. "Wow."

"Yeah," Fletcher agreed.

She looked up at him. "I'm…thrilled. This is all so wonderful."

"I agree." He shook his head. "And I can't imagine doing it with anyone else."

"Aw." She stretched up to kiss his cheek. Then said in his ear, "Now about that oral sex stuff we need to go over…"

He leaned back. "Nope. We're not talking about that." But then he pinched her ass and added, "Right now."

Nineteen

FLETCHER WAS ALREADY HOME by the time Jordan came through the door that evening. He met her halfway across the kitchen.

"Hey, how was —"

He cupped her face and brought her in for a deep kiss. She was up on her tiptoes, clutching the front of his shirt within seconds.

He was in shorts and a t-shirt and smelled like soap as if he'd just showered. The scent took her back to that morning and her entire body felt as if hot water was cascading over it.

He trailed his lips along her jaw to her ear. "I've been dying for you to get home."

"Well, I'm thrilled to be here," she told him, gasping as he nipped the soft skin just behind and below her ear.

He lifted his head, her face in his hands, staring down at her.

She gripped his wrists, meeting his gaze, a little concerned by the intensity there. "Are you okay?"

"I just realized today that I don't have to be worried about middles as long as I've got you."

She frowned. "I thought we'd established that you *are* good at all of that. With the—"

"Yes," he cut her off with a kiss. "But," he continued after he released her lips, "*you* are amazing at middles. You don't worry about the end. You make *now* great. All you've done for Sophia and the other kids and animals in the zoo—it's all about right now. Making things better in the moment. And you've always done that. That's what you did for Jason. Being there, supporting him, letting him shine. You've always done it for me too. Letting me feel like the big shot, even if I can't explain scalene triangles."

"Fletch—"

He didn't let her finish. "So… I'm going to be fine. When I get tempted to rush to the big, grand gesture or get frustrated with having to go through the slow, or hard, unexciting middle part, you'll be there showing me how."

Jordan felt the sting in her eyes and she blinked hard, not wanting to blur the look of love and admiration on his face. "I will always be here," she promised. "But I will love every single one of your grand gestures too. Life needs those too, Fletcher. Your big happily ever after tendencies are awesome. You make people feel special and celebrated and taken care of."

He ran his thumbs over her cheeks. "We're great together then."

"We definitely are."

One heartbeat passed and then their mouths came together. Jordan's hand slid into his still damp hair. He cupped her head, tipping it slightly so he could deepen the kiss. Their tongues met and tangled. They pressed their bodies together, desperate to get closer.

After a few moments of kissing and groping, Fletcher gave a little growl and clamped his hands on her hips. He walked her backward, then lifted her to sit on the countertop. Jordan immediately parted her knees, letting him step in close and then linking her ankles behind him, pressing her heels into his ass. Her arms went around his neck, bringing him close. His hand slipped under her shirt, his big, hot palms against her bare back. They kissed again, deep and hot and needy.

He trailed his lips to her ear and said, gruffly, "Need you naked."

She remembered what he said about doing lots of exploring and their talk about blowjobs and her entire body clenched and heated.

She leaned back and reached for the hem of her shirt. But as she went to pull it off, the back of her head hit the cupboard behind her.

"Ouch," she muttered.

Fletcher's hand was immediately there rubbing over the spot. "Dammit."

She reached for him, not letting him step back as he tried. "I'm fine."

She started tugging on his shirt, moving it up his torso. He lifted his arms so she could strip it off, but he had to finish the motion because of the height difference. He tossed the shirt behind him and immediately reached for the clasp on her bra.

When they were both naked from the waist up, they pressed together again, kissing, hands wandering. His muscles bunched under his hot skin as his hands ran up and down her back, around her sides, and then up to cup her breasts.

His thumbs teased her nipples, and they beaded tightly, wanting more pressure. He read her reaction perfectly, tugging and squeezing just enough to make her gasp and moan.

He dipped his knees, bringing his hot mouth against one nipple and sucking hard. She arched her back trying to get closer, but again her head thumped against the cupboard behind her.

His head came up quickly, and he scooped his hands under her ass, with another muttered, "Dammit."

She opened her mouth to reassure him she was fine, but he lifted her and turned, striding to the table instead. He swept the mail and papers to the floor and deposited her on the top, immediately returning to sucking on one nipple while tugging on the other. With more room to move, she leaned back, bracing her hands behind her and offering her breasts to him more fully. He licked, nipped, and sucked until she was hot and panting.

Jordan shifted forward, reaching for the front of his shorts, grateful he'd put on loose athletic shorts with an elastic waistband. The table wobbled under her as she leaned though and she grabbed the edge with one hand.

Fletcher's head came up and he stared down at her, breathing hard.

Oh, she didn't want him to stop now. She lifted a foot, hooking it behind his knee, not letting him step back. She ran her hands over his abs, loving the way the muscles jumped underneath her touch. Then she slid one down into the front of his shorts and along the hard hot length of his cock. He wasn't wearing underwear.

He sucked in a deep breath through his nose, his eyes sliding shut. "Fuck," he groaned.

She encircled his shaft, squeezing gently, then stroking from base to tip and back down.

"Jordan."

The way he said her name was rough and she wanted so much more of that.

"I want you," she told him. "Please."

She didn't know if she could take any more just making out. He'd learned every inch of her body, going over it with his fingers and his tongue, but no matter how amazing the orgasms he'd given her had been, she needed *more*. She wasn't exactly unsatisfied, but she was craving more. Everything.

His eyes bored into hers as he seemed to be thinking over something important. Then he gave a single nod. "Need you naked," he said again.

He put a hand on her chest and pushed gently. Her hand slipped from his shorts and she leaned back again, bracing her hands behind her.

Fletcher reached for the button on her shorts, undoing it swiftly and lowering the zipper. He tugged, sliding the shorts down her hips. She had to lift a little to get them past the curve of her butt and the table wobbled again.

"*Dammit,*" he muttered.

Rather than let him focus on the instability of the surface, Jordan moved to shove the shorts the rest of the way down her legs. They dropped to the floor and Fletcher's eyes went immediately to the center of the silky lavender panties she was wearing.

He lifted a hand and traced a finger along the lacy upper edge.

Jordan sucked in a quick breath, her stomach tightening under the light stroke.

"God, you're so fucking gorgeous," he said. "How did I keep my hands to myself all these years?"

She felt one corner of her mouth curl up. "Because you're a really good guy."

Fletcher was not the type of guy to ever try to take another guy's girlfriend.

He lifted his eyes. "Thank God that didn't cost me. I got you in the end."

She nodded. "You definitely got me."

With his eyes locked on hers, Fletcher grabbed the tops of her panties and stripped them down her legs. The purple silk dropped to the floor at his feet, but his eyes were still on hers as he stroked a hand up her inner thigh. "Time to learn something new," he said.

She didn't even need specific words for her body to react to that. It was in his voice, in his eyes, in the press of the erection behind the cotton of his own shorts. He wanted her. And Fletcher wanting her this way was doing more to her than Jason's touch had in the past few years.

Oh God. She gave a little whimper. "I'm all yours, Mr. Landry."

Yeah, the hot, naughty teacher thing wasn't going to get old any time soon.

Or ever.

Fletcher's gaze flared hot and finally dropped to skim over her naked form.

"Holy hell," he said, almost reverently, like a prayer.

He grabbed one of the chairs and pulled it around, dropping into it, then reached for her, pulling her ass to the edge of the table. The table wobbled and creaked, but this time Fletcher didn't react.

Sitting in the chair put him at the perfect height to lean in and kiss her inner thigh.

Jordan's entire body trembled with desire and anticipation.

He ran the tip of his finger up and down the outer lip of her pussy. Every muscle in her body clenched.

"So, so pretty," he said. He lifted his eyes. "And all mine."

The possessive words made her instantly hotter and wetter. She pulled her bottom lip between her teeth and nodded.

That definitely seemed to please him. He stroked his finger over her outer lip again, then moved to the center, running the big, thick pad of his finger up and down her slit. He grazed her clit and the tingles shot from that spot out in every direction through her body.

She gasped his name.

"Oh yeah, I'm going to hear a lot more of that," he said, his voice husky.

He teased her with his finger for another few moments, winding her tighter, then slipped half his finger into her tight channel. She immediately clamped down on him and he gave a little groan of approval.

"Oh, you want this," he said.

"Yes. So much." She was panting now.

"You can have whatever you want from me."

She swallowed hard. "Anything, you promise?"

He met her eyes again and nodded. "I promise. "

She licked her lips. "I want *everything*. Fletcher, seriously. Tonight. I want another chance at our wedding night."

He took a deep breath and blew it out. "Yes," he finally said.

Relief rushed through her and she lowered herself onto her elbows. "Show me what you've got, Mr. Landry."

He moved his finger, sliding in and out a couple of times, clearly not deep enough, but enough to ignite her nerve endings. Then his thumb brushed over her clit and she groaned.

She slid her knees further apart and he gave an answering groan. He teased her for a little longer with just his finger and thumb, but finally, he lowered his head and gave her clit a lick.

Jordan nearly came off the table. As her hips lifted, the table wobbled and she gripped the one edge.

"Scoot back a bit," he ordered. "You might move too much to be on the edge."

She was already feeling restless and urgent. She needed to move and arch and...she didn't even know.

She started to slide up the table, but something pinched the upper curve of her ass and she gasped.

"What is it?" Fletcher asked sharply.

"Nothing." She rolled her head back and forth on the table. "It's nothing. Keep going."

He lowered his head again and gave her a long lick, then lightly sucked on her clit as he slid his finger deeper inside her.

She cried out, just from that much. Her hips bucked and she felt the sharp sting on her butt cheek again.

"Ouch!"

Fletcher's head came up quickly. "That hurt?"

"God no," she told him. "Not you."

He frowned. "What's going on?"

She huffed out a frustrated breath. "I don't know. Something's pinching my butt."

"Fucking hell." He stood swiftly and scooped her up. She wrapped her arms and legs around him. He looked down over her shoulder. "You're right on top of the drop-leaf," he said.

"Fletcher, it's fine."

He huffed out a breath and looked around the kitchen. "You might have a point about only having sex in bedrooms."

She looked up at him. "When did I say I only have sex in bedrooms?"

"After you sprained your ankle in the shower."

She shook her head. "Stop *remembering* things. I'm fine with sex anywhere. With you, *everywhere*."

He looked down at her, then over her shoulder to the living room. "Good." Holding her straddling his waist, he strode through the kitchen and into the living room, not stopping until they got to the couch. When she thought he was going to settle onto the cushions with her, he surprised her by setting her butt on the back of the couch with her feet on the cushions.

Before she could say anything, he knelt between her legs, pushed her thighs apart, and leaned in, resuming his licking and sucking.

"Oh my God, Fletcher!" Her hand flew to his head, curling into his hair as he ate at her.

He slid a finger into her, pumping deep, then added a second.

It wasn't just his hand and mouth that got her climbing again nearly instantly. Those were magnificent of course, but it was the position, the way he knelt between her knees as if servicing her. It was also that this couch had been the site of so many things—brainstorming, heart to hearts, the massage the other night when he just took care of her. And now it seemed appropriate that one of the dirtiest, hottest moments between them happened here.

He sucked harder, curled his fingers, and she came quickly. Surprisingly quickly.

Her muscles clamped down on him and she cried out his name as the orgasm crashed over her.

"Fletcher! Oh my God, Fletcher!"

He lifted his head and slid his hand from her body, but pulled her in for a deep kiss.

She could taste herself on him and that was a whole new

level of dirty. He stroked and circled her tongue as he had her clit just moments ago.

Then he pulled back, shoved his shorts and boxers to the floor, and pulled her into his body, as he turned to sit on the cushions.

"We didn't talk about this the first time," he said. "Do we need a condom?"

She shook her head. Then frowned. "I'm on birth control. And I would say I was clean—Jason said he and Vivian hadn't slept together yet, but I don't know if you trust him." Then she frowned deeper. "But Jason and I haven't been together in months anyway."

Fletcher nodded. He stroked his hand up and down her back slowly. "I'm clean. Up to you."

She ran her hands into his hair and cupped the back of his head, staring down at him. "I would love to have sex with you without a condom. Are you sure?"

He let out a long breath. "Holy hell, Jordan. Of course I'm sure."

She reached between them, stroking her hand up and down his hard length. He was big and hot, and she couldn't wait to have him filling her up.

She moved to position him at her entrance.

He sucked in a breath.

"You ready for this?" she asked.

"I've been ready for this for years." He gripped her hips and helped guide her up and forward.

As she sank down onto his length, they both moaned.

They took it slow at first. He stretched her slowly and deliciously and Jordan felt the sensations licking her body, from the soles of her feet to the back of her neck.

"God, you feel amazing," he ground out.

"Yes," she agreed breathlessly. "Oh, yes."

"Tell me what you want. What you need," he said.

She moved her hands to his face and looked him directly in the eye. "You. Fletcher, all I need is you."

He looked at her for a long moment, then he gripped her hips and surged upward, taking over. She gasped as he completely filled her. It was so, so good.

He paused for a moment, as if letting them both adjust.

But after a moment he started moving. And it took her breath away.

She was on top, but Fletcher was very clearly in control. He lifted and lowered her, meeting each slide with a thrust of his hips. Jordan helped, sort of, but she definitely let him set the rhythm.

The position made him go deep with every stroke and she felt her body climbing quickly toward a second orgasm.

"Play with your clit," he told her. He took her hand and put between her legs. "I want you to come like this."

She really thought it was possible she could come without that, but they'd definitely established that her orgasms were strongest with clitoral stimulation. She loved that he was not put off by the idea that she needed more than just his cock.

She circled her clit, lazily at first, loving the deep, slow strokes.

But then Fletcher leaned in and took her nipple in his mouth and sizzling sensation shot through her body. Her finger began rubbing faster and he moved her hips accordingly.

Soon the rhythm was almost frenzied as he fucked up into her and she climbed closer and closer to that pinnacle. Her fingers on the other hand dug into his shoulder and she gasped his name.

"Yes, fuck, Jordan."

It was the need in his voice that finally pushed her the rest of the way. The coiling ball of pleasure exploded and she came hard, crying his name.

He was right behind her, pounding up into her and then suddenly tensing, squeezing her against him as he came.

The sound of her name on his lips at that moment was the best thing she'd ever heard. Knowing that she could push him to the brink that way, but then also give him the ultimate fulfillment and satisfaction was amazing.

She slumped against him and felt his hold on her ease slightly. But he wrapped his arms around her and she curled into his chest.

They sat entwined, breathing hard, cooling off, for several long minutes.

Finally, Jordan lifted her head and looked down at him. "Beginning, middle, and end," she told him. "Very, very nice."

He grinned, kissed her, and then said, "What do you mean end? We're just getting started, Mrs. Landry."

THE NEXT FOUR weeks were a whirlwind of activity, and happiness. Jordan and Fletcher fell into a very easy, happy, sexy routine. They didn't shower together every morning and Jordan continued to be a later sleeper than Fletcher, but they figured out that the sex in the kitchen worked just fine if he bent her over the kitchen table, without the drop leaves up in place, and that the shower bench really was something they were thankful to Zander for.

And they both got a grand finale or two every day.

Things at the petting zoo also were going well. Spreading the cursing parrots out had worked and no one had heard the word "motherfucker" in weeks—at least not from the birds.

Ana had agreed to have Sophia spend an hour with Chewie every day after school and had started bringing a friend or two with her over the past couple of weeks so he could get used to more kids.

It was working. Chewie was becoming more friendly with the rest of the herd and was eating much better. It was also adorable to watch him strolling toward the fence around three fifteen every day, anticipating Sophia's arrival. When their visit was over, the alpaca would stand at the fence and watch her go, but after she disappeared from sight he would wander back over to join the rest of the herd and would allow other children to pet and feed him at times.

The porcupines, Spike and Dill Prickles, had gotten used to Jordan handling and feeding them quickly, and everyone thought Spike was the first to animal to have a crush on Jordan.

The red panda enclosure was completed. And Griffin and Fiona had both come around to the idea of adding to zebras, much to Zeke's delight. Zebras would not be arriving in Louisiana for at least another month or so, but their barn was nearly completed.

Regan continued to give input as did her two ex-patients and Brittney, the psychologist who had agreed to consult with the petting zoo's new program, was incredibly impressed by the plans and how open-minded and passionate Jordan was about everything.

Fletcher really did try to stay out of the way. This was Jordan's project and she was amazing when it came to brainstorming and discussing new ways for the kids and animals to interact. But sometimes it was hard to hold back his pride and enthusiasm.

Sophia had completely come out of her shell. She was now participating in class discussions, her artwork and writing both showed a much more optimistic and positive attitude, and while she was still quiet during big group activities, she smiled more, sat with other kids at lunch, and played at recess. Ana thanked him at least twice a week and Fletcher continued to insist that the majority of the work was thanks to Jordan and Brittney.

Jordan and Charlie had done a few interviews about the direction of the petting zoo and the new program. They were getting great local attention and had seen an uptick in donations to the zoo. However, they were still waiting for news about the grant application that would make all the difference to Jordan and Brittney's salaries and Jordan's ability to attend more specific training and expand the program.

That news arrived two days later when Fletcher strode into Ellie's to join Jordan and the family for dinner on Wednesday evening.

The back table was nearly full and he was grinning as he approached. But his grin quickly died when he focused on his wife. She looked absolutely dejected.

Frowning, his first words to her were, "What happened?"

She looked up at him, and the disappointment on her face punched him in the chest. She handed him a piece of paper.

He knew what it was even before he looked down. Sure enough, the letterhead was from the foundation they'd applied to for the grant.

Dear Mrs. Landry, we are impressed with the program that you have outlined and your vision for the future. However, at this time, we regret to inform you that we must pass on your request for grant funding.

He didn't read any further. He looked at Jordan. "Dammit," he said. "I'm sorry."

She nodded. "We knew it was a possibility."

The thing was, Fletcher actually hadn't thought it was a possibility. He'd honestly believed they would get this grant. Why not? Their program was amazing. It was visionary, had a positive impact not only on children but also on animals, and was great from the perspective of growing a small business. They wanted to go from being a petting zoo that sold stuffed animals and snow cones to a sanctuary for animals with physical and emotional trauma and a unique, educational site with a widespread positive impact.

Which was exactly what he'd put in their fucking application. *Son of a bitch.*

They'd worked their asses off on that proposal. He'd been so proud of it. So confident. He'd reviewed and edited a grant proposal that had been awarded just last year for new computer software for the entire school. He'd helped give the presentation that had won a statewide scholarship for fine arts programs in public schools. He'd been asked to speak on behalf of the teachers in convincing the city council to spend money on improving the internet access to the school and community.

He knew how to make a big production out of convincing other people that he knew what he was doing. He was a Landry. Big ideas and too much confidence were in his blood.

But this time, it hadn't worked.

And this time, it had mattered more than any other time.

This time it was for Jordan and Sophia.

And why was he suddenly thinking about geometric equations and parallel parking?

Because, just like those, he'd only been able to get Jordan partway toward her ultimate goal.

"Fuck them." Fletcher tossed the letter onto the table. "I'll give them a call tomorrow."

Jordan looked up at him, eyebrows high. "You'll *call* them?"

"Yes."

"You'll just…call them."

"Yes, I'll call them," he repeated. "Obviously they didn't read the proposal carefully enough. I think as an educator I can help them understand the positive impact this is going to have on kids. As an educator who has a child in his classroom, at this moment, who is benefiting from this program, I think I can add some really important perspective."

Jordan actually laughed at that. But she was looking at him with clear disbelief. "That isn't how this works, Fletcher. We have to apply like everyone else and give them the information they asked for. They measured us against the other applicants and clearly felt like we weren't the best choice."

Fletcher scowled. "Well, they're idiots. There's no way there were other applicants better than us. Let me call and see what I can find out."

"Oh my God. No," Jordan said simply. "We'll reapply next year. Or we'll look for another grant somewhere."

But she didn't sound overly optimistic about that.

"We need the money *now*. In fact, we needed the money a month ago," Fletcher said. "We don't have time to wait around for another foundation to make up their minds."

"We don't get to make these rules," Jordan said. "They're the ones with the money. They decide how it gets distributed. They ask the questions. They set the timelines. All we can do is our best."

"Well, that obviously wasn't good enough." Fletcher snapped.

"And sometimes that's how it goes," Jordan said, frowning. "Sometimes our best isn't good enough and we just have to be happy with knowing we did everything we could."

"Right. Sometimes our best is only enough for a B-, right?" he asked.

"Oh for fuck's sake," she muttered.

"You finally told him about geometry?" Zeke asked.

"Shut up, Zeke," Jordan told him.

The look she gave him actually made Zeke bite back whatever he'd been about to say. That was a damned miracle.

Fletcher shoved a hand through his hair. His emotions were swirling. Sophia had shown him how important this program really was. He hadn't been able to help her himself, but he'd had a chance to be a part of something that could. That had made him feel better. It was indirectly helping her, but that was better than nothing.

And yeah, fuck, he hadn't been able to get Jordan from a B- to the A- but Zeke had. At least, in the end, she'd gotten what she needed.

So what could he do about the money for this program? If his grant proposal wasn't good enough, what other options were there? Because yes, Sophia was doing better, but what about the next kid? The one who needed even more help?

Because there would be one. Fletcher would always be the fun teacher, but he wouldn't be the teacher with all the answers. This program had given him hope that there would still be a resource for the kids when he came up short. Maybe he didn't have to always be the one fixing everything, but he needed to know that there was *someone* to turn to. He needed to at least be able to offer metaphorical Gatorade when things were tough.

"I need some air." He turned on his heel and stomped toward the front door of Ellie's.

He had to admit he was waiting for someone to call after him, to stop him. He was half expecting Jordan to run after him.

But as he stepped out into the summer evening, no one said a word.

He'd walked several yards before he realized that he'd headed for the alpaca pen. He stopped and looked up. The alpacas were grazing in the pasture, happily oblivious to the turmoil the humans were going through.

Fletcher propped a foot on the bottom rail of the fence and leaned on the top with his forearms. He took a deep breath.

He'd been working around these alpacas for months. He'd done several presentations for the kids over the summer that included the alpacas. Where alpacas were originally from, what they ate, how they interacted with each other, how they communicated. But in all that time he had no idea how important they would become to him. Because of Jordan. She hadn't brought the alpacas into his life, but she'd opened his eyes to what was already there.

That seemed exactly right. His whole life she had been making the things that were already around him, already a part of his daily routine, bigger and better. Eating ice cream was more enjoyable when he did it with Jordan. Watching a television rerun that he'd already seen three times was funnier when Jordan was watching it with him. Hanging out with his family was always a good time, but it was even better when Jordan was there.

She made everything in his life better, and now he was lucky enough that she was going to live with him as his wife for the rest of his life.

Assuming that he quit acting like a jackass and figured out how to work through these rough patches when he felt like a failure.

Something bumped against his shoulder and he looked over to find Chewie looking at him.

"Hey, man," Fletcher greeted.

He didn't interact with the little alpaca much one on one. He didn't think he'd ever hand fed or given treats to the little guy. So Chewie was not over here because he thought Fletcher had something for him.

He was probably over here because he thought Fletcher looked sad.

That was Chewie's thing—to cheer up sad humans.

With a sigh, Fletcher reached his hand out and rubbed the alpaca's snout. His brown curly coat was soft and his nose was velvety. The alpaca nuzzled him back, and Fletcher actually felt some tension leave his shoulders.

Amazing.

"So what do I do?" he asked the animal. Maybe it wasn't completely crazy to be asking. Griffin talked to the otters all the time, as everyone knew.

Chewie pressed against his hand again and Fletcher rubbed his nose a little harder.

"Yeah, I just have to raise some money, how hard can that be?" Fletcher gave a short laugh. "Right, there's gotta be *someone* with a hundred thousand dollars just stuffed in their sock drawer."

But as he continued to pet the alpaca who seemed content to just stand by the fence with him, Fletcher's wheels began to turn.

He could fix this. They just needed funding. They had everything else. The knowledge, the heart, the passion were here.

Now all they needed was dollars. And it wasn't a million dollars or anything. It was a hundred grand. They could come up with that.

He didn't have the money, but he had an idea.

And a phone number.

JORDAN STOOD STARING at the door of Ellie's bar.

Fletcher had just walked out.

She knew he was feeling like he'd failed her and Sophia and everyone else and the one thing Fletcher didn't handle well was not being able to fix everything for everyone he loved.

She started in the direction of the door, but she only got two steps before she felt a big arm band around her waist and lift her off the floor.

"Oh no you don't." Zeke turned and set her down, standing between her and the door. "You're not going after him."

"I need to talk to him."

"No, you don't. He needs a chance to think."

She looked past her brother-in-law to the door, then sighed. "I don't know what else to say anyway."

"There's nothing to say. He's pissed because he's passionate about this and his first try to fix it didn't work. He not only likes to be the go-to guy, he likes it to be easy. But this is good for him. If you'd told him you were still having trouble in geometry, he would have kept working with you until you had it, you know."

She closed her eyes and shook her head. "Fucking geometry."

Zeke laughed. "But it's true. And very symbolic. You needed help, he jumped in to save the day, he did—partially—but *you* let him think he'd solved it all and he sat back and didn't have to work at it anymore. Don't do that this time. Let him deal with having to try again. Give him a chance to think about this and figure out another plan."

Jordan was staring at him.

"What?" Zeke asked.

"That was very…insightful."

"And almost…wise," Zander added.

"I can be insightful and wise," Zeke said, seeming offended.

"Since when?" Owen asked. "Last week you jumped off the roof of a house."

"It was on fire."

Michael, the firefighter and paramedic in the group, sat forward. "*What?*"

Zeke held up a hand. "I jumped down to get the fire extinguisher. It wasn't *on fire*. A rag on the roof caught on fire from… never mind. Not important. I jumped on the scaffolding, not all the way to the ground anyway." He frowned at Owen. "You make me sound like a dumbass."

"*I* make you sound like a dumbass?" Owen asked.

"*Anyway*, as much as it pains me to say this," Zander said. "Zeke's right. Fletcher needs a chance to fix this. Not because he always gets everything right, but because he *doesn't* and he needs to realize that's okay and taking another run at it is fine. Maybe three or four runs. Nothing wrong with tryin' again."

Owen and Michael exchanged looks.

"What the hell is your grandma puttin' in the beer now?" Michael asked. "You're all actually getting *smarter*."

Zeke looked smug. "And we've all gotta be gone when Fletcher comes back in here for help. He's gotta do this on his own. Zander and me have been fixin' shit for him for too long and making him look like a big deal."

Jordan sighed. "It was like three chapters in geometry and two things on the driving test." She was never going to live any of that down.

"Still, we're headin' to Bad. Who's comin'?" Zeke asked.

"What's Bad?" Donovan asked, already getting out of his chair.

Donovan Foster had arrived in town yesterday. This time it was more than a visit to his brother. He was here to help Griffin with a black bear that had been wounded by a trap. Bailey and her partner had brought the tranquilized animal in to Griffin for surgery. He'd immediately called Donovan to come and help with the rehab.

According to the rest of the guys, unlike his brother, Donovan was up for anything, any time.

"Town up the bayou," Zeke said. "It's probably the one place Fletcher won't look for us. Or Jordan. He'd find us down by the water and he'd definitely think to check Trahan's."

Trahan's was their favorite bar in New Orleans. It was owned by two of Owen and Josh's best friends. It sat on a busy corner in the French Quarter and everyone from Autre made regular trips up there. But that was kind of far to go tonight just to avoid her husband while he worked things through.

That wouldn't take long.

Would it?

Ten minutes later, Jordan was sitting next to Zeke in the front seat of his truck with Naomi and Charlie and Donovan in the backseat. Griffin was planning to join them when he was finished at the otter enclosure a little later.

They walked through the doors of Bad Brews, the bar and restaurant in Bad, Louisiana, twenty minutes later.

"Zeke Landry, what the hell are you doing here?"

Marc, one of the owners of the bar, greeted Zeke.

"Decided to do some charity work and give money to the poor town up the road from us."

Marc flipped him off, but then laughed. "You want to sit at the bar or you want a table?"

Zeke looked at Jordan. "Need to get this girl drunk fast." He pointed at Naomi. "And need to keep that girl off the karaoke stage."

Marc laughed. "Hey, Jordan, hey, Naomi."

"Hi, Marc," Jordan greeted. "I haven't seen you in forever."

"Well, you've been a little busy. From what I hear," Marc told her. "But no worries about karaoke tonight. Sabrina's on stage."

Sabrina was Marc's fiancée. She happened to be a gifted singer-songwriter. She had left the area to pursue a music career, but hadn't had the same fortune Jason had. Sabrina and Marc were a little older than Jordan, Fletcher, Zeke, and Naomi. But because Sabrina was also involved in the country music scene, Jordan and Jason had definitely been aware of her.

"Oh, that's awesome, I'd love to hear her perform," Jordan said.

Marc nodded. "Go on in. I'll even just charge you regular price on the drinks rather than double tonight," he told Zeke.

Zeke laughed. "Thanks, man. You're a real charmer."

They headed into the bar area and found a high-top round table with four stools. They were able to drag two additional over from a nearby table. They settled in and the waitress came over to take their order.

Jordan ended up with a blue concoction in front of her that was raspberry flavored. Apparently, Marc had invented it himself.

She took one look at it and burst into tears.

Zeke lifted a brow as he took a long draw of his beer. The bar had three of their own beers on tap. Bad Brew, Badder Brew, and the Baddest Brew. The Baddest Brew was the darkest and apparently one of Zeke's favorites.

He swallowed and set his glass down. "What the hell?"

"It just reminded me of that time that Fletcher and I ate and drank all blue stuff at the fair and then he ended up getting sick and puking blue all over me."

Zeke rolled his eyes. "Very romantic."

Jordan shook her head. "The point is, I know we're just getting started on the marriage thing. I know that we have a lot of things to go through and figure out. But we've already been through a lot. This should be a little easier by now. But he has to realize that sometimes we're going to get bogged down in the middle of our plans, with setbacks and things we didn't expect."

She took a long drink from her glass. It was delicious. It was one of those drinks that was going to go down very easily. As was the next one. Or two.

Zeke sat back, cradling his beer glass. "He'll figure it out. When it comes to you and those kids in his classroom, he's always going to be super protective. And a little irrational. But he'll figure it out."

Jordan sighed and took another drink.

"So, you just need money?" Donovan asked.

Jordan nodded. "Pretty much."

"I could do something," Donovan said.

Zeke looked at him. "Something like what?"

"Like an exhibition or something. I could sign some autographs. We can put something up on YouTube."

Zeke looked confused. He looked at Jordan and then back to Donovan. "You're just going to sign some autographs.? How can that raise money?"

Naomi leaned in. "You don't know who he is?"

Zeke shook his head. "He's Griffin's brother. And?"

"He had a show on the Go Wild channel." Naomi said. "He traveled the world rescuing and rehabilitating wounded wild animals. That would pair perfectly with the animals with special needs that you have and the message you want to promote with the program. Rehabilitation, recovery, adaptation. That's what he's all about."

Donovan was staring at her.

Naomi glanced at him. "What?"

"Gorgeous and sweet *and* you know who I am?"

Naomi looked surprised and didn't say anything to that as she sat back in her chair.

Jordan watched her friend with fascination. Naomi looked… a little rattled.

Naomi took a breath, then nodded. "Yes, I've seen an episode or two of your show."

Donovan leaned an elbow on the table, a slight grin teasing his lips. He looked a lot like Griffin, but his dark hair was a bit lighter and both his hair and beard were shorter. His left arm had ink running all the way to his wrist and his skin was tan and more weathered looking, obviously from being outdoors in a variety of conditions.

Right now, looking at Naomi, he seemed downright enchanted. "Really? Which ones?"

"There was one where you rehabilitated a polar bear up in Alaska."

He nodded. "Which one was your favorite?"

Naomi cleared her throat. "I saw one with a dolphin too. That one was great."

He grinned. "Thanks. That was amazing." He turned to the others at the table. "The goal of the show was to highlight wildlife rehabilitation around the world so people were aware that it happens. We covered what to do and where to find resources if people encounter injured wildlife where they live and ways humans often contribute to illness and injury in wildlife. But it was very cool just getting to interact with lots of different animals myself." He looked at Naomi. "I think my favorite was when I rehabbed a kangaroo down in Australia."

She frowned. "You never worked with a kangaroo. There was one with an echidna, but no kangaroo."

He lifted a brow. "Maybe you missed that episode."

"No. I've seen them a—" She broke off and pressed her lips together.

Donovan laughed. "Now, don't be embarrassed about seeing my whole show. *Please*. Gorgeous women aren't often into bloody animals. Or seeing *my* blood."

Jordan couldn't put her finger on how she knew exactly, but it seemed that Naomi was a little flustered. By Donovan Foster.

Charlie laughed. "I've seen a couple episodes myself since Griffin told me about you. And yeah, saving poor, defenseless, injured, and scared animals and facing down danger and being willing to risk being bitten or stung or clawed while you're trying to help super cool things like dolphins and kangaroos." She rolled her eyes. "No woman would ever find *that* attractive."

"He never worked with a kangaroo," Naomi muttered.

Donovan grinned. "Well, sure, once I *tell* them about all of that. But very few have *seen* the show." He looked at Naomi again. "And definitely not *all* of the episodes."

She blew out a breath, clearly regretting him learning that.

Donovan's grin grew. "And have you seen my YouTube series?"

Naomi didn't respond right away. She was chewing on the inside of her cheek.

Jordan looked at Zeke. Zeke gave her a look with wide eyes and a grin.

They both focused back on Donovan and Naomi.

"I've caught a couple of those episodes as well," Naomi finally said.

"Uh-huh," Donovan said, with a knowing smile. "And how did you come across those? I ask because it's important for marketing purposes. Of course. Great to know how people find the show."

Naomi shook her head. "I don't remember. I might have been watching videos about…giraffes or something."

Donovan nodded. "I see. So you're an animal lover?"

"Yes," Naomi said. "Of course."

"And wild animals in particular?"

She nodded.

"And where's that come from?" Donavan asked. "Did you grow up around a lot of animals?"

"Wait, are you flirting or do you really not know who *she* is?" Charlie asked.

Donovan glanced at his brother's girlfriend. "Um. Naomi LeClaire. The woman with the best taste in television in Autre, Louisiana. Am I missing something?"

Charlie snorted. "Well, I mean—Ouch!" Charlie jumped and frowned at Naomi, leaning to rub her leg.

"I think she means Jordan," Naomi said to Donovan. "She's wondering if you know who Jordan is."

It was an unspoken agreement in Autre that everyone

protected Naomi's identity. If people thought they recognized her, the people in Autre generally downplayed it or flat-out lied. If people came to town looking for her, having read somewhere on the Internet that she was from Autre originally, the people in town covered. Naomi was very much living a simple, quiet, out-of-the-spotlight life now. And her town, especially her friends and family, protected that. Charlie had obviously had a momentary lapse.

Donovan looked at Jordan. "Oh, should I know who you are?"

Jordan shook her head. "Not necessarily."

"She dated Jason Young," Naomi said. "The country music singer."

Donovan frowned as if trying to place the name. Then shrugged. "I think I've heard of him."

Jordan nodded. "Yeah. We broke up. Not too long ago. So every once in a while I get recognized."

"Is he a big deal?" Donovan asked.

Charlie and Naomi both chuckled. "Yeah, he's a big deal," Charlie said. "Rising star."

"We should ask him for help too, then," Donovan said. "More celebrity power."

Charlie gave a choked laugh and Naomi frowned at her.

Naomi had done a lot of charity work back when she'd been on her show, but she'd developed anxiety about crowds and big public places toward the end of her career so she no longer did appearances.

"Maybe he could do a benefit concert or even just talk about it in some press conference or something," Donovan said, still talking about Jason.

Charlie sat up a little straighter. "Griffin's here. Hey, Donovan, go grab Griffin and on your way past the bar, get us all some refills."

Donovan looked over to where his brother had just entered the restaurant and nodded. "Okay." He slid off the stool. But he turned back to Naomi with a grin. "Don't worry, sweetheart, I'll be right back. Save my seat."

As soon as he was far enough away from the table that he wouldn't hear what they said, Jordan and Charlie both turned on Naomi.

"Oh my God," Charlie said.

"What?" Naomi asked. She was studying her fingernails.

"I have never seen you moony-eyed over a man."

Naomi frowned. "Moony-eyed? I don't even know what that means."

Charlie pointed at her. "You have a crush on Donovan Foster. Why didn't you say anything?"

"Why would I have said anything? What am I supposed to say to you? 'Oh, hey, I've seen Griffin's brother on TV and oh my God'."

Charlie nodded. "Yes, basically that's what you could've said."

"Except that I didn't want you to know."

"I could've introduced you. I could've *set you up*! He's obviously attracted to you."

"I didn't want to meet him and I do *not* want to be set up," Naomi said.

Zeke chuckled. "Yeah, why would you want to meet the guy you have a crush on?"

Naomi took a breath and blew it out. "You all know that I like low-key. I have a simple life. And I love it. I don't want to be set up with my friend's boyfriend's brother. Especially when he's a celebrity. Donovan Foster is *not* low-key."

Charlie and Jordan both snorted.

"Celebrity?" Jordan asked. "I've never heard of him."

"Well, he's a celebrity in some circles," Naomi said. She actually tipped her chin up and said it with a slightly haughty air.

Charlie and Jordan laughed even harder.

"The man *scales the side of the mountains* to go down and rescue eagles that have been injured," Naomi said. "He's swum out in the midst of sharks to rescue a baby whale. He once had to avoid a pride of lions so he could take a lioness to his rehab facility."

Charlie shook her head. "This is awesome. I mean, if I had to pick the guy that I thought Naomi LeClaire would have a crush on, it would absolutely not be a larger than life, attention hog, adrenaline junkie like Donovan."

Jordan shook her head. "I don't know, it kinda makes sense. He's into wild animals and she's always been an animal lover. They totally have that in common. Plus, she understands the TV thing. Plus, he's hot."

Charlie nodded. "I mean he does look a lot like his older brother. So he's definitely good-looking."

"And charming as hell." Jordan peered closer at Naomi. "And I think he is absolutely captivated by the idea that you know who he is."

Naomi waved that away. "A lot of people know who he is. And he was just being flirtatious when he said that women don't normally know."

"I don't know about that," Charlie said. "I don't know a ton of women who watch the Go Wild Channel. And even fewer that watch YouTube series about wild animal rehabilitation experts."

"Well, Ms. Marketing Guru, maybe you need to do some more research." Naomi said. "Animal videos? Come on. That's basically why most people start watching YouTube."

"Yeah, funny cat videos and stuff like that," Charlie said. "Not specific series that are created for YouTube."

Naomi shook her head. "I mean, it's not as polished and produced as his show on cable, but that almost makes it better. It's gritty and real. They don't always cut away when something awkward happens, or even during the boring moments. It's all on there. You really see what it's like."

"Does he ever take his shirt off?" Jordan asked, resting her chin on her hand.

Naomi rolled her eyes. But she didn't say he *didn't* take his shirt off.

Jordan laughed. "That answers my question."

Charlie leaned in. "Do you think if he did something for the petting zoo it would actually matter to his followers?" she asked Naomi. "Like could he help us raise the money online?"

Naomi shrugged. "Possibly. I mean, at least he has the credentials. Like I said, he could talk about rehabilitating animals and tie it into some of the permanent disabilities our animals have." She looked at Jordan. "I might be willing to do something too," she said softly.

"No, seriously, Naomi. You do *not* have to do that. I am not going to make anyone do anything they don't want to do." She looked at Charlie. "We will raise the funds we need. Or I'll go back to substitute teaching and volunteer my time at the zoo."

"But we won't be able to do as much then. At least not as quickly," Charlie said, clearly disappointed. But she looked at Naomi. "But I do not expect you to do anything you don't want to do. You have put Zoey at the Zoo behind you. We fully support that. We are not trying to get you to change your mind."

Naomi nodded. "Okay. I just feel bad. You have this amazing petting zoo that you're trying to grow into more right in my backyard."

"You don't owe us anything, Naomi. We're friends. Your happiness and security come first."

Naomi gave them both a grateful smile. She'd had panic attacks and since coming back to Autre had been able to manage them, but she was very strict about staying out of the spotlight.

Donovan and Griffin returned to the table with more drinks and as they talked, Jordan had to agree that while Donovan and Naomi had a lot of interesting things in common with their experiences with wild animals—though the animals Naomi had worked with had been highly trained and very safe—Donovan really was not at all what Naomi would want or need in her life. He was charming, funny, and extroverted to the nth degree. And clearly loved any chance to be the center of attention. Naomi was absolutely the opposite of all of that.

However, her friend continued to watch, listen, and laugh at the stories the hot animal expert shared as they all drank and talked.

It was so nice of Donovan to jump in with ideas about how they could raise money for the petting zoo. And for him to volunteer to be a part of it. And what he'd said about Jason…

She reached over and grabbed Zeke's forearm as a thought hit her.

"Oh my God," she said. "Fletcher is going to call Jason."

Zeke looked at her, confused. "What are you talking about?"

She nodded furiously, her heart hammering. "Fletcher is going to want to save the program. He will be willing to do whatever it takes to fix this. Just like he ended up calling Jason for advice about my migraine when he didn't know what to do, Fletcher is going to call Jason and ask him for money."

Zeke frowned and shook his head. "I don't know about that, Jordan. I mean, it's one thing for him to call Jason when you're sick, but that would take a lot for him to let Jason be the big hero here. He would have to really swallow his pride to do something like that."

Jordan shook her head. "I know, but he would do anything for me. He believes so much in this program, and he wants to do what he can to make me and all the kids happy."

She felt a strange mix of panic, frustration, and love at this realization.

Fletcher had thought he was helping with the big finale when he'd written the grant proposal for the final funding they needed. But now that it hadn't worked, he would still want to come in and save the day. Zeke was right thinking that Fletcher would just need some time to work through it all and to come up with another plan.

But he would do whatever it took.

"I can't let him do that," she said. "Jason shouldn't get to save the day on this. This program is mine and Fletcher's." She glanced at Charlie. "I mean, it's all ours of course." She reached into her purse and dug her phone out. "But it's *ours*. We can work on this. *We* can make this happen."

"Who're you calling?" Zeke asked.

"I have to fix this." She listened to the phone ring.

A male voice answered almost immediately. "Jordan?"

"Hi, Jason."

Twenty~One

EVERYONE at her table stopped talking and turned to look at her with wide eyes.

"What's going on? Are you all right?"

She appreciated that this was Jason's first question. "I'm fine. But you can't give Fletcher the money."

"Fletcher? What money?"

"The money Fletcher called and asked you for. For the program that we're putting together."

"The program with the animals and the kids? I saw a write up in the local paper about the alpaca and the little girl who lost her dad. That was really cool," Jason said. "I'm really proud of you. And really happy for you. Do you need money?"

She shook her head, then remembered they were on the phone. "No. I mean, yes, we got turned down for the grant we applied for. But we don't need your money. Fletcher is going to ask you for money to fund it and we have to work for it ourselves. We are going to have to put together… something."

"Fletcher hasn't called me, Jordan. Last I talked to him, it was about your headaches."

She frowned. "Are you sure you don't have a missed call?"

"Completely sure. By the way, I'd answer his call."

Okay, that was nice. "I appreciate that. Well, maybe he's still going to call. But you have to say no when he does."

"Why? Why not let me give the money?"

"I don't want your money, Jason. This isn't about you."

"Okay, but all the stuff you did for me, all the time you gave me, all the support, that wasn't about *you*." Jason sighed. "Come on, Jordan. I owe you. You were behind me all that time. I know you gave up a ton for me. Ask me for the money. I'd love to give it to you. Hey, it's even a local program, it makes sense. I can support the kids and a local business back home."

"I'm not going to let you use this program to boost your image," she said. "Sorry. I did do a lot for you. And I don't regret it. I'm happy for you and proud of you. You're making all your dreams come true. At the time in my life when I was with you, that was what I wanted to do. But this program is what I want to do now and I want to do it with Fletcher. Not with you."

"Okay. I get it. But I would give you the money without anyone having to know. I can transfer the money into your account right now. I still have your bank account information connected to mine. I don't even have to tell my manager or anyone. It can come from my personal account."

Jordan hesitated. She pressed her lips together and thought about what he was saying. She kind of wished she hadn't drank so much blue raspberry stuff.

Jason had the money that they needed. She could have it tonight. He wanted to give it to her. And, frankly, he wasn't wrong about owing her. Not that she would ever consider demanding anything or reminding him of that. She couldn't put a price tag on the things she'd done for him. But if Jason anonymously donated the money, the program would be fully funded within ten minutes.

Was she stupid to turn that down?

Finally, she said, "Let me think about it. I need to talk to Fletcher. But I'll let you know."

"Okay. You know where to find me. I'm happy to do it."

And she believed him. "Okay, we'll talk soon. Bye." She disconnected and looked around the table.

"What did he say?" Charlie asked.

"He wants to give us the money."

"Nice!" Donovan lifted his glass. But a moment later he set it back down. "We're not happy about this?"

"I need to talk to Fletcher," Jordan told Zeke. "We need to get back to Autre."

EVERYONE IN ELLIE'S turned as one as the front door banged open, and Jordan yelled, "Don't call Jason!"

Fletcher watched his wife find him across the room and stomp toward him. She got up close, nearly on his toes. She tipped her head back and looked up at him and repeated, "Do not call Jason."

God, he loved her. "Why would I call Jason?"

"Because he has money. And guilt. And he's actually a good guy. And we need money. And you'll do anything to make this program work. And anything for me."

He nodded. Then he glanced at his brother. "How drunk is she?"

"Not so drunk that she didn't realize that you might call Jason, but drunk enough that she called him first."

Fletcher looked down at Jordan. "You called Jason?"

She nodded quickly. "To tell him not to give you any money."

"I see."

Jordan reached out and grabbed his hands, squeezing tightly. "We can do this without Jason. I know that this is the middle, where the hard work happens and there are setbacks and disappointments. But if you stick with it, we can make it happen and it will be so much sweeter in the end."

He reached up and cupped her face. "I know. You are

amazing at middles. And you are going to teach me, firsthand, how to do this. I'm not going to call Jason. I hope ever again."

Jordan's eyes widened. "Really? You didn't think about him giving us the money?"

"Nope. I realized there are other ways for us to get the money. And working with you on projects, brainstorming and staying up late plotting and planning is one of my favorite things in the world. Why would I take the easy way out and miss out on all that?"

That was the best thing she'd ever heard. She lifted on tiptoe and pressed her lips to his.

When she let him go, he stepped back slightly so she could look around.

The whole family—minus Zeke, Charlie, and Griffin who were standing behind her—were gathered around the table. There were papers and folders on the table in front of them.

And Nancy Howell and Ashley Mason were with them.

"What are you guys doing?" Jordan asked.

"While you were out partying with my brother, I got started on some of this middle stuff on my own." Fletcher stepped back and gestured at the table where they all sat. "We've been brain-storming fundraising ideas."

"Fundraising?"

"Yeah. Nancy is a fundraising genius and Ashley is always her co-chair."

Jordan looked stunned. Then confused. "Like bake sales and stuff?"

He took her hand and led her to the table. "Yep. It will be slower but it can be done. I was thinking it would be appropriate for us to start with something with all blue food." He gave her a grin and a wink. "But we've been playing around with slogans, and I'm not sure we're getting it right. We might just have to flat-out steal the whole It Blew Me Away thing. You think that company would mind?"

She laughed and looked at the notebook he was holding.

"Well, we still remember that slogan fifteen years later and if they're still in business then their marketing is working really well, and we should absolutely 'borrow' their slogan."

He pulled out a chair and ushered her into it. "Then sit your sweet ass down and help us with this."

They sat and talked and brainstormed for an hour.

But in the end, Jordan sat back with a sigh. "As much as I love a good bake sale, and as much as I love the idea of us just working to get this money, this is going to take way too long."

"Sometimes middles take longer than we want them to." Fletcher leaned over and put his arm around her. "God knows the middle between when I first fell for you and when I finally got you down the aisle was a long-assed time."

She grinned at him. "Three years *is* a long time."

He shook his head. "That was when I first started wanting you. When I first fell in love with you was twenty years ago when you tied my shoe at recess."

Her expression softened. "Oh my God." She looked around at the table. "I'm so happy you've finally learned to slow down and do all the steps."

"I guess I just needed *you* to show me how great all the steps could be." And she had. From reading research articles, to learning handling techniques for ducklings, to brainstorming taglines that would sell socks, Fletcher really did love going slow now. Well, *slower* anyway.

She grabbed his chin in her hand and leaned in to kiss him. "That's it, Landry," she said against his mouth. "I can't do this."

He pulled back. "What?"

She sighed and shook her head. "Nope. I love all of this, but it's not enough for me."

Fletcher frowned. "What isn't enough?"

"The bake sale is sweet and I love the idea of selling t-shirts and socks and everything. But this means too much to the man I love. I'd do anything for him. And I'm thinking that maybe it's my turn to sweep in and save the day for him."

Fletcher narrowed his eyes but his heart rate sped up a bit. "What's that mean?"

"Middles sometimes really suck, Fletcher. And we've put the time in. We've worked at it. But this program, this petting zoo, this group of people, deserve a big, flashy grand gesture right now." She nodded. "And I can make it happen *fast*."

Fletcher lifted a brow. "You're going to ask Jason for the money, aren't you?"

"I'm going to let Jason donate the money," she corrected. "We deserve it. This program deserves it."

He thought about that. Yeah, she did deserve it. They all did. They needed the funding and dammit, Jason should do this. Fletcher was not too proud to take the guy's money. He had that money because of his success and his success was, in part, thanks to Jordan.

"Fine. But he can't transfer the money to you quietly," Fletcher said. "Tell him he should come and do a concert and attach his name to it. It'll be good for his image too. It'll be good to show that you two are on good terms and that he can support you as a friend after everything that happened."

She was clearly surprised. "Really?"

"Yeah. What the hell?" He shrugged. "He told me about the Gatorade."

She beamed up at him.

"And let's face it," he leaned in, so that she was the only one who could hear. "Me being chivalrous to him and letting him use this to help his image? That's a *huge* gesture from me."

She kissed him. Then pulled back, "Yours will always be the biggest, Fletcher."

He chuckled. "Damn right."

Then she closed her eyes and swallowed hard, pressing her hand to her stomach.

"You okay?" Fletcher asked.

She shook her head. "Do you remember the time, we were

sitting in Ellie's, brainstorming about how to fund the animal park and I threw up blue stuff all over the front of you?"

Fletcher processed that quickly. He shot back in his chair, hauled her up out of her seat, and headed for the back door.

They made it outside, but Fletcher still ended up with blue puke all down the front of him.

After Jordan took a shaky breath, she met his eyes.

And they both started laughing.

"I guess I owed you that," she said.

"You had to be drinking blue shit tonight?"

"Sorry." She didn't really look sorry.

"This is so gross, Mrs. Landry."

"I know."

"And I still want you more than anything I've ever wanted before."

"You're so weird." She grinned up at him with so much love in her eyes. "But damn, marrying you was such a great idea."

Two weeks later…

JASON'S BENEFIT concert was a huge hit.

And they made their goal and then some.

The locals in Autre and Bad were thrilled to have their native son back and Jason put on a hell of a show, Fletcher had to admit.

He had also been very gracious about everything he'd said to the press and on social media about their program and Jordan in particular.

It seemed that his fans, and more importantly, Jordan's fans, had accepted the fact that Jason and Jordan were no longer in love, but they were still very good friends. And they were now all following the social media accounts Charlie had created for

Jordan that were full of photos and facts about all the animals in the petting zoo. The alpacas got a lot of love.

Jason's tour was going very well, with sold-out audiences everywhere, and his team had even been able to spin his trip home as him squeezing a hometown charity into his busy schedule because he was just that great of a guy.

They'd had the concert in downtown Autre rather than at the animal park. Griffin had insisted that the huge crowd and loud music would be disruptive to the animals. However, earlier in the day, the petting zoo had been busier than ever. And they hadn't served *any* blue food.

As the Landry family clustered at the end of Main Street, watching the last of the crowd file out and Jason's crew start to clean up the stage and instruments, Griffin approached.

Charlie frowned at her boyfriend's expression. "What's wrong?"

Griffin sighed. "Good thing we got the money raised."

"Why? Did something happen?" Charlie asked.

"I just got off the phone with my friend Jillian, one of the vets from the Omaha zoo."

"What's going on?" Charlie pressed.

"Apparently she needs some help."

"Okay. Do you need to go to Omaha?"

"No. She's coming here."

"Oh. Great," Charlie said. "The more the merrier."

"I'm glad you feel that way. Because she's not coming alone," Griffin said. He held up his phone. On it was a picture of penguins. "And she's bringing eight penguins."

No one responded for several seconds.

Zeke was the first to speak. "*Penguins*? Fuck, yeah. That's cool as hell." He chuckled and elbowed Zander. "Get it? Cool?"

"You're hilarious, baby brother," Zander said.

Charlie's eyes were wide. "Penguins? Seriously?"

Griffin nodded. "Yeah, she is now the owner of these

penguins and needs a place for them to live. She thought of me and Tori first."

Charlie's shocked expression was slowly spreading into one of delight.

Griffin noticed. And sighed.

"You told her yes, didn't you?" Charlie asked.

"Penguins?" Griffin said. "Where are we going to put them?"

"We'll build them a habitat," Zeke said as if it was the most obvious thing. "This will be fun. I'll research how to get ice and all that shit in there. It will be like a super AC system."

Griffin shook his head. "Well, at least that's good news. They're Galapagos penguins."

Zeke lifted a brow. "You know I have no idea what that means."

"They're tropical penguins. The warm temperatures here will be fine for them."

"What?" Zeke looked crestfallen. "I don't have to come up with a freezer system for the penguin habitat?"

"Nope," Griffin said. Zeke sighed. Then perked up. "Could we get a polar bear?"

"No."

"*Yes.*"

Griffin was the only no. Jordan and Charlie were the yeses.

Fletcher just laughed. "So how does someone suddenly become the owner of eight penguins?"

Griffin shook his head. "It's crazy. Apparently an eccentric millionaire left them to her in his will."

They all took that in. Zeke was again the first to speak. "No fucking way. That's cool." He elbowed Zander. "Even if they are tropical penguins."

Zander rolled his eyes. "Hilarious. Seriously."

"Not sure Jill agrees with you on the cool part," Griffin said. "She's a little frazzled."

Zeke nodded. "Well, she's wrong. It's cool. In fact, it's *flipping* cool." He paused and looked at them all. "Get it? Flipping? Penguins have flippers?"

They all just sighed and started for Ellie's.

Jason and his crew were going to meet them there. They were crashing over in Bad tonight and flying out of New Orleans tomorrow to Tampa.

"Seriously. You guys, that's funny," Zeke insisted as he walked with Griffin, Charlie, and Zander ahead of Fletcher and Jordan. "It's *flipping* funny. This will be so flipping fun. I'm very flipping excited." He spread his arms wide. "I can go on all night."

"We know," Griffin said. He glanced at Zander. "Don't you have a stun gun or something?"

Zander was just smirking. "I think he's pretty flipping funny."

Griffin groaned and Charlie laughed.

Fletcher looked down at Jordan. She was grinning and seemed almost choked up.

"What are you thinking?" he asked as they walked hand in hand toward Ellie's bar down the main street of their hometown.

She looked up at him. "Honestly?"

"Of course."

"I'm thinking I'm just so, so happy that Jason Young dumped me."

Epilogue

A month later…

"I'M THINKING that maybe I embezzled money from the church."

Fletcher looked over at his mother. They were both leaning on Ellie's bar waiting for their to-go coffee orders. "Is this one of your stories about stuff you must've done in a past life?" he asked with a grin.

Elizabeth nodded. "Being punished in this life for past sins is really the only explanation for the mental anguish you and your brothers have put me through over the years." She looked up at him. "Less you than them. At least in the last few years."

Fletcher snorted. "What did Zeke or Zander do this time?"

His mother's gaze moved past him to something over his left shoulder. "Well, we're going to have to ask him."

Fletcher turned and straightened as Zeke stepped into Ellie's.

Zeke was limping slightly, and his jeans were ripped along with one sleeve of his jacket. His clothes were also dirty and covered in dust. There was a bright red scrape on his cheek and he had a huge goose egg with the gash on his forehead, which was covered with a butterfly bandage.

Interestingly, however, Zeke was grinning widely.

"Well, what the hell happened to you?" Ellie asked as he limped over and slid up onto one of the barstools.

"I just woke up after having one of the best nights of my life," he told her.

"Damn, boy, I'd hate to see the morning after a bad night," Leo told him from two stools down.

Zeke grinned at his grandfather as Ellie slid in a cup of coffee across the bar. "Met a gorgeous woman last night and she made me feel *all* better."

"So you had an accident on a backroad or something and a strange woman took you home?" Elizabeth asked her youngest, propping a hand on her hip. "Have you never seen a *single* police drama or unsolved mystery documentary on TV?"

Zeke laughed and shook his head, then winced slightly as if it hurt. "Not a backroad and not her house. Flipped my bike in front of the motel and she took me to her room."

"The motel?" Elizabeth repeated. "The motel *here*? Just up the road?"

"Yep." Zeke took a long drink of his coffee.

"Why didn't you call one of *us*?"

"Uh, because none of you have a hot brunette who will…" Zeke trailed off with a grin. "Never mind."

Elizabeth rolled her eyes. And crossed herself.

Fletcher laughed. "You're not Catholic."

"Well, it can't hurt, can it?" Elizabeth asked. "Maybe I embezzled money from a children's cancer charity."

"Is that worse than stealing from a church or better?"

"Worse. Obviously."

Fletcher nodded. His mother's musings about things she must've done in a past life to deserve the three boys she been given by the good Lord to raise were always dramatic and entertaining. And ninety percent of the time came up because of Zeke and Zander, no matter what she said.

Fletcher was regretting the fact that he had to leave shortly to get to school. But it was an in-service day, so he didn't have to be there early. And if he wandered in a little late to the first meeting, he'd be forgiven as long as he showed up with beignets from Ellie's.

"So what happened?" he asked his brother. "With the accident," he added quickly. He didn't need Zeke giving all the details about the brunette. At least not in front of their mother.

"I was coming down the road and had to swerve to miss a fucking goat." Zeke leaned to shoot a look at the back table where Charlie and Griffin were sitting with Knox, Michael, and Donovan.

Griffin held up a hand. "Don't even start."

"I figured you were around there somewhere since Sugar escaped again," Zeke said.

Griffin frowned. "You almost hit Sugar?"

Fletcher had to fight a smile. Sugar the goat had a huge crush on Griffin, and the only time she broke out of the goat pen—or, more specifically, asked for help from her goat friend, Stan, to get out of the pen—was when she was trying to get to Griffin.

Griffin acted annoyed by it, but they all secretly suspected he loved it. And Sugar.

"No, it was Sneezy, the little black one," Zeke said. "He was struggling to keep up with the rest." Zeke looked at Fletcher. "Benny had the rest of 'em rounded up, but she missed one."

Fletcher had to laugh. Benny, short for Beignet, was Jordan's new border collie puppy. She was a great dog. She was a fantastic herder. Even though she was Jordan's, she spent her time—including her nights—at the petting zoo barn.

She'd gone to work with Jordan the first day and that had been it. They'd tried to keep her at the house with them at night, but the first three mornings they'd found her back at the barn. They'd figured if that was where she wanted to be, then she'd be a great guard dog against any roaming night creatures—or humans for that matter—that tried to get into the barn. She also loved to round the goats up when they got loose. Which was very handy.

The only problem was that she didn't always take them back to the barn.

Actually, she never took them back to the barn. She just herded them into the closest structure.

Still, she'd helped keep the goats out of people's yards and out of the street so that accidents didn't happen.

Well, mostly.

"They were down by the motel last night?" Fletcher asked.

"She had them corralled up at the motel," Zeke said. "I think she was waiting for somebody to open the door to the office."

"So you swerve to miss the goat, flipped your bike, and then what?" Fletcher said, wanting the rest of the story before he had to leave.

And also wanting to change the subject away from his dog's tendencies to herd goats into places like the bridal shop downtown and into various people's garages around town.

"Wait, who got the call to take the goats back to their barn?" This came from Knox.

Yeah, that was another part of the goat shenanigans. When people found a little herd of goats and an overly enthusiastic border collie in these strange places around town, they called one of four people: Zander, Bailey Wilcox, Michael, or Knox. As city manager, he got the calls from people who didn't know who else to call. Or the people who didn't want to deal with calling Zander. Which was a lot of people.

Knox also appreciated the calls least of any of those people. And that was saying a lot. Zander *really* hated dealing with the goats.

"Well, I happened to get the call about Zeke's accident, so I was already there and we took the goats back before anyone called about them," Michael said.

Knox looked over. "You and Michael took the goats back to the barn?"

Zeke lifted a shoulder. "Sure, why not?"

"Well, I ask because *you* called *me* about coming to get the goats when you found them in the new kitchen of one of your remodels. Of course, you changed your voice and gave me a fake name, knowing I'd never show up if I knew it was you."

"It's not my fault you don't have my number in your phone." Zeke smirked at him. "Let's just say I was... compelled last night."

"Compelled by what? A concussion?" Knox asked.

"By a hot brunette who was all ga-ga over the goats," Zeke said.

Everyone's eyes went wide.

"This woman helped you gather up the goats and take them back to the barn?" Fletcher asked.

"Yeah, after she came rushing to my side to see if everything was okay."

Michael gave a little cough that sounded to Fletcher like, *bullshit*.

Fletcher looked at his brother. "So you wrecked your bike in front of her motel and she came rushing over to check on you?"

Zeke shrugged. "More or less."

"But someone called Michael?"

"Well, she called 9-1-1," Zeke said.

"Oh, wow, Zander's going to be so pissed he didn't get that call," Fletcher said.

Zeke nodded. "I know. Don't think I wasn't praying it wouldn't be him."

"So then after Michael checked you out, she invited you to stay the night? I suppose she felt the need to keep an eye on you to be sure your concussion wasn't too bad," Fletcher said dryly.

"Well, she definitely didn't let me fall asleep for too long at a time," Zeke said.

Elizabeth sighed. "Maybe your *father* did something bad in his past life too."

Fletcher snorted.

"Behave," Ellie told Zeke, swatting him a towel before setting a plate of biscuits and gravy in front of him.

"What can I say? Even banged up and bleeding, I'm irresistible," Zeke said as he dug into his breakfast.

They all laughed. But at the same time, no one could deny that things always seemed to work out for Zeke.

"So are you going to see her again?" Elizabeth asked.

"Nah, she's just passing through," Zeke said as he reached into his pocket for his phone. "I don't even have her last name. Or her number. Or where she's from." He looked down at his phone, reading a text message.

Cora reached over the bar to hand him a little glass bottle that contained a powdery yellow substance. "You take a spoonful of this if you had start hurting," she told him.

Zeke looked up. "Can't take any medicine. Or whatever you call your stuff." He gave her a wink. "The new penguin veterinarian's in town early and wants to see the penguin habitat."

"But your head," Cora said.

Zeke took the vial from her and tucked it into his pocket. "I'll keep it close." He took another big bite of his biscuits and gravy.

The guys never asked what was in Cora's concoctions. Everything she handed out worked. If she gave you a powder and told you to sprinkle it over your vegetable garden to keep the rabbits away, it would work. If she told you to mix it with water to clean grease off your tools, it would work. If she told you to swallow it for a headache, it would work. So nobody asked questions.

"The habitat is done, right?" Griffin asked.

"Totally done. And it's awesome." Zeke took another bite.

"Well, you need to be sure to go home and clean up before you meet her," Elizabeth said. "You want to make a good first impression."

"That penguin enclosure we built for her is going to make all the impression I need."

"Shower, Ezekiel," Elizabeth said firmly.

"Yeah, yeah, I will. Heading home now. But trust me, based

on the texts and emails we've been exchanging, that's all she cares about. I've been trying to get her to give me some guidance on what she wants done with the remodel on the house she bought and she hasn't answered a single question about *that*. But I got instructions down to the centimeter for where those penguins are gonna live."

Fletcher glanced at Griffin. The woman who was bringing the penguins to Autre was a friend of his.

Griffin nodded. "Penguins are her life."

Zeke took a few more bites, then slid off the stool. He grabbed his coffee and drained the last of it. "I better get going. She's already out there poking around."

He turned and limped to the door.

As soon as the door closed behind him, Charlie turned to Griffin and said, "Why didn't you tell him that Jill was here last night and staying at the motel?"

Fletcher straightened and Michael leaned in.

"Jill?" Fletcher asked. "The woman with the penguins?"

Griffin nodded. "She got into town last night. We went up to say hi. I guess that's when Sugar saw me," he added with a sigh.

"So Jill, the penguin veterinarian, was in town, at the motel, last night when all of this was going down with Zeke and the motorcycle and the goats?" Fletcher asked.

Griffin and Charlie exchanged a look.

Then Charlie grinned. "Yep."

"What's Jill look like?" Michael asked.

"Petite, long dark curly hair, petite, doesn't wear a lot of makeup, dressed in a green shirt and jeans when we saw her last night."

Michael sat back with a huge grin. "That's her."

"The woman who rushed over to help Zeke?" Fletcher asked.

"The woman who rushed over to check on the *goat*," Michael corrected.

They all laughed and Griffin nodded.

"That sounds like Jill."

Fletcher looked back and forth between Griffin and Michael. "So, Zeke just spent the night—one of the greatest nights of his life—with the new penguin veterinarian? And the woman whose house he's remodeling? Who is his new neighbor? But he has no idea who she is and thinks he's not going to see her again?"

"Yep," Michael said simply.

"Well," Fletcher said, grabbing his coffee cup. "I, for one, am really happy I stopped in here this morning on my way to work."

"I was under the impression that you were *all* really happy to stop in here for all kinds of things *all* the time," Ellie said, pretending to be offended.

Fletcher gave her a grin. "Well, some of the most interesting things do happen in this bar."

"Or at least the stories about them get repeated here" Charlie said.

Yep. And it looked like he and Jordan were coming up here for dinner tonight for sure, because there was going to more to *this* story soon. And he had a feeling it was going to be a good one.

Thank you so much for reading *Heavy Petting*! I hope you loved Fletcher and Jordan's story!

There is so much more to come from Boys of the Bayou Gone Wild and the Landry family!

Zeke and Jill are up next in Flipping Love You!

He's the tattooed bad boy her mama warned her about.
She's his hot mess-but mostly hot-next door neighbor.
Until a two-night-stand gives them the surprise of a lifetime...

Find out more at
ErinNicholas.com

ॐ

Find ALL of my books at **ErinNicholas. com**

And the best place to find out all the news about that (including upcoming books and more!) is right here!
bit.ly/Keep-In-Touch-Erin
Be sure you get those dashes and upper case letters in there!

And this is your personal invitation to my Facebook group, Erin Nicholas's Super Fans where you can get first looks, behind the scenes peeks, and daily fun with fellow romance lovers (including me!)!

About the Author

Erin Nicholas is the New York Times and USA Today bestselling author of over sixty sexy contemporary romances. Her stories have been described as toe-curling, enchanting, steamy and fun. She loves to write about reluctant heroes, imperfect heroines and happily ever afters. She lives in the Midwest with her husband who only wants to read the sex scenes in her books, her kids who will never read the sex scenes in her books, and family and friends who say they're shocked by the sex scenes in her books (yeah, right!).

Find her and all her books at
www.ErinNicholas.com

And find her on Facebook, Goodreads, BookBub, and Instagram!